TROUBLE TWISTERS

BOOK THREE

THE MYSTERY

Also available

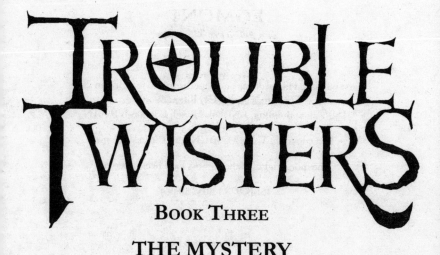

TROUBLE TWISTERS

BOOK THREE

THE MYSTERY

GARTH NIX
SEAN WILLIAMS

EGMONT

EGMONT

We bring stories to life

First published in hardback and paperback in Great Britain 2013
by Egmont UK Limited
The Yellow Building, 1 Nicholas Road, London W11 4AN

Text copyright © 2013 Garth Nix and Sean Williams

The moral rights of the authors have been asserted

ISBN 978 1 4052 5865 4

1 3 5 7 9 10 8 6 4 2

www.egmont.co.uk

A CIP catalogue record for this title is available from the British Library

Typeset by Avon DataSet Ltd, Bidford on Avon, Warwickshire
Printed and bound in Great Britain by the CPI Group

47385/2

MIX
Paper
FSC FSC® C018306

EGMONT

Our story began over a century ago, when seventeen-year-old
Egmont Harald Petersen found a coin in the street. He was on
his way to buy a flyswatter, a small hand-operated printing
machine that he then set up in his tiny apartment.

The coin brought him such good luck that today Egmont has
offices in over 30 countries around the world. And that lucky
coin is still kept at the company's head offices in Denmark.

To Anna, Thomas and Edward,
and to all my family and friends — Garth

For my grandmothers, Isobel Jean Williams and
Evelyn Mary Schiller — Sean

CONTENTS

Out of the Rain

Young Master Rourke sat upright in his armchair, startled awake by a sudden noise. Despite his name, he was actually an old man, only a few days short of his eighty-fifth birthday. He was known as 'Young Master Rourke' because his father had been the one and only 'Mister Rourke' in the area for many, many years. Old Mister Rourke had built Rourke Castle and had bought up all the railways, shipping lines and the whaling stations for miles around. In doing so he had become one of the richest and most influential men of his time.

Most of the riches were now gone, but Young Master Rourke still owned Rourke Castle. A vast rambling palace that extended across two sides of a hill, it had towers, stables, three ballrooms, a Greek temple, a Venetian canal and a scale copy of an Egyptian pyramid that was a hundred feet high. (The Pyramid looked like stone on the outside, but was in fact hollow, made of concrete slabs over a steel beam skeleton).

Rourke Castle was so big that it was spread across two towns. Half was within the bounds of a small town called

Portland, the other half in the neighbouring town. When the castle had still had staff, they used to joke about going to Portland, or going to Dogton, when crossing from one side of the castle to the other.

Over the years, more and more of the castle had been locked up and left, as it was too expensive to maintain. Young Master Rourke kept moving from larger rooms to smaller ones as his needs shrank. Finally he left the main castle entirely and moved to the old porter's lodge near the front gates, past the lake that had once boasted real icebergs and penguins, even in summer. Now the giant ice machine was broken and the penguins had been sent to a proper zoo. The lake was just a dark expanse of water, choked by rotten lilies.

The lodge and the land around it were half a mile outside the boundary of Portland. Young Master Rourke had not thought this important when he moved. He had forgotten that someone had once told him that he should take care to stay on the Portland side of the boundary at all times.

The sound that had woken him came again. Young Master Rourke tilted his head back as he tried to work out what it was. The grandfather clock in the corner of the room ticked slowly and melancholically, but that wasn't it. The time was five minutes short of midnight and the clock far from striking.

The night was quiet for a few seconds. Then the noise came a third time – a quick rush of beats that swept across the roof and were gone.

'Is that . . . rain?' muttered Young Master Rourke, blinking the sleep from his eyes.

He took off his half-moon reading glasses and consulted the ornate, gilded barometer that stood next to the grandfather clock.

The barometer's needle was sitting at FAIR.

'Stupid thing,' Young Master Rourke mumbled.

He struggled out of his deep leather armchair and crossed the room to tap the face of the barometer firmly. The needle quivered, then moved, but not towards STORMY. It kept insisting the weather should be fair.

Another round of what sounded like heavy raindrops crossed the roof. Rourke went to the window and looked out. There were still a few lamp posts working on the broad avenue that led to the castle, alongside the lake. Above, the sky was cloudy and the sky utterly empty of stars, but Rourke couldn't see any actual rain.

'Just a shower, you daft old fool,' he told himself. 'Forget about it and go to bed.'

He bent down and picked up the book, his mood improving instantly. Rourke had read *Gorillas vs The Fist* before, but it was one of many favourites that he often revisited. Reading pulpy old detective stories was one of his two main activities. The other one was looking after the only legacy of his father's that he actually treasured: the animals of the old Rourke Menagerie.

In his father's time, the menagerie had contained elephants, lions, tigers and other kinds of exotic animals. Now there were only two chimpanzees, a warthog, three lemurs, a zebra, a jackal, two wolves and a macaw called Cornelia, who was at least a hundred years old. When Young Master Rourke had been much younger, he'd believed Cornelia had been stolen from a pirate.

In old Mister Rourke's day, all the animals had been housed in a complete zoo, up past the eastern wing of the castle. But that area was a weedy wasteland now. The remaining animals lived in a much smaller collection of cages and enclosures built on the old polo field right next to the lodge where Young Master Rourke lived. It was nowhere near as impressive as the grand old menagerie had been, but it was closer and much easier to deal with.

The new cages were also outside Portland's boundary.

Rattling rain fell on the roof again as Rourke shuffled out of his study into the lodge's main corridor. This time when the heavy beat of the drops ceased, a sudden loud bang immediately followed, and then much heavier thudding along the roof.

'That's not rain . . .' whispered Rourke, looking up to follow the sound as it travelled towards the back of the lodge. His heart was suddenly thumping in his chest, faster than was good for him. 'That's footsteps.'

The sound stopped. Rourke's head snapped back down as a man-shaped shadow passed across the narrow stained-glass window to the left of the back door.

There was someone out there — someone who had apparently come down with the rain.

It was only then that Rourke remembered the warning about staying inside the Portland town limits, and what might happen if he didn't . . .

The book was still in his hand. He raised it, gnarled old fingers moving faster than anyone might expect, and flipped it open to the back page, where there was a simple white sticker with the phone number and address of a business in Portland.

Rourke stumbled to the ancient phone that sat on a seventeenth-century chestnut table in the corridor and put one shaking finger into the rotary dial.

At that moment he heard Cornelia the macaw, who had a free run of the new menagerie, but most often slept in a custom-made box under the eaves at the back door of the lodge. Cornelia normally never said anything but 'Who's a pretty girl?' and 'Nellie wants a nut'. Now she started shrieking.

'To the boats! Abandon ship!'

The other animals started braying and screaming and kicking, making noises that Rourke had never heard, not in all his long lifetime spent looking after them. They were hooting and howling, barking and biting, shaking their cages and filling the night with unnatural terror.

Frantically, Rourke dialled the number.

As the dial whirred in its final rotation, the noise of the

animals suddenly stopped, as if a conductor had snapped down his arms for a sudden finish.

Rourke held the phone to his ear, hardly hearing the sound of ringing at the other end. All his senses were focused towards the back door and the menagerie beyond.

The animals were quiet now, but there were other noises. Cages were swinging open, one by one. These sounds were familiar to Rourke, who opened them every day. There was the screech of the chimps' door, the one he had been meaning to oil for weeks. There was the scrape of steel on concrete, the bent door in the fence that surrounded the wolves' enclosure . . .

The phone kept ringing, and now Rourke could hear animals moving. Much more quietly than normal, though he still heard the soft pads of the jackal, the hooves of the zebra, and the shuffling gait of the warthog. The wolves, he assumed, remained stealthy, moving with their characteristic silence.

'What?' asked a tired voice on the phone. A man, grumpy at being woken up so late.

Rourke's mouth opened and closed. He struggled to speak, but couldn't get any air into his lungs. The uncaged animals were at the back door now – he could see their shadows against the stained glass.

'No!' he tried to say, the word emerging as little more than a croak. 'No!'

The handle of the back door slowly turned. The door edged open.

'Who is this?' asked the voice on the phone.

The back door swung open. A man stood there, a man wearing a hat and a trench coat just like the one on the cover of Rourke's book, except both were thoroughly wet. Water dripped from the brim of the hat that shadowed this man's face.

The animals were gathered round the stranger, silent companions pressing in as close as they could as he eased through the doorway.

'David?' the old man gasped.

There was something very odd about the animals. It took Rourke a second to process exactly what it was.

'Their eyes . . .' gasped Rourke. 'Their eyes are white!'

The phone fell from his hand as the man in the door lifted his head to stare at him. The shadow of the man's hat brim rose and light fell on his face, reflecting from his eyes – eyes that just like the animals' eyes were completely and utterly white, without pupil or iris.

++Where is it, old fool?++ asked the intruder. No sound came from his mouth and his lips did not move, but the voice was clear in Rourke's mind. **++Where is it?++**

Rourke opened his mouth, but only a choking rattle came out. His hand flew to his head, as if he could ward off the stabbing, awful communication that was going straight into his brain.

++Answer the question!++

Rourke suddenly clawed at his chest with both hands. *Gorillas vs The Fist* fluttered forgotten to the floor.

++No!++ shouted the stranger. He dashed forward and caught Rourke as he fell.

White began to swirl in Rourke's eyes too, but it could not outpace the other change that gripped the old man.

Young Master Rourke went limp. The white ebbed from his eyes, leaving them open and unseeing.

The stranger lowered the heavy body to the floor. He grabbed the phone and pulled it from the wall, the cord coming out with a piece of plaster the size of a dinner plate. Then he bent down and searched through the pockets of Rourke's dressing gown.

Without any sign or gesture from the stranger, the two white-eyed chimpanzees went into the study, while the other silently roamed the study as though looking for something.

The stranger flicked through the pages of Young Master Rourke's book. As he did so, a thick grey mist formed above him and several heavy drops of rain fell on to his back. He paused and looked up, and made an angry dismissive gesture that caused the mist and rain to immediately disappear.

In the study, the chimpanzees began to move books out of the bookcases, carefully opening each one before dropping it disinterestedly on to the floor. The wolves circled Rourke's fallen body as though looking for something.

"It *must* be here," whispered the stranger, using his voice this time. It sounded strangely like a growl, at first neither man nor animal, but then shifted to being fully human. 'But if it's not, there's always Plan B . . .'

Behind the chimps, the clock shook. Springs whirred inside its cavernous casing, cogs grated and a melancholy chime sounded the first of the twelve strokes of midnight.

The sound echoed through the lodge and, faintly but clearly, outside. The ancient macaw, hiding in the topmost branches of one of the great elms that lined the castle avenue, heard the clock and lowered her proud-beaked head.

'Every parrot for herself,' she muttered, and launched herself into the air, beginning a slow but steady flight to the east, towards the shimmering lights of Portland.

CHAPTER ONE
The Accident

The twins were doing maths questions when they heard the first siren scream past the school, heading north, and then stop not much further on. Back in their old home in the city, they wouldn't have paid it any attention at all. But in the small town of Portland, even a single siren was unusual. When it was followed by another, as was the current case, it became almost interesting.

'That's the ambulance,' said curly-haired Kyle, one of those people who could recognise the slight individual variations in the sirens of the local emergency service vehicles. 'And the second one is the fire engine . . .'

His voice trailed off as another more distant siren joined the mix, getting louder as it raced towards the town.

'And that's the rescue rig from Scarborough!' he exclaimed. 'Something big must be going on!'

He jumped up and rushed to the window, followed by most of the class.

'Children, children!' admonished Mr Carver, but as he

didn't actually raise his voice, only the front row heard him and stayed in place.

Jack and Jaide looked at each other and didn't immediately follow, having experienced quite a lot of disasters and emergencies in the last few weeks. Also, they were from the city and so had a reputation to uphold as not being impressed by something that probably wouldn't rate a mention on the news back home.

Then, over the cacophony of all the sirens, there came a deep, fast beat that the twins knew very well. The *wokka-wokka-wokka* of an approaching helicopter.

'Airswift Aeromedical 339, twin-engine,' said Jaide, jumping up and angling quickly between a couple of kids to get to the window. Her brother Jack followed in her wake.

'How do *you* know?' asked Kyle.

'That's Mum's helicopter,' said Jack. 'This *must* be serious. Can you see anything?'

'Not really, but the helicopter looks like it's going to land near the iron bridge,' said Kyle. He craned up on tiptoe, trying to get a better view. 'Yeah, there it goes – must be right in the middle of the road!'

'Class, I would particularly appreciate it if you would return to your seats,' said Mr Carver, still in his normal conversational voice, 'while I endeavour to ascertain if this emergency affects the school.'

His students didn't even turn round. They just keep jostling to try to get to the window, while the kids in front pushed back with their elbows to try to stay in place.

'CHILDREN! Back to your seats!'

No one had ever heard Mr Carver shout before. There was a moment of shock, followed by a sudden cascade of students rushing back to their desks, several of them tripping over the beanbags that were used during Mr Carver's 'Meditation Time'. They didn't so much sit back down as do controlled crashes into their chairs.

'Continue with your maths problems,' said Mr Carver. He wasn't shouting now, but his voice was still louder than usual, clear even over the noise of the sirens and the helicopter winding down. 'I am going to see what's going on. I expect everyone to stay in their places unless requested otherwise, by me or another teacher.'

He took his phone out of his pocket as he strode out of the class, dialling with one hand as he pushed the door open with the other.

'Wow! I've never seen him like that before,' said Tara, the newest student in the school. 'I mean, I thought he was nothing but peace and light all the time.'

'Nah, old Heath loses it occasionally,' said Kyle, using Mr Carver's first name, as he preferred his students to do, although few of his students could ever bring themselves to do so. 'Three years ago he freaked out when that tree branch fell down in the car park, just before the bus left for the whale-watching excursion.'

'That wasn't three years ago, Kyle,' said Miralda King, daughter of the mayor.

'Yes, it was,' Kyle snapped back.

'We went fossil-hunting on Mermaid Point three years ago,' retorted Miralda. 'Whale-watching was *four* years ago.'

'Actually, it *was* three years ago,' said one of the other kids, and then all the locals who'd been at the school long enough started arguing about whether they had gone whale-watching four or three years ago, and whether or not the branch had fallen that year, or in fact some other year, when the bus was leaving for some different excursion.

'I guess you have to find your own excitement in a small town,' whispered Tara to Jaide.

'Whatever's happening on the bridge is enough for me,' said Jaide. 'I wish we could see what's happening.'

'Can't be too big or we'd have to evacuate,' said Jack 'I mean, if it was a gas tanker that was going to explode or something.'

'There's a lot of sirens,' said Jaide. 'And Mum's helicopter, so someone must be badly hurt. Maybe lots of people.'

'You know, I thought I heard something before the sirens,' said Tara. 'A kind of thudding noise, like when a big truck goes past and shakes everything a bit. Just for a second.'

'I didn't hear anything,' said Jack. 'I was totally concentrating on the maths questions.'

'Yeah, sure,' said Jaide. 'You were practically asleep, I saw you.'

Jack shrugged. His twin knew him too well. He had finished the problems ages ago and been daydreaming, imagining himself using his Gift, merging into the shadow by the wall and escaping from school.

'I suppose we had better do these questions,' said Tara to Jaide. 'They won't go away on their own.'

The students were bent over their papers – all except Jack, who had moved on to imagining increasingly unlikely accidents to explain the unusual events in Portland that morning – when Mr Carver came back into the room a few minutes later. He was talking on his phone.

'So there is no danger to the school? Good, good. What exactly . . .? Into the river? Yes, of course I know . . . oh my . . . oh my . . . . oh dear!'

Jack and Jaide were not looking up, or they would have seen Mr Carver suddenly stare at them with an expression they all knew well. His forehead had wrinkled and his mouth flattened into a straight, sincere line.

Tara saw it. She nudged Jaide.

'You just got the Caring Sharing Face from Heath.'

'What?' asked Jaide. All of a sudden she felt a stab of fear. The helicopter . . . her mother! But the helicopter had landed fine. Why would they be the object of Mr Carver's Caring Sharing Face?

Mr Carver put his phone away and carefully walked between the desks over to where Jack and Jaide sat.

'Class, continue with your work,' he said brightly. 'Jack and Jaide, could you please come with me to the office? There's something I'd like you to help me with.'

Jack and Jaide stood up and started to gather their books.

'No, no, leave everything and come along,' said Mr Carver.

He opened the door and gestured to them to go in front of him. Out in the corridor, Jack stopped and said, 'What's going on? Is Mum all right?'

'Yes, I'm sure she's fine,' said Mr Carver quickly. He made some tentative gestures again, as if he was trying to herd ducklings into his office. 'Just step inside and I'll tell you when you're sitting down.'

'We were sitting down before,' said Jaide, as she and her brother sat uneasily on the shiny orange and yellow couch.

Mr Carver perched himself on the corner of his desk and fiddled with a small Tibetan prayer wheel, flicking it till the bells began to jangle.

'Yes, but this is . . . what I have to tell you . . . it's best not in class. No I think more suitable that you be sitting together . . . you may even want to, in fact I think it's a good idea if you hold your brother's hand, Jaide –'

'Just tell us!' both twins said at once.

'I'm not sure, I don't have all the details, but it seems that about twenty minutes ago, a car was forced off the road just before the iron bridge, into the river . . .'

He spun the prayer wheel more forcefully.

'So?' asked Jack, now extremely puzzled. '*What* car went into the river . . .?'

'A yellow car, an old yellow car,' whispered Mr Carver.

It felt like time froze for the twins, as if everything stopped. For a long second, neither of them could move, or think, or speak, and then everything started again and Mr Carver was gabbling about 'your wonderful grandmother', but it was meaningless. All they could think about was Grandma X's old yellow car going into the river, taking Grandma X down with it, down into the muddy depths . . .

'But . . . but it couldn't . . . it couldn't happen,' Jaide said finally.

'No,' agreed Jack. 'No way.'

'I know it is difficult to comprehend,' said Mr Carver. 'Fate is fickle, and in accidents such as these, anything can occur –'

'No,' said Jaide. 'You don't understand. Grandma X is . . . is *special*.'

She couldn't say what she really wanted to say. That Grandma X had magical Gifts, and wisdom, and . . .

There was the clatter of boots in the hall and then all of a sudden the twins' mother was in the doorway. Mr Carver nervously stood up, but she ignored him and dashed to the children.

'Jack, Jaide!'

The twins moved into Susan's hug as if she was a life belt thrown to them at sea. She hugged them just as tightly for a moment, then eased them back.

'Is . . . is she dead?' asked Jaide. She could hardly get the words out, or keep back the tears that were suddenly welling up in her eyes.

'No,' said Susan. 'But the car was in the river for some time, and they've just got it out and she's still inside. She *is* conscious, which is a very good sign. We'll be flying her to the hospital as soon as they can . . . get her free. I just ran over to tell you that Rodeo Dave is on his way and he'll drive you to the hospital. I'll be there of course.'

'Which hospital?' asked Jack. He looked at Jaide, and she knew what he was thinking. Grandma X might have to be taken beyond the wards, and neither of them knew what effect that might have.

Grandma X was the Warden of Portland, charged with secretly protecting the world from The Evil, a terrible force from another dimension. If it wasn't for the Wardens, the world would have been taken over long ago. Jack and Jaide were going to be Wardens one day, but for now they were troubletwisters, young Wardens whose Gifts were unreliable and occasionally dangerous, despite the best efforts of their grandmother to teach them how to use them. The first time their Gifts had appeared, the twins had accidentally blown up their house in the city and they had been forced to move away from the life they had always known.

Their grandmother was strict and knew a lot more about everything than she ever let on, including her name. They just called her Grandma X while everyone else mumbled when they had to call her anything. The twins had been in Portland for months now, constantly learning about their Gifts and their new responsibilities, but sometimes it seemed as though they had barely begun. There was still so much they didn't understand.

Would the four wards of Portland, which kept The Evil from breaking into the world, still work if the Warden in charge of them left?

What would happen if she died?

'She'll go to Scarborough of course,' said Susan, ignorant of their concerns. She didn't like being reminded of the legacy the twins had inherited from their father, and Grandma X had 'encouraged' her ability to forget. 'Better facilities. Not to demean Portland Hospital, but –'

Her walkie-talkie crackled and a voice said, 'Sue! Almost there. Three minutes.'

'On my way!' said Susan. She hugged the twins again. 'I have to go. She'll be OK, I'm sure of it. She's the toughest person I know!'

She turned quickly to Mr Carver. 'Dave Smeaton from The

Book Herd is authorised to pick the children up. He'll be here in a moment.'

With one last hug and one last look to the twins, she was gone.

The next five minutes were very long. Mr Carver spun the prayer wheel one more time, then put it down and picked up his nose flute, but he put that down again without playing anything. He opened his mouth to say something, and nothing came out. Finally, he got up and slid through the door, pausing to mutter something about 'leaving you to your thoughts' and 'must get back to class'.

As soon as he was gone, Jack and Jaide started whispering furiously to each other.

'She'll be OK,' said Jack. 'She probably wasn't even really hurt. Right?'

'But *hospital*, Jack. What if they fly her to Scarborough? Shouldn't we do something?' asked Jaide.

'We should call Dad,' they both said together.

'But we don't know where he is,' continued Jack.

'Custer!' said Jaide, thinking of their father's old friend. 'Custer will know.'

'We don't know how to get in touch with him either,' said Jack. 'Or the other Wardens. Grandma X did all that.'

'Mum must have a number for Dad,' said Jaide, but she didn't sound very convinced.

'He always loses his phone,' said Jack glumly. 'And he's usually somewhere weird anyway, where nothing works. But he might have, you know, secret Warden ways of knowing stuff. Maybe Grandma X sent him a . . . a thought message . . . or something.'

'I cannot reach your father,' said a faint voice behind the twins, apparently emanating from the wall. Jack and Jaide leaped off the couch as if it was suddenly red-hot.

Behind them, on the wall, was a faint image of their grandmother. She didn't look young like she did when her spirit form appeared, and it didn't look three-dimensional. This was more like a blurry photo being projected on to the wallpaper. Her white hair was even messier than it was every morning. Her eyelids fluttered.

'I am somewhat injured,' said Grandma X. 'But I will be all right, so you don't need to worry.'

'But they're taking you to Scarborough!' exclaimed Jaide. 'What will that do the wards?'

'They are *not* taking me to Scarborough,' said the blurry image with familiar stubbornness. 'Shortly, they will decide that it is better to take me somewhere closer, even if the facilities are not so advanced. Portland Hospital will fit the bill perfectly.'

Her eyelids closed completely, but not before they saw her eyes roll back upwards, into her head.

'Are you really OK?' asked Jack anxiously.

'I have a concussion . . . and my body was affected by the cold of the river,' said Grandma X, her eyes opening again. 'I don't have much time. Custer will monitor the wards. I don't expect trouble, but if anything does come up, and Custer is not available, you can . . . ow! . . . Be careful . . .'

Grandma X's voice was cut off, and the image disappeared.

'Hello, you two,' said Rodeo Dave from the doorway behind them. The twins spun round again, uncertain how long he'd been there. He bobbed his head and said, 'All ready to go? Scarborough Hospital, your mother said.'

'Uh, yeah, thanks,' said Jack. 'Only maybe we should check first –'

Dave's phone rang.

'Hang on, Jack. Dave here . . . oh, right . . . no problem. We're on our way.'

He put the phone away and said to the twins, 'Not Scarborough General. Portland Hospital. We'll be there in a jiffy. Come on!'

The helicopter lifted off as they got to Dave's white van, which he used to pick up and deliver books. They all piled in the front and, after reminding him about his seat belt, they drove out on to River Road.

'We'll have to go the long way,' said Dave. 'The bridge will be closed for a while.'

The twins peered past the willows to the bridge, which was surrounded by emergency vehicles. At the southern end, the crane truck that usually worked at the marina was up on its supports, with a chain going down to the battered, mud-strewn wreck of a yellow Hillman Minx that had been pulled out of the river.

Seeing the car made it all seem more horribly real. Jack had to look away, and Jaide found herself the victim of a sudden attack of the shivers.

'Your grandmother will be fine,' said Dave, noting both of these events. He leaned across and opened the glovebox. 'Grab a couple of the sweets there. You've both had a nasty shock.'

The sweets were nothing the twins had ever seen before, old-fashioned boiled things wrapped in paper that was hard to remove. Concentrating on getting the paper off took up most of the trip to the hospital.

Susan was waiting for them in the lobby.

'Grandma is OK,' she said. 'We were worried for a moment, but she rallied as soon as we got her here. That's amazing for someone who's been through a major accident.'

'Can we see her?' asked Jaide, as Jack said, 'Is she awake?'

'The doctors are with her now,' said Susan. 'They're going to keep her in Intensive Care until tomorrow morning probably. They may still have to move her to Scarborough. As for what happened . . . it's not that clear. She told Constable Haigh a truck or a van came up fast behind her, and tried to overtake before the bridge, then cut back in unexpectedly, forcing her off the road and into the river.'

'But didn't stop?' asked Jack. 'Wow, that's mean.'

'More than mean,' said Susan. 'It's criminal. The police will be looking for it. Things are going to be a bit complicated at home for a while. I can't get someone to cover for me immediately – you know how we're always short-handed, so you'll be by yourselves a bit more than usual. I will be home tonight though. Maybe we can find someone to check in on you until my shift is over.'

'What about Tara?' asked Jaide. 'We could hang out with her.'

'Yes, good idea, I'll give her father a call . . . but we can't rely on them every night.'

Rodeo Dave, who had until that moment been occupied with grooming his thick moustache, cleared his throat.

'Renita Daniels, that is, Rennie, has been helping me out at the shop,' he said. 'I've let her have the small apartment up top, and I'm sure she'd be happy to . . . uh . . . babysit, if you'll pardon the term, Jaide, Jack . . .'

Susan nodded with relief. 'Thank you, Dave. And thanks for bringing the twins here. Can I ask you to take them back to school as well? I hope you don't mind.'

'Of course not.' He winked at them. 'It's a pleasure.'

'Oh, and I should have said before how sorry I was to hear about Young Master Rourke. He was a friend of yours, wasn't he?'

'He was,' said Dave, his face falling. 'He bought a lot of books from me, over a long time. In fact, I'm heading up there the day after tomorrow, to catalogue his collection for the executors.'

'Young Master who?' asked Jack.

'What happened to him?' added Jaide.

'We'll talk about it later,' said Susan. 'Now remember, Grandma X is very fit and strong . . . for someone her age. So don't worry, honest —'

She was interrupted by three quick bursts of sound from her walkie-talkie. Not words, just the crackle.

'Got to go! Love you!'

There was a whirlwind embrace, then she was off.

'OK,' said Dave. His smile returned as though it had never vanished. 'Your chariot awaits.'

CHAPTER TWO
An Unexpected Encounter

Four hours later, water was dripping from the edge of the umbrella Jack Shield held and trickling right down the back of his sister's neck. Jaide shuddered and tugged her collar tight up to her throat, pulling her head in as best she could. She could see nothing outside the umbrella but clods of disturbed earth, the mud-spattered feet of the adults walking around them and the base of a heavy grey stone wall ten feet away. The rain continued to stream down on them, far heavier than it had been back in the town.

'Remind me what we're doing here?' she grumbled.

'You suggested it,' said Jack. 'You asked Mum if we could hang out with Tara.'

'But this wasn't what I was expecting!'

They were standing next to a life-sized castle – a real one, to all appearances, with turrets and a portcullis, even a deep moat filled with murky brown water. Nearby were a number of smaller buildings scattered around the edge of a large and even murkier-looking lake. A squat pyramid peeked round the shoulder of a low hill.

'Dad says this is one of the most important landmarks in Portland,' Tara said, coming up behind them. She had her own umbrella, a purple spotted thing that looked brand-new, vastly different to the moth-eaten black antique the twins had found in the back of Tara's car. It leaked and two people couldn't quite fit under it, but Jaide told herself it was better than nothing. 'He knew you'd love to see it since you're interested in old buildings and stuff.'

'Er, right.'

It was Jaide's turn to want to kick her brother, this time for the ridiculous lie he had come up with to explain their former interest in Tara's father, a property developer. It meant long lectures on the renovation potential of old warehouses and barracks and being dragged about in all manner of weather, whether they asked to go or not.

'You know, Jaide, it *is* pretty cool,' said Jack, peering out and up at the castle wall, tipping the umbrella in the process and sending another wave of water straight into Jaide's right ear. 'There was nothing like this in the city.'

Jaide braved the rain to take another look. The side of the castle seemed to go up forever, broken only every now and again by a narrow, slit-like window, for archers to fire from. Jaide didn't think there had ever been a need for archers in Portland, but there probably hadn't been any need for a moat either.

'Young Master Rourke lived here?' she asked.

'Not here exactly. He was in that little building we passed by the gates.'

'And he really just died?' Jack asked, thinking of the sadness in Rodeo Dave's eyes and the weirdness of their present position. They had only just heard about him, and now here they were, exploring where he used to live.

'Saturday night,' Tara said. Her eyes gleamed with gruesome relish. 'Dad doesn't know who found him.'

'Maybe his butler,' said Jaide.

'He didn't have a butler. He cooked and cleaned for himself, and lived here completely alone.'

Jack could make out people striding about in boots and raincoats.

'I can't believe Portland has a *castle*,' he said, wondering if it was cool for a grown-up to want to live in one, or a bit weird. He had thought Grandma X was the strangest person in Portland, but now it seemed she had some competition.

Used to have competition, he reminded himself. That thought combined with the image of her all alone in hospital to make him worry about her even more.

'I can't believe Portland has a castle either,' exclaimed Tara's dad, sticking his head into their huddle of umbrellas with a wide, white-toothed smile. He was, as always, wearing a cap with the name of his company on it, MMM Holdings. 'And it's prime land, just perfect for redevelopment. When the will is sorted out, we could be sitting on a gold mine! Do you know, the main building has thirty-seven bedrooms and hasn't been lived in for twenty years? Think how many apartments we could fit in there!'

'Dad!' protested Tara. 'The old guy only just died! And you're already moving in on the property?'

'Officially the council asked for a valuation, in case Rourke left it to the state,' he said, ruffling her black hair before she could flinch away. 'But it doesn't hurt to speculate . . . I mean, imagine the possibilities. There's a lot of work to be done. We'd have to get that bridge fixed, first of all . . .'

He hurried off to oversee four council workers who were trying to shift a footbridge that had fallen into the stream that fed the castle's moat. A sheet of water was building up behind it and spreading like a gleaming, translucent pancake across the muddy lawn. Everyone's footprints were being submerged, human and animal alike. On the far side of the lake, two more council workers were struggling to catch something that looked very much like a zebra.

'Do you think he had a pet platypus?' Tara asked. 'I've always wanted to see one of those.'

'Really?' said Jack. 'They'd creep me out, I reckon.'

'Why?'

'Well, it's like they're made from bits of lots of animals, all mixed together.'

'Like Frankenstein's monster?'

'Yeah . . . I guess.'

Tara was quiet for a moment, then she said in a distant voice, 'I had a dream like that . . . I think. There was a monster . . . or something . . . made of lots of smaller things. You were in the dream, Jack. And you too, Jaide. But I can't . . . quite . . . remember it.'

Jaide sought some way to change the subject. Tara wasn't remembering a dream, but something that had really happened to all of them. Four weeks ago, they had been attacked by The Evil, which had a nasty habit of taking over living things and mixing them together, creating very real monsters that could in turn attack people. After The Evil had been vanquished, one of Grandma X's fellow Wardens, a big-haired man called Aleksandr, had used his Gift to cloud Tara's memory of everything that had happened to her. Sometimes the memory poked up again though, like a whale breaching, before returning to the depths. What would happen if it ever came right out, Jaide didn't like to imagine.

'Look down there,' Jack said. 'Are they statues down by the creek? Let's check them out.'

Tara shook herself, sending droplets of water tumbling down her green coat. 'They don't look like anything special.'

'Come on,' said Jaide, relieved to hear Tara's voice returning to normal. 'We're going to get washed away if we stay here.'

The pool of water was spreading rapidly towards them, backed up from where the bridge had fallen into the creek. Tara's dad was waving his arms imperiously, to the annoyance of all, and the sound of raised voices was getting steadily louder as the problem showed no sign of being fixed.

Jack, Jaide and Tara gave the puddle a wide berth and headed past the impromptu dam to where a much-reduced trickle ran along the slimy creek bed. The ground was slippery underfoot and the rain showed no sign of letting up.

It was weird, Jack thought, how Portland had been sunny when they had set out after school. The clouds had only gathered and the rain begun when they reached the estate. And it was odder still how it seemed to be raining *only* on the estate, not anywhere else. It was so heavy and set in . . .

'There you go!' Tara called back to them from the line of statues. 'Men in sheets and women without any arms. What's with these old guys? Don't they have any taste?'

Jack opened his mouth to say that being rich meant you didn't have to have any taste, but Jaide's hand gripping his forearm sent the umbrella wobbling and pulled him to a sudden halt.

'Look,' she whispered, pointing in such a way that Tara couldn't see into an untidy copse at the far edge of the estate. 'There's someone in those trees, waving at us.'

'Where?'

'There!'

Jack peered into the shadows under the trees, using his Gift to see details Jaide could only guess at. His Gift was strongest at night, but the sun was so hidden right now behind heavy rain clouds that his sight was clear. There *was* someone in the copse, a lone man in a coat and hat, his eyes invisible behind dark glasses. It was hard to make out more than that, but he was definitely staring right at Jack and his sister and his right hand was above his head, waving back and forth.

'That looks like Dad' said Jaide, clutching Jack even more tightly than before.

Jack squinted. 'It couldn't be him, could it? He's not supposed to come anywhere near us.'

'What if he's here because of Grandma's accident?'

Jack raised a hand, tentatively, and waved back.

The shadowy figure raised both hands in a triumphant thumbs up.

'It *is* Dad!' exclaimed Jaide.

The twins hadn't been this close to their father since their Gifts had woken, apart from once, when the protection supplied by the four wards of Portland had broken. He wasn't allowed to be near to them because it made their Gifts go crazy.

There was, however, no denying the relief they felt on seeing him. Someone must have told him about what had happened, and perhaps he had come back to check on them from a distance.

Jaide waved too and suddenly, with long energetic strides, their father moved towards them, stepping out from under the trees and across the sodden lawn. Jack and Jaide were torn between being pleased to see him and freaking out.

'What's he *doing* here?' hissed Jaide. 'If someone sees. . .'

Jack looked frantically around. Tara was busy poking her finger into the eye socket of a statue. The council workers were hard at work shifting the bridge and chasing the escaped animals – but all it would take was one of them to look around and recognise their father.

'We need a distraction!' said Jaide. Their father had already crossed half the distance between them.

Jack thought fast.

'Use your Gift,' he said, glancing up at the clouds. Jaide's Gift was mostly tied to the sun. 'It should be kind of damped down right now. I'll go and talk to him while you keep everyone busy – and keep your distance while you're doing it.'

'I'm not sure that's a good idea,' said Jaide. 'Besides, I want to talk to him too!'

'Can you think of anything else?'

'Not right away –'

'There's no time. Just do it!'

'All right, all right!' said Jaide, giving him the umbrella. 'I'll do my best – but don't use your Gift when you're near him. Who knows what might happen?'

Jack could easily imagine. His Gift gave him power over light and shade, allowing him to shadow-walk, among other useful skills, when he could control it properly. When he couldn't, it had the power to black out the sun.

'Be careful,' he said to Jaide.

'I will. You too.'

Jack hurried towards the bank of the creek, practically vanishing into the thick grey sheets of rain.

Jaide shielded her eyes with her hand against the downpour, and turned to look up the slight rise past the dammed creek to the castle, where Tara's dad was still arguing with the council workers.

'A distraction,' she whispered to herself.

She felt for her Gift, and embraced the slight breeze, collecting it around her, building it up so that she could use it. A gust escaped her hold for a moment, pirouetting round her like an invisible dancer, sending her damp hair flying.

'That's right,' she whispered, gesturing with her free hand to usher the wind away from her. Strands of wet red hair lashed her face, but she ignored them. 'You can do it.'

The gust grew stronger, whisked twice more round her, then shot off up the slope, where it capered round the arguing men, snatched up Tara's dad's hat. He clutched at it, missed, and knocked the man closest to him on to his backside. The hat smacked the face of a third man and everything dissolved into chaos.

Jack heard sudden shouts behind him, but he didn't turn round to look. His attention was fixed on his father, who was approaching rapidly across the muddy field. The rain seemed to fall even more heavily around him, so much so that it came down in visible sheets, beating on the umbrella so hard it sounded like it might collapse under the impact.

Hector Shield raised his hat and waved it in one hand. He shouted something that Jack couldn't make out. They were close enough now that Jack could clearly make out locks of curly brown hair plastered to his father's high forehead, so like Jack's own. His glasses were completely smeared with rain. Even with the characteristic welcoming smile on his face, he looked strained and worried.

'It's not deep!' Jack called out, as Hector suddenly stopped on the other side of the creek.

Hector didn't move. He had stopped as suddenly as if he'd run into a wall, and now he backed up a few feet, taking off his glasses and wiping them on his sleeve. He squinted at Jack with eyes that were a perfect match for his son's, apart from being desperately myopic.

'It's not deep!' Jack shouted again. 'Come over!' The rain was so loud now it drowned his words. He could hardly hear himself.

All of a sudden one side of his umbrella collapsed, and a great deluge washed down Jack's back. He cried out and threw the umbrella down in disgust.

His father shouted something in return, but Jack couldn't hear him. The rain was amazingly loud. Jack pointed at his ears, then at the sky and shrugged.

Hector Shield nodded, and pointed urgently at something

behind Jack, stabbing the air with his finger.

Jack whipped round, squinting against the rain. Even through the downpour he could see what his father was pointing at so emphatically.

A thick black twister was rising up over the castle like a supernatural cobra gathering its strength to strike.

A tornado.

Jaide's Gift had gone out of control.

'No, no,' Jaide hissed into the wind. She'd forgotten about trying to be unobtrusive and was making wild hauling-in motions with her hands. 'That's way too much!'

The twister didn't listen to her. It sucked in the rain and blew it out sideways like a fire hose, knocking a council worker upside down and sending him sliding across the mud with the speed of an ice-hockey puck. Then it swooped down and picked up the bridge, raising it high above the heads of the cowering workers, spinning it round faster and faster as it took it higher and higher, ready to bring it smashing down again.

'No!' shrieked Jaide. '*Listen* to me! Obey me!'

The twister slowed and bent forward, towards Jaide, the bridge still spinning thirty feet up in the air. The huddle of council workers suddenly split, everyone running in different directions.

Jaide felt the tension in the tornado, the built-up energy

that just had to go somewhere. It needed to do *something*.

'All right,' said Jaide sternly. 'Just don't hurt anyone, and then you really have to go back to normal.'

The tornado spun faster still, crouched down like a discus thrower, and then the bridge suddenly flew out of it, sailed across the field and smashed into the distant pyramid, broken pieces of timber sliding down the reinforced concrete slope.

Downstream, Jack watched open-mouthed as the twister reared up even higher, got thinner, and then just winked out of existence.

He had to shut his mouth as a massive raindrop fell straight down his throat. Coughing, he turned back towards his father, shrouded in rain on the other side of the creek. The water level had suddenly risen, now that the fallen bridge was no longer blocking the creek upstream, so there was no chance now for either of them to get across.

'Jack! *Mmmm* the *mmmmm*.'

'What?' shouted Jack, as loudly as he could.

'Catch – the – phone!'

The twin's father pulled back his left arm and threw something small and black high across the creek bed. Jack stepped back, stretched and caught the object, and then in the next instant his feet slid in the mud and he went over backwards, landing with a jarring thud.

'Ow,' said Jack. 'Major ow.'

He looked at the mobile phone clutched tightly in his hand.

It was in a plastic bag, with a charger. The screen was still lit up, showing a message.

I heard about grandma. Will call you later. Don't tell your mother I was here!

Jack looked across the stream. His father was backing away, disappearing into the darkness of the torrential rain.

'Wait! Don't go!'

A hand tugged at his shoulder.

'Jack? Are you all right? Did the tornado get you?'

It was Tara.

'Yeah, no, I just slipped.'

'Well, come *on*. Don't just stand there! You'll drown.'

The creek was rising incredibly quickly. The rain was phenomenal – it had to be some kind of cloudburst. Jack staggered to his feet, slipping the phone and charger into his pocket as Tara helped him up. She tried to hold her umbrella over him, but one last errant remnant of the twister blew past, smashing the umbrella's ribs and turning it inside out.

'Oh no!' exclaimed Tara. 'That was Mum's! This weather is *crazy*!'

'You can say that again,' said Jaide, who had just run up. She looked apologetically at Jack, but there wasn't time to say anything more before Tara's father bore down on them.

'Are you all right?'

He pulled Tara into a hug. Tara's dad had been much more protective of her since The Evil's last attack, when she'd been

37

caught up in the train wreck. Tara had told the twins she both liked and disliked this new attention. This time, she let him keep his arm round her.

'Do you three want to go home?' asked Tara's dad. 'I can come back later by myself. You're soaked, and this rain, this amazing wind . . .'

'I think it's easing,' said Tara. 'I'm not cold. And I don't mind being soaked. I want to see the rest of the estate.'

The rain was easing, at least near the castle. Further off, towards the woods where the twins' father had gone, it was still bucketing down.

'What about you two?'

'We're fine,' said Jaide, answering for both of them. 'Lead on, McAndrew!'

She fell back a few paces as they headed for the pyramid.

'Did you speak to Dad?' she whispered to her brother. 'What did he say?'

Jack retrieved the message and held the phone out to her, keeping it cradled in his palm.

Jaide stared at it, her pale brow creased, the rain trickling down her face like tears.

'Is that all?'

'He didn't have time for more,' whispered Jack. 'Someone might have seen him.'

'But still —'

'We can ask him when he calls us. Besides, look, Jaide – he gave us a *phone*.'

The upside of their brief encounter with their father only occurred to her then. The twins had been hankering for a mobile phone for months, but neither their mother nor their grandmother had given in. It was hard to play them off against each other when they agreed so absolutely, if only on that single point. But now their father had given them one, and they hadn't even had to ask!

Despite the circumstances, it was a welcome development.

'Let's call him,' Jaide said.

'The number he texted us on is blocked . . .'

Tara glanced over her shoulder to hurry them up and Jack hastily put the phone away again. Whatever their father had to say to them would have to wait a little while longer.

CHAPTER THREE
The Mission

The phone burned a hole in Jack's pocket all the while they were on the castle grounds, following Tara's father from place to place as he inspected the other structures for their market potential. None of it was all that interesting because a lot of the internal rooms were locked. Even the pyramid was a let-down, although Jack was kind of impressed that the bridge hadn't even dented the outer face.

Ordinarily the twins would have been interested in the makeshift menagerie and its unhappy occupants, but by that stage they just wanted to get home and find out how Grandma X was.

Most of the animals were being patched up by Portland's vet after being recaptured. The vet was a slender woman with surprisingly big hair, even with the rain weighing it down. She explained that several animals were still missing, including a grey wolf and both chimpanzees.

'There's a macaw too,' she said. 'If you see it, leave it well alone. Parrots can have a nasty bite.'

'No problem,' said Tara. 'All I want to do now is get out of the rain.'

'Agreed,' said Jack. 'Can we go now?'

Tara's father was staring at the porter's lodge, no doubt thinking about how it could be redeveloped or knocked down.

'What? Oh, sure. I've seen enough.'

Susan was waiting for them when they got home. Dinner was on the stove, a stir-fry whose vegetables had been cooked so long it was hard to tell the chicken from the carrots. Neither twin cared about that though. The appearance of their father at the estate had thoroughly rattled them. His presence suggested that Grandma X was sicker than anyone was telling them.

'She had a brain scan this afternoon,' Susan reported. 'They're waiting for the results. It's perfectly routine. You don't need to worry about it. Just go and get changed and then we'll eat, OK?'

'Have you spoken to Dad?' asked Jack.

'I tried calling him while I was in the hospital. He didn't pick up, but then he rang an hour ago. I could hardly hear him, but I think he got the message about Grandma before the phone dropped out. I have no idea where he is – the middle of nowhere probably. Now go! You're dripping all over the floor.'

Jack literally bit his tongue to stop himself from telling her that Hector wasn't on the other side of the world, but practically on Portland's doorstep. But the message on the phone stopped him: *Don't tell your mother.* Whatever was going on, it was strictly Warden business.

By the time the twins were dried and warm in fresh clothes, the vegetables were even gloopier and their anxieties hardly quelled. Jaide barely tasted her mother's cooking, which was probably for the best, and Jack did little more than push his food around the plate.

'Tell me what you did with Tara today,' Susan said in an attempt to bring them out of their thoughts.

'We went to the Rourke Estate,' said Jaide, but instead of distracting her, the topic only made her think of her father again. She kept one hand on her jeans pocket at all times. The phone their father had given them was an old-fashioned model that sent text messages and took calls, but unfortunately did little else. Jack had worked out how to turn it to vibrate, and the twins were taking turns keeping it in their pockets.

'I was talking to Dr Peters in the hospital,' said Susan. 'He said people only knew that something had happened to Young Master Rourke when his animals started showing up in town.'

'Why's he called Young Master Rourke?' asked Jack.

'Mister Rourke was his father, so he was "Young Master" even when he was old,' Susan said. 'That's what everyone called them anyway.'

'Did you ever meet him?' asked Jaide.

'No, but your grandfather did. He serviced the clocks on the estate while he was alive.'

Jack's ears pricked up. They knew very little about Grandma X's husband. 'Dad's dad?'

Susan nodded, but had nothing else to add. He had died years before Hector and Susan had met. 'There's a Rourke Road. I guess that's named after either Mister or Young Master Rourke. The swamp too, and the park.'

'How did he die?' asked Jack.

'Dr Peters said he had a heart attack, although there were some suspicious circumstances. Apparently, the lodge where they found him had been turned inside out. Constable Haigh said it looked like a break-in, but nothing obvious had been taken.'

'Why weren't you called out?' Jaide asked.

'Because I wasn't on duty. Besides, a ground crew could get there easily enough.'

'Could you have done anything if you were there?'

'I don't think so, Jaide. He was an old man. There's nothing anyone could've done.'

With a soft thud, Ari, a ginger tomcat who frequently put in an appearance at mealtimes, jumped through the open kitchen window. His whiskers twitched as he surveyed the meal from the vantage point of the window sill.

'I disagree,' he said. 'Something needs to be done immediately. All the noise on the old man's estate has scared the mice away.'

'Always hungry,' said Susan, almost as though she could hear what Ari was saying. 'Don't feed him, Jack. You'll only encourage him.'

Ari looked less than impressed by the broccoli Jack had surreptitiously offered him. Turning up his nose, the cat looked pointedly at the chicken, but Susan shooed him away.

Ari jumped down and sat at Jaide's feet, rubbing his head against her ankle. Jaide put her hand on the phone for the thousandth time. It felt just like an inert lump of plastic. Mobile phones were very unreliable in Grandma X's home, losing reception and power for no reason. What if their father was calling at that very second, but he couldn't get through?

'Have they found the person who drove Grandma off the road yet?' Jack asked.

'No, but I promise you they're looking.' Susan said. 'In a small town like this, nobody gets away with anything for long.'

Across the table, Jaide jumped as though Ari had bitten her on the leg. She stared at Jack wide-eyed for an instant, then jumped again.

'Can I be excused?' she said.

Without waiting for an answer, she ran from the table. Jack fought the impulse to run after her. It was hard, since he knew that the only reason Jaide would act like that was if the phone was ringing. If only *he* had had it at that moment. He might be the one talking to their father, hearing his familiar voice in his ear.

He was so distracted thinking about the call that he ate two whole pieces of broccoli without having to be asked, all the while watching the door for Jaide's return.

A minute later, Jaide peered round the kitchen doorway, her eyes bright and the phone safely tucked behind her back. She jerked her head, indicating that he should join her.

'Can I be excused too?' asked Jack.

'What's going on with you two?' asked Susan as Jack hurried from the table. 'I'll start dessert without you if you take too long!'

Jack held his breath until he and Jaide were up in their room, well out of earshot.

'It's him,' she whispered, taking the phone out of her pocket and putting it on speaker so they could both hear.

'I'm back,' she said. 'And I have Jack with me.'

'Hello, Dad,' said Jack.

'Hello, son,' came the familiar voice over the phone. Hector Shield was almost inaudible, thanks to a roaring noise in the background that Jack realised was more heavy rain. 'I'm sorry it took me so long to get through to you. The house makes it very difficult . . .'

His voice disappeared under the drumbeat of the rain for a second. When it came back, he was still speaking.

'. . . must all be very frustrating to you, but you surely understand by now why I can't come any closer.'

'Our Gifts,' said Jack, hoping his wouldn't suddenly go crazy and ruin everything.

'. . . saw what happened today at the estate. With your grandmother incapacitated, your Gifts are even more dangerous than usual . . . can't set foot in Portland without risking a disaster.'

The twins understood, but couldn't help being disappointed.

'Do you know how Grandma is doing?' asked Jaide. 'Mum tells us not to worry –'

'But she *would* say that,' put in Jack. 'Can you tell us what's really going on?'

'I know as much as you do,' said Hector. '. . . waiting for the results of the scan . . .'

The twins leaned closer to the phone, straining for every word.

'. . . called me just before she was hit by that van . . . was on the way to retrieve a powerful artefact, hidden from The Evil long ago . . .'

Hector's voice was lost again. He sounded like he was talking in front of a waterfall.

'Dad, speak up!' said Jaide into the phone, as loud as she dared.

'Did The Evil cause the crash?' asked Jack, the thought

sending gooseflesh spreading in a wave up his arms.

'. . . not possible . . . wards still intact . . . no danger to her or to you . . .'

Jaide breathed a sigh of relief. That was one less thing to worry about. But it was still odd, the accident happening just as Grandma X was on such a mission.

'She was planning to meet me afterwards,' Hector Shield said. His voice was a bit clearer now, as if he'd found somewhere out of the rain. 'Near where I saw you at the Rourke Estate, where the artefact was hidden. *Is* hidden. It must still be there, since she didn't make it that far. It's critical we find the artefact quickly, before it's sold off and lost forever . . . might even fall into The Evil's hands . . . I've searched every inch of the estate outside the wards and it's not there . . . must be inside the castle, inside the wards . . .'

Once again a roaring, gushing sound drowned out his voice. The twins looked at each other, thinking exactly the same thought.

'We could help you, Dad!' exclaimed Jaide, struck with the idea that they could help their father. It wasn't the same as being with him, but it was close. 'There's nothing stopping *us* going back.'

'I was going to ask Custer . . .'

'He's busy minding the wards for Grandma,' said Jack.

'Or a Warden from out of town . . .'

'Why, Dad?' Jaide persisted. 'We're right here – and we were right there on the estate today. If we'd known, we could've looked for you then!'

'I'm not sure,' their father said, but they could tell he was thinking about it. 'The artefact is very powerful. It could even be dangerous in the hands of a troubletwister.'

'We'll be very careful,' Jaide promised. 'Please let us help.'

'*Please*,' Jack added. 'I know we can do it.'

The noise of the rain redoubled, smothering their father's voice. They could still hear him, speaking slowly and firmly, as though fighting to be heard, but his words were unrecognisable.

'Stupid house,' said Jaide, staring up at the ceiling and literally shaking her fist. 'Let him through! It's not going to do any harm, just *talking* to him!'

As though the house heard her, the rushing noise faded and the words became clear.

'All right, but . . . call later, hard to talk now . . . ask the *Compendium*.'

'What do we ask it?' Jack leaned close to the phone to hear as best as he could.

'. . . the Card of Translocation . . . but remember, be careful!'

With that final word, the call cut out completely, and Hector Shield was gone.

The twins sat staring at the phone for a long minute, considering everything their father had told them.

'The Card of Translocation,' said Jaide, rolling the words

round her mouth as though that might tell her what they meant. What did translocation mean? What kind of card? And why was it hidden at the Rourke Estate?

'It doesn't sound like much,' said Jaide. 'What's so special about a card?'

'Is there someone else up here?' asked Ari from the door to their room.

Jack snatched up the phone and shoved it deep into his pocket. Their father may have given it to them, but not with their mother or grandmother's permission.

'No,' he said. 'We're just, uh, talking about homework.'

The cat narrowed his eyes for a moment. 'I thought I heard someone else.'

'You couldn't have,' Jack insisted, 'because there's no one else here.'

Ari's eyes closed down to menacing slits, as if he was stalking a mouse. Jack and Jaide shifted uncomfortably, even though they weren't lying to him. They *were* the only people in the house, apart from him and their mother.

'You're sure you didn't hear anything?' asked Ari.

Jack and Jaide slowly shook their heads.

'Ah, well.' Ari's eyes opened wider, and he yawned, revealing every one of his very sharp teeth. 'Perhaps I imagined it.'

'You must have, I guess,' said Jaide weakly.

'But I have been hearing an odd voice all evening,' mused the cat. 'Hard to pinpoint . . .'

Ari suddenly shook his head once, then shook it a second time more violently, as if he might dislodge something from his ear.

'Have you seen Kleo, by any chance?' he asked.

Kleopatra was the second of Grandma X's Warden Companions, a Russian blue who was also Protector of the Portland catdom.

'I haven't seen her since yesterday,' said Jaide, only realising that fact as she said the words. Kleo was normally close at hand, keeping an eye on the troubletwisters in case they got into trouble.

'Sorry,' said Jack.

With a worried look, Ari thanked them and padded from the room.

'Oh,' he added at the top of the stairs, 'there's chocolate pudding.'

'Home-made or from the shop?' asked Jack.

'The shop. And if you're not there in one minute, your mother's going to give it all to me . . .'

The twins bolted past the cat to the kitchen, where Susan had just served up two steaming bowlfuls of Jack's favourite dessert and was in the process of adding dollops of thick farm-fresh cream to both. She placed a smaller bowl on the floor for Ari, with a wink at the twins as though to say, 'Don't tell your grandmother.'

Even as they ate, thoughts of their father, mysterious cards and their mission were far from forgotten. They couldn't raise any of those subjects, but Young Master Rourke, who had a Warden artefact hidden somewhere on his estate, was still fair game.

'He can't have been *completely* isolated up there, can he?' said Jaide. 'Surely he had friends, family, the occasional visitor . . .'

'There was a groundsman, I believe,' said Susan. 'But no one else. He was an only child who never married and didn't leave any heirs. Sorting out what happens to his estate will be a terrible exercise, I'm sure.'

'I wonder what he did all day?' asked Jack, thinking of how easily a single card could get lost among so much stuff.

'I guess he read his books,' she said. 'He was a great collector apparently, and his library was very extensive.'

'Wasn't he lonely?' asked Jaide.

'Some people like the quiet, Jaide. Remember, your grand-mother was alone until we came to live with her. Apart from the cats of course.'

She reached down to pat Ari, who had finished his pudding and looked up hopefully for more.

'It's funny,' she said, more to herself than her children. 'I thought it'd be quiet here, but there always seems to be something going on. Giant storms, trains coming off the rails, rich old men dying, car crashes . . .' She shook herself and smiled brightly. 'Well, at least it's not boring. Now, when you've finished, I believe it's your turn to do the dishes.'

'It's *always* our turn to clean up,' said Jaide.

'That's because you're so good at it.'

Jack and Jaide polished off the last of their dessert and reluctantly took the dishes to the sink, where after a short argument, Jack washed and Jaide dried. Susan wandered off to another room to do her own thing on the computer, Ari hopped back out of the window and the twins were able to whisper among themselves.

'How are we going to get at the *Compendium*?' asked Jack.

'Later, when she's asleep. I'll set the alarm on the phone.' Jaide blew soapy foam off the back of a plate. 'I'm more worried about how we get back into the estate. I mean, we can't keep going with Tara's dad, can we?'

'I don't know,' said Jack. 'Maybe we can. Besides, there might be another way. Remember what Mum said about Young Master Rourke and his books?'

'He collected them. So?'

'Rodeo Dave said that he was going back to the estate to catalogue the collection for the . . . what do you call them? Not executioners.'

'Executors. Of course! We'll ask tomorrow.'

The twins finished the dishes and the rest of their chores, and went to bed satisfied that they had at least the beginning of a plan.

CHAPTER FOUR
Forgotten Things

An ear-splitting beeping woke Jack at two a.m. He lurched bolt upright in bed, heart pounding. He had turned the phone's volume up full because he hadn't wanted to sleep through the alarm. Now the whole house would be woken up for sure! How could he have known it would be so *loud*?

The beeping appeared to have stopped, however, and only slowly did he realise that it had only *seemed* loud to him. As well as turning the volume up, he had put it under his pillow next to his right ear. Once his head was off the pillow he could hardly hear it at all.

The flashing screen was bright to his eyes, enhanced by his Gift. He switched the alarm off and slipped out of bed, tiptoeing across the room to wake up Jaide. It took him two attempts, and even when her eyes were open he suspected she was still mostly asleep.

'Is the monster back?' she asked blearily.

'No, that was last time. And it wasn't a monster anyway, remember? It was the Living Ward.'

'Oh, right.' She slowly put the pieces together. The four

wards of Portland came in different types, memorialised in a poem every troubletwister was taught:

SOMETHING GROWING
SOMETHING READ
SOMETHING LIVING
SOMEONE DEAD

The first time The Evil had attacked it had been through the 'Something Read' Ward, formerly a brass plaque at the top of Portland's lighthouse. The twins had made some romantic graffiti their parents had written the new ward and The Evil had been repelled. But a part of it had been caught inside the boundary established by the Wards, and it had attacked the Living Ward next. This was a former axolotl that had mutated into a hideous creature Portland's citizens had occasionally glimpsed, thinking it a monster. When the giant axolotl was killed, the new Living Ward was Rennie, a woman who had once been absorbed by The Evil, but who had managed to free herself, though she was horribly injured. Now she lived in the attic above Rodeo Dave's bookshop, recuperating and doing whatever it was the Living Ward was supposed to do, which the twins suspected was basically just staying alive.

The Evil had been quiet since then, and there had been no signs of it stirring. The weathervane on top of Grandma X's house had only pointed in the direction of the wind for weeks now, and none of the other magical items that she had deployed showed any signs of activity.

Jaide got out of bed and put on her father's old dressing gown. Even though there was a slight risk that it might interfere with her Gift, since anything a Warden interacted with for a long time absorbed a little of their powers, Grandma X had admitted the chance was very slight and had allowed her to keep it.

Jack took his sister's arm and guided her through the house and up the stairs to the top floor, both of them carefully avoiding the creaky floorboards that they had memorised from frequent practice.

They paused on the uppermost step, listening automatically for the sound of Grandma X's snoring. But that night there was only silence. Grandma X was in a hospital bed on the other side of town – they wouldn't be up in the middle of the night were she not. The top floor of the house was empty.

Even as they took the final step, however, they heard a faint voice calling, 'Rourke!'

'Did you hear that?' hissed Jaide.

'Yes,' whispered Jack. 'I wish I hadn't.'

'Rourke!'

Jaide felt her brother's hand tighten on her arm.

'Maybe it's the old man's ghost?'

'Why . . . why would he be calling his own name?'

'I don't know.'

'Rooooourke!'

'Where's it coming from?'

Jaide pointed at the door on the top landing. It looked like an ordinary door, but it wasn't. Although it should have opened on to a north-facing bedroom, against all laws of geometry and space, it actually led to the house's basement, where Grandma X maintained the secret workshop that was the heart of her mission in Portland.

Called the Blue Room, it contained talking skulls, silver swords, living chess sets and a thousand other things that defied easy description. There was also a huge mahogany writing desk that had no obviously special powers, but was the home of *A Compendium of The Evil*, the repository of knowledge collected by Wardens down the centuries. A thick folder full of notes, drawings and often incomprehensible essays, it was kept safely away from Susan while she was in the house. They saved their true education for the three days of every normal week when their mother was stationed in Scarborough.

The only other entrance to the basement was from the front of the house, through a blue door that was hidden from the eyes of non-Wardens. The lock on that door could only be opened from the inside, and although the twins had worked out how to manage that during their first days in Portland, it was much easier to take the stairs.

'Rooooourke!'

The distant cry came again.

'I suppose we should check it out,' said Jaide, but she didn't move.

'Maybe we should wake up Mum?'

'We'll never get the *Compendium* if we do that,' said Jaide. She took a deep breath and then forced herself to step forward.

Nervously, one synchronised step at a time, they crossed the landing and opened the door.

'Rooooourke!' cried the voice again as they stepped through. It was much louder than before and Jaide jumped, rising six foot off the ground and almost colliding with the ceiling before she got her Gift under control.

Jack fought an urge to run back to their bedroom, but instead he pulled Jaide down and led the way onward.

The Blue Room was dimly lit by the eternal candle flames of two crystal chandeliers. Little was visible in the gloom, even to Jack's night vision. There were so many competing shadows, a few of them quite dissimilar to the objects that cast them. A hat rack cast a shadow that bent into a right-angle in the middle. The broken grandfather clock cast no shadow at all.

Atop a coffee table balanced on one slender leg sat something new: a cloth-covered shape that was round about the middle, like a barrel, and domed at the top. The silken cloth shone in the candlelight, patterned with red and gold hibiscus flowers. Tassels along the bottom swayed gently, as though in a breeze.

'Rourke! Rourke! Rourke!' shouted the voice, startlingly loud in the gloom, and this time both twins nearly hit the ceiling.

'Who's there?' said a stern voice from the other side of the cloth-covered shape, which was now rocking furiously from side to side. 'Come forward, where I can see you!'

The twins knew that voice and they obeyed it instantly.

Sitting in a chair shaped like a dragon's mouth was a regal, blue-grey cat.

'Jack and Jaide,' Kleo said with the slow intonation of a judge. 'What are you two doing down here?'

'Oh, Kleo,' said Jaide, 'we came to look something up in the *Compendium*, and then –'

'Rourke! Rourke!' shrieked the voice.

'What *is* that?' asked Jack.

Kleo nodded at the cloth-covered thing.

'Take a look. She won't hurt you.'

Jaide reached out with one tentative hand, grabbed the cloth by a dangling corner and swept it aside.

Both twins stepped back in surprise.

Beneath the cloth was a big brass cage. Inside the cage, running back and forth on a thick wooden perch, was a very grouchy-looking parrot.

'Rourke!' it said, fixing them with first one baleful eye, then another, swivelling its head from side to side as it did so. Its curved beak was black and sharp-tipped. Even in the gloom, the colouring of its feathers was magnificent, a deep royal blue, apart from a dash of bright yellow around each eye and another on either side of its beak. It was easily the largest bird Jack had ever seen, its tail feathers so long and pointed they stuck out of the side of the cage.

'Rourke!' it said, and Jaide suddenly felt like giggling. Was it saying 'Rourke' or just squawking?

'*Rawk*?' she said back at it.

The bird took a step away from her.

'Cut and run,' it said in a hoarse but clear voice. 'Parrots and children first!'

'What is it?' asked Jack, coming round to look at it from the other side.

'*She* is a Hyacinth Macaw,' said Kleo, licking a paw and smoothing down the fur behind her ears.

'What's she doing down here?' asked Jaide.

The macaw clicked loudly with a thumb-like tongue and glared at her again.

'Cornelia is here because I am guarding her.'

'Guarding her from what?'

'Ari partly,' said the cat. 'Can you imagine what he'd do with a giant bird in a cage? He has no self-control when it comes to food. Begging your pardon, Cornelia.'

Jack could imagine Ari eating Cornelia for sure, even if the cat felt really bad about it afterwards. But the parrot also had a very large beak and a wicked eye. Jack smiled. Perhaps the protection was for Ari as well.

A series of sudden understandings had come to Jaide too, along with a suspicion or two. Ari had been hearing the macaw's voice long before they had, which meant the bird had been in the Blue Room for some time, perhaps all weekend – and the town vet had mentioned a macaw that had escaped from the old man's menagerie and was still on the loose . . .

'What else are you guarding her from?' Jaide asked.

'I'm not entirely sure. Cornelia doesn't want to talk about it yet. But she was at the estate the night the old man died, and it's possible she saw something.'

This was a juicy revelation.

'So you think he didn't just die of a heart attack?' Jaide asked. 'You think it might be murder?'

'And so Cornelia's in witness protection until Grandma comes back?' added Jack excitedly.

Kleo raised a calming paw.

'Don't jump to conclusions, troubletwisters. We don't know that she saw anything at all. She arrived here Saturday, just after midnight, in a terrible state. She won't talk to me because I'm a cat, no matter how much I try to persuade her that I am no ordinary cat, and she won't talk to Custer either because he turns into a cat. She just gets agitated and shouts the old man's name over and over. All I know is that something frightened her, and frightened her very badly.'

'Custer was here?' asked Jaide.

'After the accident,' Kleo explained. 'He came by to collect some of your grandmother's things, and he set up the cage for Cornelia while he was here.'

'Did he say anything about Grandma?'

Kleo's ears flattened in regret. 'Only to keep an eye on everyone in this house, and to keep Ari away.'

Cornelia was watching them with her big black eyes, rimmed with yellow so they looked permanently startled.

'Rourke,' she chirruped quietly.

Jack felt sorry for her. He didn't know much about parrots, but he knew they lived for a long time. Cornelia might have been in Young Master Rourke's menagerie for decades. Maybe they had been friends. Now he was gone.

'Perhaps *we* could try talking to her,' he said, edging closer to the cage.

Kleo stood up on all four legs, as though about to intervene, but all she said was, 'Perhaps, Jack, but be careful.'

'I know,' he said. 'I read once how a parrot bit the leg off an eagle.'

Jaide watched curiously as Jack bent over so he was eye to eye with Cornelia. The macaw studied him warily too, leaning with her weight mainly on her left clawed foot. It had a metal ring around it, he noticed for the first time, as though she had once been tagged by a scientist. Her head bobbed up and down, not encouragingly, more as though she was reassuring herself of something.

'Rourke?'

'I'm not Young Master Rourke,' Jack said, 'but I'd like to be your friend, if you'll let me.'

Cornelia tilted her head one way, then the other.

'There's a bag of seeds and nuts by the cage door,' said Kleo. 'Try offering her one.'

Jack fished around in the paper bag until he found a Brazil nut. He held it by one end and slid it between the bars.

The macaw's tongue appeared again, tapping against its beak as though tasting the treat already.

Cornelia took one step closer.

'That's it,' said Jack. 'You can trust me.'

The sharp-tipped beak reached out as though to take the nut, but then she suddenly stopped, turned her head sideways and glared at Jack's fingers, before suddenly jerking back and flapping her wide blue wings, the cage rocking violently.

'Enemy in sight!' she cried. 'Rourke! Rourke!'

Jack jerked away, so startled by her sudden violence that he dropped the nut on to the floor. He hadn't done anything except talk kindly to her and offer her something to eat. What had upset her?

'She was fine until she got close to me,' he said.

'Maybe you smell bad,' said Jaide.

'How could I!?' protested Jack. 'I've had like the equivalent of ten showers today.'

'Put the cloth over the cage,' said Kleo. 'That calms her down eventually.'

Jaide did as instructed, sweeping the silk up and over the brass bars. Cornelia watched her with avian wariness and flapped her wings, making the cover puff out like a curtain in front of a window on a windy day.

Then with a few softer 'Rourke's and one final, plaintive 'All at sea', she settled down into silence.

'Poor thing,' Jack said, almost to himself. 'I feel sorry for you.'

'I wouldn't feel too sorry if I were you,' said Jaide. 'I reckon you almost lost a finger a minute ago.'

'How would you feel if your master had just died?' asked Jack angrily. 'She must've come here for help and wound up stuck in a cage – can't you imagine how that must *feel*?'

Jack wasn't angry at his sister very often. He was by nature an even-tempered boy who shied away from serious conflict. Perhaps because he was tired and worried about Grandma X, or because he had always wanted a pet of his own, but this was suddenly one of those times. Anger flared up in him like a wild thing, and his Gift responded instinctively. The candles flickered and a deep dark shade fell across the room, as though the air was suddenly full of black smoke.

'Jackaran Shield, listen to me.'

A soft but insistent bump against his left calf muscle brought him back to himself. He blinked and looked down at Kleo, who carefully put one paw on his leg and slowly extended her claws. She didn't do anything else, but it got his full attention.

'The cage isn't locked,' she said. 'Cornelia can let herself out any time she wants. I think she's in there because it makes her feel safe. That's why she came here in the first place.'

'Oh,' he said, feeling foolish. 'Sorry, Jaide.'

'It's OK, little brother,' she said, punching him lightly on the shoulder. She rarely called him that, because the difference between them was only four minutes, and because he hated it when she did. 'I cracked a stupid joke and we're both tired.'

'I'm not surprised,' said Kleo, glancing at the nearest working clock. 'What did you say you were doing down here at this hour?'

'We came to look at the *Compendium*,' Jaide said.

'What for? It's very late to be doing homework.'

'I know, but it's about what happened to Grandma. Did she say anything to you before she left this morning?'

'Anything about a card of some kind?' added Jack, putting the matter of Cornelia behind him.

'Not that I recall.' Kleo looked from one twin to the other. 'Should she have?'

'That's OK, Kleo.' Jaide wondered if she should try to look disappointed. If Grandma hadn't mentioned the missing card to her own Warden Companion, there must have been a reason. Or Kleo had been instructed to keep it a secret from them. Perhaps it was best not to push too hard. If Kleo found out they knew, she might try to talk their father out of letting them help.

'We understand,' said Jack, 'but it would make us feel better if we could just take a quick look.'

Kleo looked more amused than suspicious. 'All right, troubletwisters. You know where the *Compendium* is kept. But don't stay up too late or you'll be tired tomorrow and get into trouble at school.'

'We won't!' they promised, heading round the cage to go up the steps to the landing where the great mahogany desk sat. There, between two other large folders, rested the enormous blue folder that now contained brief records of their own encounters with the Wardens' ancient foe, along with everyone else's. A small card stuck into its plastic sleeve said *A Compendium of The Evil.*

Jaide pulled the folder free and laid it open on the desk. A great mass of different sorts of papers rustled and shifted, sounding uncannily as though the *Compendium* itself was waking up, as she had, from a very deep sleep.

'Remember what Dad told us to look for,' she whispered to Jack, closing the folder again and putting her hands on the cover. Jack did the same and faintly, barely audible at all, she heard him whisper.

'The Card of Translocation . . . the Card of Translocation.'

Jaide closed her eyes and repeated the name with him three times more, then she opened her eyes and together they opened the *Compendium* to see what it would show them. She could never tell in advance what that might be. A picture sometimes, more often on thick parchment than photocopied; or an essay, typed or written in the crabbed hand of a long-dead Warden. Once, after asking who the first Warden was, they had opened the folder to find a collage made from feathers, shells and ochre. Neither of them knew what to make of the answer.

What they saw that night were numerous pages that appeared to have been printed on a modern laser-jet printer, held together with a thick metal clasp.

'What does it say?' asked Jaide.

The type was very small and Jack had to lean close to read it.

Along the top of the first page, underlined, was a title. Below that were names, and to the right of each name were two columns, one for 'Use', the other for 'Location'.

The Register of Lost and/or Forgotten Things
1. *The Sundered Map*
2. *The Sound of Meredith's Horn*
3. *Edgwick Bartle's Shoes*
4. *The Silver Card of Oblivion*

'What is it?' asked Jaide.

'It's a list.'

'I can see *that*. A list of what?'

'Lost and/or Forgotten Things of course.'

Jack put his finger on the page and scrolled down, then turned to the next one when the name he was looking for hadn't appeared. He found a lot of cards – and, oddly, reading glasses – but not all of the cards were made of metal. Some were ivory, while others were plastic or even crystal. He wondered what sort this one might be.

It was on the fourth page, halfway down:

261. *The Golden Card of Translocation*

Gold.

'Jaide, you know those decks of cards that Custer and Grandma have?'

Jaide nodded. Of course she did. Grandma X had used a deck of large, incredibly heavy cards of gold to try and evaluate their Gifts when they'd first come to Portland. Custer had done the same more recently. Their cards started off blank and changed to reveal a symbol when touched by someone with a Gift. No one had ever told them who made the cards or what powers they might possess.

'It's one of those cards, do you think?' she asked.

'It must be.'

'But what makes a card so powerful and dangerous?'

'Maybe the Register will tell us.'

He scanned across the page, reading as he went.

'This is weird. It says, *at this time forgotten, best so, and lost to us, if not to the world.*'

'That's not very helpful.'

Jack leaned back and rubbed his eyes.

'Well, at least we know it exists.'

'Fat lot of help that is,' Jaide said. 'I wonder what Grandma and Dad want it for?'

'What would happen if we ask about gold cards in general?' Jack asked.

'Let's try it.'

They closed the *Compendium* and concentrated on an image of the two decks of gold cards they had seen so far. When they opened the folder again, there was a picture of a blank card on the page and a brief explanation beneath written in a looping, old-fashioned script: *For the Divination of Potential Powers and Safekeeping Thereof.*

'By 'powers', do you think it means Gifts?' asked Jaide.

'I guess so,' said Jack, 'but what does it mean by "safekeeping"?'

'I don't know. Maybe Wardens use the cards to store their Gifts when they're not using them.'

'Why *wouldn't* they use them?'

Kleo leaped on to the desk next to them, making them both jump.

'Did you find what you were looking for?'

Jaide slammed the *Compendium* shut, but not before the cat saw the page they had been staring at.

'No, we didn't,' she said.

'Your grandmother's deck is securely hidden and I won't tell you where,' Kleo said with feline smugness. 'Back to bed now. Troubletwisters aren't supposed to be nocturnal creatures, like cats.'

The twins let her lead them back past Cornelia's cage, to the elephant tapestry which hid the door to the upper floor. Jack listened for any sign of life from the macaw, but heard only a faint, stealthy shuffling of feathers.

'Promise me you won't tell Ari about Cornelia,' said Kleo. 'You can come back to say hello, but no other visitors are allowed. Not until she's settled anyway.'

'All right,' Jack promised. He *would* come back as often as he could. Cornelia must be lonely, he thought, without Young Master Rourke. Surely she would get used to him and wouldn't bite his finger off.

'Goodnight, Kleo,' said Jaide, scratching the cat under her chin. Kleo leaned in with a purr. The two of them had had their differences in the past, but they were now firm friends again, even if they were keeping small secrets from each other. Jaide imagined how surprised Kleo would be when the twins completed Grandma X's mission on their own. The thought made her smile.

'At least now we know what the card looks like,' she whispered when they were back in bed. 'That'll make it easier to find.'

Jack's eyes were heavy. 'It must be especially well hidden if no one's found it before now,' he said.

That sobering thought followed Jaide into sleep, and there were no answers waiting for her in her dreams.

CHAPTER FIVE
Monsters Old and New

There was no time to ask Rodeo Dave about the Rourke library that morning because the twins slept late and had barely enough time to scoff down some toast and hot chocolate before riding their bikes to school. They had hoped to visit Grandma X on the way, but Susan explained that it wasn't possible that morning.

'I rang as early as I could,' she said. 'The results of the scan were inconclusive. Someone's coming in from Scarborough today to look at them, a specialist in brain trauma.'

The twins looked at each other with concern. 'Brain trauma' sounded like something to seriously worry about.

'Will you go and see her?' asked Jaide. 'Will you make sure she's OK?'

'I promise I will,' their mother said, giving them a squeeze. 'The nurse said they're keeping her in strict isolation so she's forced to rest. You can imagine it, can't you? I bet she's bossing them around at every opportunity, when the sedatives wear off.'

Jack could imagine it very well, but he didn't find the thought amusing or reassuring. It worried him that she hadn't tried to contact them since the brief vision yesterday. He was afraid that, once again, all the important goings-on in Portland were being kept from them because they were too young.

Mr Carver's 'Happy Song of Beginning' was already under way when they ran through the front door of school. It sounded like a flute being tortured.

'I thought you weren't going to make it,' whispered Tara as they slipped into their seats at the desk they shared. 'What's that?'

The phone had slipped from Jack's bag and slid across the desk. He snatched it up.

'Uh, it's a phone,' he said.

'I thought you weren't allowed to have one!'

'Dad thought we should,' said Jaide, which was true enough.

'Great! What's your number? I'll put it into my phone and we can text each other.'

Jack and Jaide stared helplessly at each other.

'We've forgotten it,' said Jack.

'That's OK. I'll give you mine and then you can text me.'

She wrote down her number and Jack put it into his phone's memory. He texted 'testing testing' and waited. A second later, Tara's phone buzzed.

'Got it,' she said, 'but . . . your dad must've blocked your number. Why would he do that?'

'Maybe to stop us wasting all our credit,' improvised Jaide. 'If people can't text us, we can't text them back.'

'What's the point of a phone if you can't text?'

'Phones away, please,' said Mr Carver as he came into the room, massaging his nostrils after a long session playing his welcome music on the nose flute. 'Today we're going to start with a short discussion. As many of you will be aware, Portland lost one of its most venerable citizens over the weekend: George Archibald Mattheus Rourke the Third. He was a very rich man and a recluse, but I expect he touched all of our lives in one way or another. What can anyone here tell me about him?'

'Is he really dead or just missing?' muttered a voice at the back.

There was a small amount of laughter, but less than Jaide might have expected. The boy was referring to Rennie, who had for a week or so been presumed drowned before revealing herself to be very much alive.

'He's really dead,' said Miralda, who fancied she knew everything about everyone in Portland. 'Under mysterious circumstances too. They say his face was awful, as though he was scared to death.'

'That's not true,' said Kyle.

'Oh yeah? How do you know?'

'Because my dad . . .' He stopped and looked down, as though he wished he hadn't spoken up.

'That's right,' said Miralda with a smirk. 'Your dad worked for him, didn't he? What was he, again – a gardener or something?'

'Groundsman,' said Kyle with a flash of anger. 'And there's nothing wrong with that. He was the second person to see Young Master Rourke . . . Young Master Rourke's body . . . so he knows what he's talking about.'

'Not much call for *groundsmen* around here,' Miralda said. 'Not any more anyway . . .'

'Now, now, children,' said Mr Carver, trying weakly to forestall another argument. 'Let's stick to Mr Rourke.'

'Not *Mister* Rourke,' said Miralda, voice dripping with scorn. 'That was the father. Young *Master* Rourke didn't do anything. Without *Mister* Rourke, Portland wouldn't even be here. He built the railway line and the town hall and he brought all the fishermen here –'

'Whalers, not fishermen,' said Mr Carver.

'Fish, whales, what's the difference? It got the town going properly, didn't it? Young Master Rourke never did anything with his money except sit on it. That's what my dad says, and he would know because the old guy never gave *him* any.'

'He sponsored the library,' said a girl at the back. 'His name's on a plaque there.'

'And the cactus gardens,' said another.

'And he paid for the costumes for the annual musical, even though he never went himself.'

'What about the Peregrinators?' asked someone else. 'Didn't he build their clubhouse or something?'

'The what?' asked Jack.

'A bunch of crazy guys chasing UFOs,' said Miralda with a sniff. 'And besides, it's not a clubhouse, it's the sports shed on the oval. The Portland Peregrinators only use it once a month.'

'Yeah, but he paid for it, didn't he?' said Kyle.

'Anyone can *buy* stuff,' said Miralda. 'It takes leadership to do something with it. That's what Dad says –'

'Who cares what your dad says? My mum says he's just a guy who wears an ugly necklace and likes the sound of his own voice.'

Again, Mr Carver was forced to intervene, banging on a drum until he had everyone's attention.

'The important thing,' he said, 'as I think this all proves, is that no man is an island. Or woman either. Everything we do affects someone else, even if no one notices at the time.'

For once, Jack thought Mr Carver had a point. Young Master Rourke might as well not have existed for all he and Jaide had known. But now he was gone, it was apparent that everyone was involved to some degree, either because of things he had done while alive, or because of jobs they might lose now he was dead.

Kyle simmered silently all through that morning, as the class moved on to various states and countries and the names of their capital cities. Memorising them wasn't compulsory – nothing at the Stormhaven Innovative School of Portland was compulsory – but Jack didn't mind paying attention. Thinking about geography distracted him from worrying about Grandma X, and made him think of all the places his father must have been in his long career searching for such Lost and/or Forgotten Things as the Card of Translocation. Maybe one day, Jack thought, he too would travel like that, when he became a Warden.

When the lunch bells chimed, this time without Mr Carver's nose flute accompaniment, Jaide took the opportunity to put the next stage of their plan into action.

'Let's go and see Rodeo Dave,' she whispered to Jack, just a little too loudly.

'Can I come with you?' asked Tara. 'It's boring around here when you guys sneak off at lunchtime.'

'Er,' said Jack, glancing at Jaide, 'I guess so . . .?'

Jaide thought fast. Although they had nothing secret to discuss with Rodeo Dave, involving Tara in any expedition back to the estate might make searching for the Card of Translocation that much more complicated. But there was no way to put her off without sounding rude.

'Sure,' she said. 'Come along. It's just an old bookshop though.'

'I love books,' Tara said. 'Maybe I'll find something I haven't already read.'

'You're bound to,' said Jack. 'Rodeo Dave has everything.'

That wasn't remotely true, Jack knew, but he had yet to be disappointed. He liked reading too, and when he had finished the stack of childhood favourites his father had left behind in Grandma X's house, Jack had gone looking in The Book Herd for something similar. There was row after row of old westerns. He could read for years without running out.

As they explained to Mr Carver that they were going home for lunch, Jack felt as though he was being watched. He glanced over his shoulder and saw Kyle sitting on his own, staring hotly at them. Jack didn't know what they'd done to offend him. Maybe he was just upset because his dad might lose his job at the estate. Or maybe it was because they had each other and he had no one.

For a microsecond, Jack considered inviting Kyle along, but there were too many of them already and Kyle had done nothing to initiate friendship before. The middle of a mission wasn't the time to start making new friends.

On the way to the bookshop, Tara spotted a carved memorial stone outside the fish markets that had been dedicated by George Archibald Mattheus Rourke the Second in 1923, commemorating the loss of a commercial ship to a storm just outside the harbour.

The Book Herd was open but empty of customers, as it always seemed to be, but Rodeo Dave wasn't alone. Rennie was there as well. She and Dave looked up from his desk as the twins and Tara walked through the door.

'Well, hello,' said Rodeo Dave, brushing imaginary sticking-out hairs back into line on his thick proud moustache and beaming at them. He was in his usual jeans and cowboy boots, with a red-and-white check shirt. 'I wasn't expecting you kids around these parts on a school day.'

'Hello, Dave,' said Jaide, echoed by Jack. 'Hello, Rennie.'

Tara said nothing, and neither did Rennie. The woman who was Portland's Living Ward simply nodded her head and almost smiled.

She looked pale and thin, scarred physically and mentally by her time possessed by The Evil. She was wearing a black cotton dress, which had very long sleeves that didn't quite hide her twisted right arm or the complete absence of her left hand. She wore a yellow silk bandanna to conceal her lack of hair, and the skin of her throat was pockmarked and scarred, as though she had suffered terrible acne. The Warden healer called Phanindranath had done her best, but neither Warden Gifts nor modern surgery could correct all her injuries.

The almost-smile was new though. It showed that Rennie was healing on the inside, where it counted.

'Renita's going to be minding the shop while I'm busy on the Rourke Estate,' said Rodeo Dave. 'I could close it, but with Renita living here, I figured why miss out on the custom?'

A flicker of unease crossed Rodeo Dave's face as he said the name 'Rourke', but the twins didn't notice. This was the perfect opportunity for them to get back to the estate!

'Mum says the library is huge,' said Jack. 'Won't that take longer than a few days?'

'We could help you,' said Jaide brightly. 'Then you'd be done in no time at all.'

'I'm not sure that's a good idea,' said Rodeo Dave slowly, looking from one to the other.

'We won't get in the way,' said Jack. 'We promise.'

'But it'll be very boring.'

'Anything's better than homework,' said Jaide.

Rodeo Dave laughed. 'Well, yes, that's bound to be true. All right then, fine with me, but I'll have to talk to your grandmother first.'

'She's still in hospital,' said Jack. 'Mum'll probably be grateful we're not at home alone, getting in her way.'

'Sensible thinking, but I'll have to make sure. What about your friend here? Does she want to come too?'

Tara was staring at Rennie with a blank look on her face. When Rodeo Dave spoke to her, she blinked and looked away, as though waking from a dream.

'Oh, hello. Do you have anything with vampires?'

'Over on the far wall,' said Rodeo Dave, 'next to the maps of Vanuatu.'

Tara wandered off.

'She half remembers,' said Rennie unexpectedly, in a voice as rough and soft as a burn victim's.

'Remembers what, Renita?' asked Rodeo Dave.

'Nothing important,' said Jaide hastily, keen to change the subject before Rennie said something that Rodeo Dave shouldn't hear. 'Will you call Mum and ask her? Shall we come back here after school?'

'Unless you change your mind.' His usual grin returned. 'I'm sure you can think of better things to do than hang out with an old man's books. Now, who's for lunch?'

'Me!' said Jack, opening his lunch box on the desk. It was lunchtime, after all, and his stomach was complaining. Rodeo Dave joined him, unwrapping a thick ham, cheese and mustard sandwich. Rennie didn't eat anything, even when Jaide offered her a bright red apple Susan insisted on packing for her, even though Jaide didn't like apples. Rennie just watched them eat, perched on a high stool among the books like a solitary bird in a rookery.

'You knew him, didn't you?' Jack asked Rodeo Dave.

'Knew who?'

'Young Master Rourke.'

'I suppose I did.'

Rodeo Dave thought about his own answer for a moment, then added, 'If anyone could say that. He was one of my best customers, always calling me up, looking for this or that. I would take him his books in person rather than use a courier, but George was never one for talking, just like his father.'

'Did you meet *him*,' asked Jaide, 'Mister Rourke, I mean?'

'I never really met him. But I saw him around. Always out and about the town, always talking, making his opinion known. You could see him a mile off, a tall, rakish man with an enormous nose, and you could smell him too. Not because he never bathed. He was fussy in that regard. He used to slick his hair back with this gel – I forget what it was called now – but it was ghastly, sticky stuff. The stink of it was enough to make you feel ill.'

Rodeo Dave pulled a face.

'He sounds horrible,' said Jack.

'Mister Rourke had his faults. There's no denying that.'

'What happened to him?' asked Jaide.

'He died in Africa. Some people said he was trampled trying to capture an elephant, but actually he caught malaria and wasn't treated properly. Which goes to show that money can't buy you everything.'

'Nobody's perfect,' whispered Rennie.

'Indeed.' Rodeo Dave raised the half a sandwich he had been holding, uneaten, as though in a toast. 'The dead outnumber the living. Let's not tempt fate by speaking ill of them.'

Tara chose that moment to return from the shelves, clutching a scuffed, cloth-covered book in one hand.

'This is all I could find,' she said. 'I was looking for stories, but most of the books you have in that section seem to be non-fiction, which is weird because vampires aren't real.'

'Monsters are only as real as we believe them to be, like tyrants.' Rodeo Dave took the book from her and studied the spine. 'Ah, *Dracula*. The original and the best.'

'There was no price on it.'

'That's because it belongs to you,' he said, giving her back the book with some of his usual sparkle returning.

Tara looked confused. 'You're giving it to me?'

'Books find their own owners. I just hold on to them until they meet each other. Money is often an unwelcome complication.'

'But . . . I mean, won't you go out of business?'

'Have no fear on that score, Tara,' Rodeo Dave said. 'Not with Renita here to keep the shop open.'

'There's more to living than busyness,' said Rennie in a soft but firm voice.

'Exactly!' Rodeo Dave grinned widely, as though having someone in the store to not take money from non-existent customers solved all his problems.

Jack and Jaide could understand Tara's puzzlement. Her mother ran a gift shop in Scarborough, and her father was relentless in his pursuit of the next business opportunity. It wasn't surprising that she found Rodeo Dave's philosophy completely alien.

Come to think of it, most people would find it pretty weird. Not for the first time, Jack wondered whether Rodeo Dave was secretly rich or something. Maybe he owned a cattle ranch somewhere.

His thoughts were interrupted by Tara suddenly leaning close to Rennie and staring at her, *Dracula* hanging limp in her hand, forgotten.

'Where do I know you from?' she asked.

'We drew pictures of her,' said Jaide quickly. 'At school, remember? When we thought she had . . . you know?'

Mr Carver had held a small memorial for Rennie when the town believed she had drowned in The Evil's storm, one year after her own children had drowned.

'That's right,' said Jack, picking up on Jaide's quick thinking. They had to stop Tara from remembering The Evil and the old Living Ward, everything she had seen in the cave under Little Rock. 'There was no one to give the pictures to, and you didn't want them to be thrown out. You had them in your backpack during the train crash. I guess you took them home afterwards. That must be where you've seen her face before.'

'Oh yeah,' said Tara, some of her confusion slipping away. 'That's it. The pictures. I don't know why I've been keeping them. It's like I dreamt her . . . dreamt *you* . . .'

'I would like to see those pictures,' said Rennie.

'I'll bring them in,' said Tara. 'Tomorrow.'

'Thank you.'

Tara blinked and looked away, and whether the explanation made sense or not, it seemed to have helped. Rodeo Dave pulled up another chair and she sat down with the others to eat her lunch, a cold noodle salad with a chocolate bar that she broke into five pieces and shared with everyone.

CHAPTER SIX
Treasure Hunt

It was Jack's turn to hold the phone that afternoon, and although he waited anxiously for it to buzz, it stayed resolutely silent. Jack couldn't help but wish their father would check in again. He could at least have sent them a *text* . . .

The last hour of school dragged horribly, but finally it was over and Jack, Jaide and Tara hurried off, hoping that they would be given permission to go with Rodeo Dave to the Rourke Estate.

Outside The Book Herd they were cautiously pleased to see their car with Susan sitting in the driver's seat. She tooted her horn as they approached, and a few moments later, Rodeo Dave appeared from the shop, waving at them.

'Hop in,' he called out. 'We're getting a lift.'

'So it's OK for us to go, Mum?' Jack asked as the three kids piled into the back seat.

'Of course, Jack, as long as you're home in time for dinner. I said I'd drop you there and pick you up afterwards to make sure. Your dad will collect you from our place later, Tara.'

'Great!' said Tara brightly. 'Thanks!'

On the way through town, Susan drove over the old iron bridge. There was no sign of the rescue crew that had been there yesterday, just a couple of skid marks on the road leading up to the bridge and some broken glass on the verge.

'Can we see Grandma?' asked Jaide. 'The hospital's kind of on the way to the estate.' Actually, it was in a completely different direction, but everywhere was close in Portland.

'I'm really sorry, we can't today,' Susan said. 'She's undergoing more tests. I spoke to the new specialist not long ago. Dr Witworth says she needs to double check a couple of things showing on the first scan.'

'What kind of things?' asked Jack, feeling his heart beginning to race.

'She didn't say. "Abnormalities" was the exact word she used, but I wouldn't read too much into that. That's just something doctors say when they don't know what's going on.'

Neither Jack nor Jaide was terribly reassured by the suggestion that something was going on that doctors didn't understand. Especially if it meant Grandma X staying in hospital and them not visiting her.

'Your mother's right,' said Rodeo Dave, turning round in the front seat to beam at them. 'If they'd looked into your grandmother's head and *not* seen something out of the ordinary, that would've been cause for serious concern.'

'True enough,' said Tara. 'There's no one in the world like her.'

'And I did speak to her on the phone this morning,' Susan added. 'She sends her love and reminds you to do as you're told and keep up with your homework. That sounds like her, doesn't it?'

It did, and the twins were willing to let their worries on that front ebb slightly. Until they saw her with their own eyes though, they wouldn't be completely reassured. With her suddenly absent, there was an enormous void in their lives. Jack had dreamt the previous night that he had woken to a world where no one had ever heard of Grandma X or the Wardens, and his Gift had vanished. Jaide occasionally found herself daydreaming about moving back to the city – and not in the excited way she once had. Their life was with Grandma X now. Without her, everything was at risk of turning upside down again.

The sky above was grey, mirroring their mood, but there was no sign of the rain that had saturated them the previous day, not even as they approached the high hedges and elaborate gates of the estate. Wide enough for two carriages to pass side by side, the gates rose up in a high arch over the drive, wrought-iron curlicues swirling and tangling in a pattern that Jaide hadn't been able to make out the previous day.

The right-hand gate was closed and this time, without the rain to obscure her vision, she discerned a fish's tale in its elaborate design.

Then, as the car passed through the opening on to a

thickly-gravelled drive, Jaide realised that the open left-hand gate wasn't a mirror image of the right. Instead of a fish-like tail there was a great rounded head with a single metal eye. Putting the two halves together in her mind, Jaide realised that the gate, when closed, depicted not a fish but a whale.

That wasn't all. High on the corner of each gate was a ship braving the turbulent seas, crewed with men waving harpoons, hemming the whale in.

The drive curved to the left and a stand of trees blocked her view of the gates. Rodeo Dave guided Susan along a fork leading away from the smaller building in which Young Master Rourke had been found. That stretch of drive wound round the lake and up towards the castle. The creek was now running clear and there was no sign of council workers, just one large man in overalls tending a rose garden – Kyle's father, Jack presumed – and a young, round-faced security guard sitting half on, half off the seat of a golf buggy. He stood up as the car approached and crunched to a halt in front of him.

Rodeo Dave stepped out of the car, wiped his palms on his jeans and cleared his throat.

'David Smeaton,' he said. 'And these are my three helpers.'

'I don't have any helpers on my list,' said the guard, glancing at a clipboard.

Jaide's stomach sank. If the guard wouldn't let them in, how were they supposed to find the card? She bet that wouldn't have been a problem had Grandma X been there. She would have just bossed him into it. Jaide couldn't imagine Rodeo Dave bossing *anyone* around. He was already turning to them with a look of apology.

'Thomas Solomon, isn't it?' said Susan, getting out of the car with a sunny smile. 'I used to know your mother years ago. We bumped into each other again today, in the bakery, and she said you were working up here. It's nice to meet you.'

'Ah, and very nice to . . . um, who did you say you were?'

'Susan Shield. These are my children, Jack and Jaide, and their friend Tara. I'll be back in two hours to pick them up.'

'Well . . .' Thomas Solomon looked as though he might argue the point, but then he smiled and said, 'What's the harm? Just don't tell anyone else or we'll have all the kids up here.' He put the clipboard face down on the seat of the golf buggy. 'Two hours it is.'

The twins and Tara climbed eagerly out of the car and waved as Susan drove off. Jack was impressed. He'd thought they were going to be turned back for sure, and he was amazed at how well his mother was fitting into Portland, having never wanted to come here at all.

As Jack turned to follow Dave across the drawbridge over the moat, he caught a glimpse of a huge muscular animal running through the grounds. He immediately thought of the escaped menagerie animals. No one had mentioned a tiger! But then it raised its head to look at him and he saw the enormous teeth.

There was only one sabretoothed tiger in the world that he knew of. It was the animal form of Custer, the Warden whose job it was to look after the wards while Grandma X was in hospital.

Jack automatically went to wave, then turned it into a tug at his hair in case anyone noticed. Custer winked and kept running, vanishing behind some bushes an instant later.

'You saw him too?' Jaide whispered.

'Yes.' Jack wished they could talk to him about their father. If Custer had been able to stop, he could have helped them look for the Card of Translocation. But he supposed it was hard work, minding four wards single-handedly. Grandma X made it look easy, but that, Jack was sure, only came from years of practice.

'Come on,' called Tara. 'Dave's already almost inside!'

They hurried after her, their feet making hollow wooden sounds on the drawbridge. The moat surrounding the castle was deep and dark, with smooth, steep sides. Jaide didn't want to imagine what it would be like to fall in. Luckily, despite the hollow sound, the planks of the drawbridge were as unmoving as solid stone.

Two high towers loomed over them. Thick chains connected the drawbridge to the castle walls. On the other side of the moat was an open gateway where Rodeo Dave was waiting.

'This way!' he said. 'There's a lot of books a-waiting!'

The gateway led into a small courtyard. There were archers'

notches high in the walls around them, and one solid door ahead. If this was a real castle, Jaide thought, here was where friends would be welcomed and foes stopped in their tracks.

'This is the inner passage,' said Rodeo Dave, fumbling in his pocket for a ring of keys. They jingled and clinked with the deep voices of antiquity. 'The inner door is always locked.'

'I didn't see the guard give you those keys,' said Tara.

Dave didn't quite look at her as he mumbled, 'Oh, George . . . Young Master Rourke gave me a set so I could deliver books straight to the library.'

He selected the largest key and slid it into the lock. It turned with a series of heavy clunks.

He pushed the door and it swung open with a groan. A wave of cold air rushed outwards, over the twins. Tara went '*Brrr*', which startled Jack. He didn't think anyone actually made that sound in real life.

'So you've been here bef–' Jaide started to say, but stopped at the flurry of echoes that bounced back at her from within the castle. What lay on the other side of the door was hidden in shadow.

She tried again more quietly. 'So you've been here before?'

'Not for a few years,' said Rodeo Dave. He took three steps inside and fumbled along the wall to the right of the door. 'It's here somewhere . . . I'm certain of it.'

There was a click, followed by a series of smaller clicks deeper within the castle. Fluorescent lights pinged on overhead, one at a time. Section by section, the covered courtyard within was revealed – dusty portraits on the walls, sheet-covered furniture on the floors, actual suits of armour guarding the corners, a tall grandfather clock on the opposite wall and high wooden beams above. Two particular paintings had pride of place, one of a forbidding man with receding black hair and long fingers, the other of a small oval-faced woman with startlingly green eyes. They faced each other, unsmiling, from different sides of the hall.

Jack followed Rodeo Dave inside, struck by the thought that, although it looked like a museum, this room had once been part of someone's home. Jaide and Tara followed him, looking around in awe.

'Welcome to Rourke Castle,' said Rodeo Dave, his cowboy boots sparking off the cobblestoned floor. 'George's father, Mister Rourke, had this built out of real stone from the country his family came from. Some said it was an actual castle, but that wasn't true. Just the ruins of one. But the plan was based on a real castle, so there are towers, halls and cellars, just like they would have had centuries ago. There's even a chapel and an armoury, and a solar on the top floor.'

'A solarium?' asked Tara.

'No, a solar. It's where the lord of the castle and his family could spend time alone, away from the staff and the soldiers. "Solar" here comes from "sole", meaning alone, nothing to do with the sun.'

91

Rodeo Dave was talking more quickly than normal. He seemed nervous, Jaide thought.

'Is the castle haunted?' she whispered, suddenly afraid to raise her voice too much.

He smiled at her, but there was no humour in it. 'Only by memories. See that clock? Your grandfather Giles had terrible trouble with it. It kept losing time and made Mister Rourke terribly impatient.'

Both twins admired its carved wooden panels and painted face, impressed by the fact that this was something Grandma X's husband had once touched.

'Now, come this way and I'll show you the library.'

Rodeo Dave led them from the entrance hall into a wide corridor lined on one side with tapestries depicting hunts, dances and feasts. One showed a whale being speared from two sides at once. Heavy wooden doors, all of them shut, lined the other side of the corridor. Cobwebs stirred above them, swaying in air that might not have moved for years. The castle was tomblike around them.

They reached a fork in the corridor.

'This way,' said Rodeo Dave, turning left. Then he stopped, facing a dead end. 'No, the other way, I'm sure of it.'

They took the other leg of the corridor, stopping at a double door opposite a flight of spiral stone stairs. Rodeo Dave fished out another key and with a flourish opened both doors at once, then waved the twins and Tara ahead of him.

They entered a huge room with a ceiling forty feet above them, with an internal balcony running all the way around halfway up. Electric lights in shell-like shades sent overlapping pools of illumination all across the library, banishing shadows to the furthest corners. Every vertical surface was lined with shelves, some of them protected by glass doors, all of them holding books. Big books, small books, books with gold writing on the spine, books in different languages – there were so many books that Jaide could only gasp in amazement. How did Rodeo Dave ever imagine that he might catalogue them all in just a few days!

'*You* sold him all these books?' gasped Tara.

'Good grief, no,' replied Rodeo Dave. 'Most of these were George's father's. That's the father there, as a young man.'

He indicated a marble bust sitting on a plinth. It showed a more youthful version of the man in the portrait they had seen earlier. His nose was pointed and his lips thin with the faint hint of a sneer. The eyes of the bust seemed to follow Jack as he walked round it, judging him and finding him wanting.

'He looks horrible,' said Tara, folding her arms and turning her attention to the ceiling.

'I've seen him before,' said Jaide.

'When?' asked Jack in surprise.

'I don't know.' The memory was frustratingly incomplete. She definitely knew that cruel face from *somewhere*. But no matter how she scratched her head, whatever the details were they weren't coming out.

Above the room's enormous inglenook fireplace was a painting of a smiling blonde woman in a primrose gown sitting at a table under a tree bedecked with autumnal leaves. She was playing Solitaire with a deck of old-fashioned cards, their faces yellow and white, diagonally striped. A pale clay-brick path snaked behind her, between fields of ripened wheat on one side, buttercups on the other. The overall impression was one of intense gold.

That, and the deck of cards the woman in the painting was holding, reminded Jaide of what they were supposed to be doing in the castle. The Card of Translocation lay hidden somewhere in its walls. Standing between them and finding it was only one obstacle: the hundreds and hundreds of books they had said they would help Rodeo Dave catalogue.

'Do you mind . . .?' she said. 'I mean, do you think it'd be all right if . . .?'

'Of course, Jaide,' said Rodeo Dave with a smile. 'I know why you're really here.'

She blinked in surprise. 'You do?'

'Yes. You want to explore the castle. And that's fine with me. Everywhere you shouldn't go will be locked and I'll be busy for at least an hour or so, just checking the general condition of the books. The actual cataloguing will start once I've done that. Until then, you are free to wander. Just don't touch anything. There are a lot of fragile, precious things in here, including yourselves. Don't get lost!'

'We won't. Thanks!'

'I'll ring that when I'm ready for you,' he said, pointing at an elaborate gong as big as a bass drum, suspended in a black wooden frame opposite the fireplace.

Tara and the twins ran out of the library before he could change his mind.

'Which way?' asked Jack.

'Up the stairs of course,' said Tara. 'Last one to the top is a rotten egg!'

The twins raced after her, the sound of their footfalls echoing brightly off the walls and filling every corner of the castle with life. The next floor up contained a series of locked rooms with brass plaques on the doors: the RIGHT ROOM, the WHITE ROOM, the PYGMY BRYDE ROOM, the BOWHEAD ROOM. Not until they came across the HUMPBACK ROOM did Jack guess that they were all named after species of whale. They stopped to peer through a keyhole. Jaide and Tara could see nothing, but Jack's dark-sensitive eyesight made out a four-poster bed and a cupboard and a tightly shuttered window.

They went back down briefly and explored several other labelled rooms: the BAKEHOUSE, the PANTRY, the GARRISON, the GRANARY, the BLACKSMITH and the PRISON. Their doors were open, but they contained little of interest. The door to the CELLAR was locked, so they went back upstairs and searched until they found a stairwell that led to a guardhouse in one of the corner towers. The view from the top was spectacular, right out over the lake and surrounding trees. Portland was also visible and Jaide easily found the Rock, and from that landmark she easily worked out where their house was located. She could just make out the weathervane, pointing resolutely south.

'This would be the perfect place to play hide and seek,' said Tara.

'You think everywhere's a good place for hide and seek,' said Jaide. Tara was particularly good at that game.

Jack was about to second what Jaide had said, intending to add that they had to go back to Rodeo Dave soon, but before he could speak he felt a sudden buzz in his pocket. The mobile phone was ringing.

'I agree with Tara,' he said, 'and she's it!'

With that, he ran from the guardhouse down the stairs and along the corridor, trying doors at random. Most of the rooms were locked on the top floor, but some were open. A broom closet would do, just so long as he could get there before his father hung up.

He found a door that would open and flung himself through it, slamming the door shut behind him, not seeing what the room contained. He didn't even turn on the light. Jack could see perfectly well with the lights out.

He whipped the phone from his pocket and pressed the flashing green button.

'Dad?'

'Hello, Jack,' came the voice at the other end. 'You sound out of breath. I was beginning to wonder if you were going to pick up.'

'Had to hide from Tara,' he gasped. 'We're in the castle!'

'I know. I saw you arrive.'

'You did?'

'From the trees. I've been waiting for you.'

Jack imagined Hector Shield stretched out on a branch with a pair of binoculars.

'Did you see Custer go by?'

'I did, and I'm glad you didn't interrupt his work. You mustn't interfere with his concentration. I saw your mother as well . . . you didn't tell her about me? It would only upset her, and I've done enough of that already – unfortunately Warden business must take priority over our feelings.'

'No . . . no, we haven't told her.'

'Good. I know it's difficult, but it won't be for long, I promise. Everything will be the way it's supposed to be once the card is found.'

'And Grandma's better.'

'Yes . . . that too.'

Jack's father sounded distracted and very serious. There

wasn't even a hint of his usual jokey friendliness, reminding Jack that the war against The Evil was far from a game.

'I don't have much time,' Hector said. 'Tell me what progress you've made.'

'Well, we've only just started exploring. The castle is huge. It has hundreds of rooms. Most of them are locked.'

'You'll have to find a way into them.'

'We're helping Rodeo Dave clear out the library. He has keys . . .'

'Best to keep him out of Warden affairs. Don't ask for the keys – or even think about stealing them from him. You don't want to raise his suspicions.'

The thought had crossed Jack's mind. He suppressed it with reluctance, although what Rodeo Dave had to be suspicious of exactly he didn't know. But he didn't want to attract his attention. Rodeo Dave wasn't a Warden, but he did seem close to Grandma X, and he hadn't freaked out when the whirlwind had carried him up the drive when they'd first arrived in Portland, so maybe he did know about Warden stuff and The Evil.

'If it's not in one of the open rooms, you'll have to find another way into those locked rooms, one that doesn't involve David Smeaton or his keys. Perhaps there's some way you could use your Gifts.'

Jack suddenly remembered something. 'Of course! It's just like in *The Second Spiral Staircase*.'

'The what?'

'One of your old books. Don't you remember? There was a locked room that no one could get into. The keys had been lost. But they found a skeleton key that would work on lots of doors. That's how they got it open.'

'Good thinking, Jack. Skeleton keys . . . hmmm. Father – your grandfather – wasn't a Warden, but he used to have a key for opening clock cases and they'll work on most old locks. It's probably in the Blue Room.'

'We'll look for it as soon as we can.'

'Tonight, Jack. It's vital you find the Card of Translocation as soon as possible.'

'We will, Dad. Don't worry. We'll find it soon, I promise.'

Jack spun round in surprise as a voice suddenly spoke from behind him.

'Well, you won't find anything in *here*, I can assure you of that!'

CHAPTER SEVEN
Seeking and Hiding

The voice had come from inside the room in which Jack was hiding, but it belonged to neither Jaide nor Tara. It wasn't Rodeo Dave either. It sounded like a grouchy old man.

'Who's there?' Jack scanned the room, an ordinary attic by the look of it, with boxes stacked up against one wall and lumpy furniture covered in sheets along the other. Even with his sensitive night vision, there was no one to be seen. 'Who said that?'

'Ignore me and I'll go away. It won't be the first time.'

Jack reached out to the nearest sheet and whipped it off the stuffed armchair it covered. No one.

'Why can't I find you?'

'Nobody ever wanted to before.'

'Are you a ghost?'

'Of course not!' Now the voice sounded offended. 'Although I *am* dead.'

Jack nerved himself to whip away another sheet, revealing a chest of drawers.

'Where are you?'

'If I could see, perhaps I could tell you. It's so dark in here . . . so very dark.'

Jack reached behind him to turn on the light. It dazzled him for a second, before his eyes adjusted.

'How's that?'

'I can see a white blur, a considerable improvement on my former state, but still far from ideal.'

Jack began tearing at the sheets at random, raising a thick cloud of dust and revealing more armchairs, a selection of tea chests and one broken hatstand.

'Don't trouble yourself, sir,' said the voice. 'Just turn the light off and leave. That's what I would do in your shoes. I was rather unpopular even when I was alive.'

The second-to-last sheet revealed a table. On the table was a selection of oddments: candlesticks, chipped plates, a tarnished silver service and something that Jack mistook for a scuffed plaster bust similar to the one of Mister Rourke in the library . . . until it moved.

'Gadzooks!' it said, blinking up at him. 'Are you a child or has everyone evolved into midgets during my absence?'

Jack stared at the plaster head in amazement, or the half-head, since it was really only the face with the back past the ears just a flat surface. It wasn't a very flattering head at that. The nose was too large and the cheeks too fleshy. The head had no hair, and its chin receded sharply, giving an expression of permanent disapproval. It didn't look like the kind of a thing an artist would make to flatter a rich patron. It looked entirely too . . . authentic.

'What are you?'

'Don't you mean who *was* I? Professor Jasper Frederik Olafsson, at your service. Forgive me for not bowing. You haven't answered *my* question, remember.'

'I'm not a midget,' said Jack, although he did wonder sometimes if he was growing too slowly. 'I just came in here to talk to . . . whoops, hang on.'

Jack had forgotten the phone and his father. He turned away and raised it to his ear. Nothing but silence. Hector Shield had hung up.

He had sent a text message though: **Call you tonight 9pm. Keep looking.**

'What is that contraption?' asked the head calling itself Professor Jasper Frederik Olafsson. 'The last time I was uncovered, people still spoke face to face. Is this the way people communicate in your world – via machine?'

'What do you mean, "in my world"? It's the same as your world surely.'

'Most likely, but your present is my future. Everything changes: that is the only certainty. I must therefore take nothing for granted.'

Jack put the phone away. 'We still talk face to face mainly, but there are lots of other ways too. How long have you been down here?'

'I have no way to tell,' Professor Olafsson said. 'There is no clock in this room. I cannot see the daylight coming or going, so I cannot count the days. I have no pulse even. Just the sensation that a vast epoch of time has passed – large enough that young men such as yourself are not startled by the apparition of a talking death mask. Are you considered normal for your kind?'

Jack was beginning to feel confused under the barrage. 'Yes. That is, no, not really. What's a death mask?'

In the hallway outside, Jaide could hear voices. She knew Jack must have felt the phone buzz and run off somewhere to take the call, so Tara wouldn't overhear. She had left Tara searching fruitlessly on the other side of the castle, figuring that Jack wouldn't have gone far from where they had started. But if that was him talking on the phone in the room ahead, why could she hear a *second* voice, answering his questions?

She inched up to the door and put her ear against it.

'. . . a wax impression of my face as I lay on my deathbed, then cast in plaster. It was a common custom in my time. For loved ones, you see, so they could gaze upon the countenance of their dearly departed and think fond thoughts. Except I had no loved ones . . .'

'But this is what you looked like . . . when you died?'

That *was* Jack. Jaide turned the handle and wrenched the door open, not liking the idea of dead things talking to her brother, even if he didn't sound terribly frightened himself.

'What's going on?' she said.

'Oh, hi, Jaide.' Jack was sitting on the edge of an upholstered chair, facing a head on a plinth resting on a cluttered table. 'This is Professor Olafsson. He *was* a professor anyway, before he died.'

'Oh right,' said Jaide. The white face wasn't the weirdest thing she'd seen since becoming a troubletwister and it looked harmless enough. At least it couldn't move about.

'What about Dad?' she said, not yet accepting the idea of talking to someone dead, but prepared to let it go for the moment in order to concentrate on more important things. 'I thought you were talking to him.'

'I was, but we got interrupted.'

From behind her came the sound of Tara's footsteps. Jaide ducked into the room and shut the door behind her, motioning for quiet.

'We don't have long, Jack,' she said. 'Tara's too good at this game. What did Dad say?'

'Not much. Just to keep looking.'

'We already knew that.'

'Yes, but now we know he's still nearby, watching.'

'He is?' Frustration rose up in her. 'I wish he could come closer.'

'I wish so too, Jaide, but he said he'll call us later.'

'What is it you seek?' asked the plaster head. 'I have lived in this castle a long time. Perhaps I can help you find it.'

'How?' asked Jack. 'You've been under a dust sheet practically forever.'

'Actually, I haven't been under a sheet the whole time. Death masks are collector's items, you know, and I have often been on display.'

'Why would someone put a talking death mask on display? Shouldn't you be in a museum?'

'Oh, I can't talk to *everyone*. Imagine the fuss that would cause!'

'But you talked to me.'

'There's something special about you,' mused Professor Olafsson. 'And your sister. Tell me what you're looking for, before your friend arrives, and I will help you if I can.'

Jaide looked at Jack. It was clear he wasn't afraid of Professor Olafsson, which meant something. Besides, a plaster head couldn't be Evil, not within the Portland wards as the castle most definitely was.

'We're looking for something gold,' she said, choosing her words carefully. 'Like a gold brick but flatter . . . about this big.' She mimed the size with her hands. 'It will probably be blank.'

'But it might not be either,' added Jack.

'A gold card,' Professor Olafsson said. 'Why didn't you say? *For the Divination of Potential Powers and Safekeeping Thereof*, I presume.'

Jaide gaped at him. They were the exact words the

Compendium had used. 'How did you know that?'

'Ah, I know what you are now! Troubletwisters! I was a Warden when I was alive, and a very good one too, if I can be so bold. My death mask was imbued with my Gift, and so it has in effect become me – or I have become it rather – and here I am, Professor Jasper Frederik Olafsson, formerly of Uppsala, and currently . . . wherever this is.'

Jaide was amazed that such a thing was possible, but she wasn't about to look a gift horse – or a gift head – in the mouth.

'Do you know of any gold cards in the castle?'

'Not specifically, I'm afraid, but there are many places one *might* be hidden. I will give it some thought. Perhaps –'

'Shhhh!' said Jack. He had heard a noise from the other side of the door, as though someone had stopped just outside. The handle twitched.

Jaide acted without thinking. The nearest sheet was out of her reach, so she used her Gift to sweep one up off the floor and hastily drop it over the table and Professor Olafsson's head.

Before he could protest, the door burst open.

'Aha!' Tara cried. 'I thought I heard you in here. But you know you're not supposed to hide *together*, right?'

Jack and Jaide feigned innocence. Professor Olafsson stayed quiet, although the sheet did move as he wrinkled his nose. Jaide tried to flatten it back down with a swift blast of air, but her Gift rebelled, making the tablecloth flap.

'What's that?' cried Tara, backing away with her hands at

her mouth. 'It better not be a rat! I hate rats!'

'I think it *is* a rat,' said Jack, hurrying her out of the door before a full-on tornado could erupt. After his first encounter with The Evil, he was wary of rats too, so it wasn't hard to fake. 'Run!'

Jack and Tara fled up the corridor, while Jaide did her best to get her Gift under control. The tablecloth whipped up into the air and flew around the room, trailing a hurricane of dust. The door slammed shut behind her. Coughing, she gathered the wind up in her hands and crushed it down into a ball, where it evaporated.

'Finely done,' said Professor Olafsson. The sheet had fallen back over the bust but he could still see her with one eye. 'You had best run after them or suspicions will be raised.'

'Yes, but we'll be back,' she said, brushing her hair back into its usual place and blinking dust from her eyes. 'I don't know how or when, but we will.'

'Naturally. Gold cards don't find themselves. Until next time, Jaide the troubletwister, sister of Jack.'

She stopped with her hand on the door.

'How did you know our names?'

'You used them right in front of me.' Professor Olafsson looked smug.

She exited the room, hurrying along the corridor to catch up with Jack and Tara. If they could talk Tara into another game, this time Tara would hide and the twins could search, pretending to find her choice of hiding place too difficult.

Echoes of a very real sound immediately dispelled that plan.

'That's the gong from the library,' said Jack as Jaide ran up to him. 'Rodeo Dave wants us.'

'Then I guess we'd better go,' said Tara. 'The thought that this place has rats just makes me shiver.'

Jaide consoled herself with the thought that the card might actually *be* in the library, in which case they would be poking around in exactly the right place. The trick then would be to locate it before Tara or Rodeo Dave did. If they didn't, there would go their father's chance of ever using it to fight The Evil.

It took them three tries to find the right corridor. Rodeo Dave looked frustrated when they finally reached the library, which was a surprise because normally he never looked anything other than cheerful. He had the gong's padded mallet in one hand as though he'd been about to ring it again, but when he saw them he put it down. They quickly realised that he wasn't frustrated with them, but with the job at hand.

'It's going to be a much bigger task than I thought,' he said, wiping one hand across his forehead and leaving a grey smear behind. 'The books used to be in alphabetical order by author, but they've been all mixed up since I was last here. Tara, do you think you could steady the ladder while I check the topmost shelves? Jack and Jaide, I'd be grateful if you could wipe all the shelves you can reach, using these cloths—they don't need to be dampened. We should have enough time to finish this part of the job before your mother arrives to take you home.'

The twins put their backs into their job willingly enough, peering into every corner of every shelf in the hope of seeing a telltale flash of gold. The air was soon thick with dust, and Rodeo Dave gave them masks to put over their mouths to filter out the worst of it. That made talking difficult, let alone whispering, so the twins had to be content with searching alone. The matter of their father's phone call and the Professor's death mask would have to wait until later.

Mister Rourke's stony bust watched them as they worked, still maddeningly familiar to Jaide. Every time she looked at it, it seemed to be looking right back at her, tauntingly, as though daring her to remember.

Finally, Rodeo Dave climbed down from the ladder and declared that it was time to go. They took off their masks and brushed themselves and each other down. The twins were covered with cobwebs, even though they hadn't seen a single living spider.

'No rats at least,' said Tara. 'I think I'd die if I saw another one.'

'You'll find lots of them here,' said Rodeo Dave. 'Mice too. George hated cats.'

Tara put her arms round herself and went *brrr* again. 'Why?'

'George thought they talked about him behind his back. So did his father.'

Jaide hid a smile. Knowing Kleo and Ari, the Rourkes might well have been right.

They filed through the corridors to the entrance hall, then outside. The sun was hanging low on the horizon over the countryside outside unprotected by the wards of Portland. Jack wondered if his father was still watching them and resisted the urge to wave.

Susan was already winding up the drive towards them, while Thomas Solomon's security buggy whirred into view from around the moat. The two vehicles converged on the waiting pedestrians where they stood by the drawbridge, readjusting their eyes to the natural light. Dusk shadows stretched everywhere, making Jack's feet itch.

This time it was Jaide who glimpsed the long, feline figure of Custer prowling through the estate's bushes and trees. The Warden didn't acknowledge her, and neither did the smaller feline shape following at his heels. Ari only kept up with Custer by running at full pelt. Even as Jaide watched, he fell back into a winded lope and wiped his face with a paw, giving up the chase.

'All finished?' asked Thomas Solomon. Jaide turned. The security buggy had been the first to arrive.

'Far from it, I'm afraid,' said Rodeo Dave. 'I'll be back tomorrow first thing.'

'No rest for the wicked, eh?'

Rodeo Dave didn't smile. 'It appears not.'

'Guess I'd better do my rounds,' Thomas said self-importantly. 'Can't stand around here talking all day.'

The golf buggy whizzed off and Jaide suppressed a smile, imagining what would happen if he bumped into Custer.

Susan's car swept to a halt in front of them.

'Right on time,' she said as they clambered inside. 'How was your afternoon?'

'Very educational, I think,' said Rodeo Dave. 'The children learned that a castle's solar has nothing to do with a solarium, and that being a second-hand bookseller is more about dust and cobwebs than actual books.'

Jack got in last. An orange shape slipped in with him, almost getting tangled in his feet along the way. He bent down and skriched the hair between Ari's ears to cover him whispering, 'What are you doing here?'

'I've been patrolling with Custer,' the cat said. 'He's been restless all day, like he's sensing something suspicious. I thought he could use my help.'

'*Your* help?'

'On Kleo's orders.' The cat's eyes narrowed. 'What are you trying to say?'

'Nothing. I'm sure Kleo knows what she's doing.'

Tara reached down and pulled Ari up into her lap.

'Oh, hello there,' she said. 'You look hungry. I wish I had something to give you.'

'I *like* this girl,' said Ari, though all Tara heard was a purr.

'She should come round more often. Tell her to pack lunch next time.'

'He's always hungry,' said Jaide, only half-concentrating on the conversation. Susan was accelerating back along the drive. Soon the castle would vanish behind them. They *had* to find a way back to complete the search.

'Rodeo Dave is coming back tomorrow, Mum,' she said. 'The library is really enormous. He could be there for weeks and *weeks*.'

'Hmm? Oh, not *quite* that long,' said Rodeo Dave. He seemed distracted, as if his mind was elsewhere.

'It doesn't seem fair that Dave should have to do it all alone,' said Jack, following Jaide's lead. 'He's got his bookshop to run. What's going to happen if he's not there?'

'I thought Rennie was helping out,' said Susan.

'That's true,' Rodeo Dave started to say.

'Yes, but it's not the same,' said Jaide. '*Can* we help, Mum? It would only take a couple of days. And it's not as if we do anything interesting at school, anyway. We'll learn many more interesting things in a castle than in Mr Carver's classroom.'

Susan glanced at them in the rear-view mirror.

'You're as persuasive as your father,' she said. 'Both of you. What about you, Tara? Are you trying to skive off school as well?'

'No . . .' said Tara. 'I don't think my parents would let me, and anyway, that place has lots of rats and mice. I hate rats.

Even Mr Carver's nose-flute music is better than rats.'

'So it's not been all fun and games then,' said Susan. 'And you certainly look like you've been put to good use.'

'We have,' said Jaide. 'We're exhausted.'

Susan's gaze shifted to Rodeo Dave. 'Have they really been helpful?'

Rodeo Dave didn't answer for a moment, as if the question had to travel a long way to reach wherever he had gone.

'What? Oh yes, I'd have to say –'

'I guess it's OK, then. They're all yours.'

The twins cheered. Ari put his paws over his ears and Susan raised a hand for silence.

'Just for tomorrow,' she said. 'After that, you must return to school.'

'We will, Mum,' said Jack.

Jaide promised too. 'Thanks, Mum!'

Tara looked as though she might be regretting her decision and, surprisingly, Rodeo Dave didn't look entirely relieved either. Jaide had thought he would be glad of the help, but instead he said nothing, his posture tense and unmoving, even as Tara got carried away with a story about the 'giant killer rat' that had leapt out at them in an attic.

As they came into town, Susan said, 'Now, Dave, I'll drop you home first, then I'll take the kids to see their grandmother.'

The twins sat up straighter, excited by the thought, and Rodeo Dave started out of his daze too.

'She's well enough for visitors?' he asked.

'I hope so. Dr Witworth said we should swing by on the way through, just in case.'

'May I come with you?'

'Family only, I'm afraid. Tara will have to wait outside. You don't mind, do you?' she asked Tara. 'They won't be long.'

'No problemo.' She cupped Ari's face in her hands and gave it a smoosh. 'Ari will keep me company.'

'Kill – me – now,' the cat forced out.

'I don't think Ari will be allowed in the hospital, Tara,' said Susan.

'Cats and booksellers,' said Rodeo Dave, reaching back from the front seat to save Ari. 'We've got to stick together, eh? Never mind. I'll give you a snack when we get back to the shop. Maybe Kleo will be there to keep us company.'

'If she's not,' Ari said, 'can I have her snack too?'

Rodeo Dave, perhaps understanding without hearing the actual words, smiled and tickled him under the chin.

CHAPTER EIGHT

The Sleeper

Susan dropped off Rodeo Dave and Ari at The Book Herd, then turned the car around and drove across town to the hospital, where she parked under a chestnut tree whose spreading arms easily covered the car, and several others besides. The hospital was an uninspiring single-storey building with none of the glamour and excitement hospitals sometimes had in movies. It seemed completely full of old people. Even the nurses were old.

Susan walked up to the nurses' station. 'Is she . . .?'

'Very restless this afternoon, Sue,' said a stout nurse with a beard that looked far from sanitary. 'Dr Witworth prescribed a stronger sedative. It's probably taking effect now, but you can go through and see how she is.'

Susan nodded and led the children deeper into the hospital until she reached a closed door with a low bench outside.

'Wait here,' she told them. 'I'll just check.'

She ducked through the door, leaving Tara and the twins standing awkwardly outside. None of them said anything. Jack and Jaide strained to hear what was going on inside the room, but could hear only mumbled voices.

Susan returned. 'Go on,' she told the twins. 'She's a bit groggy, but awake.'

Jaide took a deep breath and walked through the door. Jack followed more hesitantly. He didn't know what to expect. Would Grandma X look as she usually did, or would her head be bandaged? Would there be horrible bruises . . . or worse?

In the end, she looked unchanged, apart from from the fact that she was in a hospital gown and was lying propped up in a hospital bed, with her silvery hair spread out on the pillow. She looked much smaller than usual – and that somehow was far worse than anything Jack had imagined. The room was dimly lit and smelled of antiseptic. It looked like a place someone went to die, not get better.

'Come here, dear troubletwisters,' Grandma X said, waving them closer, one each on either side of the bed. She hugged them tightly, her arms just as strong as ever. 'The doctors, blast them with a thousand curses, insist on keeping me *calm* and *relaxed*, not realising that keeping me *here* is having the exact opposite effect. I'm sorry your studies have been interrupted. I hope there have been no . . .' she glanced at the door, '. . . unexpected catastrophes?'

They assured her there hadn't been. And apart from the matter of one small bridge, that was the entire truth.

'We've been out at the Rourke Estate with Rodeo Dave,' Jaide started to say.

'Really?' Grandma X said. 'Kleo sneaked in here earlier, but she didn't say anything about that. She tells me you've been in the Blue Room, helping our feathery guest to sleep.'

Jack hadn't thought of it that way, but he supposed it had been exactly like that.

'I like her,' he said. 'Can we keep her?'

'I don't think so, Jackaran. Technically she belongs to the estate, and when the lawyers agree on who will inherit what, we should really let her go.' She went to pat his hand, but missed. 'I hope you'll understand.'

'Have you spoken to Dad?' Jaide asked.

'Yes, of course, dear.' A nurse they hadn't seen before entered the room and fussed about, tightening the sheets and adjusting the pillows whether Grandma X wanted them so or not. 'He's very busy.'

'So it's OK if we . . . go back tomorrow?' Jack persisted. It was impossible to talk openly with someone else in the room, but they had to try. There was no way of knowing how long they had before Susan took them home again.

'I don't see why not,' she said. 'David will look after you. You can trust him completely.'

'He doesn't seem very happy about us being there,' said Jaide, remembering Rodeo Dave's moody silences on the way back from the estate.

'I think he's just sad about Young Master Rourke,' Grandma X said. 'David was the closest friend he had – perhaps George's only friend. At the funeral on Friday he'll be delivering the eulogy, and that's a very hard thing to do. Particularly because it would have been George's birthday.'

She looked sad too for a moment, and then brightened, as though consciously willing herself to do so.

'Kleo says the weather has been odd,' she said. 'Storm clouds and rain and yet no lightning, all confined to one area . . . it strikes me as altogether strange.'

'Could it be The Evil?' asked Jaide, still wondering if the car crash had been the work of their grandmother's ancient enemy. 'Like that storm, the first time?'

'I don't think so. Wardens are trained to recognise The Evil in many forms. This doesn't feel like any of them. It does have a familiar flavour, though . . . one I haven't felt for some time . . . if I could only remember what it was . . .'

Her voice trailed off and her eyelids drooped closed. The silver moonstone ring she wore on her right hand, with the moonstone tucked safely into her palm, looked dull and tarnished in the room's yellow electric light.

'Is she asleep?' Jack whispered after a minute's silence.

'If she is, she's not snoring.' They sometimes heard their grandmother at night, even though separated from her by several walls and an entire floor. On a quiet night she sounded like a medium-sized jet aircraft having trouble starting up.

'What do we do now?'

Jaide sneaked a look at the hand-scrawled sign above the end of the bed, but instead of a name there was just a Patient Number with seventeen digits.

'Beats me. Leave her, I guess?'

The twins went to step back from the bed, but suddenly Grandma X's eyes were open. She lunged for them, catching their forearms in an alarmingly tight grip.

'Something is going on, troubletwisters,' she said, in a voice that lost none of its power for being barely a whisper. 'I don't know what it is, but it started the night Young Master Rourke died. The wards will protect you, as they have these last weeks, but I want you to be – to be . . . very . . . care . . .'

Her fight to stay conscious was taking its toll. The grip on their arms was already weakening when a lab-coated doctor entered the room, followed by the same nurse who had fussed with the bed before.

'I think that's enough excitement for one night,' said the doctor, a woman in her fifties with grey hair pulled back into a tight bun. Her nametag said 'Witworth'. Her voice brooked no dissent. 'If you'll step outside, please . . .'

The twins retreated, dismayed by the sight of their grandmother in such a confused state. Or *was* she confused? What if everything she said was right? The twins had never had reason to mistrust her judgement before. If she was worried about something going on in Portland, maybe something *was* going on in Portland.

But what?

Susan and Tara were waiting for them outside. The doctor followed them and took Susan by the arm to talk to her privately for a moment. Tara surprised both Jack and Jaide by taking their hands and giving them a squeeze.

'I remember when my Po Po was sick,' she said. 'There was a lot of hanging around hospitals as well, watching grown-ups talk in whispers.'

'What happened to her?' asked Jack. 'Did she . . . get better?'

'Oh yeah. She comes to visit every year and makes my life miserable.'

Her grin was infectious and it made Jaide feel a little better.

'Off we go,' said Susan, returning and indicating that it was time to leave. Dr Witworth nodded as they passed, not smiling, as though glad to see the back of anyone under forty.

'She'll be OK,' said Susan in the car. 'She's had a nasty knock on the head that would leave anyone a bit muddled for a while. We'll have to take it slowly. And so does she. Some people just don't have the patience to be a patient.'

'How long until she can come home?' asked Jack.

'Dr Witworth doesn't know. A couple of days, maybe. Longer, if the swelling doesn't go down.'

'*Swelling*?' said Jaide, alarmed.

'Don't fret about the details. The important thing is that she's getting better.'

They swept up Watchward Lane with a rattle of fallen

leaves. Susan parked in the Hillman's usual spot. She had dinner ready to roll: home-made hamburgers and chips, which was something she could actually cook well, with chocolate ice cream to follow. That was what she usually cooked on her last night in Portland before going on shift. The twins knew she was spoiling them a little and they were grateful for it.

Over dinner they gave their mother a more comprehensive but still edited account of their day, lavishly describing the suits of armour, the rooms full of sheet-shrouded furniture and the apparently endless corridors, but leaving out anything to do with Professor Jasper Frederik Olafsson.

'I'm a little jealous,' said Susan with a smile. 'I'd love to take time off work and explore a haunted old castle.'

'I don't think it's haunted, Mum,' said Jaide, wondering if a talking death mask counted. 'And most of the rooms are locked.'

'Still, it's good of you to help out,' she said. 'Mr Smeaton might even pay you, if you do a good job.'

'He could pay you in books,' said Tara. 'He has enough of them.'

Dinner was soon over, and so were the dishes, which it was somehow their turn to do yet again, but with two sets of hands to dry it wasn't so bad. Ordinarily the twins liked having Tara over rather than doing their mother's version of maths homework, but tonight they had other things on their mind. Foremost among them was the knowledge that their father would call at nine. Luckily, Tara's father came long before then, and it was something of a relief when they waved off their friend and ran back inside.

In their room they conferred quickly and quietly. Their mother was tidying her room, just up the hallway.

'We have to get back into the Blue Room tonight, after Mum's asleep,' said Jaide, 'and search for a skeleton key.'

'What does it look like, do you think?'

'I don't know. A key, I guess. Probably not much like a skeleton. Let's ask the *Compendium*.'

'All right. Cornelia will still be there. Maybe she's ready to tell us something about the night Young Master Rourke died.'

Jaide nodded. They froze at the sound of their mother walking past their door, then heading down the creaky stairs.

When she was gone, Jaide shut the door and checked the phone. The time was almost nine o'clock.

'Dad will call soon,' she said.

'I hope so. If only we had the number of the phone he's calling from, we could call him instead of waiting.'

They fidgeted in silence until the phone rang. The number was hidden, but who else could it be? Jaide pounced on it and put it close to her ear, so Hector Shield's voice was as clear as it could be.

'Hello?'

'Hello, Jaide. Is Jack there too?'

There was the sound of heavy rain in the background

again, clouding Hector's voice, but it wasn't as distracting as it had been the previous night.

'I'm here, Dad,' said Jack, listening in as best he could, his head close to his sister's.

'I'm relieved,' Hector said. 'I thought the phone had been discovered when I hung up on you earlier.'

Jack supposed it had been, technically, but not by anyone who mattered.

'We didn't find the card,' Jaide confessed. She wished she had better news. 'We looked in all the obvious places, but it just wasn't there.'

'We're going back to the castle tomorrow,' Jack said.

'Well, that's good.' He sounded disappointed. 'I've been thinking about what you said earlier about a skeleton key. You should definitely look for your grandfather's. But there's something else you should look for too, something I thought of after we talked. It's a witching rod – like a divining rod for finding water, but it finds artefacts special to Wardens instead.'

'Like Grandma has for The Evil, except the other way around?' said Jack. 'Cool.'

'What does it look like, Dad?' asked Jaide, nudging Jack away. He had got to talk to Hector last time, and now it was her turn.

'Use the *Compendium* like you did last night. Let it guide you. I'll call you again tomorrow to see how you got on.'

'All right,' she said. 'But, Dad, we could go with Tara to

123

Scarborough for the day so you can come into the wards without affecting our Gifts. Wouldn't that be easier?'

'It would, but there's no way your mother would let you skip school just to have fun, and we can't wait as long as the weekend. If the card was lost or fell into The Evil's hands before then, that would be a disaster.'

'How would The Evil get through the wards?' asked Jack.

'I saw Custer on the estate,' said Jaide. 'Ari said he was picking up something weird.'

'Jack is right,' Hector said. 'The Evil would know that the wards are being closely monitored after your grandmother's accident. The slightest open attack would be noticed immediately.'

'How would it know about the accident?' Jaide asked. 'Would it sense it somehow?'

'Grandma says that some people work for The Evil without being taken over by it,' said Jack. 'There could be someone like that in town right now.'

'There probably is,' Hector said, 'and you would never know. There's no way to tell until they act against you. The Evil has even been known to plant sleeper agents that lead an ordinary life for years, decades sometimes, before they're activated to work against the Wardens. Ideally it would be someone who's around a lot and completely trusted by everyone. Someone harmless and easy to overlook.'

That was a creepy thought.

'It could be anyone,' said Jack with a shiver.

'It could be the person who drove Grandma off the bridge!' exclaimed Jaide.

For a moment there was nothing but the drumbeat of rain over the phone, and both twins feared that the call had been lost. But then Hector's voice came through.

'That's true,' their father said. 'Don't be frightened unnecessarily though. All most sleeper agents do is watch and report. Just be careful who you talk to . . . and find the card as soon as possible. You'll do that for me, won't you? You'll have good news for me tomorrow?'

'We will,' they promised over the thickening hiss.

'Good. And now, children, I must go.'

'Already?' protested Jack. They hadn't talked about Grandma X or Professor Olafsson yet. Even over the phone, though, he could feel his Gift growing restless. The shadows were lengthening and growing darker, and Jaide's Gift was scooting dust bunnies around the floor.

'I'm afraid so,' said Hector. 'Be careful, both of you. You're very . . . very brave.'

'We love you, Dad!' said Jaide.

But the call was already over. She lowered the phone and held it in her lap for a moment, unwilling to let go of the tenuous connection to their father it provided.

'We'd better put it on to charge,' said Jack. 'The battery's getting low.'

Jaide forced herself to move. The charger was in a drawer. She plugged it into the socket near her bed and attached the phone.

'I wonder if Mr Carver is a sleeper agent,' she said. 'That might explain the nose flute and everything.'

'That's weird, but it's not actually evil. And Dad said it would be someone easy to overlook. He's impossible to ignore.'

'Someone who's been around for a long time,' Jaide mused. 'Someone harmless and trusted.'

'The only person who sounds like that is Rodeo Dave,' Jack joked. 'And it can't be him because . . .'

He stopped because Jaide wasn't laughing and he couldn't think of anything to follow 'because'.

'No way,' he said. 'He can't be. Can he?'

'Why not? He's all Dad told us to look out for.'

'Yes, but . . . but . . .' Everything Jack wanted to say came back to the criteria of a sleeper agent. *But Grandma trusts him. But he's been around forever. But he's just a funny old bookseller.*

And then there were other things that occurred to him as the horrible thought took root in his brain.

'The van,' said Jaide. 'Grandma was knocked off the bridge road by a van. Rodeo Dave drives a van.'

'And you remember at school when we found out? Grandma was cut off when she was trying to talk to us and suddenly he was there.'

'And he was surprised when Mum said that she was awake.'

126

The twins stared at each other, shocked by the possibility. Rodeo Dave had given no signs he knew anything about the Wardens or The Evil, so could he really be a traitor, lying low in Portland and biding his time? How could he just pretend to be Grandma X's friend, and the troubletwisters' friend too, while planning to betray them all along?

The thought was an awful one. So too was the thought that they would be stuck in the castle with him all day tomorrow.

'We should tell someone,' said Jaide. 'Custer, or Kleo –'

'What if we're wrong? We don't have any actual evidence. Remember when we thought Tara's dad was Evil, and it turned out he was just a property developer?'

Jaide did, and that cooled some of her desire to leap up and take action. Grandma was always telling them not to be so impetuous. Perhaps she should think it through first, before making any wild accusations.

'If Grandma knew, she'd be furious,' she said.

'If we were wrong, she'd be furious at us.'

'I know. I guess we'll have to keep an eye on him tomorrow and see if he does anything suspicious. When we know for sure, we'll have to do something about it then.'

They agreed by bumping their fists, but neither felt reassured. Worst of all, Jack thought, was the possibility that Grandma X *already* knew about him. That would explain why Kleo supposedly lived at The Book Herd, to keep an eye on him. It might also be why Rodeo Dave didn't know Rennie was the Living Ward even though she was living and working there. But why would Grandma X put the twins into his hands so readily, without even warning them?

'It just doesn't make any sense,' he muttered.

'In Portland, nothing ever seems to make sense.'

The sound of footsteps outside the door interrupted them again. Jaide swung into action, throwing her backpack over the phone so their Mum wouldn't see it.

The door opened and Susan leaned in.

'Time for bed.'

She ushered them towards the bathroom, where they cleaned their teeth. Jack cleaned his much more carefully than usual, since he thought that it might be his breath that was putting Cornelia off him.

'I've changed my shifts so I'll be around in the evenings all week,' said Susan as she tucked them into bed. 'That's one good thing to come out of all this,' she added, brushing an errant hair out of her daughter's eyes. Both eyes and hair were the same colour as her own, and although Jaide had the shape of her father's face, it was be clear that she and her mother would resemble each other closely when Jaide was grown up. 'I miss you terribly while I'm away. You know that, right?'

'Yes, Mum,' Jaide said. 'We miss you too.' On an impulse, she added, 'Do you think Dad will be able to visit Grandma soon?'

'I don't know, dear,' Susan said, dropping her eyes. 'You know how . . . how busy he is right now. How difficult it is for him to come home. It's not something I have any control over. But I wish he would come back. I wish it could be the way it was when we were all together and everything was . . . normal.'

Both twins wanted to tell her that he was just outside the bounds of Portland, but even if they could have told her that, there was no way they could ever be normal again, not in the way their mother meant. That was the deep and abiding truth Susan still wrestled with, under the veil of reassurance that Grandma X had cast over her. Susan rarely thought about what had brought them to Portland – the explosion, the truth about her husband's work and the legacy her children had been born into. But even with Grandma X's clouding of her mind, the facts still swam to the surface, and there was no hiding from the more painful truths of their new lives.

Susan blinked and shrugged off the dark mood that had fallen across her. She had two wonderful children and a job she enjoyed. She was even making friends, in town and at work. Life could be so much worse.

'Sweet dreams, Jack and Jaide,' she said, giving them both a kiss. On the way out she only half-closed the door behind her, so the room wouldn't be completely dark.

CHAPTER NINE
Between The Evil and the Deep Blue Sea

It took them both forever to fall asleep, and then only seconds seemed to pass before the alarm went off again. The twins tiptoed groggily past their mother's room and went upstairs a second night in a row. They had a mission: to find the skeleton keys and witching rod. Without them, the Card of Translocation might vanish forever – into obscurity or into the hands of The Evil, which would presumably use the Gift it contained against the Wardens.

In the Blue Room they found Kleo and Cornelia in exactly the same positions as before, except the silk cover of the brass cage was off.

'Hello, troubletwisters,' said the cat, sitting up straight the instant they appeared. She hopped off the dragon-mouth chair and hurried to greet them. Cornelia watched her pad across the floor with one sharp, yellow-rimmed eye.

'Rourke?' the macaw said, but in a way that suggested she was making wary conversation rather than looking for her dead master.

Jaide gave Kleo a pat. 'Have you been in here ever since last night?'

'Yes, I'm afraid so. The life of Warden Companion isn't a constantly exciting and adventurous one, and I'm thankful for that most of the time, but I will confess to getting a little bored today.'

Jack reached for the bag of seeds and offered one to Cornelia. The great macaw was crouched on the uppermost perch, about eye level with him, and she looked at him with patient curiosity.

'Has she said anything?' he asked Kleo.

'Safe harbour,' the bird announced in a clear, distinct voice.

Kleo sat down and coiled her tail round her legs. 'Yes, there's that,' she said. 'We think that's why she came here, to get away from whatever it was that scared her. All the animals around here know or at least sense that Watchward Lane is a safe haven – unless you're a mouse or a bird when Ari's around.'

'You mean you don't eat mice and birds?' asked Jack.

'Not when they are seeking refuge,' sniffed Kleo.

'The devil and the deep blue sea,' said Cornelia, waddling over to inspect the nut Jack held. She sniffed him first, as she had the previous night, and this time after a moment's careful consideration deigned to take the offering.

'She says that a lot too,' said Kleo. 'I don't know what it means.'

'Isn't it a saying, like caught between a rock and a hard place?' said Jaide.

Jack nodded. Hector Shield liked to say that he was stuck between the Kettle and the Steeped Oolong Tea.

'So she was frightened at the estate and she's frightened here too,' he said. 'But she's safe here, isn't she?'

'Perfectly, while Custer is keeping Ari distracted,' Kleo said. 'She might be the only witness who can tell us what really happened to Young Master Rourke the night he died.'

'Can you tell us, Cornelia?' asked Jack, offering her a big shiny pumpkin seed this time. 'We just want to stop it happening to anyone else.'

Cornelia raised her head and tilted it to one side, glancing at Jack first, then Jaide, then back again. She seemed to be trying to work something out.

'Out of the rain,' she said.

'That's new,' said Kleo, ears pricking up.

'Out of the rain,' Cornelia said again, more firmly than before.

'What are you trying to tell us, Cornelia?' asked Jack.

'That's not rain . . .'

'What isn't?'

'You daft old fool. Batten down the hatches! Rourke! Rourke!'

Cornelia spread her wings and flapped them up and down, sending tiny feathers and seed husks flying all around them. Jaide retreated, spluttering, while Jack tried to calm the bird down.

'Shhh! Cornelia, it's all right! We're here – you're safe!'

But the bird couldn't be consoled, and in the end they had to throw the cover back over the cage in the hope that she would settle. Slowly, with the occasional raucous 'Rourke', Cornelia did become quiet, although Jack could hear her moving about inside the cage.

Kleo went back to the dragon-seat and sat like a sphinx, facing the twins.

'Well,' she sighed, 'that was all new. I don't think it means anything, but it's progress . . . of sorts. She likes you, Jack.'

'She still doesn't like the way I smell though,' he said, sniffing his fingertips. They didn't smell like anything more sinister than hamburger, and perhaps a small amount of dirt. Next time he would wash his hands to be sure.

'I'm just going to look in the *Compendium*,' Jaide told Kleo, giving Jack a *keep her distracted* look as she went to the desk.

'Not gold cards again, I hope,' said the cat, looking amused.

'No,' Jaide said truthfully. 'We're just worried about getting out of touch while Grandma's in hospital and we're busy . . . helping Rodeo Dave,'

She opened the *Compendium* and began to focus her thoughts on skeleton keys.

'Speaking of Rodeo Dave,' said Jack, 'has he seemed all right to you lately?'

'Not really,' Kleo said. 'He has been very tense since the old man died.'

'Were you with him the night it happened?'

'I was. The phone call woke us both up.'

'What phone call?'

'The one from the old man.'

'Young Master Rourke rang Rodeo Dave?' This was a twist Jack hadn't anticipated. 'What did he want with him?'

The cat shook her head. 'I don't know, but it was definitely him. Rodeo Dave said "Rourke" three times, then he went out to the estate in a hurry. That's why he was the first to find the old man.'

Jack sat on his knees in front of Kleo, struggling to absorb all this new information. Rodeo Dave had spoken to Young Master Rourke while he was still alive. Then he had rushed out to the estate and found the old man dead and the lodge thoroughly ransacked. Or *had* he? Had he taken the opportunity to look for the Card of Translocation while Young Master Rourke had been out of the picture? Or had he killed the old man himself because of something he had been told on the phone . . .?

That was a picture of Rodeo Dave quite unlike the man Jack thought he knew. But as Jaide said, nothing in Portland was ever simple.

'Jack?' said Jaide. 'Come look at this.'

There was something odd about Jaide's tone, and with good

reason. Her thoughts had been distracted by Jack and Kleo's conversation. Instead of focusing on skeleton keys, she had been thinking about Young Master Rourke living alone on the giant estate, the son of a man who had made such an impact on Portland's prosperity, but had not been terribly well liked.

Then she had turned the page and seen a familiar picture.

'This one again?' said Jack, leaning close over her shoulder. 'Portland in 1872.' It showed a whale carcass being winched ashore in front of a crowd of old-fashioned people. Everyone in the photo had wide, white eyes, indicating that they belonged to The Evil.

'Look at him,' said Jaide, pointing.

Standing with one arm raised, facing the camera, was a man in a black suit.

'Do you recognise him?' Jaide asked.

Jack squinted, then gasped.

'That's Young Master Rourke's father!' he said. 'The one in the portrait and the statue in the library . . . but it can't be, can it? I mean, it's too long ago . . .'

'It looks like him,' said Jaide. 'And he was Evil.'

Kleo made them both jump as she hopped up on to the desk and nosed the picture.

'That's the first Rourke,' she said. 'The grandfather. He started the whaling, but it was his son who built up everything else. They looked very alike. And the white eyes there might just be because it's an old photograph.'

'Oh,' said Jaide, disappointed. 'There's too many Rourkes.'

'Only three,' Jack pointed out. 'Grandfather Rourke, the whaler. Mister Rourke, the rich one who built everything. And Young Master Rourke.'

'I still think Grandfather Rourke was part of The Evil,' said Jaide, studying the photograph again. She shuddered and said, 'Look at all those white eyes . . .'

'Can you imagine what it would be like to have a dad who was part of The Evil?' Jack wondered aloud.

Jaide shuddered again, as though something slimy had slithered down her spine. She didn't want to imagine anything as horrible as that – not on top of Grandma X in hospital and Rodeo Dave a possible sleeper agent.

'I don't think I want to look at this for a while,' she said, shutting the *Compendium*. 'I guess we should go to bed.'

Jack looked at her in surprise.

'I don't want to go to bed. It's too early.'

'I suppose we could stay here and keep Cornelia company for a while,' said Jaide, with a wink that the cat couldn't see. 'Do you want a break, Kleo?'

Kleo's ears twitched.

'I could do with a stroll,' she acknowledged. 'The night does beckon.'

'Well, we'll stay here for say half an hour,' said Jaide. 'Would that be OK?'

'That is most considerate of you,' said Kleo. 'I'll be back shortly.'

She jumped down from the table, shot up the steps to the tapestry-covered door, whisked behind one corner and was gone.

Jaide waited for a few seconds, in case the cat came back, then shut her eyes and placed her hands on the *Compendium* and this time thought ferociously about skeleton keys and in particular the set owned by her grandfather.

She felt the book shuffle under her hands, and though she didn't lift them, when she opened her eyes the folder was open, this time displaying a handwritten note that said:

Sam didn't have the hooks. I've put all the keys in the top drawer of the snake bureau for now, will make the board when the hooks come in. And I picked up the cake, so you don't need to go.

Jack was reading over Jaide's shoulder.

'I guess that's Grandad's writing,' he said. 'Weird . . .'

Jaide looked round the Blue Room. Over in one corner there was a teak bureau wound about with carved snakes.

'That must be it,' she said, pointing. 'Check it out. I'll ask about the witching rod.'

Jack went over and pulled out the top drawer. It was full of numerous differently shaped and coloured wooden boxes. He opened the lids of each of them in turn until in one of them he found a large ring of keys. The keys ranged in size from half the length of his little finger to one big key as long as his hand. They all had ivory handles, carved in the shape of a crescent moon and the key parts were bright silver and surprisingly simple.

'We still don't know which one is the skeleton key,' Jack said, holding them up. They made a sound like a wind chime. 'I suppose we take them all and try them one by one.'

Jaide didn't answer. She was concentrating on the *Compendium* again. It fluttered open, but this time revealed only some hasty but well-executed sketches. One showed a close-up of a thick wire that had been bent in half and twisted in the middle. Underneath was an inscription in very small handwriting that said:

Makeshift witching rod, made from fencing wire, works just as well as the one the blacksmith made. Comes in handy for toasting marshmallows.

The second drawing showed a hand gripping the very end of the wire with just two fingers and thumb, and the note beneath that said:

Of the two grips suggested, this one works best for me. Hard on the fingers, but the rod responds strongly, so strongly sometimes it jumps from my grip!

Jaide stared at the drawing.

'This isn't much use,' she complained. 'It shows what a witching rod looks like, but not *where* one is.'

Jack came and looked too, bringing the keys. He tilted his head sideways, then laughed. 'I know where it is,' he said.

'Where?' asked Jaide.

'In the living room, next to the fireplace. In that box with the poker and stuff. I'll go and get it.'

'Don't wake up Mum by jangling those keys!' warned Jaide.

Jack closed his hand tight round the keys to stop their noise and went up into the house. Jaide put her hands back on the *Compendium*, ready to ask it about one more thing that she thought needed investigation.

When Jack came back, he was holding a soot-blackened wire rod with a twist in the middle. He barely had time to show it to Jaide before the tapestry twitched and Kleo returned.

'What's that?' asked the cat.

'Um, a toasting stick,' said Jack. 'For marshmallows.'

'Or sardines,' mused Kleo. 'I like a fire-toasted sardine.'

'I guess I could toast you a sardine,' said Jack, wrinkling his nose. 'Not right now though.'

'Yeah, we'd better go to bed,' said Jaide. ''Night, Kleo!'

'Thank you for watching over Cornelia, troubletwisters.' Kleo rubbed her head against both of them as they filed through the door. 'Goodnight.'

As Jack pulled the elephant tapestry back into place, he heard Cornelia quietly call out.

'The devil,' she said, 'or the deep blue sea?'

It was definitely a question, but Jack didn't feel as though it was directed at him. It might have been nothing more than random words from an old parrot. Still, it made him sad to think that she was still worried about something she couldn't communicate to anyone. If only she could talk properly like Kleo and Ari . . .

Back in their room, Jaide took the witching rod. It didn't look like anything magical, little more than a bent old coat hanger, but slightly thicker.

'Well,' she said, 'I guess this *is* it. It looks just like the picture.'

Jack took the witching rod back from her and held it as the drawing had shown, with just two fingers and his thumb. It immediately quivered and the end arched back, towards Jack himself.

'It works!' he exclaimed. 'I've got the skeleton key in my pocket.'

'I looked up something else while I was in the *Compendium*,' Jaide said.

'What?'

'The death mask you found, Professor Olafsson. He was a Warden, just as he said. He was very controversial though, even among Wardens. He had a theory that in addition to the world where The Evil comes from, there are other parallel worlds all around us that we can't see or access, but if we could work out how The Evil gets into our world, we might be able to get into all the other worlds too.'

'Wow!' said Jack. 'Interesting guy.'

'Interesting extremely *old* guy,' said Jaide. 'He died in 1763. So I guess he won't be very in touch with anything going on more recently.'

'He might still be able to help us find the card,' said Jack. 'We can ask him tomorrow.'

Jaide pulled back her covers and crawled gratefully under them.

'*If* we can get away from Rodeo Dave . . .'

CHAPTER TEN
Every Castle Has its Secrets

While they were getting ready for their second trip to the castle the next morning, there came two loud knocks at the door. Susan opened it and stared out at a high-cheeked man with long blond hair. There was something about his eyes that unnerved her – they were so close-set and disturbingly intense. He seemed to be staring right through her, or into her.

'Susan Shield, I presume,' he said.

'Yes, but I'm afraid –'

'I am a friend to your husband,' he said, offering his hand. She took it. His grip was gentle, but his fingernails were surprisingly long. 'And to your children.'

'Oh,' she said, backing away, feeling as though the wind had been knocked out of her. 'Yes, I . . . think I understand.'

Jaide had poked her head round the kitchen door. 'It's Custer!' she cried, running out to meet him. Jack followed.

'What are you doing here?' he asked. 'Is something wrong?'

'Nothing is wrong.'

'Would you . . . would you like to come in?' asked Susan. 'I've just made some coffee.'

'Thank you, but all I require is a moment with Jack and Jaide here.'

He gestured at the twins. Susan nodded, and turned as though in a fog, and walked three steps up the hall.

Custer squatted down in the doorway in front of the twins.

'We saw you yesterday,' said Jaide. 'Out on the estate.'

'Indeed you did, and I will be patrolling again today while your grandmother remains in hospital.' His upper lip curled, revealing his opinion of modern medicine. His teeth were long and sharp-looking. 'Ari tells me that you too are returning to the estate. You must be careful. The boundary of the wards stretches across the property. It would be dangerous for you to step beyond that boundary.'

'Why?' asked Jack. 'Is The Evil around?'

Custer glanced over their shoulders to where their mother stood just out of earshot, gnawing on a thumbnail.

'That is not what I am saying. I am asking merely for you to be careful.' He reached into an inside pocket of his long leather greatcoat.

'Take these. They'll tell you when you reach the boundary.'

He handed them a leather wristband each and helped them tie them round their wrists. Colourful beads dotted the bands, apparently at random. One of Jack's beads looked like a tiny six-sided dice.

Jaide opened her mouth to ask Custer the first of many questions she had, but a horn tooted outside and the chance was lost.

The three of them, followed closely by Susan, went out on to the verandah to meet Rodeo Dave. He was driving a huge red car – long, wide and rectangular, with enormous fins at the rear and a top that had been folded down behind the back seat, leaving the interior open to the sky. Two long horns adorned the grill at the front, looking as though they came from a real steer. The car's engine sounded like the growl of a giant dog, slowed down to a rumbling throb. Rodeo Dave looked small and insignificant behind the wheel, even with his enormous moustache and an equally incongruous cowboy hat, which was also new to the twins.

'The old companion?' said Custer.

'It seemed fitting,' said Rodeo Dave.

'Young Master Rourke would have hated it.'

'This isn't about George.'

The exchange revealed nothing to the twins, except that Custer and Rodeo Dave knew each other.

'Hop aboard!' Rodeo Dave called over the grumbling engine. Jack looked at Jaide, who shrugged. The chassis hardly shifted as they climbed in, Jack in the front, marvelling at the chrome-finished dashboard and the depth of the seats, and Jaide in the seemingly infinite rear.

Susan hurried out of the house carrying packed lunches, as

though they were going to school. She gave them to the twins, with a kiss each goodbye, and waved as the giant automobile slid smoothly into motion. They watched her recede into the distance behind them. Custer had disappeared as though he had never been there.

'This is Zebediah,' said Rodeo Dave over the engine noise, patting the dashboard. 'I only bring him out for special occasions.'

'What's the occasion?' asked Jaide, wondering if this had something to do with Grandma's accident. Could he be hiding the van to get rid of evidence?

'Zebediah *creates* the occasion,' he said. 'Without Zebediah, this'd just be another ordinary Wednesday. And that's absolutely what it should not be.'

Jack couldn't believe the car was going to fit down the lane, but it did, just.

'Where do you keep him?'

'Gabe Jolson lets me use the dealership's shed on Station Street. Zebediah doesn't take up much space when you park him carefully.'

Gabe Jolson ran Portland's sole car yard, Gabriel's Auto Sales. Rather like The Book Herd, the twins had hardly ever seen anyone looking at the cars, let alone buying one.

Zebediah glided through the town like a cruise liner, barely bumping when they went over the bridge and turning into corners as smoothly as cream. People stopped to look as the car swept by, and some of them even waved. It was as Rodeo Dave had said – Zebediah did create an occasion. Jack would have liked to drive around a little longer, but it seemed to take them no time at all to reach the castle gates.

Thomas Solomon waved Rodeo Dave into a parking space large enough for Zebediah. Dave put on the handbrake and turned the key, and with a smooth clearing of its mechanical throat, the car's engine shut down.

'I reckon you can leave the top open,' Thomas Solomon said to Rodeo Dave. 'No rain forecast today.'

Jaide looked up. The sky was cloudy with patches of blue. It seemed the weird weather of the previous days had passed. As she slid across the back seat to come out of the far door, she saw a ginger tail poking out from under the front seat. She reached down and tugged on it gently.

The tail retracted and Ari's face appeared.

'Hey, watch it!' he hissed.

'What are *you* doing here?'

'Shhh. I'm supposed to be keeping an eye on you.'

'Why?'

'Who knows? I think Custer wants me out of the way so Kleo can get up to . . . whatever it is she's getting up to.'

That was a possibility, Jaide thought. If Ari suspected that there was a giant vulnerable bird cooped up, who knew what he might get up to? But couldn't it also be that Custer didn't trust *them*? Or maybe it was Rodeo Dave he didn't trust . . .

She wished they'd had time to talk to Custer properly that morning. It occurred to her only then to wonder if Rodeo Dave's arrival had been timed to cut them off.

'All right,' she whispered. 'You stay there and I won't say anything. Just try not to get in our way, OK? We've got something important to do.'

'Don't worry,' he said before she could explain. 'I don't care a bit for old books. I'm mainly here for the mice.'

'Coming, Jaide?' asked Rodeo Dave.

'Uh, yeah, just getting my bag.'

Ari stayed under the seat as Jaide left the car, slammed the door behind her with an echoing boom and ran to catch up with Jack and Rodeo Dave as they crossed the moat bridge to the castle. Rodeo Dave had a backpack of his own, filled with things that rattled and clanked. He didn't explain what they were, but it certainly didn't sound like lunch. He had left his cowboy hat behind, on top of the dashboard.

Nothing had changed inside the castle. Everything was frozen just as it had been for all the years after Young Master Rourke had moved out. Jack assumed that other assessors would be moving in at some point, to look over the furniture, paintings and other valuable items. Hopefully that wouldn't happen before they had found the Card of Translocation.

Rodeo Dave put his backpack on the floor of the library and took stock of the job ahead of them.

'Right,' he said. 'Here's how we start. I've made a rough

list of the titles across these three shelves. I need you to take the books out, check them off against the list, dust the covers and put them carefully in the boxes over there. If I've missed a book, write in the title, author, publisher and year of publication, if there is one, on the right side of the list. If anything looks really fragile, leave it where it is. Don't even try to dust it. OK?'

'OK,' said Jack.

'I'm going to check the collection in the lodge. It's mostly paperbacks, but even so some of those old pulps can be very valuable. You'll be OK here while I'm gone?'

'We'll be fine,' said Jaide.

He nodded, picked up his backpack and left.

'That's great,' whispered Jack. 'Now we can start looking!'

'Not yet,' Jaide said. 'First we have to wait in case he doubles back to get something and catches us gone. We also need to make it look like we did *some* work. We don't want to make him suspicious.'

'What if the card is in the lodge?'

'He's already searched it – or someone has – and it wasn't there. I don't know why he's searching again. Let's get started, Jack, otherwise he'll come back before we've even gone.'

Together they went through about half the shelves Dave had indicated, marking off and cleaning the books, flicking through them as they went, before boxing them up as instructed. They were soon filthy, with blackened fingers, and dust and cobwebs in their hair. Jack had found an old notebook (blank) slipped between two volumes of a massive history of the steam engine, and Jaide had found the skeleton of a mouse or small rat, squashed under a giant book about ship maintenance, but apart from that they found nothing out of the ordinary. No gold card, and no map showing them where it might be hidden either. Just books, the bust of Mister Rourke and the painting of the woman in yellow, smiling to herself as though she knew something they didn't.

Jack put his latest armful on to the ground, puffing up a cloud of dust that triggered a coughing fit.

'I think that's been long enough now, Jaide, don't you?' he said when he had recovered.

'All right.' She climbed down from the low ladder she was using to check the top shelves. 'Let's go.'

They took the ring of keys and the witching rod from Jaide's pack and eased slowly through the library door, after first checking for anyone in the hallway outside. It was empty, apart from several enormous tapestries, two suits of armour and one wooden chest. The air was still and quiet. The only echoes came from the small sounds they made as they shuffled forward and stood for a moment, deciding where to go first. There was no sign of Ari.

'Let's try the keys on the chest,' whispered Jack. 'It looks locked.'

There was no doubt of that. A huge iron padlock hung off

the front, shaped like a lion and as big as two fists gripping each other.

Jack moved forward to try one of the keys in the lock, but Jaide held him back.

'Let's test the witching rod first, before we know what's in there,' she said, raising the bent wire and holding it in the way the *Compendium* had recommended. The wire was surprisingly difficult to keep still, once it was under tension. It flexed and shifted in her hand like a kitten ready to spring on a toy, and it took all her concentration to keep it steady.

She swept it across the wall in front of her, and felt nothing more than its usual jitteriness. They moved closer and she tried again. The wire felt taut in her hand, but it didn't bend down towards the chest.

'Nothing,' she said. 'OK, open it.'

Jack looked at the lock and then at the ring of keys in order to choose one at random. As he held the ring up, however, one of the keys swung out so it was pointing at the lock, as though magnetic. It looked like it would fit, so he slid it into the lock and tried to turn it. For a moment it was stuck. He jiggled it a little, and it went in far enough for him to turn it with ease.

The lock clicked open, but it took both of them to lift the mighty lid. When it fell back against the wall with an echoing boom, Jaide gasped with surprise. A hideous face was staring up at them with wide, staring eyes and long, sharp teeth.

Then she laughed.

'Another head!' she said.

This time it was a bear's head, stuffed and mounted, mouth open as though roaring. Its fur was matted and covered with dust.

Jack let out a sigh of relief. His heart was pounding too, but at least this head wasn't likely to come alive and bite them, if the witching rod was to be believed. And now they knew that the skeleton keys worked perfectly.

'Let's shut it again,' he said. 'Then go and get Professor Olafsson.'

'All right. Hey look, more whales.'

The underside of the lid was engraved with whales, whaling boats and sailors with harpoons.

'The Rourkes were *obsessed*,' said Jaide. 'There are whales everywhere.'

Together they lowered the lid, unable to avoid another loud boom as it closed. As Jack turned the key again to lock it, he thought he heard another noise, the soft chiming of a clock in the distance.

'Did you hear that?' he asked.

'What?'

'A clock, chiming . . . it was kind of faint . . .'

'Nope,' said Jaide. 'Come on. I want to talk to the Professor.'

The death mask was exactly where they had left him, dozing patiently under the dust sheet. His eyes jerked open with a sneeze when they pulled it off.

'Ah, it's you again. The midgets from the future – no, wait, children, you said. You're looking for a golden card. You're starting your collection rather young, aren't you? Perhaps that's how you do things in this future of yours.'

'What collection?' repeated Jack, confused.

'Of cards. Every Warden has one, but not usually in my time until they *were* Wardens.'

Even though the death mask only had blank spaces for eyes, Jack and Jaide had the uncomfortable feeling that that the Professor was looking right into them. 'Perhaps it is the same in this time too. 'Why do you seek this card exactly? And for whom do you seek it?'

'Our father asked us to find it,' said Jaide. She figured she could trust a Warden with the truth, even if he had been dead for hundreds of years.

'What is this card called?'

'The Card of Translocation,' Jack said. 'Do you know what it's for?'

'There are thousands of gold cards. I don't recall that one in particular. They are, in general, *For the Divination of Potential Powers and Safekeeping Thereof.* Beyond that, however, I can only speculate. The name is somewhat curious.'

The death mask raised its plaster eyebrows and dropped the left corner of its mouth in something that conveyed the feeling of a shrug.

'Can you tell us where it might be?' Jack asked.

'I can do better than that, if you put me in one of those satchels of yours. That would be a practical solution to my non-ambulatory state – my lack of legs, I mean.'

'You want to come with us?' asked Jaide.

'Of course! I can't very well help you stuck here on this table, can I?'

She had hoped for directions rather than lugging the death mask around with her, but the Professor's suggestion did make sense. And besides, he had been trapped under a sheet for more years than she could imagine. It seemed only fair that he should have a change of scenery.

She and Jack arranged his pack into a kind of harness around Jack's neck and shoulders, so it hung down his front. Then they tied the death mask of Professor Olafsson to it using the ends of the straps.

'No' 'oo 'ight – ah, yes, yes, that's perfect.'

His grin widened as they approached the door and opened it.

'What a marvellous opportunity! I imagined I would be forgotten there forever, you know. A terrible fate for a brilliant mind like mine.'

'Shhh,' Jack said. 'We're not the only people here.'

'Is someone else looking for the Card of Translocation?'

'I don't know for sure,' said Jaide. 'Maybe.'

'We should hear Rodeo Dave coming,' said Jack. 'His boots make a lot of noise on the stone.'

'Well, I will endeavour to speak quietly,' said the Professor, only slightly more quietly than he had spoken before. 'Tra la la! I see you have a witching rod. Yes, hold it like that – I believe it is the more efficacious of the two methods. Now, if we take the left corridor ahead, that would be our best course.'

'Why?' asked Jaide. 'What's there?'

'A very large window,' said the Professor with dignity. 'I have not seen the sun for many decades. After a brief interval there, I will lead you on our search.'

As quietly as they could, the twins moved off down the corridor, with the death mask of the Professor humming something softly to himself, a tune the twins did not know, but long ago had been written in tribute to the glory of the sun.

CHAPTER ELEVEN
The Hidden Door

The Professor was completely silent as Jack stood in the shaft of sunlight that came through the tall window. After a few minutes, when Jack began to fidget, he sighed and said, 'Enough. Let the hunt begin.'

The twins took turns with the witching rod. It was difficult to hold and they soon became quite sensitive to its every twitch and tremble – perhaps oversensitive. They spent a lot of time examining empty rooms and unmarked stretches of walls. They opened countless chests, drawers and doors, with the skeleton key working every time. Often Jack heard the distant chime of a clock when he turned one of the keys. Eventually he realised it must be an echo of some old power, and wondered if the keys must have been used by Wardens as well as by their grandfather. That would explain why the key was apparently pysically drawn to the locks they presented it with, as though it had a mind of its own.

Unfortunately, when the twins got the chests, drawers and doors open, they usually found nothing but dust. There were occasional surprises that under other circumstances would have piqued their curiosity: a brass bell hidden under a sagging bed; four pitted cannonballs in a pyramid in one corner of an otherwise empty attic; several coils of rope that rats had nibbled at; a shield leaning up against the side of an empty barrel; even a moth-eaten jester's hat in a glass case with a label that had faded into illegibility.

They *did* find lots more whales: in carved flourishes on the banisters, on crockery and cutlery stacked neatly in the lifeless kitchen, even on a handkerchief someone had dropped long years past behind a sagging wainscot. Jaide supposed the motif made sense, given the family's fortune was made through whaling, but it was still a bit grotesque.

They also found the castle's medieval toilets.

'Is that what I think it is?' asked Jack, pointing at a piece of wood with a round hole in it, lying flat in a niche that stuck out of the wall in one corner of the castle's solar.

'It's a garderobe,' said Professor Olafsson. 'Has the future no need of such things any more?'

'We call them toilets, and yes, we still need them,' said Jaide, looking down the hole. It led to a pit outside the castle walls. A strong draught made her shiver. The air smelled of rain. 'I wonder if the Rourkes used it? You know, being super-realistic with history and everything?'

'There were proper toilets in those bathrooms upstairs,' said Jack. 'And next to the library. Besides, wouldn't they stink?'

'Not if properly cleansed,' said the Professor. 'A few

buckets of water every time, mixed with a solution of hyssop and rosemary. Or you could lower a small child with a brush –'

'OK, OK!' interrupted Jack. 'That's enough about garderobes! Let's get on with finding the card. We're running out of time.'

'I'm not getting any twitches,' said Jaide, waving the witching rod slowly across the walls and furniture. The solar was one of the few places where the twins had found anything actually made of gold. Here it was in the form of candelabra and a cufflink case shaped like a fish. Downstairs they had found gold mugs in the dining room and a gold pen in the study, looking as though it had dropped on the desk decades ago and never been moved.

'Maybe that's a good sign,' said Jack, kicking at the foot of the bed in frustration and provoking a rain of dust. 'It never seems to point to anything interesting. Could it be faulty, Professor Olafsson?'

'That is a remote possibility,' said the death mask. 'The wire mechanism is simplicity itself. The fault might lie in the operator –'

'Are you saying I'm doing it wrong?' asked Jaide, looking under the bed and finding only an ornate chamber pot.

'– *or* in the nature of the card's hiding place. What if we can't find this card because it is not truly here?'

'Huh?' said Jack.

'There are more worlds than we can imagine brushing up

against this one, realms separated from ours by the simplest thought, the merest breath. What if the card is in one of those? The witching rod might glimpse it, but we cannot because we lack the key to enter the realm the card occupies.'

The twins glanced at each other. The *Compendium* had mentioned Professor Olafsson's ideas about parallel universes and how they were controversial among Wardens, with the majority not believing him. But they didn't want to show signs of scepticism in case he became offended and wouldn't talk to them any more.

'We have the skeleton key,' said Jack, hefting the ring in his hand. 'Could they help us?'

'I don't mean that kind of key,' Professor Olafsson said. 'These locks aren't physical. They are mental. Only with the greatest effort of mind can we unpick them. I was working on such keys when I died, but my work was sadly incomplete.'

'So the card could be here and at the same time . . . *not* here?' said Jack, trying to get his head round the idea.

'Exactly. We are surrounded by things we can't see that *are* there and things we *can* see that aren't. Like salt dissolved in water, or a reflection in a mirror. Have you never wondered where The Evil comes from, what its reality is like? It has its own world from which it attempts to break into ours, a world with its own rules . . . horrible ones no doubt, quite inimical to our own.

'I'm not saying that the card is with The Evil,' he added

hastily, seeing the alarm blossoming on their faces, 'but that it might be somewhere like that. Another world with its own rules, connected to our own by some means of passage that *someone* fathomed, and which we too now must.'

Professor Olafsson looked satisfied with that conclusion, but the twins were still frustrated.

'Like a secret passage?' said Jaide.

'Yes, exactly like that, between one world and the next.'

'Do you know if the castle had any secret passages?' asked Jack.

'None that I saw, in the attics or the areas in which I was on display.'

'You wouldn't put a secret passage where just anyone could bump into it,' said Jaide. 'You'd put it somewhere safe, somewhere private.'

'Somewhere like the solar,' said Jack excitedly.

'Exactly!'

Jaide leaped off the bed and began poking things at random – carved knobs on the mantelpiece, gas-lamp brackets and joins, looking for loose panels or hidden switches. Jack did the same, abandoning the mysteries of the witching rod for something more concrete.

'I didn't mean to be taken so literally,' said Professor Olafsson, jostling from side to side as the twins competed over likely possibilities. 'I hardly believe that a passage between worlds would be revealed in such a vulgar way as –'

He stopped talking when, with a solid click, a carved whale sunk one inch into the wall under Jack's insistent thumb and a panel slid aside next to it, revealing a dark, dank space beyond.

'Oh my,' said Professor Olafsson. 'You do appear to have found something.'

Jaide peered inside the hidden panel and saw narrow stone steps leading downward. The walls of the secret passage were wood, once polished but now stained with age and damp. There were brackets for torches, all empty, and the light from the solar petered out after a few steps. Beyond that point, Jaide could see nothing at all.

Jack fared better thanks to his Gift, but even he could see just ten feet forward, to the point where the stairs turned left. The ceiling was very low and he was horribly reminded of the sewers under Portland, where The Evil had once chased him. He still had nightmares about those terrible experiences. Here at least there was no slime, and the air just smelled stale, not foul. And the odds were that the realm of The Evil probably wasn't at the end of the tunnel . . . he hoped.

'After you,' he told Jaide.

'*You* found it,' she shot back. 'Besides, you can see in the dark. I can't.'

He swallowed his fear with a gulp and stepped inside. As though sensing his reluctance, Jaide put one hand on his shoulder and followed closely behind him. He was glad of his sister's presence. In the sewers he had been entirely alone, and that had been the worst thing of all.

They descended four steps. Behind them, the panel closed with a soft click, plunging them into total blackness.

It was Jaide's turn to be frightened, and to be grateful for Jack's confident guidance. Fortunately the dark didn't last long. Four more steps took them to the corner and as they turned it, she found that a slit in the wall further down allowed a sliver of dim light into the tunnel. To her dark-adjusted eyes it was more than enough to see by. As they passed the slit, she saw that it opened on to a room they had visited before: a pantry on the first floor that had seemed utterly unremarkable.

'There might be holes like this all over the castle,' she whispered.

'We should've checked the paintings,' said Jack. 'You know, like in old movies. There's always someone peeping through the eyeholes.'

That prompted a creepy thought. What if someone had been watching them as they searched the castle? They might be in the tunnels with them right now . . .

Don't be silly, she told herself. *There's no one in the castle but us.*

But the creepiness remained as they followed the tunnel down through tight bends and past several more peepholes. At the bottom was a narrow storeroom, one of several judging by the arched doorways leading from it, with curving ceilings above, like a vault. There were no chests or drawers, just stuff piled up or leaning against walls in apparently random fashion.

Some of it was unidentifiable – implements or machines made from metal and wood, some of it rusted or rotten almost to nothing – but much was eerily familiar, after three visits to Rourke Castle. It was the legacy of two generations of whaling.

There were harpoons corroded and stained by the blood of all the whales they had killed. There were carving knives as big as scimitars, with grips large enough for two hands. There were hooks and ladles and spades and tubs, along with compasses, cables and oars that could have had innocent uses, but probably hadn't, considering the company they were keeping. There were sheets of whalebone in its raw form, which Professor Olafsson called baleen, plus numerous white objects that he assured them were whale's teeth, carved decoratively by the crews of the long-gone ships.

Jack and Jaide moved among them slowly and carefully, feeling a kind of revolted reverence normally reserved for graveyards and their father's old record collection. There was other stuff too – a collection of artefacts from Asia and Polynesia, consisting of leering carved heads and wooden spears, and other objects difficult to identify – piled high in places like backyard junk, although once it had been precious to *someone*, Jaide thought. It might have been an exhibit, in a time when taking such things from the people who owned them was acceptable.

'What's it all doing down here?' Jaide asked. Echoes whispered back at her like a hundred voices.

'I guess he had to put it somewhere,' said Jack. 'Mister Rourke, I mean. What with whaling being banned and so unpopular and everything.'

'But why keep it at all?' She flicked open an old journal, the topmost of several stacked in a pile. The copperplate handwriting within was hard to decipher, but it seemed to be a captain's log from 1891. 'He should've just thrown it all out.'

'Whaling is banned?' said Professor Olafsson in amazement. 'What oil lights your homes then? What material strengthens your ladies' corsets?'

'Uh, we don't do stuff like that any more,' said Jaide. 'Whales are almost extinct. It's wrong to kill them.'

'Maybe he kept it for a reason,' said Jack, getting out the witching rod. 'To hide something else.'

He gripped the wire tightly and swept the business end over a pile of rotting tarpaulins. He tried the walls in case there was another secret passage. He scanned everything he could see, even if it didn't gleam or couldn't possibly contain anything.

Nothing – until the rod was pointing at the third entrance on the right. Then the wire twisted in his hand like an eel, so powerfully he almost lost his grip on it.

'Through there!' he said. His feet moved as though of their own accord. The rod was tugging him forward, pulling him towards the doorway.

Jaide fell in behind him, breath tightly held. They entered another narrow storeroom, lit by the faint light shining through two narrow peepholes. This storeroom held more of the same, with one important difference.

Next to a doorway on the other side of the room was a large suit of armour – but this wasn't the usual plate and mail variety. This was made of overlapping leather, gilded at the edges, with a wide skirt and sloping shoulders. The helmet was crested in red, sporting a nose guard and a gorget, a long, spreading collar that protected the neck. Ornate serpent-patterns covered the chest and shoulders.

'Chinese,' said Professor Olafsson. 'Ceremonial, by the looks of it.'

Jack shushed him. The witching rod was pointing at the suit of armour. He approached warily. The space inside the helmet was dark and empty. Could the Card of Translocation be hidden inside?

They had barely got halfway across the storeroom when the rod twitched again, tugging Jack to one side. At the same time, the light coming through the peepholes brightened, and they heard footsteps.

Jaide's breath stopped in her throat. They weren't alone!

The beams of light shifted as though someone holding a torch was moving on the other side of the wall. Someone coughed – a man. Jack put a hand over the death mask's mouth and inched closer to the peephole, Jaide close alongside him. They crowded together and peered through to see what lay beyond.

It was a cellar filled with wine barrels. A man moved among them with a light strapped to his head – like a miner's lamp but modern, with LED globes. It was hard to see his face for the shadows it cast. His hands held simple L-shaped pieces of wire that Jaide recognised from the *Compendium*: it was another sort of witching rod, different to theirs, but designed to do the same thing. If they were pointed at something magical, the weighted ends would swing together.

'Where is the wretched thing?' the man asked himself.

Jack suppressed a gasp of recognition. The face might be hidden, but the man's voice was immediately familiar.

'It *must* be here,' muttered Rodeo Dave, pointing the witching rod methodically at each of the barrels in turn.

And Jack understood. It was Rodeo Dave's rod that their rod had detected – which meant . . .

Jaide realised before him, but pulled him away a second too late. Rodeo Dave's rod twitched at the same instant the one in Jack's hand did. They had detected each other!

Rodeo Dave's head came up. He stared for a long moment at the unbroken wall before him. The miner's light shone directly through the peephole. Jack and Jaide retreated from him. Rodeo Dave seemed to be staring *right at them*.

Jaide's foot kicked a fallen machete, which scraped along the cobbled floor with a terrible grating noise. Rodeo Dave froze.

'Who's there?'

The twins acted instinctively. Jack reached out with his Gift to snuff out the miner's light, while Jaide whipped up an obscuring whirlwind, thick with choking dust. Darkness and grit blinded Rodeo Dave's sight. He staggered back with a howl, tripped over his feet and fell heavily on to his backside, blinking uselessly.

'Run!' Jaide hissed, pushing Jack ahead of her.

CHAPTER TWELVE
Meet the Menagerie

Jack was already moving. Wiping grit from his eyes, he took his sister's hand and tugged her towards the nearest doorway. He couldn't remember which one they had come through, but that didn't matter. Getting away from Rodeo Dave was the important thing. The death mask bumped against his chest as they ran from storeroom to storeroom, past a seemingly endless exhibition of humanity's cruelty to whales, fleeing the sound of Rodeo Dave cursing and spluttering behind them. He seemed constantly close on their heels – a result, perhaps, of the acoustics of the cellars, but the effect was the same. The twins didn't let up their pace.

Jaide could see nothing at all as she ran, and Jack could barely breathe through the roaring dust. Only dimly did he perceive a door larger than any of the others looming ahead, double the width, made of sturdy aged oak with a beam lying crossways across the middle, sealing it shut. He fumbled at the beam and eased it as quietly as he could to one side. The door creaked open, letting in a rush of fresh air and natural light. Jaide lunged forward, not caring what lay on the other side. She could see again. Her Gift rose up and pushed them forward, lifting both of them off their feet for an instant, then setting them back down.

They stumbled up a flight of stairs, the light growing brighter with every step. At the top was a metal gate, easily unlocked with the skeleton key. Through its bars they could see the green mayhem of an overgrown kitchen garden. They passed through the gate, out of the secret storerooms and into daylight that seemed bright to them, even though the sky was overcast. They were outside.

Jack slammed the gate behind him and ran with Jaide through the garden. He didn't know if Rodeo Dave was behind them or not, but every instinct told him not to take any chances. They headed for a clutch of nearby outbuildings, over a low stone bridge that crossed the moat in a graceful arc. Dark water churned below, as though stirred by invisible beasts. Thick dark clouds gathered above. A natural, gusty wind tugged at them, made them hurry.

They reached the outbuildings and stopped, gasping.

'Did we lose him?' asked Jaide.

'Probably – that is, I'm sure we–' Jack was interrupted by a low growl coming from very close nearby. '–did?'

Only then did the twins notice the inhuman faces staring from all around them, a ring of hostile visages. They stepped closer to each other, and the growling doubled in volume.

'Is that a wolf?' asked Professor Olafsson, rolling his eyes around to look in every direction at once. 'I'm not edible per se, but I'm undoubtedly chewable.'

A gangly, humanoid figure leaped at them, shrieking like a banshee. The twins retreated until their shoulder blades crashed into iron bars. Another set of bars caught the attacking figure in mid leap, and that seemed only to enrage it more.

'It's a chimp!' said Jack in relief. 'We're in the old menagerie!'

Jaide drew in a sobbing breath. 'Of course. They must've reopened it when the animals escaped from their other pens.'

A monstrous howl came from right behind them, and they leaped away from the bars. Turning, they saw a tremendous grey wolf standing alone in the cage with its legs braced wide apart, poised to spring. It growled again. If the bars hadn't been between them, thick and sturdy despite their age and the weeds sprouting from their base, the twins would have instantly bolted.

The wolf's and chimp's cages were just two of at least two dozen cages of varying sizes to match their inhabitants. There were at least ten animals scattered across the cages. Quite a few were ones the twins had never seen before outside of a nature documentary, including a warthog, who looked asleep until they realised his eyes weren't completely closed and the very end of his tail was twitching slightly.

At least the animals' eyes were normal, Jaide reassured herself. There was no sign of The Evil here. But there was something strange about the animals nonetheless.

'Why are they all staring at us like that?' she asked. 'They look they want to eat us – even the ones that don't normally eat meat.'

'That's because you're troubletwisters,' said Professor Olafsson. 'And you've recently used your Gifts. Surely this can't be the first time animals have acted strangely around you?'

Jack shook his head, remembering kamikaze insects that had been drawn towards him, only to die on touching his skin.

'Could that be why Cornelia has been weird with me?' he asked.

'Who's Cornelia?'

'A macaw. She used to live on the estate too. A couple of other animals escaped and –'

'Can we go somewhere else, please?' Jaide asked. The staring animals were putting her on edge. 'I don't like it here.'

'Back to the library?' Jack suggested, peering round the cages to the gate they had passed through. There was no sign of Rodeo Dave, who Jack was now convinced had to be a sleeper agent for The Evil. Why else had he lied to them about what he was doing in the estate?

And more than that. Rodeo Dave was looking for the Card of Translocation too. It was now a race between them and The Evil to get to it first.

'We'd better get back there before Rodeo Dave does anyway. Otherwise he might wonder if it was us he detected in the cellar.'

'All right, but not the way we came,' said Jaide. She didn't want to retrace her steps through the storerooms, with the stained harpoons and whalebones, and the brooding armour guarding the doors. 'Let's go round the front.'

They set off, leaving the staring, restless animals behind them. Jaide was glad to put them behind her. They had disturbed her far more than they had Jack.

'So how *are* we going to find the card?' he said.

'We keep looking,' said Jaide. 'When we can.'

'But where? We've gone all over the castle.'

'Maybe it's in the grounds somewhere, not in the castle itself.'

'That's not what Dad said.'

Jack was firm on this point, even though he knew Hector Shield wasn't infallible. He was always losing his glasses for one. And his phone, keys, wallet and way. But Warden business was different. He would never make a mistake about something *important*.

'Maybe there are other secret passages we haven't found yet,' said Jaide.

'Don't forget my other-world theory,' said Professor Olafsson. 'All we need is the right doorway and right key, and we will have that card found before you know it!'

Neither twin shared his optimism. As well as being worried that they might let their father down, they were nervous about facing Rodeo Dave again. What if he *did* know they'd been in the cellar, and it was their Gifts that had struck him down?

There was a slight rise on the south side of the moat, partly covered by a copse of ancient fruit trees. They trudged uphill, tired, dirty and hungry. Jack stopped at the top to reach into his bag in search of the lunch Susan had packed. As he did so, a gleam of sunlight caught the corner of his eye.

He looked up. The gleam came again. It was reflecting off something in the woods bordering the estate, where his father was hiding. The light flashed like Morse code, fast and slow, fast and slow – an unmistakable signal.

Jack gripped Jaide's arm and pointed.

'Look!'

She had seen it. 'Is it him?'

'It must be.' He smacked his forehead with the palm of his hand. 'Jaide, we forgot to check the phone. I bet he's been trying to call!'

They pulled it out of Jack's bag. They had kept it on vibrate so Rodeo Dave wouldn't hear. There were several missed calls from an unlisted number, but no messages. For the millionth time Jack lamented the fact that they didn't have their father's number. 'If only we could call him back!'

Jaide waved the phone above her head and jumped up and down, hoping he could see her through his binoculars, or whatever he was using to watch the castle. But the flashing continued and the phone didn't ring. Maybe he was looking at the drawbridge, not the back of the castle.

'We'd better go to him,' said Jack, already moving down the

hill away from the castle, Professor Olafsson bouncing once more against his chest. Jaide followed closely behind. They cut a straight line across the estate, not needing to cross the creek because that was the other side of the castle.

As they approached, the flashing grew brighter, then ceased.

'He's seen us!' said Jack, starting to run. Jaide ran too, and Jack put on an extra burst of speed to keep ahead of her.

That was when he felt a sharp tug on his left wrist as though someone had grabbed him. But Jaide was on the other side of him and there was no one else around. No one with a body anyway.

'Ouch! Hey, Professor – what are you doing?'

'I have done nothing but attempt to hang on with my chin!'

'It's the wristband,' Jaide said, holding up her right arm. 'Custer gave them to us, remember?'

Jack had forgotten completely about the narrow coil of leather wrapped round his wrist. It tugged at him again, uncannily as though an invisible hand was holding him back, almost pinching his skin. He imagined the ghostly form of Custer reaching across the horizon to remind him of what he shouldn't have done.

They had left the wards.

Jack broke his pace for a second as reason undermined his original sense of urgency.

'We should go back,' he said. 'We can tell Dad about Rodeo Dave when he calls us later. He's bound to, isn't he?'

'Yes, but we can't go back *now*,' said Jaide. 'He's on his way – and I'm sure if we're quick and don't use our Gifts, nothing will go wrong.'

Jack put his head down and pressed on, but even though the ground was perfectly flat, he felt as though he was running uphill. Worse, the slope was increasing, so every step took more energy. No matter how he huffed and grunted, he slowed down rather than sped up.

Beside him, Jaide was experiencing the same problem. To her it felt as though the invisible hand on her wrist was not only slowing her down, it was pulling her back to the safety of the wards. She gritted her teeth and fought as hard as she could, but there was no resisting the power of Custer's charms.

'This is useless,' she gasped, as both of them were practically running on the spot. 'We're never going to make it!'

The treeline was still some dozens of feet away.

'Where is he?' asked Jack. 'I can't see him.'

Jaide scanned the trees for any sign of their father.

'There!' she pointed.

A shape was moving through the undergrowth, low and hunched, like someone trying not to be seen. Jack waved his arms and Jaide called out, 'Dad! Over here!'

The bracken parted. Something stepped into view.

It wasn't their father. It was something totally unexpected.

A chimpanzee, riding on the back of a very large, very

savage-looking grey wolf. The chimp grinned, showing its huge yellow teeth.

But it wasn't the chimp's teeth the twins were looking at. It was its eyes. Eyes that were completely white, without pupils of any kind. The wolf's eyes were just as white, horrible milky orbs set in the deep fur.

Jaide gasped. 'The Evil!'

'Retreat!' shrilled Professor Olafsson, just as Jack shouted, 'Let's get back!'

Jack was already moving as he spoke. Jaide was barely a pace behind him. This time the bracelets worked in their favour, pulling them back towards the wards' influence.

Behind them the chimp pointed at them and the wolf broke into a trot. They looked like a miniature horse and jockey, heading right for the twins. The ape lowered its arm as the trot became a run, hanging on tightly to the thick grey fur.

Jack looked over his shoulder and was shocked by how fast the wolf was moving. The boundary of the Wards was invisible so there was no way of knowing how far they had to go. Could they outrun a wolf?

Ten scrambling, panicked steps later he glanced over his shoulder again and wished he hadn't. The grinning wolf was almost close enough to snap at his heels. The chimp was crouched low on its back, like a champion jockey, its arm whipping the flank of the wolf with a twig.

++Turn back, troubletwisters,++ said The Evil, directly

into their minds. **++There is no escaping us!++**

Jack and Jaide unleashed their Gifts at the same moment, though not under control. A sudden darkness fell upon them, but vanished just as quickly, even before Jaide could cry out in fear, closely followed by a wind that roared past ahead of them, flattening the grass, but not doing anything else.

The chimpanzee chittered and the wolf howled, and though Jack didn't dare look, he knew that any moment he would feel the wolf upon him or, even worse, might see Jaide fall under its great weight.

++Your Gifts are strong, troubletwisters. We will use them well when they are ours!++

At that moment, a cloud formed above them and rain bucketed down, lashing the twins like whips, turning the already sodden grass into a slippery slide. Jack lost his footing and in reaching for Jaide, tripped her over too. They fell on to the suddenly muddy soil and slid to a stop.

++Ours at last! All ours!++

The wolf leaped towards them, the chimpanzee jumping from its back to target Jaide as the wolf sprang at her brother.

But they did not land. They were met in mid-air by the rain, a solid *force* of rain, like a giant baseball bat made of compressed water. It met wolf and chimp with a liquid snapping sound, both animals disappearing right into it, before they were suddenly ejected out again and sent flying back up the slope in an explosion of mist and raindrops.

'What was *that*?' gasped Jack.

'Who cares!' said Jaide, slithering backwards through the mud. Even the ordinary rain was torrential, getting in her eyes and making it hard to see which way she was going. The castle was a distant blur, far out of reach. 'Let's get out of here!'

The wolf sprang up and headed back towards them, the mud-spattered ape struggling along at its side.

++One of you,++ growled The Evil inside their heads. **++Grant me one of you and we will let the other go free.++**

'No!' cried Jack as he tried to get up and slipped over again. He reached for Jaide's hand and gripped it. 'Never!'

++Never is a long word for such a small boy.++

'You're just trying to drive us apart!'

++We merely hasten the inevitable.++ The wolf was prowling towards them, the chimp clambering on to its back. There was no sign of the mysterious watery force to protect the twins now. **++Spare yourself the agony, troubletwister, before she decides for you!++**

The raindrops suddenly got bigger and fewer. They were so large each made a sound like a small gunshot as they hit the ground. Then a really enormous raindrop fell, and there was a thunderclap, though neither twin saw lightning.

Wiping their half-drowned faces, the twins saw a sodden figure appear out of the rain.

'Dad!'

'Stay back!' said Hector Shield, splaying the fingers of his right hand wide to drive them away from him. 'This is my fight.'

++You dare? Do not come between us and our troubletwisters,++ said The Evil.

'Keep away from them.' Hector's voice was faint but strong through the rain swirling around him. 'Don't do this.'

++You know we do what we must do. You cannot fight us!++

Hector Shield did not answer. Instead, he raised both arms, and with another thunderclap so loud the twins felt it in their chests, an absolute river of rain fell out of the clouds to smite The Evil where it stood. Stinging spray blinded the twins, and they recoiled from where their father had been standing, calling for him and hearing only the roar of water all around them.

Then two strong hands grabbed each of them by an elbow.

'Hurry,' said their father, pulling them twisting and sliding back down the slope. 'Get inside the wards!'

'Come with us, Dad,' pleaded Jack. 'I swear we can control our Gifts –'

But already the light was flickering and the rain was swirling round them with the beginnings of a hurricane.

'Listen to me, Jaidith and Jackaran.' And they did. There was no arguing with their father's tone, and he only ever used the twins' full names when he was mad or in a hurry.

'The Evil is trying to distract us,' he said. 'It wants to

stop us finding the card before it does.'

'But we know who's looking for it,' said Jack. 'The sleeper agent is Rodeo Dave!'

'That explains a lot, but it doesn't change anything. You still have to go back. If he doesn't know you know, he won't act openly against you. The search for the card will keep him busy – he won't hurt anyone else now.'

'Can't you just . . . I don't know . . . have him arrested?' said Jaide. 'Or whatever it is Wardens do?'

She could feel Hector's hand shaking where he held her. Not only was he drenched, he looked and sounded like he'd run a marathon. His glasses were askew on his nose. He pushed them back up as he hustled the children closer to the castle, bringing his eyes back into focus.

'It's not that simple, Jaide,' he said. 'The Evil already senses your grandmother's weakness. That's why it's here, now, acting so openly against the wards. If she finds out that Rodeo Dave is an enemy agent, it could weaken her even further, and not even Custer could keep The Evil out then. What have you told her Companions?'

'Nothing,' said Jack. 'We only just found out.'

'Then we'd better keep it that way. Act as though nothing has happened and let me and the other Wardens keep The Evil at bay. We'll do our job while you do yours. OK?'

'Yes, Dad,' said Jaide, even though it warred with her instincts. First Rodeo Dave was a traitor, then The Evil was actively looking for the card too, and now they were keeping secrets from Grandma X and her Warden Companions. But it wasn't their fault, she supposed. It was The Evil's, for putting them in this situation.

'I'm sorry we came out to see you,' said Jack. 'We should've waited for you to call.'

Hector shook his head.

'Never mind, what's done is done. It'll all be over soon, once the Card of Translocation is in our hands.'

++Come back to us!++

Hector pushed the twins violently the last few feet and they fell sprawling again. This time there was no tug from their wristbands. They were inside the boundary of the wards.

But their father did not follow.

++Come back to us now!++

'Go! Find the card, quickly!' Hector Shield shouted to them.

With that, he flung himself back into the rain. Back towards the wolf and the chimpanzee, back towards The Evil.

'Dad!' cried Jack and Jaide together, but he was gone.

CHAPTER THIRTEEN

The Lady in Yellow

Jack started to get up to run after his father. Jaide grabbed him around the waist and pulled him back into the mud.

'Don't, Jack!'

'This is not for troubletwisters,' agreed the Professor's muffled voice between them. 'Live to fight another day – thus we keep The Evil at bay. But could you get my face out of the mud first?'

'What if he loses?' Jack said, but he did stop trying to get up and instead took his bag off and started carefully scraping mud from the death mask. 'What if The Evil beats him?'

'It won't,' said Jaide, although she was worried about that too. 'It can't.'

'Jack! Jaide!'

The twins heard their names, muffled by the rain and looked around, wondering who was calling them. It didn't sound like Rodeo Dave.

It was Ari, running across the lawn with dripping, rain-flattened fur.

Jack flipped the Professor round so he could look the death mask in the eye.

'Don't say anything about what you just heard,' he whispered. 'We have to keep this a secret!'

'Why?'

'Because Dad says so!'

'But –'

'Maybe we'll just put you back in the backpack for now,' said Jaide, taking him from Jack and zipping up tightly so the sound of his muffled protests was inaudible over the rain.

'What are you doing out here?' asked Ari as he came within earshot. 'Custer sent me to bring you inside while he braced the wards. The Evil is about. It hasn't breached the wards, so there's no reason to panic, but you're dangerously close to the boundary.'

'Oh, really?' said Jaide innocently, glancing anxiously over shoulder. Behind them, in the thick of the squall, there was no sign of either their father or The Evil. 'I guess we got lost in the rain.'

'How did you get past me?' asked Ari. 'I've been watching the front door all day.'

'We came out the back way,' she said.

'Oh. But what are you doing out here in the first place? Why aren't you sensibly inside the castle, where it's dry and you're supposed to be anyway?'

Jack said the first thing that came into his head.

'We, uh, came to shut the car's roof to keep the rain off. And then we got lost.'

'All you had to do was follow the castle wall around. Even a mouse couldn't get that wrong.'

'All right,' said Jaide, throwing up her hands in mock-surrender. 'We were exploring.'

'In the rain? I will never understand humans.' Ari lifted his nose to sniff the air. 'Hey, that smells like wolf. Wasn't the vet looking for one of those earlier?'

That galvanised the twins into action.

'If it is a wolf,' said Jack, heading towards the castle at a brisk pace. 'We don't want to get any closer to it.'

'Good thinking,' said Ari, trotting close by his heels and looking nervously over his shoulder.

The three of them hurried back to the castle, the rain slowly petering out behind them. By the time they reached Rodeo Dave's car – whose roof was closed – there was little more than a drizzle. The damage had been done though. The twins were soaked through, covered in mud and felt exactly like Ari looked. Thomas Solomon waved from where he'd taken shelter in his golf buggy, wrapped up in a raincoat, but didn't offer them a lift.

They stopped in the courtyard to try and clean and wring out their clothes. They managed to get most of the mud evenly distributed, if not actually off, and their clothes moved up from sodden to no longer dripping. They particularly didn't want to drip everywhere on the way to the library, or get any water on the books. Ari shook himself like a dog and sent a fine spray into the air around him.

When they were merely damp, they retraced their steps through the castle, past the chests, tapestries and suits of armour – which now seemed perfectly ordinary to them after the discovery of the secret cellar, or *the dungeon* as Jaide had begun to call it to herself – back to where they had started that morning.

Rodeo Dave was waiting for them there. The twins had been nervous all the way back to the castle, knowing that they would have to face him again, the sleeper agent who put Grandma X in hospital. They braced themselves for what might come if he suspected they were seeking the card as well, but he seemed merely concerned, not angry. In fact, Jaide thought, she had never seen Rodeo Dave angry, or overly excited, or anything. It was almost as if he was never entirely in the moment, a watcher rather than a participant. He had obviously learned to keep his true self deeply concealed.

'I've been looking for you,' he said. 'Where did you get to?'

'We heard the rain,' said Jaide. 'We were worried about your car.'

'You left the roof open,' added Jack. 'It could've been ruined.'

Rodeo Dave put a hand on each of their shoulders. They held their breath. Did he know that they had in fact been out of the library for hours and that they had seen him in the dungeon?

'That's kind of you to think of Zebediah,' he said. 'I'm sorry you got wet doing it. At least it washed off the dust, eh?'

'I think it turned the dust to mud,' said Jaide, thankful for one less thing they would have to explain away on their own. Her elbows and knees were brown from where she had fallen on to the ground outside.

'I'd better take you home. You must need a warm shower and a change of clothes.'

'That's OK,' said Jack, not yet ready to give up the chance to look for the Card of Translocation, impossible though that task seemed now. 'We'd rather stay and help you.'

Rodeo Dave frowned and looked at them and then back at the library. Clearly he was torn between what he wanted to do, what he thought he ought to do and what The Evil had told him to do.

'I see you've made a dent in the work . . . I guess we could have lunch first and then see how you're both feeling?'

'An excellent idea,' said Ari to Jack. 'I've had a small appetiser of mice, but I am still hungry. I don't suppose you'd consider sharing what's in your lunch box . . .?'

They sat on some upturned tea chests and opened the lunchboxes Susan had given them. Jack fished out the ham in his sandwich and gave it to Ari, who swallowed it in two gulps.

'So he followed us here, eh?' Rodeo Dave tossed Ari a

pickle, which he sniffed warily then ignored. 'Curiosity and cats. Imagine what he could find, digging around in here . . .'

The twins stared at Ari, struck by the same thought at exactly the same time. He could look for them, in all the places they couldn't get to, while they were stuck in the library.

'Excuse me,' said Jaide, putting down the last bit of her sandwich. 'I need to go to the bathroom.'

'You remember where it is?' asked Rodeo Dave. There were toilets just up the hall that must have seemed modern when the castle was renovated, but now looked hulking and antiquated to the twins. Though at least they were better than the medieval garderobes.

'Yes. I won't get lost this time, I promise. Come on, Ari. Let's see if we can find some mice on the way.'

'If wishes were fishes the sea would be full,' he said, 'and I would be down at the beach.' But he trotted after her anyway.

'How many Wardens have you met, Ari?' asked Jaide when the library door was safely shut behind them.

'Quite a few.'

'Do they all have collections of gold cards?'

'You mean like Custer and your grandmother? I don't know. All of them collect something though. They're like magpies.'

'Jack and I want to collect gold cards, but we don't know where to start looking.'

'You need somewhere the other Wardens haven't

already picked over, somewhere full of old stuff and – hey, like this castle!'

Ari scampered ahead of her and jumped on to the nearest chest. He did a quick turn, as though chasing his tail, then looked down the back.

'Nothing behind here. Want to have a look inside?'

The twins had already checked that chest.

'I don't have time, Ari, or a key,' she said. 'I have to get back to the books. But why don't you have a look around for us, now you're inside the castle? You'll probably find more mice to eat as well.'

'If I didn't know you better, I'd suspect you're up to something.' Ari looked at her suspiciously. 'In fact, because I *do* know you, I'm sure of it. Do you really think there are cards here or are you just trying to get me out of the way?'

'Grandma thought there were,' she said. 'She was on her way here when the accident happened.'

'Was she? I don't know anything about that.'

Jaide tried her best to look innocent.

'Well, I just thought . . . you know, collecting stuff, it's a Warden thing, and I want to be a Warden so I should start now . . .'

Her voice trailed off as Ari's eyes got narrower and narrower.

'All right,' he said, 'if it'll stop you from going exploring again. Custer's instructions were quite explicit.'

'Done,' said Jaide, kneeling down and hugging him. 'Ari, you are a prince among cats.'

'Of course,' sniffed Ari, and expertly wound his way out of her embrace. 'Don't go home without me. It's a long walk.'

'We won't,' called Jaide, as Ari disappeared round the corner.

Returning to the library, Jaide found Rodeo Dave high up a ladder, passing books down to Jack, who put them in piles up against one wall. They were mainly histories and biographies of people he had never heard of, some of them running to many volumes. Jaide helped, and between the three of them they emptied one of the long bookcases that lined the enormous space. There were many more to go, and the twins stared around them with heavy hearts. While their father was out in the storm fighting The Evil with the other Wardens, they were stuck with Portland's traitor, helping him catalogue books.

Jaide consoled herself by remembering what their father had said. While they were watching him, Rodeo Dave couldn't be getting up to any more mischief – and he wouldn't hurt them unless they revealed what they knew about him. The key was to act normal until the card was found and Grandma X was better. Then, they supposed, the Wardens would pounce.

The woman in the painting above the fireplace played on as they worked, eternally picking up the same card, over and over again. It was the two of hearts, something Jack wondered about as he worked. Had the number been significant to someone? Had the suit? Could she have been the painter's wife perhaps? Or could she have been the wife of one of the Rourkes?

Sometimes she seemed to be looking at him out of the corner of her eye, not as creepily as the bust of Mister Rourke, but twice as enigmatically.

'You two are very quiet,' said Rodeo Dave as he moved the ladder over to the next long bookcase they were to tackle.

'I was just, um, wondering about the painting,' Jack said, saying the first thing that came to his mind. 'Do you know who she was?'

'The *Lady in Yellow*?' he said. His forehead wrinkled, as if he was trying to recall some distant memory. 'I'm afraid I have no idea. She's been there as long as I can remember. It's my favourite painting in the whole place. And just look how dusty she is . . .'

Rodeo Dave tut-tutted and turned his end of the ladder, guiding Jack across the room so they stood below the painting.

'Here, give me a hand getting her down.'

Together they lifted the painting off the wall and put it on the ground. The rectangle of wallpaper exposed by its removal looked as good as new, not faded at all. Producing a huge spotted handkerchief from his pocket, Rodeo Dave lightly brushed dust off the paint and wiped down the gilded frame.

'There,' he said, standing back to get a better look.

'Considerably improved, don't you think?'

Jaide had been half expecting to see a secret door behind the painting. They hadn't thought to check there before.

'She looks a bit like Grandma,' Jaide said.

'Do you think?' He cupped his chin in one hand. 'Yes, I suppose she does, as she was as a young woman. You must have seen her in photos.'

'Er, yes, that's right,' said Jack. He couldn't let on that they had seen Grandma X's younger self when she appeared in spectral form. 'Did you know her then?'

'We met in our teens, a few years older than you are now.' His eyes took on a slightly glazed look. 'She was a firecracker back then, let me tell you . . .'

Jack cut him off in some alarm. 'But it couldn't *be* her, could it?'

'What? Oh no. I'm sure your grandmother would have had nothing to do with the Rourkes back then. They were bad seeds, through and through – but not George. It always amazed me that such a rotten old branch could still grow true at the end. It's a shame he never settled down. Besides, this painting is much older than your grandmother, or the Rourkes. It looks like early eighteenth century to me . . .'

His eyes drifted back to the painting.

'There *is* something about the *Lady in Yellow* though, isn't there? Just can't put my finger on it . . .'

They left the painting where it was and moved on to a series of shelves that contained hundreds of novels all bound in the same stiff leather with gold letters pressed in the spines. Some of them looked as though they had never been opened. In the middle of a shelf at eye level, not placed with any particular prominence, were three narrow, grey books where the gold letters spelled out: *The Whale* by Herman Melville.

'Didn't Melville write *Moby Dick*?' asked Jaide.

'That *is Moby Dick*,' said Rodeo Dave, delicately removing the three volumes and placing them in a special pile of their own. 'The first British edition had the simpler title and is extremely rare. Mister Rourke was an excellent collector, if not much of a reader. His son George was quite the opposite and the happier for it.'

'So why did Mister Rourke have all these books?' asked Jack.

'To impress people. How does that line go? "Of all tools used in the shadow of the moon, men are most apt to get out of order." Never a truer word spoken, by Mr Melville or anyone.'

Rodeo Dave glanced at his watch.

'It's getting late in the day,' he said. 'You've worked long enough and I thank you for your help, but now I'd better be getting you home. I promised your mother I'd have you back before dark.'

'What about you?' asked Jaide. 'Will you be coming back?'

'Not today.' He sighed and rubbed his back. 'I'm afraid this old boy needs some rest. And a bit of a read too. Looking at all these books has definitely put me in the mood.'

'Good idea,' Jack said, thinking that if Rodeo Dave really was going to stay in and read, there was nothing he could do to help The Evil. He wiped his hands on his trousers, but feared it would take a good wash to get the dusty smell off them. 'We'll come back with you tomorrow.'

'No need, no need.' Rodeo Dave avoided their eyes as he cleaned up the remains of their lunches. 'You've been a big help, but there's your schooling to consider. I've been lucky to have you this long.'

They tried to change his mind all the way back to the moat, but he was adamant. It bothered Jack to the very core: Rodeo Dave seemed perfectly normal, his usual friendly self, but it was clear he didn't want them in the castle any longer. The only reason Jack could think of was so Rodeo Dave could keep searching for the Card of Translocation.

But how could Rodeo Dave possibly be a good enough liar to fool both of them *and* Grandma X, whom he had known most of his life? It didn't seem possible, but it had to be. There was no other explanation.

Jaide looked around outside for any sign of either The Evil or their father and the other Wardens, but the woods were empty and the rain had blown away. There was no movement along the fringe of trees. Maybe The Evil had been driven off, for now.

As Thomas Solomon drove up in his golf cart to see them off, Jaide remembered Ari. She called his name into the entrance of the castle and seconds later he came loping out to join them.

'You've got him well trained,' said Rodeo Dave. 'Not like my Kleopatra. I think she's trained me.'

'Any luck?' Jaide whispered as they climbed into Zebediah, whose roof seemed to have opened itself now the rain had passed.

Ari jumped on to her lap. 'Just bones and old feathers.' He stuck out his tongue. 'All I can taste is dust.'

Rodeo Dave put on his hat and started the car. Zebediah rumbled deep in its belly and the castle fell away behind them. If Jack concentrated, he could imagine that Zebediah was perfectly still and the world was moving around it. The gates of the estate, the outskirts of town, the town hall, the fish markets, Watchward Lane . . .

Susan was standing on the steps by the front door as though she had been expecting them. She waved as they drove up the drive and came down the steps to meet them, then she waved again as Rodeo Dave drove back up the lane, minus his passengers.

'How was your day?' she asked.

'What's wrong?' asked Jaide. There was an odd look in her mother's eyes that told her there was something up. 'Is there something wrong with Grandma?'

'With Dad?' added Jack, feeling his heart thump hard suddenly in his chest.

'Why would you think that?' Susan asked them in return. 'All I did was ask you how your day was.'

'It was . . . fine,' said Jack slowly. He looked down at his mud-streaked clothes, wondering if that was where the problem lay. 'We got pretty dirty though. All that dust and grime in the books.'

'Nothing a bath and laundry won't fix.'

The twins took a step forward to go inside, but Susan didn't move out of the way. She stood there, as if waiting for them to confess something.

Jack and Jaide just stared at her, completely at a loss. Which part had she guessed? That Grandma X's accident was the work of The Evil? That Rodeo Dave was a sleeper agent? That their father was not on the other side of the world at all, but in their very neighbourhood, fighting to keep them all safe?

Susan did something entirely unexpected. She took her hand from behind her back and held up a small black box with an electric cord dangling from it.

A mobile phone charger.

'Perhaps one of you could tell me what this is and *who* it belongs to?'

CHAPTER FOURTEEN
Multiplication and Division

The twins stared at the charger with their mouths open. Jaide felt a wild urge to laugh hysterically. This was about nothing more than the secret of the mobile phone?

'It's the charger for our phone,' blurted out Jack in relief. 'Dad gave it to us – ow!'

Jaide kicked him in the shin. One secret led to another. If they started down the path to the truth by telling their mother where the phone had come from, it would all come out and they would never be allowed to keep looking for the card, no matter how much they wanted to help.

Luckily, Susan didn't believe them.

'Your father and I agree that you're much too young to have a phone. And besides, how could he give you a phone when he's in Italy? Tell me the truth, this time or you'll be in real trouble.'

They had to say something.

Jaide opened her mouth, but nothing came out. Fortunately, this time Jack was closer to the mark.

'We know you said you weren't going to give us a phone,'

he said, 'but we really need one to text Tara about homework and stuff, and everyone else our age has one, so we got it for ourselves from one of the kids at school. It's an old one that doesn't do very much. See? They would've thrown it out if we didn't take it. We're not wasting time or money on it. We pay for the credit out of our pocket money.'

Susan looked at the phone in Jaide's hand, clearly weighing up the veracity of their explanation. She had no reason to suspect that the phone came from their father, though it was clear she was still not entirely satisfied.

'Please, Mum, we can we keep it?' asked Jaide.

Jack's heart sank as Susan shook her head.

'I don't like you going behind our backs like this, she said. 'It sets a bad precedent. If you're good, maybe you'll get it back one day, but not today."

The twins argued, but they had no choice but to hand over the phone. It joined the charger in Susan's back pocket, firmly switched off, and eventually she raised her hands to bring their pleas for clemency to an end.

'All right, enough! Go inside, both of you. I've got some homework for you to do, after you've had a shower. I'm just going to the shops to get ingredients for dinner. There's a recipe I saw on the Internet at work – it sounds delicious.'

'That's my cue to go elsewhere,' said Ari, who had watched the confrontation from the sidelines. 'If it's anything like last week's chilli con carne with white chocolate, I'd rather be patrolling with Custer in the rain.'

He sprang off into the dusk, leaving them to their fate.

Jack and Jaide hurried up to their room as their mother scooped up her keys and bag and headed out to the car.

'I can't believe it,' said Jaide. 'This is a disaster!'

'I know,' said Jack. 'But what else could we have said to Mum to make her change her mind?'

'You could tell her the truth,' said a muffled voice from inside Jack's backpack.

The twins had completely forgotten about the death mask. When they peered in the bag, Professor Olafsson was indignantly tangled up in an old plastic bag and a damp sock.

'She'd never believe us!' said Jaide.

'Not about the devices you people employ to avoid talking face to face,' he said. 'About everything. You should tell your grandmother too.'

'We can't,' Jack told him. 'Mum wouldn't want to know about it and Dad told us not to worry Grandma.'

'Do you trust him?'

'Of course,' said Jaide. 'He's our father!'

'*And* he's a Warden too,' said Jack.

'What kind of father knowingly puts his children into danger?' Professor Olafsson asked them. 'What kind of Warden keeps the near presence of The Evil secret from the Warden in charge of the wards?'

'He hasn't really put us in danger . . . has he?' said Jack.

'I guess he has, kind of – if Rodeo Dave ever finds out what we know. But he won't do that,' Jaide told Professor Olafsson. 'We're good at keeping secrets.'

'Secrets, like lies, multiply in the keeping,' said the professor. 'Have you never thought to ask *why* this card is so important?'

'Of course!' said Jack again. 'There hasn't been time, and we keep getting interrupted.'

'And we're just troubletwisters,' said Jaide miserably. 'No one tells us *anything*.'

Professor Olafsson's expression softened.

'I too was once excluded from Warden activities,' he said after a moment, 'because I argued too strongly for my theories to be tested. You know your father best. Perhaps you are right to do as he says, and I am wrong to question him. As a fellow Warden, I will keep the secrets he has asked you to keep, and I will help you find this Card of Translocation for him.'

'But how *are* we going to find it?' asked Jack. 'If we can't go back to the castle tomorrow, Rodeo Dave will beat us to it.'

'Was that Rodeo Dave you were talking to earlier, when we left the castle?' asked Professor Olafsson. 'Talking about someone called Kleopatra?'

'That's his cat,' said Jaide, 'although she's not anyone's cat really. She's Grandma's other Warden Companion.'

'Odd. I recognise his voice from somewhere, but I can't recall where . . .'

Jaide zipped up the backpack and headed to their room.

'I want to check on Cornelia,' said Jack, continuing on up the stairs. He needed to do something other than brood over the lost phone.

'OK,' she called after him, 'but don't think I'm doing your homework for you!'

Jack found Cornelia and Kleo sitting in the Blue Room exactly as they had been last time. The macaw's royal blue head came up as soon as she saw Jack and she began walking rapidly from side to side as though pleased to see him. He crossed to the cage and fed a nut through the bars.

'Hello, Cornelia. How are you doing today?'

'Shipshape and Bristol fashion,' she declared, taking the nut.

'Is that good?' he asked Kleo.

'I think so,' said the cat, extending her chin so Jack could skritch under it. 'But she still hasn't said anything sensible. Maybe she will now that you're here.'

'You can trust us,' said Jack. 'Whatever you have to tell us, we'll believe you.'

Cornelia bobbed up and down, sending bits of nut flying in every direction.

'Rourke!'

With short but confident strides, she walked along the perch and climbed down the inside of the cage to the door. Gripping the wire in her powerful beak, she pulled the door upward and, with a deft and obviously well-practised manoeuvre, flipped herself through it. Then she climbed to the top of the cage and fluffed up her feathers.

Jack took a step backwards, unsure where this was going, while Kleo watched from the dragon chair.

'Is this the first time she's left the cage?' he asked.

'Hasn't so much as put her head through the door,' said Kleo, 'until now.'

Cornelia looked at Jack and then Kleo. The presence of the cat didn't seem to worry her.

'Rourke!'

The macaw's wings unfolded, flapped and suddenly she was airborne. She didn't fly far, just to the other side of the room, where her beak tugged the elephant tapestry aside. Two swift hops took her through the door.

Jack heard her wings flap again. He ran to lift aside the tapestry to see what she was doing. He had a fleeting glimpse of blue flying down the stairwell, then she was gone.

'Why did she do that? Is she coming back?'

Kleo shrugged. 'If she won't tell us, we can't know.'

'But she *can't* tell us. She's not like you, a Warden Companion.' Frustration boiled in him. Had they let Cornelia down somehow by failing to understand?

'What if we made her a Companion?' Jack asked. 'Is there a way to do that . . .'

'There is, and it's very difficult. Far too difficult for troubletwisters,' said Kleo firmly. 'Speaking of which . . .

Custer left exercises for you. You'll find them on the desk. I'm to make certain you do them before you go to bed.'

Jack groaned. *More* homework? It wasn't fair.

'I advise getting it over with,' said the cat. 'Let me fetch your sister for you. I'll keep guard for your mother's return, and check on Cornelia too, in case she's thinking of getting up to any mischief.'

'All right,' Jack said, rubbing his stomach. He was still looking at the tapestry, worried about Cornelia, but at the same time their late lunch felt like days ago, *and* he had shared it with Ari.

He slouched up the short flight of stairs. There he found the homework as promised, a series of fiddly optical illusions for Jack (involving mirrors and lenses and beams of light in a wild variety of colours) and for his sister twelve triangular flags that she had to make flap in a particular order using carefully targeted jets of air. Jaide joined him, and they set to their tasks unwillingly and with their minds on other things, so half the time their efforts were to no avail. Flags whipped back and forth, lights flashed on and off, and inevitably their Gifts began to interfere with each other. One particularly uproarious mishap had both of them running for cover under a bureau as objects swept round the room in the grip of an invisible tornado.

The twins each felt five tiny pinpricks of pain in the small of their backs. Startled, they turned round.

'I'll take this as a sign that you are tired and in need of dinner,' Kleo said as the wind ebbed, normal visibility was restored and a hundred tiny knick-knacks fell with a clatter to the floor. 'I suggest you call it a night and head down, once we've tidied up here.'

Jaide brushed her fringe out of her eyes. 'Can I take the *Compendium* with me to read later?'

'You may – although your grandmother says it's terrible bedtime reading. It gives her bad dreams.'

'Did Custer say anything when he came by today?' asked Jack as they picked themselves up off the floor.

'Only that he has observed several unusual meteorological phenomena near the estate.' Kleo followed them and began batting hidden trinkets into view. 'He mentioned a storm and all three of you getting wet. But there was no lightning, at least none that he saw. Did you see any?'

The twins shook their heads, wondering why that might be important. Their father travelled by lightning using his Gift. They didn't know what the absence of lightning might mean.

'But the wards are strong, aren't they?' Jack asked. This was as close as he dared to asking outright if the fight against The Evil that afternoon had gone well.

'Were The Evil was to seriously test the wards, I would know,' said Kleo, rounding up a series of chess pieces that were trying to run away from her. 'Wardens aren't infallible, and as you now know, sometimes they fall ill. They can be distracted by human concerns and affections. That's why they have Companions: we can see things they do not. We are their eyes and ears when they are blind and deaf.'

With a gentle nip, like she was picking up a kitten, Kleo scooped up the last wriggling pawn and tossed him into the box with the other chess pieces.

'Thank you, Kleo,' said Jaide, rubbing the fur under Kleo's ears. 'We'd better go back upstairs before Mum gets back.'

At that moment, the crash of breaking glass sounded from the drawing room.

Kleo led the charge to find out what was going on, Jaide almost treading on the cat's tail as she ran after her.

Cornelia was crouched on the mantelpiece, clinging to the edge with her powerful claws and peering downwards. On the ground below her was a picture frame lying in a field of glass shards. She glanced up at them, then back at the wreckage. Instead of exhibiting remorse at the accident, Cornelia flapped down and landed gingerly among the splinters and began pulling at the frame with her powerful beak.

'That's no way for a guest to behave,' said Kleo, running towards her.

Cornelia looked up and outstretched her wings, flapping them violently.

'Rourke! Rourke!'

Kleo retreated and Cornelia returned to the frame, tossing it back and forth with wild jerks of her feathered head until it broke and the picture within spilled out face down on to the carpet.

She tossed the frame away, nipped the corner of the picture in her beak and flipped it over. The picture was a black-and-white photograph of the twins' family taken when they were nine, showing them all dressed in Wild West outfits. Hector looked out of place in a cowboy hat, sheriff's badge and chaps, but Susan looked totally convincing with a six-shooter in her hand, despite her frilly dress. The twins were dressed in old-fashioned Sunday best. Jack remembered the way his stripy suit had smelled, of mothballs and faintly of sick, as though the last person to wear it had thrown up in it.

''ourke!' said Cornelia, hopping across the floor to him, holding up the photo in her beak.

'What's that, Cornelia?' he asked, crouching down to her level. 'Are you trying to tell me something?'

''ourke!' She dropped the photo in front of him and nodded her head up and down. 'Rourke!'

'Something about the photo?'

She stretched out and tapped it with her beak. 'Rourke! Killer!'

'Yes, that's me in the photo, and Jaide, and Mum and –'

Cornelia tapped more insistently, putting a hole in Hector's face. 'Rourke! Killer! Rourke!'

'I don't understand, Cornelia. That's my dad, yes, but –'

The tapping became more insistent, and the hole bigger still.

Jaide squatted down next to Jack.

'Cornelia, are you saying that Dad was the one who frightened Young Master Rourke the night he died?'

Cornelia stopped tapping, hopped backwards and waddled around in a circle. The message was clear: *Finally!*

'But that's impossible,' said Jack. 'Dad wasn't there. He couldn't have been.'

'Was he the one who frightened you?' asked Jaide.

Cornelia nodded. 'Visitor! Killer!'

'And is that why you were frightened of *us*, because you could tell we were related to him?'

Cornelia's blue head bobbed rapidly up and down. 'Visitor! Killer!'

'Stop saying that!' shouted Jack. The parrot stopped squawking, but gave Jack a very beady-eyed look.

Jack backed away until he bumped into Jaide's shoulder.

'Cornelia can't be right,' he said, shaking his head. 'Dad wasn't there, and even if he had been, he wouldn't have hurt Young Master Rourke. He wouldn't have!'

Jaide was just as bewildered, but she was trying to think it through. 'There must be some explanation. Perhaps he *was* there, and Master Rourke died of fright for reasons we don't know anything about, or –'

'There's very little we can be certain of right now,' said Kleo. 'Let's just be glad that Cornelia is starting to talk about what happened, and worry about making sense of it later.'

'You don't believe her, do you?' asked Jack.

'I believe your mother will be home soon, and we have some cleaning up to do. It would be best to hide Cornelia too, to avoid making a scene.'

'Good thinking,' said Jaide. 'Come on, Jack.'

'But if Dad didn't frighten Master Rourke, who did?' he said in a dazed voice. 'I bet he wasn't there at all! You're just making stuff up!' he shouted down at the parrot. 'And I thought you were my friend!'

The parrot lunged for the photo, but Jack yanked it out of the reach of her sharp beak. He ignored her when she flapped and squawked in protest, thinking only of his father hiding in the forest in the rain, mistrusted by everyone, even his own mother. He couldn't have killed Master Rourke; he wouldn't kill anyone.

Jack wanted to run back to the estate and find his father, to be told the truth of the matter and comforted. Instead he settled for fleeing upstairs and flinging himself on to his bed, clutching in one hand the ruined photo that, for a reason he could never admit to himself, he was unable to look at.

Chapter Fifteen
The Cornelia Conundrum

Downstairs, Jaide felt similarly stunned. Cornelia quietened when Jack left the room, and eyed Jaide warily, as though sizing her up.

'You're a weird old bird,' she said. 'Maybe your eyes are going.'

'Walk the plank! Keelhaul the landlubber!'

'All right, I'm sorry. But I just don't see how you could be right. I mean, it can't be Dad.'

But for the life of her, Jaide couldn't think why Cornelia would pick out her father and screech 'Rourke! Killer!' like that, and she couldn't talk about it with the parrot.

'I'll keep guard,' said Kleo, heading for the front door. 'You do what you can to make it look like nothing happened here.'

Jaide sighed in frustration and confusion. There was nothing else to do until Jack came out of his funk, so she took the dustpan and broom from the laundry cupboard. Watched by Cornelia every second, she tipped the remains of the picture frame into the bin and brushed up every last splinter of glass as best she could.

Kleo came running back in. 'She's here!'

Jaide met Cornelia's beady eye.

'You've got to go back in the Blue Room,' she said. 'After the business with the phone, I have no idea how to explain where *you* came from. Either you go now, or I'll throw a rug over you and carry you there. That way you won't be able to bite me.'

The parrot bobbed her head low and made a low clicking noise, as though considering her options.

'I'm serious,' Jaide said, doing her best Grandma X impersonation.

'Rourke!' Cornelia came up to her full height and flapped her wings. Two mighty sweeps saw her in the air, and a third sent her swooping for the door. The front door opened as Cornelia vanished up the stairs to the top floor and through the door leading to the Blue Room.

'Finished your homework already and doing your chores?' asked Susan, seeing Jaide with the dustpan and broom. 'That deserves a treat. Now, I couldn't find all the ingredients I needed so I got us stuff for sandwiches instead. How's that?'

Sandwiches at dinner time might have been a bit weird, but it was better than the alternative. 'Great, Mum.'

'Don't look so pleased. I know that when it comes to cooking I make a great paramedic.' She gave Jaide a quick hug, regretting their tense words earlier. 'Where's Jack?'

'Upstairs finishing his homework.'

'OK. I'll make him something and you can take it up to him later.'

Jaide put the cleaning materials away and helped her mother unpack. The thought of eating dinner led to the unexpected discovery that she was actually hungry. Susan had bought fresh bread with sliced meat, cheese and salad, creating a spread almost identical to the first meal they had ever had in Portland. Jaide made herself a lettuce, ham and tomato sandwich, and contemplated all the things that had happened since that first day. They had learned about their Gifts and The Evil. They had made several new friends, two of them cats. They had been in danger many times, and would certainly be in danger again. Maybe they were in great danger at that moment and didn't know it. She thought of her father and wondered how he was doing, but there was no way to find out unless Hector called or Custer dropped by.

'Can we go back to the castle tomorrow?' Jaide asked.

'That wasn't the deal,' said Susan. 'You've missed enough school for one week.'

'But Mum –'

'No buts. David Smeaton's been very good to put up with you two, but I think it's time you let him get on with his work.'

Jaide wanted to protest that this was exactly what they didn't want him to do, but she couldn't say anything like that. If Grandma X had been there, maybe they could have talked her around.

'Is Grandma any better?'

Susan sighed and looked down at her plate. 'I'm sorry, Jaide. Dr Witworth has her under heavy sedation in the hope of reducing the pressure on her brain. Maybe we can go and see her tomorrow, if she improves.'

Jaide put down the rest of her meal, her appetite gone.

Susan made Jack a sandwich and Jaide took it upstairs to him, but not before detouring through the Blue Room to pick up the *Compendium* on the way. The chances of finding anything in it were slim, but she had to try.

Jack was lying face down on his bed and didn't look up when she entered.

'Are you hungry, Jack?'

'No.' He rolled over on to his side, his back to her.

'Well, here you are anyway.' She put the plate next to him and sat on her own bed, setting the *Compendium* down in front of her. Concentrating briefly on the notion of Warden Companions, she opened the folder and began to read.

After a minute or two, Jack stirred.

'Where's Cornelia?' he asked, still without looking up.

'Back in the Blue Room. Do you want me to get her? I could probably sneak her in here without Mum noticing.'

'No. I never want to see her again.'

One hand reached out and snagged half the sandwich. The smell of it had reminded Jack that there were more immediate concerns than what a mad old parrot thought of his father.

The first mouthful went some way towards filling the aching void inside him. The second mouthful did more.

'Listen to this,' said Jaide. '*One of the earliest steps towards inviting an animal to be your Companion is to spend three days in their mind, experiencing everything they do.* That means Grandma has been inside Kleo's and Ari's mind. I wonder if they got to be in hers in return . . .'

'It doesn't work that way,' said a muffled voice from Jack's bag.

'Professor Olafsson!' Jaide jumped off the bed to rescue him. 'We forgot you again. I'm sorry.'

'No apology necessary,' he said when released from captivity and placed on the chest beside Jaide's bed. 'But it is nice to be part of the conversation again.'

'So what *does* happen when a Warden makes a Companion?' Jaide asked him, putting the *Compendium* aside.

'May I ask why you're asking?'

'Well, I thought that if we made Cornelia Jack's Companion she'd be able to talk to us properly about what she saw that night.'

Jack rolled over.

'No way!' he exclaimed. 'I don't want anything more to do with that treacherous old bird.'

'Calm down, Jack. It's possible we're still misunderstanding her, isn't it?'

'I don't think this could be a misunderstanding.' Jack held

up the photo, where Cornelia had bitten a hole right through Hector Shield's head. 'She kept saying *killer.*'

'That does seem most definite,' said Professor Olafsson. 'But in any case, I assure you that enlisting the services of a Companion takes a great deal of time, energy and trust – three things I fear you entirely lack at the moment.'

It was Jaide's turn to flop hopelessly on the bed.

'We can't just lie here and do nothing,' she groaned.

'I want to talk to Dad,' Jack said. 'I'm sure he could tell us what really happened to Master Rourke. I mean, we know Rodeo Dave went over there that night. It's more likely that he was the one who did the frightening, if The Evil told him to.'

'I don't want to think about that,' said Jaide. 'It's too horrible, and besides, there's no way to talk to him without the phone. We just have to find the gold card first. Then everything will be all right.'

'How?'

'I don't know, but it will be!'

'I mean, how are we going to find it? We tried a witching rod. We used a skeleton key. We got Ari to look around for us. We've found nothing, and now I'm out of ideas.'

'The solution might be right in front of you,' said the death mask, 'or behind you, or above you, or all around you. If it's in the universe next door, it could be anywhere, and nowhere.'

'But how does that help us?' asked Jack. 'If it's in another universe, we can't get to it because it's . . . in another universe, right?'

'Not so. All we need is a cross-continuum conduit constructor.'

'Is that something Grandma might have?'

'Not likely. It was never considered . . . uh . . . mainstream Warden equipment. Very few were made, though now I come to think about it, I suppose more must have been built since I've been . . . ah . . . resting . . .'

'If Grandma hasn't got one of these construct things then I don't think there's much hope –' Jack started to say, when he was interrupted by the gleeful Professor.

'That's where you're wrong! There's one in the castle. I saw it while we were searching the second floor.'

Jaide and Jack sat up at the same moment.

'What!?'

'The castle contains a cross-continuum conduit constructor that I suspect now was used to hide the card you seek in the first place. If we go back, I can show you where it is. I can even show you how to use it!'

'Wait.' Jaide rubbed at her tired eyes. Her brain was beginning to shut down from exhaustion. 'You're telling us that with this thing you can open a tunnel to another world, where the Card of Translocation is hidden.'

'Yes. A world among many possible worlds.'

'What kind of world?'

'It could be like ours, or it could be infinitely stranger, built from an entirely different number of dimensions and physical laws. I glimpsed some of these places during my own research – endless flat plains with no height or depth at all, giddying vistas boasting an extra version of left and right –'

Jack cut him off. 'Could someone use one of these conduits to connect to somewhere else in this world?'

'Yes, of course.'

'So *that's* how the back door to the blue room works!'

He felt pleased to have worked that much out, even though he was no closer to a solution to their current problem.

'OK, so it could be done,' Jaide said. 'But we can't search every possible universe. That would take us forever.'

'That's true. Fortunately, in this case you would simply look for an existing doorway into the world where the card is hidden, not create a new one. Then we would use the cross-continuum conduit constructor as a key to open it.'

'Would the witching rod help us find the doorway?'

'Yes, just deduce where such a doorway would likely to be, point the rod at it and see what happens.'

'And how exactly do we do the deducing?' asked Jaide.

'Well, in my day people tended to make other-worldly doorways in things that already looked like doors. You know, they tend to the rectangular. A window, for example. Or even an actual door, since it would only open to the other world if it was activated by the device.'

'That's all great, but we still have to go back to the castle,' said Jack.

'Somehow.' Jaide felt gloomy again.

'I find,' said Professor Olafsson with persistent cheer, 'that the best ideas come when the concerns of the mundane world are set aside and the conscious mind submits to the ruminations of the unconscious.'

'When *what*?' asked Jack.

'When you get a good night's sleep, in other words, and that's what I advise for both of you right now. By the time you wake up, I'm sure you will have the answer.'

'I hope so.' Jack was too tired to argue, even with a full belly. He got up and slipped into his pyjamas.

Jaide went to the bathroom to clean her teeth. There was no sign of Cornelia or Kleo, and by the time she went back, Jack was already out cold, the damaged picture sitting on his chest, resting under his limp hand. The bracelet charm Custer had given him gleamed in the low light. She browsed through the *Compendium* until Susan came and told her it was time for sleep.

'Do *you* sleep?' Jaide asked Professor Olafsson as she got into bed.

'No, but there are times where I fade out. When nothing is happening and there is no one to talk to.' He smiled at Jaide. 'I would not want to sleep now. This puzzle has given me much to think about!'

'Well, that's good,' she said. 'Happy thinking. Maybe one of us will have the answer by morning.'

'I believe that is entirely likely, Jaide.'

Jaide closed her eyes and, within moments, started to snore.

'Cards, parrots and cats,' said Professor Olafsson softly to himself. 'Now, where *did* I hear that voice before . . .?'

Jack woke the next morning from a nightmare about giant parrots picking up members of his family one by one and biting their heads off, while Jaide had dreamt about flying in the rain and dodging lightning bolts. Neither dream brought any kind of revelation or solution to any of their problems. Professor Olafsson had nothing either, and he didn't look happy about it. The night's fruitless thinking had put him in a sullen mood.

'The entrance could be anywhere in the castle,' he said. 'It could be disguised as anything. We need another clue to guide us.'

'Will you be OK if we leave you here?' asked Jaide. 'I don't think we should take you to school.'

Jack agreed, fearing what Miralda King would make of the death mask if she got her hands on it. Professor Olafsson assented. He was getting bored with sitting around thinking, but it wasn't as if he had many choices.

Susan was distracted and irritable over breakfast, as though she hadn't slept well. Jack assumed she was worried about

Grandma X and their father, as they were. She didn't know anything about The Evil, but distance and car crashes were enough to make anyone unhappy.

'I don't want to hear any more talk about going to the castle,' Susan said, although they hadn't said anything about it at all. 'I checked the homework I gave you. You didn't do any of it. You're going to school and that's where the matter ends.'

They knew better than to argue with that tone, just as they understood when to obey their father. Feeling trapped between two parents who weren't talking to each other about what really mattered, they had no choice but to grit their teeth, make their own lunches and get themselves to school.

'What are we going to do?' Jaide asked as she untangled their bikes and pushed hers out of the laundry room.

'Beats me.' Jack followed her, almost running over two feline shapes sitting by the back door, one scruffy ginger and the other a glossy blue-grey.

'So *this* was the big secret from the other night?' Ari was looking up at the rail of the widow's walk high above, where Cornelia was visible as a blue smudge against the tiles of the roof. His eyes were narrowed and suspicious. 'What's so special about a bird? They're just dinner on legs.'

'Exactly what we thought you'd think,' said Kleo. 'I asked Custer to keep you busy so you wouldn't scare her off.'

'So he didn't really need my help?'

Ari looked hurt and Jaide hastened to distract him.

'Not all birds are stupid,' said Jaide. 'This one can talk.'

'About what, how she really wants a cracker? *Pffft.*' Ari rolled his eyes. 'No respectable animal would eat *crackers*.'

'I'm on your side, Ari,' said Jack. 'Why doesn't she just fly away?'

'Because she's still trying to tell us something,' said Kleo. 'She stirred when you awoke, troubletwisters, and came out through one of the upper-floor windows. I don't know what she's doing, but she definitely has a purpose.'

Jaide climbed on her bike. 'Come on, Jack, or we'll be late.'

Ari returned his attention to the bird.

'Just come down here,' he called, 'and we'll see whose claws are sharpest . . .'

They pedalled down the lane, leaving Ari to his fantasies of a parrot breakfast. Neither of them saw Cornelia stretch one wing and then the other, as though waking herself up, then launch herself into the air. She flapped twice, banked to avoid a tree and disappeared from Ari's frustrated sight.

CHAPTER SIXTEEN
A Twin Thing

Zebediah was just pulling away from the kerb with Rodeo Dave behind the wheel as the twins approached The Book Herd. *On his way to the castle, to renew his search for the Card of Translocation*, Jaide thought glumly. He waved, but their return waves were half-hearted at best.

'Good morning, troubletwisters,' Rennie called from the doorway with her rough voice. She waved too, and it took both twins a full second to realise that she did so with a complete left hand. They screeched to a halt, not believing their eyes. Grandma X had told them that there was no way even the Wardens could heal so great a wound.

'Come inside,' Rennie said, crooking one impossible finger. 'I want to talk to you.'

They propped their bikes against the window and followed her into the shop, where she led them through the door at the back and up a narrow flight of stairs, to the room she slept in. It contained very little in terms of furniture, just a single bed and a cupboard with one door, but was plastered floor to ceiling with hand-drawn pictures.

They were the pictures of Rennie their class had drawn when they'd thought she was dead, Jaide realised, looking around in wonder. Tara must have given them to her.

Rennie sat on the bed, surrounded by pictures of herself, and brought the twins to her for a quick hug. She was like that sometimes. The Evil had used her when she was grieving over the deaths of her own children. Now she was a ward of Portland that protectiveness had been transferred to them.

Jack felt hard, mechanical digits digging into his shoulder and realised that the hand wasn't real flesh at all.

'Rodeo Dave gave it to me,' Rennie said, holding up the hand for closer inspection. It was strapped to her wrist, a device of fiendish complexity made of thin slivers of wood and metal, with thousands of tiny gears connecting them to a complex of nested springs within. They could hear the mechanism ticking when it was still, then whirring into busy life when Rennie moved it. 'He said your grandmother had ordered it from her "special connections" before the accident, but it only just arrived.'

Jack stared at it more closely, looking for evidence that it had come from The Evil. What if the hand went crazy and attacked them? But it showed no immediate sign of going on a rampage.

'Does being touched by The Evil change you permanently?' Jaide asked, emboldened by desperation. Everyone else who understood The Evil was busy fighting it, or forbidden by their father to be talking about it. 'I mean, would there be some way to tell if it had happened to someone we know, even if it was a long time ago?'

'Maybe,' Rennie said. 'Why do you ask? Have you been threatened by someone?'

'Not exactly . . . but he has been acting pretty weird lately.'

'Who? Tell me at once, Jaide.'

Rennie took her by the shoulders. There was no refusing that anxious stare.

'Rodeo Dave,' Jaide said in a weak voice. 'I mean, he was friends with Young Master Rourke, whose grandfather was definitely Evil, and he's doing some pretty strange stuff out at the castle, and we thought Grandma might have sent you here to keep an eye on him, and –'

Jaide stopped as the mechanical hand closed firmly over her mouth.

'I still have much to learn about The Evil, the Wardens and the wards,' said Rennie. 'But I do know that people who have been taken over by The Evil have been released without permanent damage. In rare cases, people have even managed to free themselves, without the intervention of Wardens. But if you are part of The Evil for too long, it changes you. It steals away your humanity, your love. You become hollow, twisted, lost . . .'

She hesitated and looked at her artificial hand.

'I was a part of The Evil for long enough to feel that I was lost, but I wasn't. And now I am a Living Ward. Such a thing has never happened before, and it is hard to deal with. Rodeo Dave . . . David has had some similarity of the experience, so he can help me –'

'You mean Rodeo Dave was once part of The Evil!'

Rennie hesitated again, biting her lip.

'Don't jump to conclusions,' she said firmly. 'David's history is his story to tell. Ask him and perhaps he will share it with you. Let me just say that he too has known sorrow and loss, and he has helped me.'

Jack and Jaide looked at each other. That explained why Rodeo Dave was somehow connected with Warden business, and wasn't freaked out by weird stuff happening. But if he had once been part of The Evil or working for it . . . maybe he wanted to go back to it, and finding the card was how he would make up for leaving The Evil before.

'I didn't bring you here to show off my new hand,' Rennie said, snapping its fingers to bring their attention back to her. 'I want to tell you something important. I have felt The Evil nearby, through the wards. It has come very close in the last few days, to the West and North, but not once has it directly tested the strength of the wards. I sense that it is waiting for something.'

'Like what?' asked Jack.

'That I do not know,' she said. 'But I feel it . . . where I felt it before.'

'In your hand?' asked Jaide.

Rennie shook her head. 'The Evil burns like a fire, but it is not fire. It is nothing, and it leaves nothing behind. I feel it in the *absence* of my hand.'

She raised the clockwork hand and flexed it again, marvelling at its complexity.

'In losing much I have gained much,' she said, 'but I would not lose any more. Be careful, my troubletwisters. If you leave the boundary of the wards again, as I sensed you doing yesterday, I will have to tell your grandmother.'

Jaide and Jack nodded very seriously, sobered by the thought that Rennie could barge into the hospital and wake up Grandma X if they didn't obey the rules, even if it was for a good purpose.

'Listen, Rennie,' Jaide started to say, wanting to explain.

Rennie cut her off. 'You are late for school. You'd better get going before I land you in more trouble.'

'But we just want to tell you –' tried Jack.

'Enjoy your ordinary life while you can,' Rennie insisted, ushering them down the stairs. 'It won't stay ordinary for long.'

Outside, they found Cornelia sitting on Jack's handlebars.

'What are you doing here?' asked Jack angrily. 'Are you following us?'

'Rourke!'

'Well, don't. Go away and leave us alone.'

Jack tried to shoo her from his bike, but one sharp lunge

reminded him of the vicious hole in the photo where his father's face used to be.

'Here, Jack, let me.'

Rennie held out her clockwork hand. Cornelia nipped at it, but soon realised it was immune to her formidable beak. Leaving barely a scratch, she gave up and hopped on to the hand, and was lifted away.

'Off you go now,' said Rennie. 'I'll find something to keep her occupied.'

The twins pedalled furiously down the street, leaving Rennie and Cornelia behind to take each other's measure.

School had never seemed more pointless or tedious. After the usual welcome and group discussion about dreams (which the twins joined halfway through, making stuff up), the first lesson was Artistic Expression, which involved drawing or writing while Mr Carver improvised on a variety of musical instruments. Students were encouraged to join in, or even to dance, but no one ever did that. While the others sketched horses or spaceships, Jack concentrated hard on drawing a map of the castle from memory, looking for any secret spaces they hadn't visited yet. Maybe one of them had been where the entrance to Professor Olafsson's other universe was hidden.

Tara, who normally sat with them, had greeted them warmly enough that morning, but soon picked up on their mood and went to join Kyle, who had been sitting alone at the table in front of them. Ever since he had argued with Miralda, no one else would talk to him.

Now the two of them were whispering excitedly with their heads close together, and Jaide was unable to avoid hearing what they were saying.

'. . . Peregrinators pick a mystery every month, and they explore it until they figure it out or get bored,' Kyle was saying. 'I followed Dad once and listened in. They were talking about giant rats living in the sewers. Some of them wanted to go down there and check it out.'

'Eww.'

Jaide agreed with Tara. She had seen what Jack had looked like after he had been down there. But it wasn't that that made her want to join in the conversation.

'Did the Peregrinators ever hear anything weird about the Rourke Estate?' she asked, switching tables while Mr Carver wasn't looking.

'Sure,' said Kyle. 'I was just getting to that bit.'

But with a sniff Tara leaned back with her arms folded.

'So *now* you want to talk to us – when we have our own thing going?'

Jaide stared at her in surprise. 'What?'

'It's really difficult being friends with you and Jack. You know that? You're always whispering and skulking around, keeping things secret from me. Sometimes I wonder if you want to be friends at all.'

'I do,' said Jaide. 'That is, we both do. It's just really hard to explain.'

'Is it?'

'It's a twin thing,' said Kyle. 'I've got identical twin sisters, Esther and Fi. They can be real pains too, but it's not their fault. It's the way they are made. You just have to get used to it.' He smiled calmingly at Tara. 'Don't let it get to you. That's my advice.'

'All right . . . I guess. But why do I have to do all the work?'

'I'm sorry,' said Jaide. 'We'll try harder, I promise.'

Tara relented a little. Her arms unfolded. 'OK. Good. Because I want to hear about how you got on yesterday.'

'You first,' said Jaide to Kyle. 'What were you about to say?'

'What? Oh yeah. The Rourke Estate.' Excited to have doubled his audience, Kyle recommenced his story. 'A few months ago, Dad had this thing in his head that there was buried treasure there.'

'What kind of treasure?' Tara asked.

'Gold.'

Jaide leaned in even more closely, excitement rising in her.

'Did they find anything?' she asked.

'No,' said Kyle.

'So why did your dad think there was a treasure there in the first place?' asked Tara.

'There's always been rumours, and then a few months ago Dad found this weird thin strip of cloth with some words stitched on it. Not stitched very well, like maybe a kid did it for a craft project, but you know what?'

'What?' asked Tara and Jaide together.

'The thread was pure gold wire. And the cloth was velvet. So Dad went out a few nights in a row to search – I guess it was easy for him, since he's the groundsman and no one would've thought it weird if he was poking around with a shovel. But he never found anything. I assume he didn't anyway, because we didn't suddenly become rich or anything.'

'Maybe it never existed,' said Tara.

'Or it's still there, waiting for someone to find it,' said Kyle. 'Wouldn't that be cool?'

'What were the words embroidered on the cloth?' Jaide asked him.

Kyle nodded. 'It was a verse. Dad used to walk round the house saying it under his breath. We all knew it eventually.'

He leaned in closer and in a low, breathless voice intoned:

'The path between fields,
the season grows old,
the deuce is revealed –
there lies the gold.'

'What does that mean?' asked Jaide.

'If only we knew! There are fields on the estate, and lots of paths too. The rest though is a bit of a mystery.'

'How big was this cloth again?'

Kyle held up his ruler. 'About the same size as this, only half as long.'

'Sounds like a bookmark,' said Tara. 'A bookmark of velvet with gold embroidery . . .'

'Where did your dad find it?' asked Jack, who had overheard and come over.

'Just on the ground near the new menagerie cages, outside the lodge. Around the time Young Master Rourke moved there.'

'Did he ask Young Master Rourke about it?'

Kyle put his ruler back under his desk and mumbled something that sounded like 'Finders Keepers'.

Jaide leaned back, frowning. The bookmark must have fallen out of one of Master Rourke's old paperbacks, and it certainly sounded like a clue to something. But if the groundsman of the estate hadn't worked out the landmarks, how would she and Jack possibly do it?

'What's a *deuce*?' asked Tara.

None of them knew.

The school's small dictionary proved to be of some use, unlike the last time Jaide had used it. There were two definitions for the word *deuce*. The first was 'an expression of annoyance or frustration'. She could see how that could come in handy at that moment, but it didn't help. The second was all about sports and games. Deuce was when two tennis players were tied at the end of a game. It was when someone rolled two in a game of dice. A deuce was also 'a playing card with two pips'.

Jaide blinked. Suddenly she knew. She knew what the path between fields was, and what it meant when the rhyme talked about the season growing old. That and interworld doorways being rectangular! It had been staring them in the face all along!

But before she could whisper to Jack, a commotion on the other side of the class distracted her. Fingers pointed and a cluster formed round the windows, oohing and aahing.

'Isn't he just adorable?' exclaimed Miralda King. 'I think he wants to come in.'

'Don't open the window,' said Mr Carver hastily. 'He could be dangerous. They carry parasites, you know. And just look at that beak!'

Kyle and Tara hurried to see. So did the twins. There was a large blue bird pacing up and down outside the window, craning to see past the faces peering out at it.

'Oh no, not again,' said Jack. 'What's she doing *here*?'

CHAPTER SEVENTEEN
Hidden in Plain Sight

On seeing Jack, Cornelia began to pace more quickly, rolling her head from side to side.

'Rourke! Rourke!'

'She's a she, not a he,' said Jack, feeling defensive of Cornelia despite everything, 'and she doesn't have parasites.'

'You know this bird?' asked Mr Carver.

'You could say that. But I don't know what she's doing here.'

Jack pushed through to the front of the throng.

'Go home, Cornelia,' he said, waving his hands at her through the glass. 'Go on! Get out of here!'

The bird just watched him with a quizzical expression, as though he had gone mad.

'Rourke?'

'Is that all she says?' asked Miralda. 'I thought parrots were supposed to be intelligent.'

'She *is* intelligent,' said Jaide. 'We just can't understand her.'

'Rourke!' Cornelia tilted her head and bit at the window frame, pulling free a chunk of wood. Spitting it aside, she began digging again, widening the hole with her sharp beak.

'Shoo!' said Mr Carver, flapping at the window with an open book. 'That's school property!'

'Rourke!'

She kept on digging.

With a sinking feeling, Jack realised that Cornelia was his responsibility. She thought he was his friend, even if he didn't feel the same way in return any more. If he didn't do something about her, she would only get into more trouble.

'I'll take her away,' he said. 'If I can be excused . . .?'

'Yes, yes, do what you need to to get rid of that feathered vandal.' Mr Carver was normally a fervent advocate of animal rights, but not for anything that disrupted his class, it seemed. He gathered up Jack and practically pushed him out of the door. 'Don't come back until it's safely locked up!'

Jack came round the side of the school, acutely conscious of everyone watching him. Cornelia stopped digging at the wood the moment he appeared and waddled over to him.

'All aboard,' she said. 'All aboard.'

'What? Cornelia, I can't understand what you're saying.'

She opened her wings, flapped mightily and launched herself on to Jack's shoulder.

He almost fell over backwards in surprise. Cornelia rocked from side to side, her powerful claws digging into his shirt and not letting go.

'What are you doing?' Jack asked her.

'Shake a leg,' she said, folding her wings and doing an

odd and slightly painful dance on his shoulder.

'You want me to take you somewhere?'

'Rourke!'

'I'm not allowed to take you to the estate. I'm at school.'

But her dance got only weirder, shuffling from foot to foot and pushing one knobbly leg into his face.

'Everyone is watching, Cornelia. Wait . . . is *that* what you're talking about?'

Jack had forgotten the tiny metal ring attached to Cornelia's left ankle. She was waving it under his nose, trying to get him to look at it.

Jack gingerly took her leg in his hands. She didn't protest and she kept her claws carefully away from the palm of his hand so she wouldn't scratch him.

There was a piece of very thin paper tucked into the ring. He pulled it out and delicately unfolded it, expecting a note or even – his heart pounded – another clue, perhaps more of the treasure poem Kyle had recited.

Instead it was a page from an old dictionary with a hole in one corner where Cornelia's beak had gripped it.

'Did you take this from Rodeo Dave's shop?' he asked her.

'Rourke!' She tapped the page with her beak.

'Rennie must have folded it for you. Which means you're trying to tell us something again.'

He scanned the page. It came from the *T* section of the dictionary. The word *twister* leaped out at him.

'Hey,' he said, 'that's a secret. You're not supposed to tell people.'

'Rourke!' She tapped the page again. 'Rourke!'

'I know, but what does that have to do with anything?'

She tapped so hard her beak slashed the page and almost cut Jack's thumb, making him drop the paper on to the ground. She threw up her wings and squawked in frustration.

Jack sympathised. It *was* frustrating, constantly banging up against this block in communication. Cornelia mainly talked in nautical phrases, probably picked up from the captain of a whaling ship long ago. It was lucky, he supposed, that she wasn't singing rude sea shanties. Maybe it was some kind of trauma, a throwback to an earlier phase of life brought on by what she had seen the night Young Master Rourke died – understandable, but not terribly helpful.

'I don't know what you're trying to tell me,' he said, 'but I know my dad had nothing to do with what happened to your old master. He just couldn't have. Still, I don't think you're lying or trying to trick us – and you're definitely not Evil. Just a bit destructive sometimes.'

He picked up the torn piece of paper and put it in his pocket.

'One of us is wrong.'

Cornelia headbutted him on the nose. The message this time was unmistakable.

You are.

'We have to figure this out, Cornelia,' Jack said, 'but I'm

supposed to be at school. If I don't go back in, I'll get in trouble. Why don't you go home and we'll try again later?'

Cornelia looked uncertain.

'Oh, right – Ari. That was why you didn't come down earlier, wasn't it? OK. I'll come with you and see if we can find a way past him.'

She nodded, then said, 'Anchors aweigh. Push the boat out!'

'Just let me get my bike.'

Jack glanced at Jaide, who was peering out at him with the others. Jaide was practically bouncing up and down on the balls of her feet, as though there was something she desperately wanted to tell him, but there was nothing he could do about that now.

Cornelia stayed put as he pedalled up to speed and as they swept over the bridge at the centre of town, she opened her wings and held on so the wind of their passage could ruffle her feathers.

'Full steam ahead!'

If only, thought Jack.

There was no sign of Ari back at the house, or anyone else. Jack and Cornelia sneaked inside without incident. The house was empty and silent, apart from the usual creaks and ticks that made it sound sometimes like a giant clock. Cornelia didn't want to go back into the Blue Room, so Jack put her in the bedroom he shared with Jaide, where she seemed happy enough.

'I'll be back later,' he said. 'Please don't bite any more books or photos. Or Professor Olafsson. He'll be here if you need to talk to someone.'

'Indeed, I appear to be going nowhere,' said the death mask grumpily.

Cornelia nuzzled her downy head into Jack's hand and softly clucked her tongue. He grudgingly tickled her under the ridge where her ears would have been and said goodbye to both of them.

Satisfied that they would keep each other company, Jack returned to school the way he had come, conscious of the curious stares of his classmates and enduring Miralda King's sharp remark that she hoped he had the proper licence for such a wild and dangerous animal.

'I mean, it's bad enough that some of Young Master Rourke's menagerie animals are still prowling about town,' she said, 'but when they could swoop down on you from above, at any moment . . .?'

She shuddered in theatrical horror.

'Captivity is just as cruel for animals as it is for people,' said Mr Carver, eyeing the damaged woodwork. 'Perhaps your feathered friend deserves a home somewhere else, Jack, somewhere far away from here. In a forest.'

Jack slipped into his seat, hating the blush he felt boiling up over the collar of his T-shirt and turning his face pink. Mr Carver had written a series of mathematical equations on the board, and Jack tried to concentrate on what they said in order to blot out his embarrassment.

But Jaide was still bouncing.

'I know where it is!' she whispered to him when everyone's attention returned to the front.

'What?'

'The card!'

She nodded furiously, and pointed to her exercise book where she had written out the words Kyle had told them.

The path between fields,
the season grows old,
the deuce is revealed—
there lies the gold.

'It's the painting,' she whispered.

'What painting?'

Jack had spoken more loudly than he intended, loud enough for Mr Carver to come over. Jaide hastily shut her exercise book and Jack looked up at their teacher and gave him an innocent smile.

'Do you need help with the questions?' asked Mr Carver. 'If so, that is what I am here for, and I expect I will be able to answer your questions more effectively than your sister, smart as she is.'

'No, no, I'm OK now,' said Jack. 'I just got a bit distracted, what with the parrot and all.'

He looked at the maths questions and realised that he did need help. But it was too late to ask now. Sighing, he bent his head and tried to concentrate.

It wasn't until just before lunch that they got the opportunity to talk again, because Mr Carver had to go to the office five minutes early to play his Welcome to the Midday Meal song over the PA system.

As soon as he went out of the door, Jaide leaned in close.

'The painting in the library – the woman playing Solitaire – remember? The leaves on the tree are brown, so it's autumn. *The season grows old.* There are fields behind her with a road between them. And she's holding the two of hearts. The *deuce* of hearts! Jack, it has to be her. It has to be – and it was right under our noses all the time!'

Jaide's excitement was infectious. Jack felt himself getting caught up in it even as he got stuck on the obvious question.

'But there's nothing behind the painting, remember? We took it down. The wallpaper is unbroken.'

'That's because it's not behind the painting. It's *in* it.'

'How can the gold card be in a painting?'

'Think, Jack!' sighed Jaide. 'It's just like Professor Olafsson said. It's a door to another dimension. All we have to do is open it and we can go through!'

'Yeah, right,' said Jack. 'All we have to do . . . How are we going to get back to the castle in the first place? Mum won't let us go.'

'I don't know.' Jaide deflated a little at that. 'We'll just have to think of *something*.'

They sank back into their seats, minds whirling with possibilities, most of them discarded instantly.

'I wish we could call Dad,' said Jack. What if he hadn't escaped The Evil after all? What if he was out there, needing their help? What if, this time, being troubletwisters wasn't enough to help anyone?

'Oh, hey, that reminds me . . .' He pulled the scrap of paper from his pocket and laid it out flat on the table. 'Cornelia gave me this.'

Jaide scanned it, but the mystery was as opaque to her as it was to Jack. It seemed relatively unimportant too. So what if Cornelia knew they were troubletwisters? The main thing was that they had figured out where the card was. All they had to do was get their hands on it before Rodeo Dave did, and then get it to their father.

Tonight, thought Jack, as the now-familiar notes from the nose flute came drifting through the speakers in the corridor outside. *Tonight could be our last chance.*

Tara and Kyle had also been whispering all through class, and they took their conversation out into the playground, where the twins interrupted them.

'Can we tell Mum that we're going to stay at your place tonight?' Jaide asked Tara.

'All right,' she said, 'but only if I can tell my parents that I'm going to be staying at yours. Kyle and I are going to the estate to look for the treasure!'

For a second, Jaide just blinked at her in surprise.

'But . . . but aren't you afraid of rats?'

'They're only inside the castle, Jaide,' Tara said. 'We're going to look outside. I think *season* refers to seasoning, which is like spices, and Kyle says there's an old herb garden on the estate. He's going to sneak out and show me where.'

'Sometimes there are advantages to being the youngest in a big family,' Kyle grinned.

Jaide's instincts were to try to talk them out of it. The Evil was still sniffing about the wards after all.

'Do you really think the treasure's still there?' Jaide asked. 'What if it never existed at all?'

'What if you're planning to go treasure hunting too?' said Kyle. 'I saw the way you two have been twin-thinging all day. You don't want us to go because you want to find it first!'

There was no denying that, because it was utterly true. But if Jack and Jaide were inside the castle, where Tara wouldn't go, there was no possibility of being in direct competition.

'It'll be like a race,' said Jack. 'The first to the gold wins.'

Kyle's green eyes twinkled with the challenge. 'It's *so* on.'

*

The afternoon seemed to drag and race by at the same time. Jack's stomach was full of butterflies as the farewell song sounded and the class dissolved into chatter and scuffling feet. Kyle and Tara hurried off in one direction, waving and promising to see them later, while Jack and Jaide got on their bikes and rode up the street, keeping their fingers mentally crossed that Susan would let them go. That was the first hurdle to overcome.

They skidded their bikes to a crashing halt by the back door and ran inside.

'Mum?' Their voices echoed up the stairs and through the house's many rooms. 'Mum, where are you?'

There was no answer.

'The car isn't there,' said Jack. 'Maybe she went to work.'

'Or maybe she's at the hospital . . .'

Both twins jumped at the sound of a crash from upstairs, followed by a distant squawking.

'That was Cornelia,' said Jack, already running for the stairwell.

Jaide overtook him, her Gift lifting her up so she could take four steps at a time. What if something was attacking Cornelia so she couldn't tell them what she knew? *Inside the house!*

'Rourke!'

There was another crash. It came from the bedroom. The door swept open ahead of Jaide and the twins crashed through it.

Within they found a scene of utter chaos. Curtains were torn, books had been knocked over, the sheets were pulled off their beds and their clothes were scattered into every corner. It looked like they had been burgled by a thorough but incompetent burglar.

The source of the mess, a rather harried-looking Ari, was currently running in circles in the middle of the room being dive-bombed by Cornelia.

'Rourke! Rourke!'

Ari took a running leap for the macaw, but only succeeded in knocking over Jack's bedside lamp.

'What are you doing?' Jack asked, skidding to a halt with his sister at his side. 'Ari, what's going on?'

With one last squawk, Cornelia landed on the top of Jaide's four-poster bed frame.

'She started it,' said Ari, looking up at Jack with slightly addled eyes. He looked that way sometimes on a full moon, but this time he didn't have that excuse. The old moon was barely a sliver in the evening sky.

'Started what exactly?' asked Jaide. 'Have you been trying to kill each other?'

'I've been trying to make them stop,' said the death mask from where it had been tipped into a half-empty bin.

'Professor Olafsson!' Jack fished him out and put him upright next to where his lamp normally went.

'I'm so sorry,' said Jaide, then turned on Ari and Cornelia.

'You two should be ashamed of yourselves. What were you thinking?'

She sounded very angry. Even Jack was scared of her when she was like this. Ari stood behind him with only his tail and his face showing.

'Were you trying to eat Cornelia?' Jaide asked him.

'A fat old bird like that? No thanks.'

Jaide ignored Cornelia's squawk of indignation. 'So what were you doing?'

'She was calling me names,' Ari said, scuffing at the ground with one of his front paws.

'Sound the bell, Mr Dingles!'

'See? Why you —'

Ari ran for the bed, but Jack caught him. Cornelia danced from foot to foot, cackling, 'High and dry, high and dry.'

'Cornelia, stop it,' said Jack. 'That's not very nice.'

'I tried to explain to your furry friend here,' said Professor Olafsson, 'that Mr Dingles was probably a ship's cat Cornelia once served with, but he won't listen.'

'I don't even know who you are!'

'He's a former Warden,' said Jaide. 'We found him in the castle. You should do as he says.'

'Why, when *she* won't?'

'Is that it, Cornelia?' asked Jack. 'Do you think Ari is Mr Dingles?'

Cornelia looked down at him with one yellow-ringed eye

and slowly nodded her head. Jack didn't know if Cornelia genuinely understood or not, but that was something.

'Ari, if I let you go, will you leave her alone?'

'Oh, all right,' said the cat, going limp in his arms. 'But why does she get to call *me* anything at all? What's she even doing here? I'm the Warden Companion, not *her*.'

Jack and Jaide exchanged a glance. It hadn't occurred to either of them that he might be more jealous than hungry when it came to the new animal in their midst.

'You *are* one of Grandma's Warden Companions,' Jack said, 'and you're still our friend. Having Cornelia here doesn't change that one bit.'

'Jack's right, honest,' said Jaide, bending down to give him a hug.

'You promise?' he said into her neck.

'We promise,' said the twins together.

'OK then. You can let me go now.'

Jaide stood back, and Ari put his rear down and began licking his fur flat again.

Only then did it occur to Jack that they couldn't talk to Professor Olafsson with Ari in the room. Grandma X may have given them permission to go back to the estate when they visited her in hospital, but if she knew the full story about Rodeo Dave and The Evil, it would only make her upset, which their father had told them not to do.

'Erm, Ari, we need to talk in private,' he said.

'About what?'

'I can't tell you . . . it's private.'

Ari narrowed his eyes and looked from one twin to the other.

'But the bird gets to stay?'

Jaide glanced at Cornelia, who looked back at her innocently.

'I guess not,' Jaide said, holding up her arm for Cornelia to climb down.

One swift jab with the beak made her reconsider the wisdom of doing that.

'Jack, could you . . .?'

He coaxed Cornelia down from her perch and took her out of the room and put her on a banister. Once she was outside, Ari followed, taking a seat a foot or two away from Cornelia. They did nothing but glare at each other as Jack closed the door behind him. He hoped it would stay that way.

Jaide was crouched down at eye level with the death mask in the wreckage of their room.

'We've done it, Professor Olafsson,' she said. 'We've found out where the card is, and we think it's in one of your weird universes.'

'Really? How absolutely marvellous!' Professor Olafsson grinned from ear to ear. 'Well, the first thing we must do is get back there and apply the cross-continuum conduit constructor to the portal.'

'I know,' said Jack, 'but –'

He stopped at a shrill noise coming from the chest next to Jaide's bed.

'That's the phone!' she cried.

Jack couldn't believe it. The phone was sitting on a piece of paper covered in Susan's neat writing, charger plugged into the wall, as though it had been there all day. They both lunged for it at the same time, but Jaide got there an instant before her brother's grasping hands. Susan's note fluttered to the floor, unread.

'Dad? Dad? Where have you been? We've got good news!'

'How can you have good news?' Hector Shield said, voice harsh through some kind of heavy interference, perhaps even rain again. 'I've been calling you all day and you didn't come to the castle even once. I'm beginning to wonder if I made a mistake entrusting this mission to you. Perhaps it's not too late to give it to someone I can truly rely on.'

Chapter Eighteen
The Fields of Gold

The twins rocked back on their heels, feeling as though they had been punched in the guts. The lights flickered and the air swirled round them as their Gifts reacted. They had never heard their father speak so cruelly before, not even when he was mad at them. He was never mean to anyone really, and only ever raised his voice when certain household appliances didn't behave as they were supposed to. Which was pretty much everything with an on/off button, all the time, for him.

'But we couldn't come today,' said Jack, feeling sick to his stomach. 'Mum wouldn't let us. And she took the –'

'Your mother has nothing to do with this. The Card of Translocation is what's important, not the petty rules and regulations of the ordinary world.'

'We tried, Dad,' said Jaide, fighting hard not to stammer. 'And now we know where the card is. All we have to do is get it.'

'Why should I believe you?' The static was so thick they could hardly hear him.

'Because it's true!' Jaide stamped her foot, something she

hadn't done since she was five years old. It wasn't fair that he should treat them like this, not when they were so close to getting the card. 'It's in a painting in the library. And we know how to get it out. We can do it – I know we can!'

'I gave you a simple task,' Hector Shield said through the background noise. '. . . I'm really disappointed . . .'

'We just need a little more time,' said Jaide.

'. . . no time left . . . can't hold it back much longer without the card . . . taking all our energies just to protect the wards . . .'

Behind their father's distant voice they heard the sound of a wolf howling. Jaide shuddered and Jack reached out to take her hand.

'We can do it,' Jack told him. 'Mum's not here, but we can leave her a note –'

'But what if she calls Tara's parents?' Jaide asked, seeing the flaw in that plan immediately. 'She'll know we're not where we're supposed to be.'

'Yes, but she won't know where we are, right? As long as we find the card, we can deal with her afterwards.'

Jaide groaned. Success was dangling just out of their reach, but to attain it they would have to play one parent off against the other. It would be so much easier if they could just talk to Susan about what was really going on!

There was a moment's roaring silence over the phone.

'Dad? Are you there, Dad?' she said. 'We can do it. I know we can.'

'All right,' he finally said, 'but you mustn't fail me! This is your final chance.'

'You can trust us,' said Jaide. 'You really, really can.'

'We honestly won't let you down, Dad,' said Jack.

'Be sure you . . . I mean, we're counting on you . . .'

The static rose up, cutting the call off. The twins sagged, feeling emotionally drained. Their father must have been under incredible pressure to speak to them like that. Whatever was going on out there in the fight against The Evil, it was their job to help their father, Custer and whoever else was involved.

'You write the note,' said Jack, leaping to his feet and grabbing the death mask and putting it in his pack. 'I'll get torches and . . . is there anything we'll need, Professor Olafsson?'

'Perhaps some rope,' he said. 'The way through the portal may not be in the same horizontal plane.'

'What do you mean?' asked Jack.

'It might be the top of a hole, for example. Or you might come out on the side of a wall, a hundred feet up a tower.'

'OK. Rope.'

Jack opened the door to find Ari and Cornelia exactly where he had left them. Ignoring them, he ran downstairs to the ground-floor closet, a dark and cobwebby space full of all sorts of domestic odds and ends. Coiled up at the back was a length of slender, green nylon rope, which he scooped up and also stuffed into his bag.

Jaide looked for a piece of paper on which to write the note telling Susan that they would be going to Tara's house for dinner, and found the note the phone had been sitting on. She started to read the message from Susan explaining that, on further thought, maybe Jack and Jaide were old enough to be entrusted with a phone, provided they understood that it was a responsibility . . .

Jaide's eyes crossed. There wasn't *time*. Turning it over, she wrote *Going to Tara's for dinner. Thanks Mum. Love J & J*.

Running downstairs, she left the note on the kitchen table where Susan was sure to find it. When that was done, she turned she found Ari watching her.

'What's going on?' he asked.

She didn't have the heart to lie to him. He was their grandmother's Warden Companion. He was one of the Protectors of Portland. He deserved to know at least part of the truth, didn't he? The only thing stopping her was the promise she had made to her father.

'Find Custer,' she said. 'He'll tell you.'

'Mmm-hmm,' he said. 'Like how he told me how useful I was yesterday?'

'Forget about that,' she said. 'This is a whole different thing. This is *important*.'

'My feelings aren't important?'

She threw her hands in the air in frustration. 'I don't have time for this!'

Jack was already outside, untangling their bikes. 'All OK?' he asked when she appeared.

'I hope so,' she said.

They put their heads down and rode furiously up the lane.

As they turned into Parkhill Street, a blue blur whizzed overhead in a flurry of feathers and wings.

'Rourke!' cried Cornelia, settling on to Jack's shoulders.

'Yes,' he said with a grin. 'This time we're going to the estate. Are you sure you want to come with us?'

The macaw bobbed her head up and down. 'All parrots on deck.'

'OK. Let's go!'

Behind them, the weathervane turned against the wind to point north-east, directly at the Rourke Estate.

Clouds gathered overhead as they neared the castle. Sunset was still some way off, but the light failed steadily, until it seemed more like twilight than late afternoon. There was no rain yet, but Jaide had no doubt that it was coming. There was a thick, heavy feeling to the air, as though a storm was brewing. Somewhere nearby, Jack was sure, The Evil and the Wardens were doing battle.

They rode cautiously up the long drive past the lake, watchful for Rodeo Dave, or Kyle and Tara, but the only person visible was Thomas Solomon. He held up a hand as they approached and drove the golf buggy out to meet them.

'You've missed him,' he said as they came alongside him. 'Rodeo Dave just left.'

'I know,' said Jack, thinking fast. 'We saw him and he said he'd left something behind.'

'We volunteered to get it for him.' said Jaide. 'It might take us a while to find it though.'

'OK, I guess,' he said. 'But I'll be closing the gates at six so don't take too long.'

'We won't,' said Jaide. She hoped that this was true.

Barely a minute later, they reached the moat and trundled their bikes over. A rising wind whipped around them and made Cornelia grip Jack's shoulder more tightly. Apart from that, she was quiet and still, and looked all around her as though nervous. The shadowy courtyard appeared to be empty, but that was little consolation.

Jaide put the skeleton key into the lock, despite the serious mismatch in size, and turned it as hard as she could. She needed both hands, but eventually the door groaned open and Jack and Cornelia slipped inside.

As Jaide stepped over the threshold, a ginger shape darted out of the shadows and leaped on to her shoulders, clinging tight to her with what felt like hundreds of pinprick claws.

She fell forward with a scream that made Cornelia lift off in a flurry of wing beats and squawks. Jack spun round to drive off the thing that had attacked her, his Gift turning the dim light inside the castle even darker than before.

Ari rolled free of Jaide's flailing limbs and stood upright with his legs apart and hair raised along his back.

'I knew you were up to something,' he said. 'The note said you were going to Tara's. What are you doing here?'

'Something important,' Jaide said, getting up and dusting herself down. 'For Dad. You have to believe us, Ari. We wouldn't sneak around like this without a reason.'

'What counts for reasons among troubletwisters is notoriously unreliable.'

'But this is different! We're looking for a golden card – the Card of Translocation. Remember? You helped us look for it on Wednesday.'

'Not intentionally! If it's so important, why don't I know about it already?'

'Maybe Grandma just hadn't got round to telling you about it yet,' said Jack. 'Young Master Rourke had only just died. And then she had the accident. And then Kleo was busy keeping you away from Cornelia – it's been a mess, but I swear this is all we know!'

'We can't stand here arguing, Ari,' said Jaide, feeling desperate. 'The Evil is just outside the wards, trying to get in. We have to do this now.'

'How are you going to do it if no one else has been able to?'

'Everyone's been looking in the wrong place.' Jaide grinned triumphantly. 'Come with us and we'll show you.'

'Oh . . . all right,' he said, cat curiosity winning in the

end, as it always did. 'I'm all eyes. And nose and whiskers and tail.'

Jack called Cornelia back to him and together they walked up the corridor to the library for the third time that week. A wide line of footsteps marked the way through the dust. Jack gave Jaide a torch, but they didn't turn them on just yet. There was still enough light coming through the high windows to show the way.

The library was empty. Most of the books had been cleared. A stack of boxes rested behind the door, tagged with labels in Rodeo Dave's handwriting. Whatever else he was up to, he had been genuinely busy.

'So,' said Ari, walking round the base of the boxes and emerging with his tail high, 'where is it?'

'There,' said Jaide, pointing at the painting. It was still leaning against the wall where Rodeo Dave had cleaned it. The resemblance of the *Lady in Yellow* to a young Grandma X was more striking than ever, despite the old-fashioned clothes.

'Behind the painting?'

'*Inside* the painting,' said Jack, putting down his backpack and taking out Professor Olafsson and the rope. 'Tell us where you saw that constructor thing and I'll go and get it.'

'On the second floor, two doors along on the left from the main flight of stairs,' he said. 'It's a long brass tube that looks a bit like a telescope. You'll need both of you to carry it.'

'OK,' said Jaide. 'We'll be right back.'

The twins hurried through the castle, past all the chests they had uselessly searched before, stiff-limbed suits of armour that contained nothing but wooden frames and cobwebs, and door after door of abandoned rooms. The room Professor Olafsson had identified was little different to the others, except for a tubular shape lying on a desk, six feet in length and not tapering, as a telescope would. The sheet covering both tube and desk had pulled away, revealing one brassy end, capped with a smoky glass lens.

The twins uncovered it and took one end each. It was too heavy to be hollow, but not so heavy that they couldn't lift it. Treading carefully, taking turns to go backwards, they retraced their steps to the library, where Cornelia, Ari and Professor Olafsson were waiting.

'Now what?' asked Jack, mopping his brow.

'Make two stacks of books three feet high,' Professor Olafsson said. 'Put the constructor on top of them so it's lined up with the centre of the painting.'

Jaide hurried off to get some books from a pile that didn't look particularly valuable.

'How do we switch it on?' she asked.

'Switch what?'

'You know, make it work, like a machine.'

'This isn't a machine in the usual sense of the word,' he said. 'It doesn't require activation. In the right environment, with the right operator, it simply does what it's supposed to.

Now, let's make certain we do in fact have the portal before us first of all. Jack, did you bring the witching rod?'

After a flicker of panic during which Jack thought he had left it behind, he discovered that it was indeed still inside his backpack.

'Yes, Professor.'

'Please direct it at the painting and tell me what you feel.'

Jack did so and was rewarded by an immediate tremor through the wire. In fact, when he lifted his hand, the wire bent noticeably down, striving to reach the painting.

'It's pulling me,' he said, 'pulling me closer!'

'As expected. Good. Jaide, can you make absolutely certain that the constructor is aligned with the centre of the frame?'

'Yes, Professor.' She bent over the tube and sighted along it, shifting it an inch to the right. That was better, but it still wanted a book or two under the end closer to her to make it perfectly level. Once she had done that, she nodded.

'Now, Jack, tie the rope round your sister's waist. I trust you can tie a good bowline?'

'A what?'

The Professor explained how to tie the knot and Jack quickly caught on, making a loop secure around Jaide.

'Now wind the rope round that column a few times and hold the end.'

Jack wound the rope round one of the columns that supported the balcony above them and busied himself with another knot. Two of them, to be completely sure. Perhaps three.

'Are you sure this is safe?' asked Ari, peering out from behind the stack of boxes as Jack did as he was told, keeping a tight hold on the other end as he did so.

'Is a door safe?' asked Professor Olafsson.

'Of course it is,' said Ari, 'unless it slams shut on your tail. It's what might be on the other side that worries me.'

'There's no reason to be fretful. This is a hiding place, nothing more. Were we attempting a journey to the Dimension of Evil on the other hand . . .'

'What?' asked Ari nervously.

'The Dimension of Evil,' said the Professor calmly. 'Where The Evil comes from.'

'So this doorway could go *there*?'

'Oh no, very little chance of that!' chuckled the death mask. 'No Warden would hide a gold card there. You might as well just hand it over to The Evil.'

'Little chance . . . that's still a chance,' said the cat. 'Maybe we should think about this. Jaide?'

Jaide wasn't listening to him. She had got the tube almost perfectly aligned. It just needed a nudge back to the left. She checked again. Perhaps a touch more . . .

The moment her fingers touched the brass, she was wrenched off her feet and fired along its length like a cannonball down a cannon. The shelves of the library blurred around her. Jack's face, his mouth open in an *O* of shock and the rope whipping through his hands, flashed past in an instant. The canvas ballooned ahead of her and the frame swept by, flashing gold all around.

She jerked to a halt, wobbling in space as though she'd landed on an invisible trampoline. Gasping, she looked around her.

Jaide was inside the painting. There was the girl playing cards just a step or two away, as three-dimensional as life, albeit frozen into immobility under the spreading branches of the tree. There were the fields, rising and falling in golden waves to the distant hills, and there was the brick path that snaked between them.

Funny, Jaide thought. They had never noticed that the path was made of yellow bricks.

Follow the yellow brick road, she thought, and raised her right foot to walk further into the world of the painting, where the sky was smudged and the hills were blurry, as though painted in a hurry.

'Jaide!'

The voice came from behind her, wobbly and distant as though it had travelled through miles of water.

'Jaide, come back!'

It was Jack. She turned to look behind her and saw his face in the frame, as though he was now a painting. A moving painting, hanging against an endless sunset-hued sky. He was banging as though against glass, calling her name. The rope around her waist pulled insistently at her, vanishing into thin air like the brass tube, where it entered the real world.

'Jack, what's wrong?'

'You have to come back!'

'But I'm perfectly safe here. See?'

She indicated the calm world around her with a sweep of one hand. What could be safer than a painting of a girl playing cards? All she had to do was find the gold card and she could go.

'Jaide, quickly! We're under attack!'

There was an edge of panic to his voice that couldn't be denied. She took one step towards him and was instantly snatched up by the cross-continuum conduit constructor and whisked back to her world in a breathtaking rush.

She staggered. Jack grabbed her arm and stopped her from falling. Before she could ask what was going on, there came a booming crash at the library door. Cornelia took off from the head of the Mister Rourke statue and flew squawking up to the landing. Ari stood between the twins and the door, staring up at the shivering wood with his fangs bared.

'What is it?' asked Jaide.

'I don't know,' Jack said. 'But I don't think the door's going to hold.'

Another crash shook the door, then another. The wood splintered inward, making a gaping hole. A metal-clad hand reached through the hole and twisted around to grab the handle.

CHAPTER NINETEEN

Booby Trap!

'Quick!' said Jack, who had let go of the rope and was lifting a box of books. 'We've got to barricade the door!'

Jaide was frozen for a second by a glimpse through the hole of a domed, metallic head. She thought it was a monster of some kind, but then she realised it was actually a suit of armour – the suit of armour that normally stood right outside the library, now moving on its own!

She ran to help Jack pile boxes against the door and was pulled up short by the rope catching on something. Quickly stepping out of the loop, she pushed a box up against the door. The armoured gauntlet couldn't quite reach the doorknob, so it was making the hole larger, pulling off splinters of solid mahogany the size of Jack's hands as easily as he might snap a matchstick.

'What's making the armour move?' shouted Jaide. 'Is it The Evil?'

'It can't be. We're inside the wards!' exclaimed the Professor. 'I don't . . . ah . . . It must have been you!'

'Me?' exclaimed Jaide. 'I didn't do anything.'

'You went into the painting. That's what woke them up. They're guards!'

'We triggered a booby trap?' said Jack, thinking of his father's old adventure novels. That was what criminals used when they really wanted to keep something hidden. 'How do we switch it off?'

'I don't know, dear boy.'

'There must be a way,' cried Jack. He threw another box on the makeshift wall in front of the door, just as another hand punched through the wood, emerging just above his head. The jointed metal fingers lunged at him, snapping open and shut like the jaws of a metal mouth. Jack staggered back, the hand missing the collar of his T-shirt by a fraction of an inch.

With a deafening crash, the doors burst open, sending the twins and boxes of books flying everywhere. One metal figure thrust through the jagged splinters with arms outstretched, closely followed by a second. The visors on the second one flipped open, revealing that the space within contained nothing but a startled spider.

'Back!' shouted Jack.

He retreated, snatching up Ari, who looked like he was prepared to stand up to an army of magical armour but was more likely to get squashed before they even noticed him, and ran to join Jaide who had fallen back near the painting.

A breeze was beginning to whip up around Jaide, as she raised her hands and called upon her Gift. Jack's Gift was also stirring, reaching out to the shadows cast by the setting sun, which was painting dark lines down the walls and bookcases. Jack could hide in them, but that wouldn't do the others any good. Although maybe, he thought, if he held on very tight, he could take Ari with him . . .

The leading suit of armour barged through the hanging remnants of the door and the fallen boxes, and clanked towards them. As it reached the first line of shadow, Jack had another idea. He reached out with his Gift towards the shadow, and it responded by twitching like a snake, the clear line from the window now rippling under his invisible hand.

Jack focused upon it, dragging it up the suit of armour and then wrapping it around the helmet like a scarf of darkness. Even though the armour was nothing but metal and there were no eyes within the helmet to be confused or blinded, it still stopped and clutched at the veil of darkness that grew thicker and thicker around its head. Its strong metal fingers found purchase on nothing more substantial than air.

Jaide launched a very different attack. The helmet of the second suit of armour was still partly open, thanks to a splinter that had wedged in the hinge of the visor. Moving her fists as though wringing out a tea towel, she built a rapidly spinning rope of air that quickly took on solidity and form, like a spear. As the second armour pushed past the first, which was still held back by shadows, she raised her right arm and threw the spear as hard she could.

It flew straight into its face. The air rushed through the open visor down into the armour and ricocheted loudly off the hollow metal. Jaide's Gift made the wind steadily stronger and faster until, with a thunderous clatter, the staggering armour exploded. Its head went straight upwards and its arms went in opposite directions. The torso fell in halves like an exploded iron turtle. The legs stayed standing for a split second, then shivered into their component plates.

Jack cheered, perhaps prematurely, for the collapse of the armour also freed the force that had destroyed it. Both twins staggered backwards as a whirlwind erupted in the middle of the library, sending books flying in a mad spiral up to the ceiling. Cornelia was swept up into it, and she flashed in and out of sight, screeching madly. When the wind hit Jack's web of shadows, their two Gifts became entangled. Long black streaks spread upwards through the funnel of air, threatening to snuff out all light with it.

'Control yourselves, troubletwisters!' The voice of Professor Olafsson was barely audible over the wind. He had been swept into the fireplace and wedged there. 'Don't let your Gifts control you!'

'What he said!' added Ari from where he clung to Jack's chest with all twenty claws digging in.

'Stop it . . . please,' said Jaide through gritted teeth. She clutched at the whistling air, trying to slow it down, but it slipped through her fingers with playful ease. 'Stop it now!'

The remaining suit of armour stumbled into the maelstrom and was lifted off its feet. It turned around in accelerating pirouettes with both arms extended, creating a propeller effect that threatened to chop the twins' heads off when it came close to them. They clutched the fireplace to stop themselves being swept up as well. Between the two of them, they kept the painting safe.

The spinning armour's left glove hit a bookcase, sending slivers of wood and iron fingers flying like bullets. The armour ricocheted into a wall, which hastened its disintegration even further. Jaide ducked her head as bits of curved metal whizzed around her, screaming for the wind to be still before it killed them all.

Finally it listened. With a series of crashes and clatters, the whirlwind dropped its load of metal and books and shrank into a self-contained spiral. Cornelia flew out of the top and clung to the upper level's balustrade, feathers in brilliant disarray. The cross-continuum conduit constructor dropped on to the ground at the twins' feet. With a sigh of regret, the wind shrank down into a breeze and vanished.

There was no time to relax. From the hallway outside came the clanking of more metal feet.

'What are we going to do?' asked Jack. 'We can't give up now.'

'Why not?' asked Ari. 'That's what your father would want. If whatever's in the painting is so important, he should be the one looking for it.'

Jaide was pale, but she shook her head.

'No,' she said. 'Our Gifts are too dangerous when he's around, and besides he's needed outside the wards. We have to finish it ourselves.'

Ari stared up at her with wide eyes. 'Your *Gifts* are dangerous? What about those suits of armour?'

More clanking metal shapes filled the doorway, pushing among themselves to get through first.

'I urge a strategic retreat,' said the death mask from the fireplace.

'All right,' said Jack. 'We can go upstairs and watch from there.'

Jaide nodded, even though it felt like running away from the problem rather than solving it. She picked up Professor Olafsson and together with Jack and Ari they hurried to the spiral staircase that led to the second tier of books in the library. Rodeo Dave hadn't cleared out up there yet. The shelves were still full, thickly coated with dust and cobwebs that not even Jaide's hurricane had disturbed.

Cornelia greeted them with a weak croak from the balustrade. Some of her feathers had come loose and stuck out at weird angles, but apart from that she seemed unharmed.

'Three sheets to the wind,' she said, which didn't make

much sense to Jaide, but it made Professor Olafsson chuckle.

'Look,' said Jack, still holding Ari close to his chest with one arm. His free hand pointed into the room below.

Three suits of armour burst through the doorway, knocking off chunks of wood and stone with their broad shoulders. None of them was carrying a sword, for which Jack was extremely grateful – particularly as one of them headed for the stairs while the other two stayed behind to protect the painting.

'We'd better get out of here,' said Jaide.

There were no doors from the upper level, but there was a window that was just wide enough for the twins to fit through, which hopefully meant their armoured pursuer couldn't pass. It was latched but not locked, and when Jaide tugged it open, cool, fresh air rushed inside. The light was fading fast, but she could see out to the tiled roof beyond.

'We could stay and fight,' said Jaide, emboldened and energised by the breeze.

'There are dozens of those suits of armour all over the castle,' said Ari. 'And what's going to stop your Gifts blowing you up too?'

'There must be a way to switch the booby trap off,' said Jack. 'Maybe . . . maybe we can look in the *Compendium*.'

'We can't go back home,' said Jaide. 'If Mum's there, she'll never let us leave.'

'Let's worry about that later,' said Jack nervously. 'I think getting out of here is top priority.'

He raised Ari so the cat could wriggle through the gap. Then he put his hands on the frame and hoisted himself up through it. Jaide pushed him from below, trying not to think of the heavy tread coming up the stairs behind her.

Cornelia flapped through next, calling 'Rourke' softly until Jack put out his hand for her to climb on to. They were just behind one of the crenulated walls that ran round the outside of the castle. The sky above was as black as pitch and the air smelled of rain. His dark-sensitive eyes made out a way across the roof to another set of windows on the far side.

'Come on, Jaide,' he said, hearing the crunch of heavy footsteps on the stairs.

Jaide started to climb out, then suddenly dropped back.

'Jaide!'

'There's someone down there,' she said. 'What if it's Kyle and Tara?'

She ran to the railing. As one of the suits of armour was laboriously clanking up the circular stair, down below, in the ruins of the doorway, stood Thomas Solomon. He was holding a torch limply in one hand and looking around in horror at the scattered books and wooden splinters that now filled the room.

'Get out of there!' Jaide shouted. 'Run!'

'What the blazes –?'

'Run!!' shrieked Jaide. The suit of armour that was after her had almost reached the top of the stairs, and there were two downstairs that were turning towards Solomon.

'Why? What is going –'

He stopped talking suddenly, his eyes widening. Jaide sensed movement behind her and ducked just in time. A heavy iron first whizzed over her, missing her head by inches. Her Gift came to life as she rolled away, whipping books off the shelves and flinging them at the armour. It batted them away like flies, following her with thunderous footsteps. She tried to stand, but the books slipped underfoot, and her crablike backwards crawl was taking her away from the window, into a corner . . .

Finally she got to her feet and looked about for some kind of weapon. There was nothing. The suit of armour lumbered closer, drawing back its fist for another all-iron punch. She froze, unable for an instant to think or do anything but stare at the gauntlet that was raised to deliver a killing blow.

'Jaide! Move!'

Jaide moved, ducking under the blow and diving past the suit of armour. The wind gathered round her like a cloak, lifting her feet off the ground so it didn't matter that they were slipping on books every time she tried to run. She wasn't really running any more. It was more like flying, except this was nothing like having wings. This felt like being caught up in a hurricane, moving with the wind wherever it wanted to take her.

Luckily it was taking her right for the window. Jack held out his arms, and then fell backwards as it became clear she was coming like a rocket, right for him. For an instant it felt like she was shooting down the cross-continuum conduit constructor again, except this time it was a window frame, not a picture frame, and what lay on the other side was freedom not the golden card.

Something cold and hard grabbed her ankle and yanked her back into the library.

'Jaide!' Jack gaped as his sister disappeared just as quickly as she had emerged into the night. 'Jaide!'

He scrambled to the window and peered in. Horrified, he stared at the suit of armour looming over his sister.

Neither of them believed their eyes when the armour let go of her, drew itself upright and raised its right fist and saluted.

CHAPTER TWENTY
To Translocate or not to Translocate

Not very far away, in Portland, the man best known to the twins as Rodeo Dave sat upright at his desk.

'Oh my,' he said, as a series of very strange and unlikely memories suddenly rushed back into his head at the instigation of a signal. A signal that had been prepared long ago in case certain events ever came to pass.

He was still for a long moment, absorbing everything: the what, the where and most especially the why. He had chosen to forget so much – his memories had been hidden for good reason. Now the reason had come back to him, he wished he didn't know again.

Then another signal came to him, hot on the heels of the first.

'Oh my, oh my, oh *my*,' he said, leaping to his feet and reaching for Zebediah's keys.

Jaide gaped up at the suit of armour that had gone from trying to kill her to saluting her, all in one second.

'Jaide, get away from it!' called Jack. 'Now!'

She slithered backwards. The armour didn't move. It hadn't reacted to Jack, and didn't react now as she stood up and faced it again.

'Jack?'

She dashed forward and waved a hand in front of the armour's face, jumping straight back in case it was a trap. But why would it *need* a trap? It could have had her dead if it had wanted that just seconds ago.

'Jack . . . I think they've been turned off.'

He climbed through the window and hesitantly approached the armour. When it didn't move, he tapped it on its cuirassed chest. The only thing that provoked was a deep, resonant *bong*.

'I guess they have,' he said. 'But why? And by who?'

'Let me see,' said a muffled voice from his backpack. 'Perhaps I can tell you.'

Jack pulled out Professor Olafsson. He examined the armour with interest, squinting and pursing his lips until at last he nodded with satisfaction.

'Yes,' he said. 'Quiescent. Very clever use of the Gift for animating inanimate objects, very tricky too . . .'

'So why are they suddenly *quiescent*?' asked Jaide.

'Again, I can only imagine that it was your doing.'

'Mine? But I didn't do anything.'

'You must have. Did you make any unusual signs or gestures?'

'No.'

'Call it by any particular names?'

'No.'

'Touch it, by any chance?'

Jaide opened her mouth to say *No* to that too, but then she remembered otherwise.

'It grabbed my ankle,' she said. 'It touched me then.'

'There you have it,' said Professor Olafsson. 'I expect it was designed to recognise a Warden – even a junior troubletwister Warden. The moment you touched one of its agents, the booby trap realised you weren't hostile and stood down.'

'I'm glad it did,' said Jaide. 'But what about Thomas . . . oh no!'

She peered over the balustrade. Two suits of armour were frozen in mid-motion, with the unconscious form of Thomas Solomon hanging between them, his shirt bunched up in their gauntlets.

'Is he dead?' whispered Jack.

'I . . . I think I can see him breathing,' said Jaide.

'We'd better go and check,' said Jack. He looked around to make sure there were no other moving suits of armour lurking anywhere and suddenly added, 'Where's Ari?'

'I don't know,' said Jaide. There was no sign of him on either level of the library, or on the roof, when Jack stuck his head out of the window to have a look.

'Perhaps he ran away,' said Professor Olafsson.

'He would never do that,' said Jaide.

'Unless it was to get help,' Jack groaned. 'I hope he hasn't gone to wake up Grandma.'

They ran down the stairs, Cornelia zooming ahead of them and perching on the picture frame.

Together, the twins gently lowered Thomas Solomon to the ground, though they ripped his shirt in the process.

'He *is* breathing,' said Jaide. 'But . . . I guess we'd better call an ambulance.'

'What if Mum comes?' asked Jack, gesturing at the destruction all around. 'How do we explain all this? Shouldn't we go and get the card first?'

'The man is not hurt,' pronounced the Professor. 'He has merely fainted. He will come round in his own time.'

'Are you sure?' asked Jaide.

'I am sure,' said the death mask.

'OK, let's go and get that card,' said Jack, 'before something else gets in the way.'

'Indeed,' said Professor Olafsson. 'I am curious to see the cross-continuum conduit constructor in action again. It was a little quick that last time.'

The cross-continuum conduit constructor was undamaged, apart from a small dent near one end that Professor Olafsson assured them would not affect its working.

As they lined it up again Jack asked, 'What's it like in there? Did you see the card?'

Jaide explained what she had experienced, then confessed that no, she hadn't actually found the Card of Translocation yet.

'I'm going to come with you this time,' Jack said. 'Two sets of eyes are better than one.'

'Who's going to watch out for more booby traps and hold the rope?'

'Cornelia and Professor Olafsson will yell if something happens. We can tie the rope to the column and pull ourselves back.'

'Actually, I guess we don't need the rope,' said Jaide. 'I've been through and we know it isn't straight down or anything. Come on. Let's line it up and we'll touch it together on three.'

When the controller was aligned, Jaide counted.

'One . . . two . . . three!'

The twins pressed their hands to the cool, brassy surface. Once again Jaide felt herself being whisked along from the normal universe of the castle to the one inside the painting. She blinked, momentarily dazzled. There was no visible sun, but everything was lit by a warm, yellow light. She hadn't noticed how dark it was getting back in the real world.

There was a rushing, tearing noise, and suddenly Jack was standing next to her, rocking faintly on his heels and blinking around him as she had done a moment earlier.

'Wow,' he said, 'that was amazing!'

There wasn't time to gawp at the scenery.

'I'm going that way,' Jaide said, pointing along the yellow brick road to the horizon. 'You look around here.'

'Don't go far,' warned Jack. 'There could be other guards or traps.'

'I'll be careful. I won't go out of sight.'

Jack stared up at the strange yellow sky, devoid of a sun, and across at the blurred horizon. Then he put aside his amazement at being inside a painting to concentrate on the task at hand. Where would he hide a gold card if he was the one doing so? There weren't many places, or at least not many he could see, close by.

First he tried the tree, peering round its roots and branches and into every knothole. Then he tried the ground around it, looking for signs that it had been dug up, but the ground was undisturbed. It didn't even look like real soil. When he poked at it, it dimpled like rubber instead of crumbling.

Next he tried the table on which the young woman who looked a bit like Grandma X was playing cards. There was nothing taped underneath and there were no visible drawers. The cards themselves were all ordinary cards, much too small to hide something made of solid gold. The young woman was wearing a voluminous yellow dress that Jack was afraid he might have to look under, but it too was rubbery like the ground and seemed solid all the way through. Her hair too had the same texture, close up. There was no way to hide anything there.

A gleam of light caught his eye as he was examining her hair. There was something around her neck, something real: a silver locket suspended from a crimson ribbon, studded with tiny jewels. He peered closer, irrationally afraid that she might come to life if he tried to touch it. But she remained exactly as she was, a facsimile of someone, not alive in her own right.

His fingers lifted the locket. It *was* real, not part of the painting. Thinking there might be a clue inside it, he untied the ribbon and pulled the locket free. It rested lightly in his hand and opened easily when he flicked the clasp with a thumbnail.

Inside was a lock of hair and a photo. The photo had once been black and white, but was now mostly brown. It showed the woman in the painting standing on a jetty, looking out to sea. Next to her was a young man with a broad, infectious grin below a moustache so fine it might have been drawn on with a pencil. Both wore old-fashioned clothes, but not as old as the woman in the painting, maybe early twentieth century. Behind them and to one side was the Portland lighthouse.

On the inside of the locket was written: *To Lottie, With Love.*

'Found anything?' asked Jaide from behind him.

He jumped. 'No, nothing important.' He put the locket in his pocket for thinking about later. 'What about you?'

'Not a thing.' She looked as frustrated as she felt. The yellow brick road had taken her over the rubbery hills, past fields of rubbery plants, and nowhere had she seen anything that looked like a gold card. And then, just as Jack and the tree had vanished from behind her, they had reappeared again in front of her. The road had looped back on itself, taking her to where she had started with nothing to show for it.

'This can't be a dead end,' she said. 'The card has to be here somewhere.'

Jack agreed, but he couldn't see any way around it. They had searched everywhere and found nothing. There was just the tree, the table, the girl and the yellow brick road.

Suddenly he wanted to laugh. 'Of course!'

'What?'

'It's like the painting itself, hidden right out in the open. What's the one thing you didn't look at?'

'Just tell me, Jack. This isn't a game.'

'I know, but it's really very clever . . .' He stopped at the look on Jaide's face. 'Come on, I'll show you.'

He tugged her by the hand.

'It's the road itself, see?'

And she *did* see, all of a sudden, as though a veil had been pulled from her eyes. The yellow bricks were the exact size and shape as the golden cards. Any one of them could be the Card of Translocation. All they had to do was find it.

They ran back and forth at random at first, and then more methodically, scanning backwards and forwards across the road surface, looking for telltale gleams of gold. Jaide didn't know how quickly time passed inside the painting, but it soon felt like hours. She tried not to think about how the fight with

The Evil was proceeding. They could only go as fast as they could go.

And then, off to her right, she saw a brick that gleamed differently to the others. It had a distinctly flatter surface, and as she ran up to it she saw herself reflected back at her.

'Got it!' she cried, and Jack came running to join her.

'Are you sure?'

'Positive.' She slipped the tips of her fingers under the card and lifted. It came free with a click. The Card of Translocation was released from its long hiding place and into their hands.

'Finally,' Jack breathed. 'Can I hold it?'

For such a small thing, it was amazingly heavy. About the size of a book but much thinner, it was featureless on both sides and rounded on the edges. Jack turned it over in his hands, marveling at the reflections sweeping across it. As he stared, a faint black X formed on one side, and he felt an odd sensation, as though the gold was becoming icy cold under his fingertips.

For the Divination of Potential Powers, the *Compendium* had said. He wondered if this particular card was divining something in him at that very moment.

Jaide took the card back from him and put it in her back pocket.

'Now,' she said, standing up and wiping her hands on her jeans, 'let's go and find Dad so he can translocate The Evil.'

They hurried back to where the end of the constructor

stuck out of thin air and they put their hands on it at the same time, returning to the real world in a wild, breathtaking rush. Nothing had changed in their absence: the suits of armour remained immobile, Thomas Solomon was still sprawled unconscious between two of them and the mess of books lay under a pall of settling dust.

'Pieces of eight,' said Cornelia, dancing admiringly across the frame. 'Pieces of eight!'

'We've been watching through the picture frame,' said Professor Olafsson. 'Congratulations, troubletwisters. You have accomplished something wholly singular and remarkable!'

'It's not over yet,' said Jaide, gathering her things together and telling herself not to get too excited too soon. 'We've still got to get this to Dad so he can use it to fight The Evil.'

Jack checked the phone. Three missed calls, but those were from earlier. No texts.

'We'll have to go out to him,' he said. 'You saw those clouds before. He's got to be nearby.'

'What about The Evil?' Jaide asked.

'We'll be careful. Anyway, we've got the card. We can uh . . . translocate it, right?'

'You do know what *translocate* means, don't you?' asked Professor Olafsson.

'Sure, we looked it up. It means to move something somewhere else. So it must like get rid of things.'

'Get rid of things?' asked the Professor. 'But to where?

And what kind of things are translocated *exactly*?'

'I don't know . . .' said Jack.

'It doesn't matter,' said Jaide. 'We've got it, and we need to get it to Dad.'

Jack picked up the death mask and tucked it into his backpack.

'What do we do about Thomas?' he said. 'We can't leave him here like this.'

'Let's put him in a ground-floor room,' Jaide suggested. 'There's a bed in one of them, I'm sure. When he wakes up, maybe he'll think he sneaked off for a nap and dreamed it all.'

That seemed a remote possibility to Jack, but together he and his sister managed to hoist the unconscious man's arms over their shoulders and drag him along the corridor, to the accompaniment of encouragement from the Professor and comments about drunken sailors from Cornelia. At the door to the room Jaide had in mind, Jack took the skeleton key from Jaide's pocket while she held Thomas unsteadily aloft with her Gift. Jack unlocked the door, and Thomas rushed inside on the back of a tiny tornado and crashed on to a sheet-draped bed. The wind howled once around the ceiling and escaped up a chimney, leaving the room considerably less dusty than it had been before. Somehow Thomas slept through it all.

Jaide nodded in satisfaction. 'OK, that's done. Let's go.'

Cornelia flew down on to Jack's shoulder as they hurried through the silent castle, Jaide lighting her way with a torch,

Jack seeing by his Gift alone. They felt buoyed by their success in finding the card, but nervous all the same of what was to come.

There was no one outside, just Thomas Solomon's abandoned golf cart sitting slightly askew on the cobbled driveway. The air was thick with the threat of a storm. Jack could practically taste rain, and he braced himself for another soaking. They hadn't thought to bring raincoats.

Distantly, they heard a wolf howl and Jaide shivered.

'Which way, Jack?'

Before he could answer, headlights flashed in the distance as a car pulled through the gates. A car engine growled low and deep, getting louder as it accelerated up the driveway. Even from far away, they recognised the light gleaming off the tips of long steer horns.

'Jaide, that's Rodeo Dave's car,' Jack said.

'Quick,' she cried, 'into the buggy!'

They leaped aboard, even though neither of them knew how to drive. Luckily it was as simple as could be: there was a button that started the engine, and from there, all Jack had to do was push down the accelerator and turn the wheel.

The buggy accelerated down the hill, bouncing across the lawn and round the back of the castle. Jack left the headlights off so the person coming up the drive might not see them. He didn't need the lights: he could see the ground ahead perfectly well. For Jaide it was a far more terrifying experience, clinging to the dashboard in front of her as the buggy hurtled off into the darkness, swerving round obstacles she couldn't see. Cornelia jumped ship immediately and followed above, shouting such well-meaning but unhelpful advice as, 'Trim the mainsail!' and 'Hard to starboard!'

As they passed the menagerie, they heard the animals calling in alarm. Something had riled them up, Jaide thought. Perhaps they could sense The Evil gathering outside the wards.

Two shadowy figures appeared from the nearest animal enclosure, waving their arms and running in front of the buggy.

Jaide gasped and ducked. Jack wrenched the wheel to one side, narrowly avoiding a collision.

'Hey, that's cheating!' called a familiar voice after them.

'Come back here and give us a ride!' shouted another.

Jaide twisted to look behind her. It was Tara and Kyle. They jumped up and down in their wake, hollering for the twins to come back.

'I forgot all about them,' she said. 'I hope they're going to stay out of it.'

Jack just grunted. The field ahead was rough and bouncy, and he was having trouble maintaining a straight course. He could see the copse where his father had been hiding that week. Getting there was all he could concentrate on at that moment. A heavy rain had started to fall, making it hard to see, and if the ground became too boggy they might get stuck and have to run on foot.

When a glowing blue figure appeared in front of them, the figure of a young man with outstretched arms, Jack gasped and slammed on the brakes.

++Stop, troubletwisters,++ the figure said. **++You don't know what you're doing!++**

'What is that?' asked Jaide, who had only just managed to stop herself from falling out of her seat, such was the violence of their abrupt, halting skid. 'Who is that?'

'I don't know,' Jack said, spinning the wheel with the intention of going around the phantom.

++Jack, Jaide, turn back!++

'Is that The Evil?' asked Jaide, plugging her ears, but the voice in her mind was impossible to keep out.

Jack didn't know. When Wardens talked to them through their minds, they sounded just as echoey and strange. Besides, he was busy trying to get round the phantom. Everywhere he went it stayed steadfastly in front of them. Stranger still, he could almost believe that he had seen the phantom's imploring face somewhere before.

++Listen to me, troubletwisters – you're making a terrible mistake!++

Another voice struggled to make itself heard over the whine of the buggy's motor. It was coming from Jack's backpack.

'That's him!' Professor Olafsson was shouting. 'That's the voice I've been trying to remember!'

Jaide pulled the death mask out and pointed him forward.

'Him?'

'Yes! I knew I recognised him from somewhere. He was in the castle, a long time ago. He – *eeeeargh*!'

Jack braked again as a long red car roared to a halt in front of them, driving right through the phantom and dissolving it into mist. Professor Olafsson flew out of Jaide's hands and went spinning out the window, striking the side of the car with a resounding crack and splitting in two, right down the length of his face.

'Professor Olafsson!' Jaide stood up in her seat, but couldn't see if either piece was still moving. 'Jack – he's hurt.'

Jack was too busy trying to reverse, but the wheels were spinning in the wet grass.

In the rear-view mirror, Zebediah's driver's door opened with a creak and a grim-looking Rodeo Dave stepped out.

'Jack, get us out of here!' cried Jaide.

'I'm trying!'

The buggy's engine whined uselessly.

'Don't run, troubletwisters,' called Rodeo Dave over Zebediah's long bonnet. 'I know what you've done, but it's not your fault. You've been tricked!'

'Hurry up, Jack!'

'Don't listen to him!'

Rodeo Dave was coming round the front of the car now. Zebediah's blinding headlights cast his face into deep shadow. The buggy was going nowhere. They would have to get out and run for it and hope youth would win out over his longer stride, or –

'The card, Jaide,' Jack gasped. 'Use it – quickly!'

'What?' Jaide fumbled at her back pocket. 'Use it to do what?'

'Translocate him!'

'Translocate Rodeo Dave? But we don't know where he'll go –'

'We have to! He'll stop us from getting to Dad if you don't!'

Jaide pulled the card out into the light. It gleamed wildly in the reflected headlights. A wave of cold made her fingertips numb as she held it up in front of her. A series of black symbols swept across its face, settling on a bold, black X.

She called up her Gift and felt it swirl around her in the night air. Lacking any idea at all how the card was supposed to work, she simply raised it in front of her and said the first things that came to mind.

'Go, card – do your stuff!'

'Jaide, no!' said Rodeo Dave, holding up his hands in alarm. 'Don't do that!'

But it was too late. The Card of Translocation had been activated.

CHAPTER TWENTY-ONE

Remembering Rodeo Dave

Jaide's Gift vanished like the air leaving a burst balloon. She felt it going, bleeding out of her in a few seconds, leaving a terrible emptiness in its wake.

'What?' She shook the gold card as though it was a malfunctioning gadget. 'My Gift's gone! That wasn't supposed to happen.'

'Give it here,' said Jack. 'You probably didn't concentrate hard enough!'

He took the card and tried exactly what she did.

'No, Jack, wait!' cried Rodeo Dave, stepping out of the light and coming closer.

'Translocate!' said Jack.

Suddenly he could no longer see in the dark. His Gift was sliced away, leaving him blind apart from the dazzling headlights.

'It's not too late, troubletwisters,' said Rodeo Dave urgently. 'I can make everything right. Just don't run. I'm nearly there.'

Jack almost gave in. The card was useless in his hands. They had no Gifts and no means of defending themselves. Perhaps if they gave him the card, they would live to fight another day, as poor Professor Olafsson had put it. Perhaps he would let them go.

Then a voice called out of the darkness to their right.

'Jack and Jaide! Over here!'

Hope returned. It was Hector Shield, and he sounded close.

'We're coming, Dad!' cried Jack, grabbing his sister's hand and tumbling out of the cab.

Rodeo Dave lunged for them, crying, '*No, wait!*'

They dodged, and then they were running across the muddy grounds of the estate, following their father's voice.

'That's it! A little further!'

Jaide had her torch on. Hector Shield was just feet away. He waved them closer. He looked dishevelled and his glasses were askew, but his face was eager, excited and relieved all at once.

'The card has taken our Gifts,' Jaide called to him. 'Translocated them somewhere!'

'That's what it's supposed to do,' he called back. 'But don't worry – it translocates them into the card itself, with all the other Gifts he stole.'

'I didn't steal them,' puffed Rodeo Dave from behind them, 'and you know it!'

'Shut up, old man. In a moment the card will be mine, and then I'll deal with you once and for all.' Hector Shield hurried the twins onward, into his waiting arms. 'That's it, children. Almost there. *Almost mine . . .*'

Jaide hesitated then. There was something so gloating and horrible about the way her father was speaking now that she hardly recognised him. She had never heard him sound that way before, and she remembered Professor Olafsson asking *What kind of father . . .?* Her father would never talk like that. Her father would never threaten anyone.

'Wait, Jack,' she said, slowing him by tugging on his backpack. 'Something's not right.'

'Don't listen to her, Jack,' said Hector Shield, reaching towards him. His feet stayed just outside the invisible line marking the boundary of the wards. 'Just come . . . a little bit . . . closer . . . Oh, curse you, I'll come in there and get you myself!'

With that he lunged over the line, caught the card in one hand and pulled it from Jack with a cry of triumph.

'No!' shouted Rodeo Dave. He grabbed the twins and pulled them further back inside the boundary of the wards, away from their father. 'This is the worst possible thing! Behind me, both of you.'

'Nothing you can do will save them now.' Hector Shield capered on the spot, holding the Card of Translocation over his head. Black symbols danced over its surface like numbers on a digital clock that was running too fast. 'You were foolish to allow them near the card. Now I have their Gifts, and soon The Evil will have them too.'

'The Evil?' Jaide asked. 'What are you talking about, Dad?'

'Just get back,' said Rodeo Dave, putting himself in front of them.

'Dad . . . but you can't be Evil. You can't be,' Jack said.

'Can't I, Jackaran Shield?' Hector Shield stared at him. 'Just you watch.'

He tapped the gold card with his right index finger and the symbols stopped moving. It showed a square with a straight line through it. What happened next, Jack and Jaide didn't understand at first, but the air changed around them. The ground beneath their feet changed too, and the rain hitting their faces, and the clouds high above. Hector Shield changed too. He stood straighter. His face grew longer, more haggard. He didn't look like their father now. He looked like a different man hiding behind the same face.

'Dad . . .' said Jaide again, but the word sounded uncertain in her mouth.

++Will you tell them or will we, David Smeaton?++ Hector Shield said in the voice of The Evil.

Not very far away, in Portland, Renita Daniels jumped at a searing pain between her ribs. It felt as though a dagger had stabbed deep inside her, so keenly and smoothly that she hadn't even felt it, until it reached her heart.

'No,' she gasped, pressing her wooden hand to her side. 'Not again.'

*

And not very far from her, a much older woman who no longer had a name at all, opened her eyes and took in the dim gloom of the hospital room around her. Her mind felt fog-bound and sluggish, the exact opposite of how she prided herself on being, and for a long second she struggled to remember how she had come to be that way. There was a car . . . the river coming up to meet her . . . a series of doctors and nurses in white coats . . . a dark figure creeping in at night, fiddling with her drip . . .

. . . the worried faces of Jack and Jaide . . .

She sat bolt upright, startling the regal cat sleeping at her side, tucked under the sheet so a passing nurse wouldn't see her. The feeling that had woken her from her artificial slumber was startlingly clear. It was also unexpected and urgent. She was needed, and needed badly.

There was no phone by the bed, but she didn't require one. She was awake now. Fully awake. Soon her powers would return, and until then she was sure there was an ambulance she could borrow.

'A mother,' Grandma X whispered to Kleo as she swung her legs out of bed and began looking for her clothes, 'never abandons her son.'

'Run, kids,' said Rodeo Dave. 'Run!'

'No,' protested Jack. 'His eyes are normal. He can't be Evil. This can't be happening!'

Hector Shield bent forward and pulled down his bottom eyelid. Around what looked like perfectly normal brown eyes was a ring of white.

'Contact lenses!' gasped Jaide.

'But you can't be in here,' said Jack, clinging to one last piece of hope. 'The wards will drive you out.'

++You would like to believe so, troubletwister, wouldn't you?++

To Jack's horror, the hideous parody of his father did another gleeful jig inside the wards' invisible boundary. And only then did the twins realise what had changed when Hector Shield had used the card. The wards had failed.

As though from very far away, they heard Rennie cry out in pain.

++Come to us now,++ said The Evil, raising the card and studying the symbols flashing across its face. **++This family reunion is long overdue.++**

++Indeed it is,++ said a voice to their right. **++Put the card down and step away from the troubletwisters.++**

'Grandma!' cried the twins. For it *was* her, as young and beautiful as she always looked in her spectral form, standing just feet away.

++You can't tell us what to do,++ snarled The Evil. **++We are beyond your authority.++**

It thrust the card at Grandma X's image and a psychic whip lashed out at her, sending her reeling.

++Stop, H–!++

With a cry of pain, she vanished.

Aghast, the twins stared at The Evil as it turned, gloating, to face them again. It raised the card to attack them in turn.

'Rourke!' cried a voice from above. A blue winged shape flashed in front of Hector Shield and snatched the gold card out of his grasp. 'Repel boarders!'

++No!++

'Cornelia!' Jack cried in amazement. 'Good bird!'

'Everybody run!' shouted Dave. 'Get back to the castle!'

He turned to face Hector Shield, who was advancing upon the older man with his teeth bared in a furious expression the twins had never before seen on their father's face. There were lines of white around his eyes, where he had dislodged the camouflage lenses.

++The wards are gone, and you are old and feeble, Warden. The castle will offer no protection to the children. Come to us! We don't need the card to deal with you.++

'Go!' ordered Rodeo Dave. 'It can't be very strong or it would have taken us already. Take Zebediah! Go!'

Powerless and terrified by the defeat of their father and grandmother, the twins had no choice but to obey. Zebediah's doors were open, and Jack ran to the passenger side, nearly treading on the two halves of Professor Olafsson where they lay in the mud. He scooped them up and jumped into Zebediah's expansive front seat. The doors slammed shut behind them, the engine roared, and Jaide took the wheel as the mighty car leaped forward.

The pieces of Professor Olafsson stared up at Jack from where they lay in his lap, frozen in shock, mirroring the exact way he felt.

'I don't believe it,' said Jack.

'Dad being Evil or Rodeo Dave being a Warden?' Jaide couldn't believe either shocking revelation herself.

'Everything!' he exclaimed. 'The wards are down and it's all our fault!'

'If the card had only done what it was supposed to do . . .' Jaide suppressed a sudden feeling of panic that her Gifts might be gone for good.

Jack remembered Professor Olafsson asking them if they knew what *translocate* meant. He raised the two halves of the plaster mask and, figuring he had nothing to lose, pressed them firmly together.

Professor Olafsson sprang back to life with a start.

'Good grief,' he said. 'Where am I? What caused this terrible headache?' His rolling eyes caught sight of Jack. 'Oh yes. I remember now. The Warden who found me in the castle and asked for my advice. He's an old man now, but I still recognised him . . . eventually. It must've been he who hid the card in the first place, set the booby traps and everything!'

'What?' asked Jack. 'Rodeo Dave can't be a Warden! And why would he hide the card? What does it do?'

'To *translocate* something is indeed to move it somewhere else. Judging by the way the card affected you two, I'd say it moves not things, but *Gifts*.'

'But The Evil said that it has our Gifts now, or will do soon,' said Jaide. 'That they're in the card!'

'That sounds like a reasonable hypothesis. *For the Divination of Potential Powers and Safekeeping Thereof* . . . although it's not usual for cards to hold more than one Gift at a time. Perhaps this one is special because it holds the Gift of Translocation, which gives the Warden who possesses it the power to take other Wardens' Gifts.'

'Who would want a Gift like that?' asked Jaide.

'The Gift chooses the Warden, not the other way around.' Professor Olafsson stared at her out of the corner of his eyes. 'This card must *not* fall into The Evil's hands again or it will have all the Gifts it contains, as well as the ability to steal more. That's what makes it so valuable as a weapon.'

Jaide brought the car around the estate. She had lost sight of Cornelia momentarily behind the castle. As they passed the menagerie, there was no sign of Tara or Kyle.

'How would we get our Gifts back out of the card?' asked Jaide.

'I suppose you would do the same thing you did before, only backwards.'

'Yes, but how exactly?'

Professor Olafsson shrugged with his eyebrows.

Zebediah bounced in and out of a deep rut. As they came up the other side, Jaide saw the golf buggy accelerating towards them, headlights burning with a cold, Evil light. There was no driver behind the steering wheel.

'Look out!' cried Jack.

Jaide wrenched the wheel as hard as she could. The buggy turned in the same direction, and the vehicles collided head-on. Jack and Jaide were flung forwards on to the floor. The two halves of the death mask flew apart. Zebediah's engine coughed and died with a hiss, its radiator pierced by one half of the steer horns on its grill.

The twins picked themselves up and tried the doors. Jaide's was stuck, but Jack opened his fine. The Evil buggy was a twisted mess of metal and plastic. As they stepped out of the car, it twitched as though still trying to get at them.

++Come to us, troubletwisters. Be one with us!++

They ran for the castle.

'Cornelia?' called Jack, scanning the skies. The torrential rain made it hard to see anything. 'Cornelia, where are you?'

They heard a faint 'Rourke' from up ahead.

'Jack? Is that you?'

'Over here!' That didn't sound like Cornelia, but it didn't sound Evil either.

Tara and Kyle came running towards them out of the rain.

'What are you doing?' asked Jaide.

'Trying to round up the menagerie animals,' said Kyle.

'Their eyes went really weird, and then Chippy opened his cage somehow and they all ran away –'

'Chippy?' asked Jack.

'One of the chimps. They all have names. I visit them sometimes, when Dad lets me.'

'Which way did they run?' Jaide asked.

'That way,' said Tara. 'We were following when we heard you.'

'Let's go,' said Jaide, leading the charge.

They ran round the curving moat and the drawbridge came into view. Next to it was the strangest thing Jack had ever seen: a giant creature made up of all the menagerie animals combined into one. The warthog and the zebra were at the bottom, holding up the lemurs and jackal, which in turn held up the wolves, on whose backs rode both chimpanzees, with all the forest creatures mixed in for good measure. It looked a bit like a gymnastic pyramid, but for the fact that it moved as one. Even through the rain, Jack could see how the fur mixed and mingled, creating a terrible hybrid of all of them at once.

The chimps were at the tip of two reaching limbs that swayed and clutched at something in the sky, gibbering excitedly.

'Cornelia!' shouted Jack.

'Rourke!' The macaw was a blue speck staying just out of reach of the monster.

Jaide was amazed. 'Why is *she* still herself? Why hasn't The Evil taken her over?'

'The card must be protecting her,' said Jack. 'We have to help her!'

Cornelia was struggling to stay out of reach of The Evil. With the gold card heavy in her claws and her feathers full of water, it was amazing she was flying at all. But without their Gifts, what could the twins do?

'What's happening?' asked Kyle, his eyes wide with horror.

'I remember,' said Tara in an amazed voice. 'How could I forget? These guys are like superheroes. Kyle, wait until you see what they can do!'

'We're not anything at the moment,' said Jack, thinking furiously. They couldn't attack The Evil directly, but there might be another way, by luring it to the cross-continuum conduit constructor. If they could get The Evil to touch it, it would be sucked into the painting and there maybe they could trap it.

'Cornelia,' he called, 'go to the library! We'll meet you there!'

'Aye aye,' she squawked back, banking sharply towards the window they had left open on the second floor. The motley creature lunged for her, lost its balance and toppled with a roar into the moat.

'That's our chance,' said Jaide. 'Let's go!'

They ran across the drawbridge, dodging mutated limbs that reached up for them from below. They passed under the portcullis, which Jaide briefly considered trying to close. It looked merely decorative though, so she kept running. When they were through the front door, she slammed it behind her and locked it with a skeleton key.

'What . . . what was that thing?' asked Kyle, his face pale.

'It doesn't matter,' said Jack. 'Don't worry about it.'

'Don't *worry* about it? If my dad was here, he'd go mental. So would the Peregrinators. They'd never stop talking about it! That's if it didn't kill everyone first.'

'You can't tell them,' said Jaide. 'It's a secret.'

'There's this guy,' said Tara. 'Big beard . . . deep voice . . .'

She was getting vague and sluggish again. Jaide tugged her down the corridor after Jack, with Kyle bringing up the rear.

'Is this something to do with the treasure?' he called after them. 'Did you find it?'

'We'll tell you later,' lied Jaide.

As they ran for the library, they heard the distinctive *tramp-tramp* of marching metal feet.

'Don't worry,' said Jack. 'That's just a booby trap to stop people stealing the, uh, treasure. Rodeo Dave must've switched them back on again.'

But as they rounded the last corner, it wasn't the usual sort of armour they saw at the far end of the corridor. It was one of the suits from the hidden basement, covered with golden serpents. A ghostly white light shone from its eyepieces.

++Your father is ours,++ said The Evil. **++He has been all along. Join him now and give us the Card of Translocation, and we will spare your friends. If not, they will all die.++**

CHAPTER TWENTY-TWO
The Wrong Gifts

'It's lying,' said Jaide.

'I know,' said Jack.

'That voice,' said Tara with a shudder. 'I dream about it sometimes . . .'

Jack judged the distance to the library door. If they were quick they might just make it, and if they got there first they could retrieve the golden card from Cornelia and start fighting back. 'Let's go!'

They sprinted for the door. Jack, normally the fastest runner, took the lead, but he was soon overtaken by Tara, thanks to her slightly longer legs. Once again Kyle fell behind and Jaide slowed to help him along, even though she could see the armour lumbering rapidly towards them, picking up speed with every step. Jack felt as though he was running right for it, but when it was still several yards away Jack and Kyle took the turn through the doorway, feet skidding on the dusty floor, barely staying upright.

Jack looked wildly around for Cornelia.

The library was exactly as they had left it, with the two

ordinary suits of armour standing on either side of the painting, the cross-continuum conduit constructor directly in front of it and books scattered everywhere.

'Cornelia!' Jack shouted again, struck by the sudden fear that someone – or something – had got her.

Then his torch picked out a flash of blue wings fluttering towards him.

'Mind the yardarm,' she squawked, letting the gold card drop heavily into his hands and flying to her usual perch on the top of the bust of Mister Rourke.

Jack caught the card with both hands and turned it over to examine it from all angles. Now what? He'd got this far, but what could he do next? He didn't have a Gift any more. Would the card even listen to him?

There was more skidding behind him as the others followed in his footsteps. Tara and Kyle turned to look at the armour as it reached the doorway and came to a complete halt.

Only Jaide didn't stop. She kept running, following a wild guess, right up to the nearest of the booby-trapped suits of armour, without hesitation, she rapped twice on its chest.

'That thing's Evil and it's after us,' she said, pointing, 'and we're troubletwisters so you have to help us!'

The armour came grindingly to life. It looked at its neighbour and seemed to confer with it.

'Don't take too long. It's right behind us!'

The armour inclined its head and the other nodded too.

Clenching their fists, they moved forward to tackle The Evil head-on.

Armour clashed with a sound of metal meeting leather. Jaide stepped hurriedly away from them, leading the others to the base of the spiral staircase.

'What did I tell you?' said Tara to Kyle. 'They can do anything!'

Kyle was staring at the card. 'Is that *real gold*?'

Tara's confidence washed away Jack's uncertainty. Gift or no Gift, they were still troubletwisters. And now they had the Card of Translocation, he could get his Gifts back.

He raised the card. Symbols were flicking across its surface, almost too quickly to see.

'Give me my Gift back,' he told it.

Something crackled through the skin of his fingers and rushed up his arms, making his hair stand on end and his legs go weak. He felt instantly complete, but weirdly his eyesight didn't change. The shadows were still impenetrable. Maybe it took time to settle back in, he told himself.

'Did it work, Jack?' asked Jaide.

'I don't know,' he said. Things did look a little different, but not in the way he had expected. Everything around him seemed to be growing taller, including Jaide, Tara and Kyle.

'I think I'm shrinking,' he said.

'No you're not,' said Tara. 'You're *sinking*!'

He looked down at his shoes, which were already up to the

laces in the library's stone floor, as if he was being sucked into quicksand. He lifted one foot, and then put it down and lifted the other. All that happened was that he sank even further, up to his shins.

'You've got the wrong Gift,' said Jaide.

'What use is this?' said Jack in frustration. The floor was up to his knees now. If it continued he would soon be in the basement – and what happened if he *kept* falling? Would he go right down to the centre of the Earth?

With a weird, slippery sensation, the gold card fell through his fingers and clattered to the floor. Jaide snatched it before Kyle could.

'Here,' said Tara, offering Jack a hand. 'I'll pull you up.'

But her hand went right through his without even slowing down.

Panic was rising as fast as the floor. Jack told himself to keep calm and breathe slowly. This was a Gift like any other. He could presumably learn to control it. *Someone* must have after all, before it ended up in the card.

He concentrated on making himself solid again, but a sudden pain warned him off that route. What would happen if flesh and stone tried to occupy the same place at the same time? Instead he thought about just his hands, and bent down and pushed against the floor. That worked. He could feel the stone distinctly against his skin. With an awkward push-up move, he brought his legs up out of the stone, concentrated on his feet and managed to stand without slipping down again. It took constant focus, but he could do it.

Jaide studied the symbols flashing by on the card.

'You obviously have to pick the right one,' she said.

'Can I have a Gift too?' asked Tara. 'I'd love to be able to walk through walls.'

'I'd like to be invisible,' said Kyle.

'Hang on,' said Jaide, concentrating on a symbol she recognised: two connected curves like a kids' drawing of a bird with squiggly lines underneath that might represent air. She had seen something like that the first time Grandma X had shown them the cards.

That was the best lead she had to go on, so the next time she saw it she said 'Give me that one!' in a loud voice before it could flash away.

The Gift came in a rush that felt like going down an elevator really fast and for a moment she wondered if she might actually take off.

But she didn't, and when she performed a quick, exploratory jump, she found that she weighed just as much as before. She wasn't falling through the floor, but she hadn't gained a new Gift either.

'Jack, I don't think it worked.'

He didn't answer, except with a long drawn-out yawn.

She looked at him. He was sagging where he stood, eyes falling shut and his arms dangling limp at his sides. Tara and

Kyle were the same. As Jaide watched, Kyle drooped to the floor and started snoring.

'What's going on?' she asked. 'Am I doing this?'

'So . . . sleepy,' said Jack, beginning to sink into the floor again. Tara slumped down next to Kyle, struggling but steadily losing the fight to stay awake, and Jaide knew she had to do something before she was the only one left standing.

Like Jack, it was a matter of finding enough control over her new Gift to make it stop working. Concentrating on Jack, she willed him to stop falling asleep. To wake up in fact.

'Wake up now!'

Jack's eyes flew wide open, and he shot up out of the floor so fast she thought he might keep on going, right up to the ceiling.

'Are you all right?' she said.

'Wow, Jaide. What happened?'

'The gold card happened,' she said. 'It's not fair! You got a really useful Gift, but all I can do is put people to sleep, like I'm really boring.'

A sudden crash returned their attention to the duelling suits of armour. One of the friendly ones had just been knocked to pieces. The other was still putting up a fight, but it was looking severely dented and its helmet had been wrenched off and was being used as a metal boxing glove by its attacker. A series of thudding footsteps announced the arrival of the third suit of armour from the library's upper floor, but at the same time a second suit of Evil armour appeared in the doorway, and up above, a window shattered. Something big and angry growled.

'What are we going to do, Jack?' Jaide asked. They were hemmed in on all sides, with Tara and Kyle slumped at their feet.

'We'll just have to get some more Gifts,' Jack said, bouncing up and down on his toes and sinking a little bit into the stone each time. He felt a bit too wide-eyed and alert now, but that was better than the alternative. The wave of sleepiness that Jaide had hit him with had felt like being buried in a landslide of cotton wool. 'One of them is bound to be useful.'

Jaide raised the card and randomly selected another Gift.

Nothing happened.

She tried another.

Still nothing.

'Jack, it's not working!'

'Maybe we can only have one at a time.'

'Fiddly thing! Translocate!'

She felt something, presumably the sleeping Gift, leave her, and quickly shook the card and watched the symbols flash by. How to choose? At random, she supposed . . .

Meanwhile, Jack considered his original plan of luring The Evil into the painting. That might fix one suit of armour, but not both, and not anything else The Evil might throw at them.

'Perhaps we could hide in the painting while we find a better Gift –'

The second suit of armour staggered backwards into the cross-continuum conduit constructor and tripped over it. The copper tube ended up in an L-shape, and the armour in numerous pieces.

'Or not.'

'Lucky we didn't,' said Jaide, 'or we'd be trapped now.'

'Like we aren't already – what the . . .?'

Jaide was shootings sparks out of her hair. Her skin prickled and tingled with swirling electricity. She pointed her finger at one of the suits of armour, but instead of a lightning bolt all she got was more sparks.

'Try again!' Jack cried, ducking into a ball so he wouldn't get scorched.

'Translocate!'

There were two Evil armours versus one, slugging it out in the doorway, and when Jack peered out from his ball, he saw two grey snouts nosing through the balustrade, sniffing for them.

With a flap of wings, Cornelia circled Jack's head.

++Join us,++ she crowed.

Jack ducked back down as the hideous white gaze of The Evil swooped him at very close range.

'No!' he cried.

++Join us,++ growled the wolves from the floor above.

'Never!' cried Jaide, blinking in alarm at a world that had suddenly gone inside out, thanks to the new and useless Gift of X-ray vision.

++**Join us,**++ said the two suits of armour. Thomas Solomon, Tara and Kyle stirred, murmuring the same words weakly in their sleep.

'Stop saying that!' shouted the twins at the same time.

The suits of armour went still. So did the wolves. Cornelia turned a circle over Jack and then flew back to the bust of Mister Rourke, where she twisted her head from side to side and ruffled her feathers. Her eyes were black again.

'Out of the rain,' she said, twisting around to face the doorway, where, with a clatter of metal on stone, the last surviving good suit of armour staggered and fell over, revealing someone new standing there.

++**Join us,**++ said Hector Shield. ++**Don't you want to be reunited with your family?**++

Jack and Jaide drew together. Their father's eyes were hypnotically bright, growing brighter and brighter the closer they came. The natural brown colour faded from them until two shrivelled contact lenses fell down his cheeks, revealing in full the terrible whiteness beneath. The light made his face look cold and cruel.

He held Rodeo Dave with an arm twisted behind his back, and with one painful wrench walked him into the room.

'You're not Dad,' said Jaide. 'You're The Evil.'

'We're never going to do what you say,' shouted Jack.

++**But you did, didn't you? And so well too. You found the Card of Translocation for us – you even rid**++

yourselves of your own pesky Gifts. We are proud of you, troubletwisters. You are practically one with us already.++

Jack and Jaide shook their heads.

'We'll never give you back the card,' Jack said. 'We know what it does now.'

'We know you lied to us.'

++Too late, troubletwisters. The wards are defeated. How long can you withstand us on your own?++

'Don't listen to him,' gasped Rodeo Dave. 'He's not – ah!'

He gasped as The Evil viciously wrenched his arm up his back.

'Leave him alone!' shouted Jaide.

++Would you trade his life for one of yours?++ The Evil asked.

The twins glanced at each other, wondering if it was being serious. It had made a similar offer earlier, but they had had no doubt then that it was just messing with their heads. And they came to the same conclusion now. Besides, neither of them was going to let the other go. There *had* to be a way to fight The Evil, even now. Perhaps with their new Gifts . . .

++We didn't think so,++ said The Evil with a sneer.

And with that, Hector Shield's eyes began to clear as The Evil left him and all its other hosts, withdrawing from them so it could gather all its strength to move into the troubletwisters.

The weight of The Evil bore down on the twins. They

had felt this before, the terrible soul-sapping emptiness that wanted to get inside them and make them hollow and lifeless, like all of its creatures. It was the blackness at the bottom of the ocean, the coldness of winter at the South Pole and the emptiness of deep space all rolled up in one. They fought it with all their willpower, but The Evil at its full strength was too powerful. The colours in Jack's vision faded to white. Jaide felt her fear peak and then begin to dissipate – and that was the most terrifying thing of all. When she stopped feeling afraid, she would know that The Evil had her completely.

Hector Shield watched it happen with sad brown eyes.

'Help us!' gasped Jack.

'Dad . . . do something!' Jaide said. '*Please!*'

They were shuffling forward like zombies, their limbs operating without their conscious control.

Hector Shield opened his arms to welcome them in.

CHAPTER TWENTY-THREE
No Escape

With a deafening crash, a bookcase collapsed in front of the twins, directly on top of their father. The falling bookcase dislodged the one next to it, which dislodged the one next to *it*, and soon the library was full of tumbling books and the shelves that had once held them. The twins reeled backwards, released from The Evil the moment its attention was diverted. They blinked and shook their heads, feeling the horrible soul-sapping influence ebb.

'Got him!' cried Kyle, hopping in victory among the tumbled books and high-fiving Tara.

'Is that really your dad?' she asked the twins, poking a limp, outstretched hand with her toe. 'And I thought *mine* was a loser.'

'He's not a loser,' said Jack, hoping Hector was just unconscious under the mountain of books. 'He's just . . . it's not . . .'

'He's not your father,' said Rodeo Dave, clambering out of a pile of books. 'This is what I've been trying to tell you. He's not who he seems.'

'Then who is he really?' asked Jaide. 'Dad's identical twin?'

She had meant it as a joke, but even as she spoke the words, she was struck by the force of them. So was Jack. It couldn't be true, could it? If it was, that changed everything . . .

'There's no time to explain,' Rodeo Dave said urgently. 'Make for the gates and get the card to safety.'

'What about you?' asked Kyle.

'I'll follow. Don't worry about The Evil attacking me. The card is what it wants. Go!'

They didn't need to be told twice. Jaide and Jack led the charge through the castle and back out into the grounds, with Tara and Kyle hot on their heels and Cornelia above, matching their pace.

Outside, the night was storm-wracked and furious. Wind buffeted them from all sides. Rain lashed their faces. It was difficult to talk and very nearly impossible to see where they were going. They could only find the road leading to the gate and remain on it by bending low, holding each other to stay together as they ran around the lake.

Jack glanced behind him and saw several dark shapes running after them. It was hard to tell from the water in his eyes, but it looked like chimps on wolf-back again. Their eyes shone like cold stars, fixed permanently on the children's retreating backs.

'And The Evil is . . .?' shouted Kyle over the sound of the storm.

'Evil!' said Jack.

'Why?'

'I don't know.'

'Like you didn't know your dad had an identical twin?'

'We don't . . . that is, he doesn't . . . I mean . . .'

The unreality of the situation struck him hard. He couldn't decide what was weirder – that The Evil had somehow created a mirror image of their father to lure them into a trap, or that Hector Shield really did have a twin brother he had never told them about.

Despite the storm and The Evil and everything else that was going on, the weirdest thing in Jack's life was suddenly the realisation that he might have an uncle he hadn't heard of before.

'Where are the reinforcements?' shouted Tara as the gates loomed ahead.

'I can't see anyone,' said Jaide, scanning the road outside. She had been randomly trying Gifts while they ran and had stumbled across Jack's Gift by accident. Using the Gift, she could see the white-eyed animals trailing them with chilling clarity. The chimps weren't riding the wolves: they were now part of them, like miniature wild centaurs. And they were catching up fast.

Any hope of escape through the gates was snatched from them when the gates themselves came alive and slammed shut in their path.

++Halt!++

311

The metal whale woven into the gates flapped its tail and snapped its jaws at them. The four kids retreated.

'That way!' shouted Jaide, pointing. Through the wind and rain the stone walls of a building were visible near the gates. The porter's lodge, Tara's father had called it. It wasn't much, but if they could barricade the doors behind them, that would at least slow The Evil down.

Jack used his grandfather's skeleton key to unlock the front door, and they tumbled inside, one after the other.

'This is where he died, isn't it?' said Tara, flicking on a light switch and looking around. 'Young Master Rourke, I mean.'

'I think you're right,' said Kyle.

Cornelia swooped with practised ease around light fittings, coat racks and high-backed chairs, and occupied a familiar perch on a curtain rail in the main room.

'Rourke,' she said, dipping her head. 'Daft old fool.'

A chill wind whipped round the room, riffling book covers, swaying the sheets that covered the furniture and making Tara shiver from more than just nervousness. It felt ghostly, but had a natural origin. Jaide had finally got her Gift back.

She tossed the gold card to Jack. 'You want the one that looks like two black eyes.'

'And then it's our turn?' said Kyle.

'I . . . don't think it works like that. Look around for weapons. Anything will do.'

Jack found the symbol Jaide described and swapped his

new Gift for the one he had been born with. His confidence returned the moment his shadow sight was restored. This was a Gift he knew. It might be wild and crazy sometimes, but he understood it. It was part of him.

'Here,' he said, giving the card to Tara. 'Keep hold of it and it'll protect you like it protected Cornelia. If Kyle's eyes start to glow, give it to him.'

'We can share it,' she said, offering one edge of it to Kyle, who gripped it tightly between the fingers of his left hand. In his right, he held two pokers that he had found next to the fireplace. He gave one to Tara and she hefted it with relish. Cornelia launched herself off the curtain rail and landed awkwardly on her shoulder.

'Man the cannons,' she squawked.

'I just want to say,' said Kyle, 'that this is the best fun I have ever had.'

Before either Jack or Jaide could reply, the windows smashed in. At the same time something large and heavy came down the chimney in an explosion of ashen mud.

The four protectors of the golden card instinctively put their backs to each other, facing outward to meet the enemy equipped with nothing but pokers and their Gifts.

This time The Evil attacked without words, sensing its goal was within reach. The animals were silent too, not wasting energy on snarling or growling. They just came for the twins and their friends in a silent rush, armed with teeth and claws and all the cold force of the alien intelligence controlling them. There were the two wolf-chimps, plus the other members of the menagerie crossed with all the night creatures The Evil had scared from burrow or nest across the estate. There were at least three owl-lemurs, six deranged possums with eight legs and two heads, and one zebra-warthog that was too horrible to describe.

Behind them all came the stifling will of The Evil, striving to snuff every human thought from those who stood in its way.

Jaide whipped up several whirlwinds that plucked The Evil's creatures and tossed them round the room. The whirlwinds also tipped up furniture and rattled the roof and doors, threatening to tear them from their hinges, but for once this was OK. Jaide wanted her Gift to go crazy and she found it harder than expected to really let go. She had spent so long trying to control her Gift, it felt wrong to do otherwise.

Jack's struggle was no different. Putting out all the lights wasn't going to help anyone except him, since Tara and Kyle needed to poke their pokers every time an inquisitive snout snapped too close, but apart from that he was free to do anything. He threw palm-sized patches of darkness like shadowy daggers, temporarily blinding his targets. He pushed possessed creatures into the shadows at his feet, where they struggled and flailed until they finally emerged into full solidity and the light. He danced round the room like a ghost, shadow-walking too fast for anything to get a solid grip on him.

But still, despite all their efforts, the twins were nipped and scratched and clawed. Their clothes offered little protection against wild animals filled with the fury of The Evil. Steadily and silently, not caring how *they* were injured, the circle of animals pressed closer and closer to the card.

Jaide decided to risk all on a desperate gambit.

'When I say duck –' she cried.

'We duck?' said Tara, clouting a determined wolf across the snout with her poker.

'Exactly.' Jaide took a deep breath, gathering as much air into her lungs as she could. 'OK . . . duck!'

The four of them dropped to the ground, even Cornelia, who adopted a dive-bombing posture and landed in Kyle's lap. Jaide blew upwards with her lips pursed as though whistling, but what emerged was a new vortex, one denser and more powerful than any she had created before. It hung above them, sucking all of the smaller hurricanes into itself, dragging all of the animals they held with them, and becoming stronger in the process. The vortex whirled and roared above their heads, pulling in furniture and everything else not fastened down.

Jack grabbed Jaide's wrist and pulled her out from under the base of the vortex. He could tell from the way the funnel was dancing that it wanted to touch down, but it was trying to avoid hurting them. Tara pulled Cornelia and Kyle after them.

The moment they were out of the way, the vortex snapped

like a living whip, smashing down through the floor and up against the ceiling, flattening out in a spreading mushroom cloud, gaining more strength as it grew. Even the largest of The Evil's creatures, the hideous zebra-warthog, was pulled steadily into it, no matter how its clawed feet scratched at the floor. It fell sideways with a roar, and they saw it tumbling and flailing in ever tightening circles, mixed up with the other animals, its white eyes blazing in anger.

The Evil wasn't done yet. Confined to the vortex as they were, it was easy for the animals to merge into the giant monster they had seen by the castle. But Jack was ready for it. He stretched the night in through the windows like toffee, winding it round the creature's many heads and blinding it.

The creature roared and reached out for them anyway, flailing with hand and hoof and claw.

Every time one of the limbs threatened to come close, Tara and Kyle whacked it with a poker, forcing it to retreat.

The vortex spun. The animals spun with it. For a long minute, nothing else changed.

Slowly, warily, Jaide, Jack, Kyle and Tara stood up and faced The Evil in its prison of wind and darkness.

They looked at one another, bloodied and soaked through, clothes torn and dishevelled, the Card of Translocation gleaming in Tara's hand.

'Is that it?' asked Kyle. 'Have we won?'

At that moment the ceiling burst open and something

bright flashed down into the centre of the room. An explosive force flung the four children back against the walls, stunning them momentarily. The vortex trembled and Jaide reached out with both hands to control it. Jack pulled more of the night into the room, winding ropes of deepest black round the creatures it contained.

'Wait,' said Tara, 'I think there's someone in there!'

Jack peered through the roiling wind. A flash of lightning blinded his sensitive sight, but he did glimpse the figure of a man spread-eagled in the tumultuous wind. Lightning flashed again, and the vortex rocked and swayed. Jaide tried to bring it into line, but when lightning flashed a third time, the vortex wriggled like a belly dancer and spat a familiar figure out on the ruined floor.

A man who looked exactly like Hector Shield landed on his hands and knees, spluttering, glasses completely missing, a familiar pitted iron rod raised waveringly in one hand.

Jack and Jaide just stared at him, the echoes of a very loud thunderclap still ringing in their ears. Was this man their father or some Evil impersonation?

Then with a roar, a sabretoothed tiger leaped through the hole in the roof, closely followed by a much smaller ginger shadow. Custer and Ari took a protective stance between the twins and the vortex as above them all a helicopter swung into view, downdraught and spotlight only adding to the confusion.

'Keep back,' said the man who might or might not be their father. 'Let us . . . uh . . . that is . . .'

The vortex had returned to its former state, with The Evil firmly trapped inside. To illustrate the point, Kyle jabbed a passing possum with his poker, making it retreat into the swirling mass of mixed-up bodies.

The sabretoothed tiger circled the vortex once, then sat on its haunches at Hector Shield's side.

'We've arrived too late, Hector,' it said in Custer's voice.

'Do you think?' added Ari, staring up in awe at Jack and Jaide.

The twins had eyes only for their father. It had to be him now, if Custer said so.

'Come here, troubletwisters,' he said, opening his arms as his twin had, and this time they ran to him without hesitation.

Above them, the chopper came low over the ruined roof, swaying from side to side in the vortex's updraught.

'Is anyone harmed?' came Grandma X's voice over the helicopter's loudspeaker.

Hector took his arm from round Jaide's shoulders and gave her an enthusiastic thumbs up.

'Good work, troubletwisters,' said Grandma X, and the twins glowed with pride. 'Your mother says that this time the grown-ups will do the cleaning up.'

CHAPTER TWENTY-FOUR

Not All Twins are Troubletwisters

The helicopter put down behind the porter's lodge, allowing its passengers to step out on to solid ground. Grandma X was wearing a long coat over her hospital gown. Susan Shield raised an umbrella once they were clear of the rotors and steadied the older woman as they crossed to the lodge's back door. Kleo ran with them, keeping close to their heels in order to share the umbrella.

Arrayed around the lodge, next to several incongruous suits of armour frozen in mid-step, were a number of familiar faces: Aleksandr, Roberta Gendry, Phanindranath . . . The Wardens had come when called, but they were keeping well back now. They understood that this was no ordinary attack by The Evil. This was personal.

Custer greeted them inside the lodge, in human form.

'I'm on my way to get him,' was all he said.

Grandma X nodded with a weariness that had nothing to do with tranquillisers or other modern drugs.

'Be kind,' she said, 'but firm. I want to see him.'

He nodded. They went inside.

The lodge was ruined, gutted by wind and rain. Everything Young Master Rourke had owned that wasn't already boxed up was now soaked through or torn to shreds. The ceiling sagged. Floorboards curled under sodden carpet. Even the wallpaper was peeling from the walls.

The source of the destructive force stood on either side of their father. Behind them were two more children and a parrot. They should have been shivering in the cold and wet, but their faces said it all. They were beaming, proud of what they had done. Success kept them warm.

Near them, hissing like a fat, bloated snake, was the black-striped vortex containing what remained of The Evil, evidence that they had done very well indeed.

'Grandma!' the troubletwisters cried, interrupting their explanation of what had happened to greet the new arrivals. 'And Mum – what are you doing here?'

'Your grandmother . . . appeared to me,' said Susan. 'She said you were in danger. The chopper was the fastest means we had of getting here.'

'I heard the call of the Living Ward,' Grandma X explained. 'Custer was summoned by Ari.'

The ginger cat looked smug. 'He didn't believe me at first, but the smell of wolf on me was a bit of a giveaway.'

Susan looked around in amazement and alarm at the damage, at the vortex, and finally at the twins' father.

'*Were* you in danger?' she asked them all. 'Because that wasn't why we moved here.'

'That discussion can wait,' said Grandma X, opening her arms. 'Come here and give me that wretched card.'

They ran to her and hugged her, and after a moment Susan hugged them too.

Tara hesitantly approached the huddle, holding the Card of Translocation tightly in one hand. She was reluctant to give it up. She had seen its power and wanted more than just a glimpse of it.

'Here,' she said, winning the war within herself and offering it to Grandma X. 'I guess you'll know what to do with it.'

'Thank you, Tara. So, the Gift of Translocation. That's what this is all about.'

Grandma X took the card from her and studied it for a long moment.

'Let's see. It must be here somewhere . . . ' Symbols flashed by, as mysterious as the Gifts they represented. One appeared, one they had glimpsed before – a square with a straight line drawn through it. 'Ah yes. Butler's Gift, lost for forty years.'

Grandma X raised the card and something changed. Jack and Jaide felt it, although they couldn't have defined how or where they were feeling it.

Then the animals in the vortex started howling in terror, and they knew what had happened. The wards were back, reactivated by the Gift Grandma X had found. With the return of the wards, The Evil was driven out, and that left its creatures behind, afraid and confused.

'Oh,' said Jaide, 'those poor animals.'

She clapped her hands as she had seen Grandma X do and her Gift, weary from so much exertion, relaxed instantly. The vortex collapsed, the binds of blindness that stopped the animals from seeing unwound too, as Jack followed Jaide's lead. The animals staggered dizzily free.

Kyle stepped forward. 'Hey, Chippy, here.'

One of the chimps lurched to him and climbed up into his arms, scratching its head in confusion.

'Flippy?'

The second chimp joined him.

'We'd better get them back in their cages,' Kyle said, 'and all the others before they run away again.'

'Tara, will you help him?' said Grandma X.

Tara eyed the wolves with wary scepticism. 'Will they do as they're told?'

'Sure they will,' said Kyle, 'if you call them by name. Come, Tasker. Come, Kress. You'll be good for me, won't you?'

'Ari, Kleo,' said Grandma X, 'go with them. They should be safe, now the wards are back up. I have shifted the boundaries slightly to include the lodge and the rest of the estate.'

The wolves shook their furry flanks and followed as Kyle led the animals out of the room in a ragtag line.

All except Cornelia, who flapped warily back to her perch as Ari passed by.

'You don't have to worry about me,' the cat said as he trailed after the other animals. 'I only eat free range.'

That left just Grandma X, Susan, Hector and the twins. Jack and Jaide returned to their father's side, so glad to be near him again, but wary of their Gifts playing up. Fortunately both Gifts were exhausted and content to remain quiescent, for now.

'How did you know to come?' Jaide asked him.

'The Evil was keeping me busy in Bologna,' he said. 'Much busier than usual, which should have made me suspicious, on top of your grandma's accident. I called a couple of times, but kept missing everyone. That was The Evil distracting you too, I guess. But then I felt you begging me – like I was there talking to you, when I couldn't possibly be. There was only one way that could be happening.'

'It was dangerous for you to come here,' Grandma X said to him, 'but I'm glad you did. We need to be together for what comes next.'

'I wish someone would explain what's going on,' said Susan in a strangled tone, as though she didn't really want to know at all.

'You're right, dear,' said Grandma X. 'Some of it the troubletwisters might already have guessed, because they are always so curious . . . so determined to know everything. I can assure you you won't be any gladder for having the answers, Jack and Jaide. I wasn't. And neither was your father.'

There was movement in the doorway. They turned as one to see Rodeo Dave and Custer leading a beaten man into the room. He looked almost but not exactly like Hector Shield. Now they were face to face, the twins could detect subtle differences between them. One had a harder expression, as though he had known more doubt and suffering in his life, while the other – the father they knew and loved, *their* Hector Shield – had laughter lines and kindly eyes, even when directed at the man who had tried to give them up to The Evil.

'This man,' Hector said, as though confessing to a terrible crime, 'is Harold . . . my twin brother.'

Susan gaped at him, and the twins were no less surprised, even though the possibility had occurred to them earlier. Fantastical though it seemed, it was the only explanation that made any sense. But it opened up a whole new world of questions. If their father was a twin just like them, why had he kept that a secret from them all their lives? What had happened between him and his brother to make them hate each other?

'Don't look so appalled, troubletwisters,' said the uncle they had never known they had. 'Blood is thicker than water. Isn't that what they say?'

'You shouldn't have come here,' Hector said in a low, almost dangerous tone that the twins had never heard before. 'But I suppose you've wanted this ever since you fell to The Evil.'

'*Fell?*' Harold Shield's eyebrows went up into his sopping fringe. 'I gave myself up willingly, so you could live! The least you could do is be grateful.'

'For putting everyone I love in terrible danger? I'll never forgive you for that. And neither will Mother.'

'Oh, yes, take her side, just like you always did.'

'Only because she's right, and you know it.'

'You never see my side.'

Hector took a deep breath, visibly controlling himself. 'You pretended to be me. You sent an agent of The Evil into Portland to put Mother in hospital. You kept Custer and me busy so we would be out of the picture. You stole what wasn't yours.'

'*He* gave it away,' Harold said, tipping his head at Rodeo Dave. 'He hid it so well he even erased his own memory of it, so he couldn't get it back when the old man died. The fool!'

'Killer!' squawked Cornelia from her perch.

'*Did* you kill Young Master Rourke?' asked Jack.

'No! I wanted to ask him what he knew, but his heart was weak. He died before he could tell me anything.'

'So you tricked the children instead, *my* children.' Hector Shield had never looked so angry as he did at that moment. 'You *used* them.'

'I just wanted to know them!'

'You could have known them,' Hector said. 'You would

have been welcome. But you chose a different path. You chose The Evil.'

Harold Shield sagged with a cry of pain and put his hands over his face.

'It chose me,' Harold sobbed. A light rain began to fall inside the room. 'It knew I was the weak one. But I've tried to hold it back. I honestly tried to save the troubletwisters. The Evil said it would spare them if I gave the card to it . . . it said . . . it said . . .'

'It deceived you,' said Grandma X, looking even older and smaller than she had in the hospital. 'That's all it ever does.'

He just shook his head.

'What are you going to do with him?' asked Jaide.

'Do?' Grandma X turned to face her, and some of her usual stature returned. 'Wardens don't have executioners. We don't have prisons, or even laws, as the rest of the world would understand them. We have only one punishment for those who betray us.'

'Please,' sobbed Harold. 'Please . . . don't . . .'

Grandma X shook her head. Hector turned his back. Susan and the twins watched, unable to look away.

'I'm sorry, Harold,' she said, raising the Card of Translocation and pointing at him, 'more sorry than I suppose you can imagine . . . but you brought this upon yourself.'

The gold card turned blank for an instant, then revealed a new symbol, a curling raindrop – Harold Shield's Gift.

He hung his head and wept in silence. The gentle rain falling in the porter's lodge turned to mist and faded away.

Grandma X put the card in the pocket of her overcoat.

'I believe I saw some armour outside,' she said. 'They can hold him while we attend to other business.'

She snapped her fingers. Thudding footfalls sounded in the corridor and two formerly Evil suits of armour entered the room.

'Watch this man,' she told them. 'Do not let him leave. I will return you to your rest when I come back.'

They bowed and took Rodeo Dave and Custer's places at Harold's side, gripping him with strong metal fingers.

'Now,' said Grandma X, 'is there anyone we haven't accounted for?'

'Thomas Solomon,' said Jack. 'And Professor Olafsson.'

'Professor who?' asked Custer.

'A rather unique individual,' said Rodeo Dave. 'He advised me on how to hide my Gift.'

'And he helped us find it again,' said Jaide. 'We left him in Zebediah.'

Grandma X nodded. 'We'll go and get him now, and pick up any other pieces that might reveal what happened here.'

'Literally,' said Jack, thinking of the broken death mask as well as the bent cross-continuum conduit constructor, abandoned in the library.

They filed outside, leaving Harold Shield slumped in the

arms of the suits of armour. The lingering rain lacked the fury of earlier bursts, but the ground remained sodden and treacherous. Jaide hung back to help Rodeo Dave, who she only now realised was wearing slippers instead of proper shoes. He slipped several times on the slick grass before reaching the rougher road surface.

'I'm sorry we crashed Zebediah,' she said.

'No matter,' he said. 'My old companion still has a few tricks. The dents will be gone by tomorrow.'

'The car was your Warden Companion?' she asked, amazed.

'Never a finer example,' he said with a grin.

She supposed that wasn't the weirdest thing she had learned that night.

'I can't believe my dad's a twin,' she said.

'Not all twins are troubletwisters,' said Rodeo Dave, as though reciting a riddle, 'but all troubletwisters are twins.'

Jaide had heard something like that before, from her early days in Portland. *All troubletwisters are twins, but not all twins are troubletwisters*, Grandma X had told them, but Jaide hadn't stopped to untangle it then. There had been more pressing concerns, like discovering she had Gifts and her father and grandmother were Wardens. She thought about it now though, and began to understand that it was a thing of great importance.

'So just because someone's born a twin,' she said, 'that doesn't automatically make them a troubletwister.'

'Correct, Jaide.'

'But every troubletwister has a twin, like I do. And dad does. And you do . . .?'

'And Custer, and your grandmother. All of us do.'

'So where's *your* twin?'

'She . . . well, she's dead, Jaide. Her Gift gave her the power of language: she could understand and be understood by anyone. But she didn't understand herself, and that, ultimately, was her undoing.'

They curled slowly round the lake, far behind Grandma X and the others. Jack walked between Susan and Hector. Jaide felt a tiny pang of jealousy. She wished she was in his place, standing next to her father and mother like everything was normal.

'The Gift I was born with was the Gift of Translocation,' Rodeo Dave said, although Jaide hadn't asked. 'It's a great burden, one only a few in every generation bear. It's only ever used on Wardens who have gone bad, as you've seen, so The Evil can't gain their Gifts for its own use, or so their Gifts won't be used against ordinary people, but it's still robbing a Warden of everything they are, leaving them empty. I began to feel like an executioner. It made me hate my Gift, and the way my fellow Wardens made me use it, but I couldn't give it up completely. That's why I made the card and put my own Gift into it, along with all the other Gifts I had taken. Then I hid it in a place I thought it would never be discovered. I set charms to protect it and warn me if it was ever disturbed. I made a bookmark to remind me where it was, if I ever needed it again.

'But everything went wrong,' he said with a hangdog look. 'I forgot too much. I even lost the bookmark – I guess it went with a book I gave to George. And Harold must have watched me for years, noticing how much time I spent on the estate with my old friend, and guessed that was where my Gift was hidden. When George died, I knew I had to recover the card before it fell into the wrong person's hands – I remembered that much – but I couldn't remember where I had hidden it of course. I couldn't go back to your grandmother to ask for my memories back, because that memory was hidden with the card. I didn't even remember asking her to take the memories out of my head, along with most of my memories of being a Warden. It was too hard, you see, to live life as an ordinary man, knowing what I had lost.'

Jaide couldn't imagine what it would be like to voluntarily give up her Gift, or come to hate it as much as he had. But she had never once thought of Rodeo Dave as *ordinary*.

'We thought the card would just move you somewhere else,' she said. 'That's why we used it. I'm really sorry about that too.'

He smiled. 'No need to apologise. I would have done the same in your shoes. And you've learned to your cost what it really does, haven't you?'

She nodded gravely, thinking of what had been done to her uncle.

'Somewhere deep inside,' Rodeo Dave said, as though reading her mind, 'I believe that Harold is still fighting. He has not, and perhaps never will be, totally subsumed by The Evil.'

At the head of the group, Hector was answering some of Jack's questions, with Susan listening in, not saying anything for now. Harold had betrayed the Wardens a year before Susan had met the twins' father. His betrayal had taken place in the Pacific, during a mighty battle Custer had mentioned briefly once before. He had returned several times since then, during the twins' childhood, but Hector had always managed to keep him at bay.

'The Evil is cunning,' he said, 'but not as cunning as a person. And Harold was always the smarter of the two of us. I don't know exactly what he was doing, but it is clear he can operate independently of The Evil, at least for a time. He had his own agenda. When Harold fought off The Evil when you left the wards, he was acting to prevent The Evil from jumping the gun, not out of any kindness for your sakes.'

But Jack remembered Harold saying that he had wanted to see them. He was sure that part of him wanted to meet his niece and nephew, even as another part planned to betray them in the near future.

'What happens to him now?' asked Jack. 'Are you just

going to let him go? He could still be dangerous, even without his Gift.'

'We'll take his memories,' said Hector. 'He'll forget being a Warden, like Rodeo Dave did. He'll forget his Gift, The Evil . . . all of us.'

'I don't know if that's a mercy,' said Susan, 'or the cruellest thing of all.'

Hector reached round behind Jack's head and took her hand. 'You and me both.'

Jack looked up at his parents, together again for the first time in months.

'Is Mum going to forget this too?' he asked.

'Not unless she wants to,' said Hector, glancing back at Grandma X. 'As events proved, she needs to know what's happening at all times, just in case anything ever happens to your grandmother again.'

Susan sighed. 'I think you're right. If I had known what was going on . . . if you and Jaide had been able to talk to me about it, none of this would have happened. So yes, I think it's for the best I stay in the loop. For good.'

Jack smiled with relief. Keeping secrets was hard. He didn't know how Grandma X did it.

The came up the main drive. The wreckage of the golf buggy and Zebediah were to their left, across the sodden lawn. Jack pointed, and they set off through the mud.

They had barely gone five paces when Jack saw a dark

figure rise up out of the car and turn to stare at them.

'Hey, look,' he said. 'There's someone there.'

'Who?' said Grandma X. 'Tell me what you see, Jack.'

'It's not Tara or Kyle, or Custer, or Thomas Solomon . . .' He squinted, straining his Gift to the utmost. Zebediah was still some distance off and it was very dark. But the figure was faintly familiar. It was small . . . a woman perhaps, with tightly pulled-back hair . . .

'It's that new doctor,' he said.

'Dr Witworth?' said Susan. 'What's she doing here?'

'Don't let her get away!' shouted Grandma X.

Witworth had seen them and was already moving, running round Zebediah and across the lawn with something tucked under her arm. Custer snarled and leaped after her. In tiger form he easily outpaced Hector, who had started running the moment Grandma X had shouted. Jack wanted to follow them, but Susan held him back, and his Gift was still too weak to do anything. The twins could only watch as Dr Witworth fled across the estate with the Wardens on her heels.

At first Jack thought she was running for the castle, and Custer clearly thought so too, for he ran at an angle to cut her off. But then she suddenly changed direction, and put on an extra burst of speed. She didn't seem to be running anywhere in particular at all. Just running at random, Jack thought.

'The edge of the estate,' said Jaide coming up alongside him, breathing heavily. 'She's making for the boundary!'

'It's not where it used to be,' said Grandma X, raising the gold card. 'But not much further and it's stretched as far as it can go. There must be *something* I can use in here . . .'

'Sandler's Quake?' suggested Rodeo Dave.

'Too dangerous.'

'What about the Noose of Ceylon?'

'We don't want to kill her, David.'

'What about the one I had for a while?' suggested Jack. 'Running's impossible when your feet are sinking into the ground.'

'Or you could put her to sleep with my other one,' said Jaide, wishing her normal Gift wasn't so exhausted. 'Quickly! She's almost at the trees!'

Witworth looked behind her, and on seeing Custer closing the gap in a long powerful lope and lightning gathering round Hector Shield's upraised hand, she put her head down and took the final yards in a desperate lunge.

Grandma X pointed the card and the trees ahead of the escaping woman shook and rustled. Their branches came alive and laced together, forming an impenetrable net.

Custer leaped, and so did Witworth, right into the arms of the trees.

'Why'd she do that?' asked Jack. 'She can't possibly escape now.'

But then, unbelievably, one of the trees changed. Its knots glowed white and its branches untangled themselves from its neighbours. With a weird, grinding cry, it pulled Witworth up above its crown, so its branches pointed straight up along its trunk, then suddenly it dropped down into the earth, pulled by its roots into the safety of the soil.

It all happened too quickly for Grandma X, Hector or Custer to respond. One second Witworth was there; the next she was gone, rescued by The Evil.

Grandma X muttered something about 'that wretched woman' under her breath and put the card back into her pocket. The trees returned to normal, while Custer and Hector peered warily over the edge of the hole that was all that remained of the tree. The sides were already falling in, softened by the downpour.

'You need a Warden who can turn into a mole,' said Susan.

'Yes indeed,' said Grandma X, putting a hand on her daughter-in-law's shoulder and sharing some of the weight of her suddenly weary body. 'But unfortunately she's in Angola.'

EPILOGUE
The Legacy of the Dead

'So Dr Witworth worked for The Evil,' said Jaide as they waited by the drawbridge for the police to arrive. Thomas Solomon, currently standing guard by the gates, had called Constable Haigh about a natural disaster at the estate once he had woken up and had his memories rearranged to erase anything too weird. The same with the helicopter pilot. Luckily they had seen very little and needed only a small amount of Grandma X's influence to incorporate what they had seen into a freakish weather event, different only in scale to the one that had destroyed the bridge three days earlier.

'So it seems,' said Grandma X.

'But she couldn't have been the sleeper agent,' said Jack. 'She only just arrived in Portland.'

'What makes you think there was a sleeper agent?'

'Well, someone drove you off the road . . .'

'I got a look at his face,' Grandma X said. 'He wasn't from Portland.'

Jaide knew better than to ask if she was certain she knew

everyone in Portland. She probably knew what they had had for dinner every night too.

Hector Shield and Custer returned from a thorough inspection of Zebediah.

'No booby traps,' Hector announced. 'And no Professor Olafsson either.'

Cornelia flew down out of the sky and landed on Jack's shoulder.

'Man overboard,' she said.

'Dr Witworth took him?' Jack said. 'Why?'

'Will he be OK?' Jaide asked.

'That depends on what The Evil wants him for,' said Grandma X. 'He has no Gift, being an echo of himself rather than his true self. He can't be consumed like living things. There seems no obvious reason to kidnap him, apart from his knowledge . . .' She looked around, taking in the night sky, the castle and the Wardens patrolling the estate, looking for any remaining sign of The Evil. 'I wonder if he was what The Evil wanted all along, and everything else was a ruse?'

This was just one more mystery to add to a night full of them.

'Time for some quick final words,' Hector Shield said, squatting down to look both his children in the eye. 'I know you thought Harold was me, and he told you to keep secrets from your mother and your grandmother, and I think we'd all agree that this put everyone in very grave danger. Never again listen to anyone who tries to drive a wedge between you and your family, no matter how trustworthy they might seem.'

They nodded very seriously, wishing they could take back everything that had happened since Monday, when they had first come to the castle . . . except for seeing their real father for the first time in weeks.

He opened his arms and embraced them tightly.

'Do you have to go?' Jack asked, muffled by his shoulder.

'I do,' he said, 'and you know I do. Your Gifts won't stay still much longer. But you also know that I love you and miss you every second of every day. Maybe your mother will let you buy a new SIM card for that phone Harold gave you, so I can tell you so more often.'

Susan looked down at them and, after a moment, nodded.

'This time the communication breakdown was not just at the troubletwister end,' Hector said, standing and turning to Grandma X. 'Harold was always angry at you for keeping secrets. That's a mistake best not repeated, by all of us.'

Grandma X's expression became very hard when her second son's name was mentioned.

'That too,' she said, 'is a discussion that can wait.'

Mother and son embraced briefly in the rain. They separated with shining eyes.

Hector shook hands with Rodeo Dave.

'Thanks for trying to keep the twins out of trouble,' he said.

'Ever a challenge, ever a reward.' Rodeo Dave winked, stepping back.

Hector turned to Susan. 'Are you sure you're OK with this?'

'Nothing you can say will make me feel any better about it,' she said, kissing him firmly on the lips. 'Just stay alive.'

'I will,' he said. 'I've got a lot to live for.'

Susan let Hector go.

'All right,' he said, patting his pockets as though looking for his car keys, 'yes, now it's definitely time to go. Goodbye, goodbye! Wipe that beer from your eye!'

The twins smiled at the latest of their dad's weird sayings as he walked a safe distance from them and slipped the iron rod out of his coat pocket. He waved it in front of him and the rain took on an electric smell. Jaide put her fingers in her ears. Last time she had seen Hector do this, her ears had rung for an hour.

Lightning stabbed out of the sky, striking the ground exactly where he was standing. The thunderclap felt like the world ending.

When light and sound had passed, Hector Shield was gone.

'Whoa,' said a voice from behind them. 'Did you see that?'

'I told you, Kyle. These guys are incredible.'

Tara ran to examine the smoking ground where the twins' father had stood, then she looked straight up.

'Gone, just like that! Amazing.'

'Are the animals back in their pens?' Grandma X asked in a calming voice.

'All accounted for,' said Kyle, 'except for Nellie here.'

Cornelia did her best to hide behind Jack's head, but her tail feathers gave her away.

'I don't think she wants to stay here,' Jack said. 'Can she come home with us, Grandma?'

'If that's what she wants, I don't know how we could stop her. Susan?'

'Sure, but Jack has to feed her and clean her cage whenever he's told to.'

'Easy!'

Cornelia bobbed up and down. 'Nellie wants a nut.'

Pleased, Jack reached into his pockets to see if he had anything edible in there to give her, but found only a scrap of paper and something round and metallic.

Grandma X waved Tara and Kyle over to her. 'You two, I want to have a private chat with you about what you saw tonight.'

'No way,' Tara said. 'This happened last time. I don't want to forget. I want to tell everyone how incredible Jack and Jaide are!'

'That's exactly what we can't have you doing.'

Grandma X raised the moonstone ring she wore on her right hand and held it before Tara's eyes.

'Oooh, pretty,' Tara said in distant voice. 'So . . . pretty . . .'

Kyle's eyes crossed and his mouth drooped open.

'Very good,' said Grandma X. 'Now, I can't go erasing your memories every time you see something you shouldn't. It's bad for a young mind to be tampered with too often. Instead I will silence you. Not completely; on every other subject you can speak as freely as you ever did. But on anything to do with The Evil and the Wardens and my two troubletwisters here, you can say nothing at all – unless it is to one of us. Do you understand?'

The pair nodded with a solemnity beyond their years. Then Kyle sneezed with such explosive force that Cornelia took off with a squawk, dispelling the seriousness of the moment.

'Let's head back to the lodge,' said Susan, 'Much better than standing here, catching colds.'

She took Kyle and Tara in her arms and guided them down the hill, closely tailed by Grandma X. The twins and Rodeo Dave lingered a moment, looking up at the castle wall.

'George wants all this to go to the town, you know,' said Rodeo Dave, 'to be turned into a whaling museum. A memorial to the whales themselves too.'

'Do you think that'll happen?'

'Oh, the mayor will fight the idea of a memorial, and we both know that developers are already itching to get their hands on it, but I figure it will work out how George wanted. He had a stubborn streak, expensive lawyers and a good heart. That's a rare combination.'

He glanced at Jack, who was examining the two things he had found in his pockets. The paper was the scrap of dictionary Cornelia had given her in school earlier that day, with the word *twister* on it. Looking at it again, he saw another word, one that had a whole new significance after the night's revelations.

'Look.' He showed Jaide. 'Cornelia wasn't telling us that she knew we were troubletwisters at all.'

She looked at the word he was indicating. '*Twin*. She was telling us Harold was Dad's brother and we never realised!'

'Rourke,' said the macaw smugly, although now it sounded more like an ordinary squawk than anyone's name.

'That's one smart bird,' said Rodeo Dave, peering down at Jack's left hand. 'And what's the other thing in your hand?'

Jack held up the locket he had taken from the painting. He opened it and the three of them looked inside.

'I thought so,' said Rodeo Dave. 'Dear me, that takes me back.'

'Is that . . . you?' asked Jaide, recognising in the picture the phantom of a young man that had chased them across the estate. 'With *Grandma*?'

'No,' he said. 'That's your grandmother's sister.'

'Her twin?' asked Jaide.

'Of course,' said Rodeo Dave. 'I didn't even recognise the painting of her until my memories returned.'

'Was her name Lottie?' Jack asked.

'How did you . . .? Ah, the inscription. Yes, that's what we called her.'

'That wasn't her real name?'

'No. It was . . .' He stopped himself. 'I know where this is headed. If I tell you, you'll only try to find her in the Portland records, and then you'll be one step closer to finding out the name your grandmother was born with.' He shook his head. 'Well, that's none of my business. If she wants to tell you about that, she can do it herself. So you can forget about me giving you any help on that front. All right?'

The twins nodded. They hadn't been thinking anything of the sort, but they were now. How many Lotties could there be in one small town?

'What happened to her?' asked Jaide.

His face fell.

'That was a long time ago,' was all he would say. 'What's done is done and best put behind us.'

'David?'

He looked up when Grandma X called his name and waved to indicate that he would come over.

'And now I'm going to forget it all over again,' he told the twins. 'It's a relief frankly. I feel better knowing that you'll remember – and I'll be grateful to both of you if you say nothing to remind me afterwards.'

They stared at him, stunned, and nodded, one at a time.

'Thank you.'

He strode heavily to join their grandmother, who whispered into his ear too softly for anyone else to hear.

'Something terrible must have happened to Lottie,' whispered Jaide.

'Maybe she died,' said Jack. 'Or The Evil took her.'

'Like Rodeo Dave's sister.'

'And Dad's brother . . .'

They stood with their heads together, both struck by the same terrible thought.

All the Wardens they knew had been twins, just like Jack and Jaide. All of them had lost a sibling too. Now they were all alone.

'What are the odds of that?' Jaide asked.

Jack shook his head, remembering something The Evil had told them when it had killed the last living ward.

One always falls. Thus it has always been, and thus it will always be.

Could this have been what it was talking about?

'No more secrets,' said Jaide in her most determined voice. 'From now on we make Grandma tell us about our family, about The Evil, about being troubletwisters . . . everything.'

Jack nodded, although he suspected that convincing Grandma X of this might be the hardest thing they had ever attempted.

The rain was easing off. Somewhere nearby, a frog was croaking. The flashing lights of a police car were coming up the drive. Together, Jack and Jaide went down the hill to where the others were waiting.

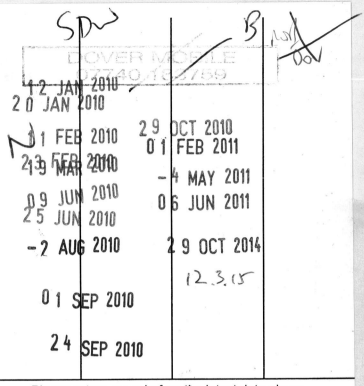

*Published by Constable & Robinson Ltd

www.constablerobinson.com

Sheer Folly

A Daisy Dalrymple Mystery

CAROLA DUNN

ROBINSON
London

Constable & Robinson Ltd
3 The Lanchesters
162 Fulham Palace Rd
London W6 9ER
www.constablerobinson.com

First published in the US, 2009 by
St Martin's Press, New York

First UK edition published by Robinson,
an imprint of Constable & Robinson Ltd, 2009

A copy of the British Library Cataloguing in
Publication Data is available from the British Library

ISBN: 978-1-84901-121-1

Printed and bound in the EU

When lovely woman stoops to folly,
And finds too late that men betray,
What charm can soothe her melancholy?
What art can wash her guilt away?

The only art her guilt to cover,
To hide her shame from every eye,
To give repentance to her lover,
And wring his bosom is – to die.

– Oliver Goldsmith, 'When Lovely
Woman Stoops to Folly'

CHAPTER 1

'Daisy, do you really need to stay away over the weekend?' Alec asked plaintively, folding the *News Chronicle* and pushing back his chair from the table. 'There's just a chance I may actually get a couple of days off. You've got egg on your chin.'

'No! How careless.' Daisy dabbed with a napkin. 'As far as my work is concerned, I could easily manage the writing part for the book in a couple of days, though I do hope I might get an article out of it as well. Lucy's photographs are the trouble. She has to hope the weather will cooperate, and one can't exactly count on it in March. Three or four days gives her a better chance of getting decent conditions.'

'Surely you don't have to stay to hold her hand!'

'But you see, darling, in this case I rather do.'

'Are we talking about the same Lucy? Lady Gerald?'

'Yes, of course.'

'I don't believe Lucy ever needed her hand held in her life!'

'The trouble is,' Daisy explained with a sigh, 'she doesn't care for the man who presently owns Appsworth Hall and its folly.'

'What's wrong with him? I don't know that I want to let you go and stay with – '

'Darling, you've gone all medieval again. Victorian, at least. This is 1926! You don't *let* me do things, remember? Anyway, there's nothing wrong with the poor man except that he's a manufacturer of bathroom fixtures.'

Alec burst out laughing. 'I can't see how you persuaded her to visit him in the first place! Not that she has any justification for such an attitude. Didn't you tell me her great-grandfather was a manufacturer of umbrella silk?'

'Great-great, I think. I suspect that's why she's so touchy,' said Daisy, the origin of whose family's title was lost in the mists of time.

Lucy, granddaughter of an earl and Daisy's closest friend, had been very difficult when Daisy first started going about with a middle-class policeman, albeit a Detective Chief Inspector from Scotland Yard. In fact she had disapproved quite as strongly as had Daisy's mother, the Dowager Lady Dalrymple. Unlike the viscountess, she had revised her opinion and given a qualified approval when he promised to support Daisy's writing career even after they married. Lucy, too, was a career-woman, continuing her photography studio since marrying the easy-going Lord Gerald Bincombe.

But writing, photography, and even detecting were one thing. Manufacturing bathroom fixtures was another, quite beyond the pale.

'It wasn't easy to get her to agree,' Daisy admitted.

'Haven't you collected enough follies for your book to skip this one?'

'We have towers, temples, cloisters, pillars, and fake medieval ruins aplenty, even a campanile, but not a single grotto. Appsworth has the best grotto in the country. There are a couple of others, but they've rather been let go to rack and ruin. Mr. Pritchard – '

'Of Pritchard's Plumbing Products?' Alec laughed again. 'The man behind the blue PPP insignia in half the wash-basins and lavatories in the country? Instigator of a million vulgar jokes?'

'Lucy seems to think it makes it worse that it's one of the biggest concerns in the country. Our Mr. Pritchard is semi-retired and Chairman of the Board – or something of the kind – I believe. But if he weren't so successful, he wouldn't be rich enough to have bought Appsworth Hall and done a marvellous job of restoring the grotto. Or so we've heard.'

'All modern plumbing?'

His teasing grin made Daisy's lips twitch, but she said, 'It wouldn't surprise me in the least. There's a stream running through it, and it's chalk and limestone country, the Marlborough Downs, where streams tend to appear and disappear whenever they feel like it.'

'Do you have to go this week?'

'March isn't the best time of year for outdoor photography, but our publisher is baying at our heels. Besides, we're invited for this week, for the long weekend, and having accepted, one can't simply say, "Oh, sorry, it's rather inconvenient, may we come next week?" That's another reason it wouldn't be at all the thing to duck out and come home for the weekend.'

'I could ring up, when I know whether I'm really getting time off, and claim a family emergency.'

'Darling, I'm shocked!' she told him severely. 'A policeman inventing an alibi? Well, not an alibi, exactly, but I call it disgraceful. What is the world coming to? I'll tell you what, though: When I get down there, I'll see if I can cadge an invitation for you to join us.'

'All I wanted,' he said mournfully, 'is a quiet day at home with you and the babies.'

'Oh dear, I can't very well expect the poor man to invite the twins and Nurse Gilpin, too.'

'No, that would be a bit much. How on earth did you manage to wangle an invitation from Pritchard's Plumbing in the first place?'

'It's a long story, involving a cousin of Gerald's in the Ministry of Health, an old school friend, Mr. Pritchard's fondness for titles, and ... But you're going to be late, darling. In spite of her reluctance, it's Lucy's doing. I'm not sure I've got it all straight, and you wouldn't believe it anyway.'

Alec came round the table and kissed her. 'I wouldn't believe it from anyone but you, love. You're leaving this afternoon?'

'Yes, Lucy's coming to lunch, then we're driving down.'

'Lucy's driving?' At her nod, he groaned.

'You may need our car.'

'True. Ring up this evening to tell me you got there safely, will you? Leave a message if I'm not home yet.'

'Right-oh, darling.' Daisy stood up and gave him a hug. 'I'll probably see you Sunday evening. We can stretch the weekend till Monday if necessary, but Lucy's not likely to want to, as long as we have decent weather for her shots. Unless you'll come to join us?'

'I'll leave it to you to assess the situation. It's up to you to decide whether I want to meet the Bathroom King, work permitting, and whether he wants to meet me.'

Alec went off to catch criminals, and Daisy went up to the nursery.

Mrs. Gilpin ruled the nursery, but she had long since been induced to concede that Daisy and Alec might visit Miranda and Oliver whenever they chose. They were even allowed to take their own children out for a walk without Nurse tagging along, though the nurserymaid, Bertha, usually acted as her deputy. Nonetheless, Nurse Gilpin was always cock-a-hoop when Daisy went out of town for a few days, as her work sometimes required, leaving the twins in their nanny's sole charge.

This led Daisy to put off informing her of an impending absence till the last minute. Of course she always gave the housekeeper, Mrs. Dobson, plenty of warning. From Mrs. Dobson to the parlourmaid, Elsie, was no distance; from Elsie to Bertha, little further; and whatever Bertha knew, Nurse Gilpin knew.

As Daisy opened the nursery door, five pairs of eyes turned her way. Three small bodies launched themselves towards her. Naturally the dog, Nana, arrived first, her cold wet nose bumping Daisy's knee in greeting. The twins toddled in her wake; Oliver in such a hurry that he sat down unexpectedly and completed the course crawling, still a faster means of locomotion as far as he was concerned. Single-minded, he beat Miranda, who put much of her effort into shouting, 'Ma-ma-ma-ma!' as she came. Daisy, as usual, ended up sitting on the floor so as to accommodate everyone in her arms.

'You'll spoil them, Mummy,' said Mrs. Gilpin disapprovingly.

Bertha bobbed a curtsy and went on ironing nappies. The twins used positive mountains of nappies. How on earth,

Daisy wondered, did mothers manage who couldn't afford to pay nannies and nurserymaids and laundrymen? Presumably their babies survived without beautifully pressed, crease-free nappies. Ironing them seemed an unnecessary expenditure of time and energy, but Mrs. Gilpin certainly wouldn't tolerate such a suggestion. Daisy decided to save her energies for the battles that were sure to arise as Oliver and Miranda grew older.

'I'm going to be away for a few days, Mrs. Gilpin,' she said. 'I'll leave a telephone number, of course, in case you need to reach me.'

'Oh, I'm sure that won't be necessary,' said Nurse with a smug smile.

And there – as Hamlet would no doubt have said had he taken any interest in child-care – was the rub. It was nice to know the babies would be very well taken care of while she was out of town, but depressing in a way that they didn't really need her.

'Will you miss me?' she whispered in Miranda's little pink ear, half hidden by her froth of dark curls.

Miranda giggled. Oliver stuck his tongue out and blew a raspberry, an act so screamingly funny that he roared with laughter and then repeated it.

'All right, Master Oliver,' Mrs. Gilpin commanded, 'that's quite enough of that!'

But Daisy couldn't help giggling, too, especially when Miranda tried to copy her brother, with indifferent success.

Perhaps it was just as well that Nurse Gilpin ruled the nursery, Daisy thought as she stood up half an hour later. Otherwise the children might grow up to be horrid undisciplined brats. Or perhaps, like Daisy herself, they had the best of both worlds: Nurse to make them mind their *p*'s and *q*'s, and Mummy to indulge and laugh with them. All one could do was love them and hope for the best.

'I'll only be gone a few days,' she assured Oliver, and stooped to tickle his tummy one more time. 'I'm going to stay with a plumber,' she said to Miranda, who regarded her solemnly. 'It should be interesting, as long as your god-mother controls the bees in her bonnet and isn't rude to the poor man.'

CHAPTER 2

Lucy braked her Lea-Francis two-seater in a swirl of gravel, having exceeded the speed limit practically every inch of the drive from town.

'Gates welcomingly closed,' she said sarcastically, glaring at the ornate ironwork two inches beyond the bonnet. On either side, a stone pillar topped with a Triton guarded the gate. She leant on the horn.

'There are deer in the park,' Daisy pointed out as soon as she could hear herself think. 'Look, over there. Darling, I do hope you're not going to spend the next four days finding fault. The sun is shining, the lambs are gambolling on the hillside' – she waved at the surrounding chalk hills, their short-cropped grass scattered with sheep busily cropping – 'and it's really too kind of Mr. Pritchard to invite complete strangers to stay and to photograph his grotto.'

Lucy was determined to take a gloomy view. 'He'll probably expect me to let him use the photos to advertise his beastly bathroom stuff.'

'Keep your hair on till he asks you, which he may very well not. Here comes the gatekeeper.'

A boy of ten or eleven, wearing grey-flannel shorts and a school jersey, came out of the neat stone lodge. 'Sorry, miss,' he called, swinging the gates open without difficulty. Well-oiled, Daisy noted. 'I were eating me tea.'

'Miss' rather than 'ma'am' worked its wonders: Lucy gave him a gracious nod and sixpence. To Daisy's relief, she didn't then shower the lad with gravel but proceeded in a stately manner – as stately as a sports car could attain – up the curving avenue of chestnuts. On the trees, brilliant green leaves were just beginning to unfold from the sticky brown buds. They moved slowly enough to see clumps of primroses and violets blooming on the verge. Fallow deer, including antlered males and a few spotted fawns, lifted their heads to watch the intruders.

They rounded a beech copse, and Appsworth Hall rose before them, spread across the hillside. Built of the local limestone, the northwest front took on a rosy cast in the slanting light of the sinking sun. Though large, in size it was more comparable to Daisy's childhood home, Fairacres, than to Lucy's family's vast nineteenth-century mock-Gothic mansion, Haverhill.

With any luck, Daisy hoped, the comparative modesty of Appsworth Hall would avert another outburst from her friend. In that respect, at least, Mr. Pritchard could not compete with the Earl of Haverhill.

Daisy had a chance to admire the house because Lucy was sufficiently struck by the sight to stop the car. In fact, she jumped out to get her tripod and camera from the dicky. In style, Appsworth Hall was similar to neither Haverhill's fantastic elaboration nor Fairacres, which had grown haphazardly over centuries rather than being planned. The Hall was pure neo-Classical, with symmetrical wings on either side of a central block marked by a portico with a pair of

Doric columns on each side. The pediment was adorned with a simple laurel wreath.

In the quiet with the motor turned off, Daisy heard the first cuckoo of spring. The first she had heard, anyway.

'Blast,' said Lucy, 'I'll have to walk across the grass to get a good shot. Look at the way those shadows make every feature stand out! The light's perfect but it's going to change in just a moment. Bring the plates, would you, darling? That satchel there.'

'I'm wearing new shoes, and it rained yesterday!'

Intent on finding exactly the right spot, Lucy ignored Daisy's protest. Somehow she managed to look stylish even while tramping heavily laden across the park.

It had been a beautiful day, though it was chilly now, threatening a frost tonight. Fortunately for Daisy's shoes, the chalky soil had dried quickly. The shoes survived unscathed, a matter of some importance as Lucy's equipment had left little space in the dicky for luggage. True, anticipating this situation, they had each sent ahead a suitcase to the nearest station, Ogbourne St. George. However, one could never be certain that the Great Western Railway would regard the matter with quite one's own degree of urgency.

Daisy was wondering whether their host would mind sending for the bags or if they'd have to go and fetch them themselves, when a large open touring car sped round the spinney. With a blare of the horn, it stopped behind the Lea-Francis, abandoned by Lucy in the middle of the drive. It dwarfed the sports car.

'Darling, be an angel and move it for me?' Lucy begged. 'Just a couple more shots.'

'All right, but you can jolly well carry the plates back yourself. They're heavy.'

Daisy waved to let the newcomer know his plea had been noted. He climbed from the Bentley as she approached, and took out a cigarette case that glinted gold in the last of the sun. Fitting a cigarette into an ebony holder, he lit it with a gold pocket lighter.

He looked vaguely familiar. His admirably cut suit of country tweeds could not disguise the bulky figure and heavy shoulders. When he raised his hat to her, she saw that his neck was as thick as his head was wide. He had small eyes set close together on either side of a pedigree nose perfected over centuries by his noble family.

He was unmistakable. She had met him a couple of times, and remembered hearing about him from her brother, Gervaise, who had attended the same public school. His distinctive appearance had led an unkind schoolfellow to nickname him 'Rhino.'

It would have been easier to sympathise had Rhino not been an exceedingly rich earl.

'Hello, Lord Rydal,' she called. 'Sorry to be in your way. Half a tick and I'll move it.'

'Please do so ... er ...' His voice had a singularly irritating timbre, rather like a well-bred crow.

Or like a rhinoceros, perhaps, Daisy thought, suppressing a giggle. But she had no idea what sort of sound a rhino was likely to produce.

'Mrs. Fletcher,' she prompted him. 'Daisy Fletcher. We met quite a long time ago, I can't recall where or when.'

'Fletcher? I haven't the slightest recollection – '

'You were at school with my brother, Gervaise Dalrymple.'

'Oh, Dalrymple, yes, how do you do.' He didn't offer her a cigarette, not that she wanted one. He continued, complaining, 'Miss Beaufort seemed to think I was the only person who could be spared to fetch your bags from the station, yours and Lady Gerald's.'

Daisy decided not to enquire as to why, with such reluctance, he should have done Julia Beaufort's bidding. 'Did you get them? Splendid. How kind of you. You see, Lucy's – Lady Gerald's – car is too small to carry all our luggage.'

'Just large enough to block the drive.'

'I'll move it!'

'Hold on, darling!' Lucy had approached unseen and unheard across the grass, carrying her camera and bag of plates. 'Let me get my stuff in first. Hello, Rhino.'

'Good afternoon, Lady Gerald.'

'What on earth are you doing here?'

'Running other people's errands, it seems. I just picked up your luggage at Ogbourne St. George.'

'How kind. While you're at it, I left my tripod back there. Would you mind frightfully . . . ?'

'I suppose not,' he said grumpily, 'as I can't get past till you go on.' He loped off across the grass, the cigarette holder gripped between his teeth.

'The perfect gentleman,' said Lucy sarcastically.

'I'd forgotten.'

'Forgotten what?'

'Gervaise said it wasn't just his looks and money that earned him the nickname. The rhinoceros is also noted for its thick skin.'

Lucy laughed. 'He has that all right. But we ought to make allowances for his being disappointed in love.'

'What do you mean?'

'Didn't you know? He's crazy for Julia.'

'Oh, so that's why he so demeaned himself as to fetch our bags! She persuaded him to.'

'Probably just trying to get rid of him for a while. Of course Lady Beaufort wants Julia to marry him, but Julia doesn't want anything to do with him. One can't really blame her, however rich and noble he may be. I expect he drove them down here – they haven't a car – and talked the plumber into letting him stay on.'

'I do think you might have warned me, darling. One needs some mental preparation before being plunged into the throes of someone else's unrequited love affair. And you *must* stop calling Pritchard "the plumber." You'll slip up and call him that to his face.'

'No fear. However ghastly he is, now I'm here I'm not leaving till I've got some decent shots of the grotto. I just hope it's all it's cracked up to be.'

'You're not telling me Lady Beaufort has the slightest interest in the grotto. If she's so determined to catch a rich earl for Julia, what do you suppose has brought them to Appsworth Hall?'

'That's easy: a rich plumber's rich nephew.'

'The plot thickens,' Daisy remarked with a sigh. 'Intended to make Lord Rydal jealous?'

'Unnecessary. He's absolutely potty – '

'Hush! Here he comes.'

Without missing a beat, Lucy continued in her penetrating soprano: ' – about cars. Aren't you, Rhino?'

'Aren't I what?' He bunged the tripod into the Lea-Francis's dicky on top of the camera and satchel, with a carelessness that made Lucy wince.

'Mad about cars,' she said through gritted teeth. 'Daisy was admiring your Bentley.'

'Cars?' he said incredulously, lighting another cigarette. 'What is there to be mad about? As long as it's comfortable and clean and runs properly. My man sees to all that. I'd have sent him to fetch your stuff, but he had to get a grease spot off the sleeve of my dinner jacket. Should have been done last night, of course, but he claims he couldn't see it till he looked in daylight. Lazy as a lapdog. But aren't they all? It's impossible to get decent servants these days.'

Daisy had been working for a couple of years, in a desultory manner, on an article about various aspects of what middle-class matrons called 'the Servant Problem.' She was aware of the complexities of the issue and was quite ready to discuss them, but Lucy muttered in her ear, 'Don't waste your breath.'

'Well, what are we waiting for? Are you going to move your car out of my way or not?'

Lucy's withering look, a masterpiece of its kind, had absolutely no effect upon the thick-skinned Earl of Rydal. Her stony silence as she got into the Lea-Francis and pressed the self-starter was equally lost on him, Daisy was sure, although she didn't deign to look back. However, their glacial pace as they proceeded up the middle of the avenue irritated him to the point of honking his horn again.

'Rather childish, don't you think?' said Daisy. 'You, I mean. It doesn't need saying where he's concerned.'

'I'm admiring the view. It's a splendid building, isn't it?' Lucy slowed still more, and the Lea-Francis stalled.

She got out, folded up one side of the bonnet and peered inside.

Rydal stormed out of his Bentley. 'What the deuce is the matter?'

'I'm not sure. How lucky you're on the spot. Perhaps it would start if you crank it for us.'

'Why don't you crank it yourself?'

Lucy sighed. 'Gallantry is dead. Never mind, we'll just sit here until your man has cleaned that grease spot, then no doubt he'll be able to repair whatever's wrong, since he takes care of yours.'

'Good lord, he doesn't do the mechanical stuff himself. He takes it to a garage. In town.'

Lucy turned a glittering smile on him. 'What a pity. I'll tell you what, why don't you push us up to the house?'

His mouth dropped open. 'Push you? *Me?*'

'It's a small car. I don't expect it will be too heavy for a big, strong chap like you. Daisy, you don't mind walking, do you, to lighten the load, while I steer?'

'Not at all. But I have a better idea. Why don't I drive the Bentley, then Lord Rydal won't have to come back for it after pushing you up the hill.'

'What a good idea,' Lucy said approvingly. 'You drive almost as well as I do. You probably won't do it too much harm.'

'I'll do my best, and he did say he didn't much care about it. If you'd just show me which pedal is the brake, Lord Rydal, then – '

'No! No, no, no! I won't have you driving my car. I didn't say I don't care about it. I just said I'm not crazy about cars. In general. But I won't let you drive my Bentley. I'll tell you what, I'll drive it and push yours bumper to bumper, Lady Gerald.'

'Not on your life! You'd probably step on the accelerator too hard and run right over me. I'll give it another go.'

The Lea-Francis started at the first try.

'Miraculous,' Daisy commented, as they rolled onwards. 'How did you stall it?'

'Simple. I just shifted up to top gear and took my foot off the clutch. Don't tell me you didn't stall a few times while you were learning to drive.'

'Of course, but I'm not sure I ever really worked out what I did wrong, just learnt to do it right. Well, honours even, I should say, but definitely childish.'

'At least I pierced that insufferable shell of complacency, however briefly. Besides, you did your bit. That was a neat touch, asking him which was the brake.'

'Yes, that's all very well, but I do hope you're not going to spend our time here sniping at him.'

'Hardly, darling. We have work to do. It was a perfect demonstration, though, of why we mustn't let Julia weaken. Lady Beaufort's the sort who still believes parents can tell their daughters whom to marry.' Lucy stopped the car in front of the portico. 'Here we are.'

They got out. As the Bentley swept past them and disappeared round the side of the house, Lucy retrieved the tripod from the dickey and handed it to Daisy. She shouldered her precious camera herself and heaved out the satchel of plates.

'Do you suppose the plumber will provide someone to garage the car for me, and bring in the rest of our stuff?' she added plaintively.

'If not, I'll do it,' said Daisy resignedly. She had been worried about her friend's attitude to Mr. Pritchard. Apparently she was going to have to protect Lord Rydal and Lady Beaufort from Lucy's scheming, too. She rather hoped Alec would be able to come down for the weekend to lend a hand.

CHAPTER 3

A very proper butler admitted Daisy and Lucy to the hall.

'Mr. Pritchard's chauffeur will convey your ladyship's motor to the garage, my lady,' he assured Lucy.

The grand staircase, black-and-white chequered marble floor, and pillared niches in the walls were just what one would expect to find behind the classical façade. However, Mr. Pritchard was clearly not bound by tradition. Illuminated by electric wall-sconces, the cold stone of the floor was half hidden by a broadloom Axminster in green and gold chequers, and, instead of marble gods and goddesses, the niches held a selection of ewers. These ranged from white china decorated with forget-me-nots and rosebuds to elaborate gilt-rimmed porcelain with scenes from classical mythology. Gods and goddesses in fact, Daisy thought, amused – as well as reminders of the days before modern plumbing.

'At least, no chamber-pots!' Lucy hissed in her ear. A modern career-woman she might be, but like Queen Victoria, she was not amused. She instructed the butler in the proper handling of her camera equipment.

A short, spare, grey-haired man in a navy pin-striped suit came bustling through a door on the right side of the hall. He greeted them with a cheerful smile.

'You must be Lady Gerald and Mrs. Fletcher.' He spoke the King's English with a slight Welsh intonation. 'I'm Brin Pritchard. Very pleased to meet you, I'm sure. And I'm delighted my grotto's going to be in your book.'

Lucy muttered, 'How do you do?' without offering her hand.

'We're looking forward to seeing it, Mr. Pritchard,' Daisy assured him, shaking his hand. 'It's very kind of you to invite us.'

'Not at all, not at all. I had a marvellous time restoring it to its old condition, or maybe even just a bit better, and I like to show it off. I wish you'd been able to arrive in time to see it in daylight this afternoon. Barker,' he said to the butler, 'bring a fresh pot of tea. Or perhaps you young ladies would prefer a cocktail at this hour?'

Regarding her host with a somewhat more kindly eye, Lucy declared that a cocktail would exactly fill the bill, while Daisy opted for tea.

'I expect you'd like to powder your noses before you join us,' Pritchard suggested, adding with an air of gallantry, 'not that I mean to suggest your noses need powdering. The cloakroom's just through there, first door on the left.'

As they followed his directions, Lucy said, 'Thank heaven he didn't offer to demonstrate the plumbing!'

'I wish you'd stop expecting him to drop a brick. I think he's rather a nice little man.'

When they returned to the hall, the butler, Barker, was waiting to usher them into the drawing room. It was a large room, furnished with an eye to comfort and cheerfulness. The only sign of plumbing was several radiators, augmenting with their welcome warmth the fire crackling in the Adam fireplace. The delicate plasterwork of the mantel was complemented by the ceiling's wreathes, rosettes, and ribbons. If Mr. Pritchard had been tempted to embellish these with depictions of urns, fountains, or other evidence of his trade, he had resisted the temptation. The walls hinted of watery influences, however, being papered in willow-green with a slight sheen, narrowly striped in pale blue.

Pin-striped, in fact, Daisy thought, as their equally pin-striped host bounced up from a easy-chair and came towards them. He must be in his mid- or late-fifties, she thought, but he was as spry as a man half his age, and his hair, though grey verging on white, was still thick.

'Come in, come in do, come to the fire and get warm. Let's see, now, you know Lady Beaufort, don't you, and Miss Beaufort? A reunion of old friends. What could be better?'

Sir Frederick Beaufort's widow, a large stately woman in forest green, seated at the fireside, gave a small stately bow, but her smile was friendly. 'Lady Gerald, Mrs. Fletcher, how pleasant to see you again. Julia has been looking forward to your arrival.'

'I have indeed,' Julia said warmly. 'Hello, Lucy. Daisy, it's ages since I saw you.'

'Years,' said Daisy. Seven years, since her father's funeral in 1919. What with the death toll of the War and the influenza pandemic, which had killed Lord Dalrymple, his funeral had not been well attended, but Julia had been there.

They had not been particularly close friends at school, in spite of both being fonder of books than sports. Julia had been shy, at that age a crippling affliction, one that Daisy never suffered from. Julia had been cursed with spots, while Daisy's Nemesis was freckles, much easier to live with. And though Daisy had never attained slimness, and now likely never would, Julia in her teen years had been positively pudgy.

But Julia, in her late twenties, had emerged from her chrysalis and was absolutely stunning. Her hair could have been described as spun gold without too much of the usual gross exaggeration. Worn in a long bob, it framed a spotless peaches-and-cream complexion with no need of powder or rouge. Without being rail-thin, she was slender enough to look marvellous in a silk tea-dress in the still-current straight up-and-down fashion, with hip-level waist, which Daisy had hoped would die a natural death long since.

Daisy looked at her with admiration and envy. The envy faded as she reminded herself that despite her own unmodish figure and merely light brown hair, worn shingled, she had Alec, whereas Julia apparently faced a choice between a rhinoceros and a plumber's nephew.

Not that Daisy had anything against plumbers.

Mr. Plumber . . . Mr. Pritchard, rather, next introduced a short, tubby woman, sixtyish, her coils of white hair sternly confined in a net, her plumpness sternly confined in a black frock embroidered with jet beads. 'My sister-in-law, my late wife's sister, Mrs. Howell, who keeps house for me.'

'Acts as your hostess, Brin!' Mrs. Howell hissed crossly. Any hint of Welsh in her voice had been carefully obliterated. 'You'll be making the ladies think I'm the housekeeper. I've been acting as Brin's hostess since my poor sister went to her reward, Lady Gerald. How do you do? My husband was Brin's partner, you see.'

'Partner?' Lucy enquired languidly, as though she had never heard the word before, though Daisy was pretty certain Gerald was a partner in a City firm, something to do with stocks and shares, as well as sitting on numerous boards.

'Business partner,' Mrs. Howell elucidated.

'Sleeping partner,' Pritchard corrected her mischievously.

'Owen's your Managing Director!' she snapped.

'My dear Winifred, you were talking about Daffyd.'

Short of an actual yawn, Lucy could hardly have shown her lack of interest more clearly.

To compensate, Daisy said, 'I've always wondered what a sleeping partner is exactly. Presumably not one who comes into the office, puts his feet up on the desk, and slumbers away the day?'

Pritchard laughed. 'Indeed, he doesn't usually turn up at the office at all, Mrs. Fletcher. It's what we call someone who invests in a private business without taking part in the running of it. Daffyd Howell was – '

'Really, Brin, I'm sure the ladies don't want to hear about the business.'

'Daisy's a writer,' said Lucy. 'Writers are interested in the most unexpected subjects.'

'Later, perhaps,' Daisy suggested. Not that she was particularly interested in the financial arrangements of Pritchard's Plumbing Products, but she didn't like the way Mrs. Howell had snubbed her brother-in-law.

'Just say the word.' He gave her a cheerful wink. 'Your tea will be here any minute, Mrs. Fletcher. Now, what can I get for you, Lady Gerald?'

'Gin and It, please.' Lucy followed him over to a huge oak Welsh dresser, beautifully carved. It had been converted into a drinks cabinet. The shelves were crowded with bottles, decanters, and glasses. One side of the top of the base section lifted to reveal a small sink – with running water, of course, given their host's business – and the cupboard below concealed an ice chest.

It was very neatly done, without spoiling a splendid piece of furniture. Daisy considered it vastly preferable to the current fad for glass and chromed stainless steel bars.

'Anyone else for a cocktail?' Pritchard invited, pouring Lucy's drink.

'I wouldn't mind a pink gin,' said Julia, going to join them.

Mrs. Howell muttered something disapproving about it being much too early for drinks.

Lady Beaufort said soothingly, 'Young people today are very different from the days of our youth, aren't they?'

Though Daisy thought it was very kind of Lady Beaufort, who surely could have given the other a good decade, Mrs. Howell didn't appear to be mollified. 'Not so young, neither,' she snapped.

'Old enough to decide for ourselves what we want to drink,' Daisy commented, 'though the three of us are too young to vote for a couple of years yet.'

'Why women want to vote I simply can't see,' Mrs. Howell declared. 'One thing I'll say for Brin, he's stuck by Mr. Lloyd George through thick and thin. So what need have I for a vote?'

Daisy refrained from pointing out the fallacy in this argument. 'Ah, here comes my tea,' she said with relief.

Lord Rydal came in just behind the butler. He made a beeline for the drinks – or was it for Julia?

'I fetched your friends' bags from the station, Miss Beaufort,' he told her irritably, jabbing with his cigarette holder towards Lucy. 'But I still don't see why one of the servants couldn't have gone. Slackers!' he said to Mr. Pritchard. 'You should give them all notice.'

'But . . .' Pritchard caught Julia's alarmed eye and continued with a look of enlightenment, 'but the only one who can drive is my chauffeur, and it's his afternoon off, I'm afraid. Sorry, Lady Gerald, I ought to 've changed his day.'

'That's all right,' Lucy said dryly. 'I'm sure Rhino was delighted to make himself useful.'

Rydal snorted.

Daisy didn't hear any more. Mrs. Howell, having dismissed the butler with a brusque 'That will be all, Barker,' asked her if she took milk and sugar in her tea. 'The scones are all gone. I hope you didn't want any, because they're busy with dinner in the kitchen.'

'They're better hot from the oven anyway,' Lady Beaufort pointed out.

'There's plenty of Welsh-cakes,' Mrs. Howell went on. 'Brin insists on Welsh-cakes. I myself consider sponge cake far superior.'

Daisy politely disclaimed any interest in scones. She accepted a Welsh-cake.

Without any reason that Daisy was aware of, Mrs. Howell seemed to have taken against her, not even having greeted her properly. Her curiosity was piqued. It didn't make sense. For one thing, if the woman disapproved of cocktails at half past five, she should have approved of Daisy's choice of tea. She could at least have apologised for the dearth of scones, or better, not mentioned it at all rather than aggressively announcing the lack thereof.

Lady Beaufort cast a mildly malicious glance at Mrs. Howell and enquired, 'Well, Daisy, how is Lady Dalrymple? The Dowager Viscountess, I should say. She seemed very well when we met her in town at Christmas.'

'Oh yes, Mother's flourishing, thank you.' Even though the lady in question bitterly resented living at the Dower House and still refused to admit that the present Lord and Lady Dalrymple had any right to Fairacres – but Daisy's mother wouldn't have been happy with nothing to complain about. 'Did you see my sister, Violet, and Lord John? They didn't bring the children up on their last visit, alas. I don't see enough of my nephews and niece.'

'Lady John was there, but her husband had already gone back to Kent. I understand you have little ones of your own to keep you busy.'

'Twins, a girl and boy. They're just over a year. And my stepdaughter, of course. Belinda is nearly thirteen already and away at school.'

'I wish Julia would hurry up and give me grandchildren.'

During this conversation, the most extraordinary change had come over Mrs. Howell. Scarlet in the face and pop-eyed with indignation, she had jumped up and rung the bell (an electric button rather than a tasselled rope, as befitted Pritchard's discreet modernisation). When the butler came in, she berated him.

'Barker, why didn't you bring scones for Mrs. Fletcher?'

Surprised, Daisy was about to assure her she was perfectly happy without, when Lady Beaufort gave her a slight shake of the head. While the butler apologised with proper impassiveness and went off to repair the deficiency, Daisy finished off her Welsh-cake.

The reason for Mrs. Howell's change of heart was all too obvious. Until Lady Beaufort enquired after the Dowager Viscountess, their hostess hadn't realised that Daisy was a sprig of the nobility. The daughter of a viscount must not be denied scones just because the kitchen staff were busy preparing dinner.

On the whole, Daisy preferred Mrs. Howell's discourtesy to her sycophancy. However, she felt obliged to eat a buttered scone, though she really didn't want it after the delicious but rich and sugary cake.

Bolstered by Lucy's admonitory gaze – Lucy was sure she could slim if she tried – Daisy adamantly refused a second scone. She returned the admonitory gaze, however, when it looked as if Lucy was about to accept a second cocktail. It really was a bit early for drinks.

'Hadn't we better go up to our rooms, Lucy?' Daisy suggested. 'You wanted to get your frock ironed before changing for dinner, didn't you?'

Mrs. Howell looked horrified. She prised herself from her chair, saying, 'Oh dear, Mrs. Fletcher, I'm afraid your room may not be ready. I must go and have a word with the housekeeper.'

'Why don't I take you both up to Lucy's room?' Julia gracefully extracted her arm from Rydal's grasp. 'It's next to mine. Willett can iron Lucy's frock for her, can't she, Mother? They came in Lucy's sports car and didn't have room for her maid.'

'Of course,' said Lady Beaufort with a gracious nod.

Mrs. Howell scuttled out ahead of the three young ladies. She was disappearing into the nether regions as Julia led the others into the hall and up the grand staircase.

'What was all that about, Daisy?' Lucy demanded as they ascended. 'When that woman said your room wasn't ready, you looked as if you were about to burst, trying not to laugh. It's disgraceful. They've known we were coming for ages!'

Daisy let a giggle escape. 'It was so funny! Mrs. Howell apparently hadn't realised my august antecedents, until Lady Beaufort asked after Mother. She's probably put me up in the garrets with the servants. It suddenly dawned on her, when I said we'd go up, that it wouldn't do.'

Julia smiled, but Lucy was inclined to take umbrage on Daisy's behalf.

'Calm down, darling. The garret room is pure fantasy.' Daisy wished she'd kept it to herself. 'Besides, if you want to stay long enough to photograph the grotto, you can't go accusing Mrs. Howell of insulting me. She can't help being a snob.'

'She is one, though,' said Julia, turning left on the landing. 'You wouldn't believe the treatment she puts up with from Rhino, without a murmur. He acts as if she's the housekeeper she's so anxious not to be taken for.'

Daisy slipped her arm through Julia's. 'I hope you're going to tell us all about Rhino and everything. I'm dying to hear what's up.'

'Nothing's "up,"' Julia said grimly, as she opened a door off the passage, 'and won't be if I can help it. Here's Lucy's room. I'll just pop into to mine and ring for Willett. Back in half a tick, then we can catch up on each other's news.'

Lucy went ahead into her bedroom. 'The Beauforts know you married a policeman,' she said. '*I* didn't tell them, but Lady Beaufort kept up with the English papers while they were living in France.'

'Darling, half the world knows I married a policeman.'

'What they *don't* know is that you keep getting mixed up in his cases.'

'You're the only person who knows about more than one or two of those. Except Scotland Yard, of course, and they do their best to hush it up.'

'Thank heaven!'

'Don't you think it's really very unfair that I never get any credit for all the help I give them?'

'No! You're not going to tell Julia, are you?'

'Why not? I'm sure she's not the gossipy kind.'

'Daisy!'

'Just teasing, darling.' With a mournful sigh, Daisy continued, 'I'm quite used to hiding my light under a bushel. I don't suppose anyone at Appsworth Hall will ever have a chance to find out what a brilliant sleuth I am.'

CHAPTER 4

Lucy's bedroom was a typical Edwardian country-house guest room. Daisy guessed the Pritchards must have taken over the furnishings along with the house from the previous owners. Things had been refurbished, but fundamentally everything was much as the unfortunate Appsworths had left it, with none of Pritchard's – or the late Mrs. Pritchard's – individuality. Rather, Mr. Pritchard's stamp was purely practical, a modern radiator under the window and hot and cold running water in the wash-basin. Lucy could hardly object to these evidences of their host's trade, adding as they would to her comfort.

Spotting her camera case on the dressing-table, Lucy visibly relaxed. She went over to check the contents thoroughly before she conceded, 'It seems to be all right.'

'I'd be very surprised if it weren't.'

'Surprised?' Lucy prowled to the wardrobe and found her frocks hanging neatly. She took out the one she wanted ironed for this evening and laid it on the bed. Daisy wondered whether her own clothes were being hurriedly repacked, or whether they hadn't been unpacked for her in the first place. 'Why surprised?' Lucy asked.

'Because Mr. Pritchard must be a pretty efficient manufacturer to make enough money to buy this place, and efficient people usually won't stand for inefficient servants. Come and sit down, do. You were talking to him. Prejudice aside, what's he like?'

'Not too bad. No kowtowing, at least.'

'Mrs. Howell seems to be the kowtower of the family. You should have seen her attitude change when she heard that Mother's a viscountess.'

'Mrs. Howell?' Julia came in. 'The poor woman's in quite a quandary.'

Daisy was intrigued. 'A quandary?'

'How many courses to serve her august company for dinner,' Lucy guessed languidly.

'Rhino put her straight on that question the first night we were here, when the soup was followed directly by a leg of lamb. "What, no fish?"' Julia produced a very creditable imitation of Lord Rydal's caw. 'Mr. Pritchard said he didn't like fish, and didn't like the smell of fish. Rhino insisted that liking had nothing to do with it, a proper dinner must have a fish course.'

'What did Mr. Pritchard say to that?' Daisy wondered.

'I was hoping he'd tell Rhino to pack his bags, but his manners are much better than Rhino's. He let the subject drop. Mother murmured something soothing about the odour of fish tending to penetrate and linger. And I said the lamb smelt simply delicious, which it did, and as it was Welsh lamb, Mr. Pritchard was delighted. He's rather a dear. If only Mother . . .' Julia sighed.

'Don't tell me you'd rather marry the plumber than the Earl of Rydal!' Lucy exclaimed. 'Apart from anything else, he must be sixty if he's a day.'

'Fifty-five,' Daisy amended.

'Good heavens, there's no question of my marrying Brin Pritchard. Mother's worried, not demented.'

'Why don't you start at the beginning,' Daisy said.

'The beginning? I suppose it all goes back to the War, really.'

Lucy groaned.

'Careful, darling,' Daisy warned her. 'You'll turn into another rhinoceros.'

'Don't worry,' Julia said with a smile, 'I shan't rewrite *À la recherche du temps perdu*.'

Lucy looked more puzzled than reassured. Neither of the others bothered to explain.

'Your father was a general, wasn't he?' Daisy asked.

'Yes, but the widow's pension of even a general doesn't go far these days. Mother decided she'd rather be poor in France than in England.'

'Hence the Christmas cards from Dinard, these past few years,' said Lucy.

'Yes. We moved there in '21. I didn't mind at all. I was able to get English books, and then my French improved enough so that I could read it just as easily.'

'Julia, don't tell me you read the whole of *À la recherche du temps perdu* in French?' Daisy asked, awed. 'I've never got through it even in English.'

'I had plenty of time. There wasn't much else to do. That's really why Mother hated it. What got her down was not so much having only one servant and only three courses at dinner, usually fish because it was cheap – '

Daisy and Lucy looked at each other and laughed.

'What's so funny?' Julia asked. Daisy couldn't blame her for looking a trifle resentful.

'Sorry!' she gasped. 'It's just that when Lucy and I shared digs, we didn't have a live-in servant at all, just a daily, and we practically lived on eggs and mousetrap cheese and sardines. To this day I simply can't face sardines. Of course, it's different for someone like Lady Beaufort.'

'But, as I was saying, pinching and scraping wasn't the trouble. It was not having enough to do. Army wives are used to being busy. Writing letters and playing an occasional game of cards with the few other English residents just wasn't enough. She had too much time to worry about me.'

'I suppose an army pension doesn't go on forever,' said Daisy. Lucy's attention was elsewhere by now. The Beauforts' maid had come in and had to be advised about ironing the evening frock, a dazzler in crimson charmeuse with a fringed, scalloped hem designed to play hide-and-seek with the knees.

'It's meant for the widow, not grown-up children,' Julia explained, confusing Daisy until she realised that 'it' was the pension, not the frock. 'Mother used to have nightmares – I told you she's not much of a reader; well, all the books she did pick up seemed to feature impoverished young ladies working in hat-shops and starving in garrets.'

'Why hat-shops, I wonder?'

'I can't swear some of them weren't dress-shops. I don't know where she found them! I told her to stop worrying because if the blasted things were so popular, I could probably write them as well as anyone and make my fortune.'

'So have you written one?'

'As a matter of fact, I'm about halfway through. But it isn't exactly –. I found I simply can't manage the right tone.

It's more like *Northanger Abbey* in relation to *Udolpho* or *The Castle of Otranto*.'

'What fun! I can't wait to read it.'

'I was hoping you might take a look and tell me if it's worth the effort of going on with it. Not right now. I left it in town.'

Lucy rejoined them. 'You've been living the high life in town for a couple of months now,' she commented, her tone questioning.

'Mother came into an unexpected inheritance and decided to blow it all to give me a last chance to find a husband. So we came to London, hired a lady's maid, refreshed our wardrobes, and looked up old friends. The trouble is, the few men I've met whom I could bear to marry have either not been interested in a penniless bride past her first youth or failed to meet my mother's criteria.'

'One of which, I assume,' Lucy drawled, 'is money.'

'Well, of course,' said Daisy. 'Lady Beaufort wouldn't want you to have to live on sardines for the rest of your life. And you wouldn't want to, either, unless you were absolutely nutty about him. But surely she can't want you to marry someone just because he can keep you in seven-course dinners for the rest of your life.'

'Hence the unlovely Rhino,' said Lucy, 'but this doesn't explain the intrusion of plumbers into your high life, nor Mrs. Howell's quandary.'

Julia laughed. 'We met her son, Mr. Howell, at a perfectly respectable dinner party in Richmond. Apparently Pritchard's Plumbing is trying to get some huge government contract or other. Mr. Howell, as Managing Director, went up to talk to Sir Desmond Wandersley, the man in charge of plumbing at the Ministry of Health – not bathtubs for bureaucrats, it's something to do with slum clearance, I gather. Sir Desmond invited him to dine, much to Lady Ottaline's fury.'

'Lady Ottaline Wandersley?' Lucy asked. 'Yes, she wouldn't be happy to find a plumber at her table.'

'Especially as it was a last-minute invitation and ruined her numbers. What's more, he's a quiet chap and didn't pay for his dinner with sparkling conversation.'

'One could almost feel sorry for her.'

'Who's Lady Ottaline Wandersley?' Daisy enquired.

'Darling, you are so out of the swim! She was a Barrington, the Marquis of Edgehill's daughter.' Trust Lucy to know the pedigree of any member of the aristocracy. 'She was rather a vamp in her day, they say. The trouble is, she's rather desperately trying to go on vamping.'

'When was her day?'

'Before the War. A siren, they'd have called her, I expect, or a *femme fatale*. She must be in her forties, don't you think, Julia?'

'Early forties, perhaps.'

' "She may very well pass for forty-three, in the dusk, with a light behind her"?' Daisy quoted.

'Oh no, she can't be more than forty-five, and she's kept her looks and figure.'

'With a lot of help,' Lucy said cattily. 'Though I must admit she positively bristles with nervous energy. She can still dance all night. But the Wandersleys are beside the point. I suppose the junior plumber fell instantly in love with you, Julia, and begged you on bended knee to visit his unancestral home, but why on earth did Lady Beaufort accept the invitation? She can't possibly want you to marry a plumber.'

Julia sighed. 'He's well-off. And presumably will be richer when Mr. Pritchard dies, as there are no young Pritchards. But I don't think Mother really regards him as a desirable son-in-law. She expects the contrast with the noble Lord Rydal to illuminate hidden virtues in the latter.'

'And has it?' Daisy asked.

'Good heavens, no! If anything, Mr. Howell has better manners, but like Lady Ottaline, he's over forty. And I'm not half as convinced as Mother is that he's interested in marriage. If you ask me, the firm is his only love. His father made plenty from his investment in the business without dirtying his hands, but our Owen chose to get involved.'

'So if he's not mad about you, darling, how is it you're here?'

'The invitation didn't drop into our laps; Mother had to prise it out of him. In any case, I don't intend to marry either of them, even if it means living on sardines for the rest of my life.'

'Well, that settles that, but I'd stick with the mousetrap cheese, if I were you.'

'Which leaves the question of Mrs. Howell's quandary,' Lucy pointed out.

'She can't make up her mind –. Oh, here's Willett with your dress, Lucy.'

'I hope it's satisfactory, madam.' The middle-aged maid held up the frock by its exiguous straps for inspection.

Lucy approved the result and tipped her.

'Thank you, madam. Miss Beaufort, her ladyship said to remind you it's time you were changing for dinner.'

'All right, Willett, I'll be along in a minute. Daisy, we'd better go and find out where they've put you.'

'I can show madam, miss. It's just along the passage.'

Julia went with them. 'Do you need a frock ironed?' she asked Daisy.

'Probably, but I haven't anything half as elaborate as Lucy's. A chambermaid should be able to cope.'

'Certainly, madam. They keep a very good class of servants here, no matter what some people may say. Here you are, madam, this is yours. There's a bathroom next door, with a connecting door, and another down the passage a bit on the other side. Mr. Pritchard's put modern gas geysers in every bathroom, so there's always plenty of hot water, and no fear of them blowing up like the old kind, and that's a blessing I can tell you. I'll tell her ladyship you'll be along in a minute, miss,' the maid said to Julia and as she bustled off.

'No matter what "some people" say?' Daisy asked as Julia followed her into the room.

'Rhino.'

'Of course. He told me all servants are lazy good-for-nothings within three minutes of our meeting this afternoon. Whereas you have yet to reveal whatever is bothering Mrs. Howell.'

'She's afraid that if Owen marries she'll lose her position as chatelaine of Appsworth Hall to her daughter-in-law. On the other hand, she'd love to be able to talk about her son's mother-in-law, *Lady* Beaufort. But against that, she strongly disapproves of Mother, as a widow, not wearing black. She simply can't decide whether to encourage Owen's suit or scotch it. Such is my impression, at least. Naturally she hasn't confided in me.'

'Wouldn't it be simplest just to tell her – or him – that you're not interested?'

'Certainly, if he were in hot pursuit!'

'But as he hasn't actually displayed any serious interest . . . Hmm, yes, I see the difficulty. One can only hope she'll decide lording it over Appsworth Hall is more important to her than your mother's title.'

'Isn't it lucky Mother's merely the widow of a knight, not the wife of a marquis?'

'Except that marchionesses never – hardly ever – have to survive and provide for their daughters on a widow's army pension, so you wouldn't be in this fix to start with.'

Julia sighed. 'You know, Daisy, I haven't really got anything against Owen Howell except his mother. He is a managing director after all. It's Mother who thinks I have to marry into society. You didn't.'

'And I'm very happy with my policeman,' Daisy said firmly. 'But I'd appreciate your not mentioning his profession unnecessarily. You wouldn't believe how presumably law-abiding people suddenly start twitching when they find out my husband's a detective.'

Julia laughed. 'Not really!'

'Really. And now we'd better think about getting changed or we'll be in hot water with your mother, Mr. Howell's mother, your maid, and the butler when we're late to dinner.'

'Not to mention the cook. I'm on my way.'

It was all very well, Daisy thought, to compare a managing director of a plumbing factory with a detective chief inspector of Scotland Yard, but she had married Alec because she was madly in love with him. Without that, she could never have coped with the hostility of his mother and her own, let alone the move from the upper class, however impoverished, to the middle class, however comfortably off.

Because, however modern and egalitarian one was, there *were* differences. Different expectations, different ways of doing things, a different group of people around one, not necessarily better or worse but indubitably different. Alec's love had pulled her through the complex adjustment.

Unless Julia unexpectedly fell in love with Owen Howell, she ought not to marry him. Daisy looked forward with interest to meeting him.

CHAPTER 5

Daisy and Lucy went down together. Lucy looked spectacular in the crimson frock, rather too spectacular for an evening in the country, in Daisy's opinion. It was designed to be shown off in a West End nightclub, or at least for dining and dancing at the Ritz. Lucy was usually frightfully particular about the right clothes for the right occasion. Perhaps her intent was to show off to the plumber. Perhaps, Daisy thought more charitably, she simply wanted to keep her end up vis à vis Julia, who would probably look lovely in rags. Or, most charitably, perhaps she hoped to distract Rhino from his persecution of poor Julia.

Three men in dinner jackets stood by the drinks dresser, Mr. Pritchard, Lord Rydal, and an unknown man, somewhere between the other two in age, with slicked-down black hair. Taller by a head, Rhino outweighed his companions combined. He was talking in his abrasive voice, punctuating his words with stabs of his cigarette holder.

As Daisy and Lucy entered the drawing room, Mr. Pritchard stepped forwards in what Daisy was coming to regard as his usual welcoming way.

'Lady Gerald! Mrs. Fletcher! What a pleasure to entertain so many lovely ladies here at Appsworth, eh, Owen?' He frowned at Rhino's disparaging snort. 'This is my nephew, Owen Howell, ladies.'

'My pleasure,' said Howell, politely but without any great interest. 'You've come to see my uncle's grotto, I hear? What can I get you to drink?'

Lucy stuck to gin and It. Daisy opted for Cinzano and soda. As Howell picked up the syphon, Daisy said, just for something to say, 'It's an ingenious device, isn't it, the soda syphon.'

'The invention of the soda syphon to add carbonation to drinks is not more than a century old,' he told her with unexpected enthusiasm, 'but the principle of syphoning has been understood since ancient times. It's of great importance in modern plumbing.'

'Really?' she murmured.

He continued to expound upon the subject. Daisy listened with half an ear, the rest of her attention on Lucy, Pritchard, and Rhino. She was relieved to hear that Lucy, far from being rude to the plumber, was sparring with the earl. He was disparaging what he called her mania for her 'hobby' of photography and she was mounting a spirited defence. Mr. Pritchard appeared to be enjoying the battle. He even put in few words supporting the right of women to have careers. After that, Lucy looked on him with a much kindlier eye.

In the meantime, Mr. Howell had moved on to the latest safety improvements in gas geyser water heaters. True to Lucy's joking remark about writers being interested in everything, Daisy found herself pondering an article on new inventions and their effect on modern life.

'I can't really follow the technical stuff without seeing

it,' she told him. 'Would you mind demonstrating for me sometime?'

'Not a bit!' He pulled out a gold pocket-watch and consulted it. 'We've just time enough before –. Oh, here are the Beauforts. I'd better get them drinks. But I'll give you a proper demonstration before you leave, that's a promise!'

'What are you going to demonstrate, Mr. Howell?' Julia asked gaily, coming up to them. 'I hope you don't mean to exclude the rest of us from the show.'

'I hardly think you'd be interested, Miss Beaufort,' he said candidly.

'How can I tell until I know what it's all about?'

'Plumbing, no doubt,' put in Rhino with a sneer.

'Can you imagine what life was like before plumbing?' Julia demanded.

Lucy gave a delicate shudder. 'It doesn't bear thinking about.'

Daisy stared at her. Rhino must have really offended her to make her take up the cudgels in defence of plumbing.

'In the course of my life with the Army,' said Lady Beaufort, 'I lived in a number of places without plumbing of any sort. I can assure you, it was extremely disagreeable. Yes, thank you, sherry if you please,' she added to Mr. Pritchard who was waving a decanter at her.

'Leave it to me, Uncle,' Howell offered. 'What can I get you, Miss Beaufort?'

'Sherry, thanks.' Julia waited until her mother had moved away, following Owen Howell, then she said in a low voice to Daisy and Lucy, 'Mother thinks drinking cocktails is fast. That's the trouble with being out of the country for so long. She doesn't realise how times have changed.'

'Fast!' Lucy said indignantly. 'I don't know anyone who doesn't – '

'Calm down, darling, Mother's not saying *you're* fast. Or rather, she believes a certain degree of rapidity is acceptable in daughters of the aristocracy, particularly married ones, but not in the spinster daughter of a mere knight, even if he was a general.'

Lucy blinked. 'Rapidity?'

'Well, fastness doesn't seem quite the word I want.'

'I wish we had a well-fortified fastness to retreat to,' said Daisy. 'Here comes Rhino, and he's already on his second cocktail.'

'Your sherry, Miss Beaufort.' Handing Julia the glass, he ignored Daisy and Lucy. 'This place is too boring for words. Can't you persuade Lady Beaufort to go back to town before Monday?'

'I'm sorry you find us boring,' Julia said sweetly. 'You really mustn't feel obliged to stay. Mr. Pritchard or Mr. Howell will certainly drive us into Swindon to the mainline station when we leave.'

'You're not boring, it's all these others.' He made a sweeping gesture that encompassed everyone in the room, and nearly sent Daisy's glass flying.

She didn't bother to protest.

'How has he survived all these years with no one throttling him?' Lucy marvelled. She made no attempt to lower her voice, but Lord Rydal gave no sign of hearing her.

'If it was summer,' he continued to Julia, 'we could go for a stroll, but at this time of year there's no chance to be alone together.'

'Thank heaven,' she murmured.

'Your mother won't let you go out in the car with me. Doesn't she realise you're much too old to need a chaperone?'

'Rhino, how crass!' Lucy said in disgust, and stalked off to speak to Lady Beaufort.

Daisy exchanged a glance with Julia, who appeared to share her feelings. They combined a pressing desire to giggle, alarm at what Lucy might say to her ladyship, and amazement at Rhino's apparent belief that he could win his beloved by insulting her.

' "A mad-brain rudesby," ' said Julia.

' "Full of spleen," ' Daisy finished off the quotation. '*Taming of the Shrew*?'

'Yes. Kate, speaking of Petruchio, of course.'

'If you ask me, you need to be a bit of shrew to cope with a rhinoceros.'

For once Lord Rydal seemed to realise he had offended. At least he made a feeble attempt to explain himself: 'I don't care for schoolgirls.' Or perhaps he was simply objecting to their display of erudition. With a sulky look, he tapped out his cigarette butt in the nearest ashtray and his lighter flashed as he lit another.

In a way it was just as well that he was so obviously appalling. Surely after a week at close quarters, Lady Beaufort would be forced to abandon her plans to see her daughter a countess.

Daisy had just reached this comforting conclusion when Mrs. Howell burst into the drawing room.

'Brin,' she cried, her face tragic, 'Cook says the soles have gone bad!'

'Good job you invited the vicar,' Pritchard quipped.

'Really, Brin, you mustn't joke about such things.'

'Sorry, I thought you were talking about fish, not religion,' he said. He sounded penitent, but he looked pleased with himself, and Daisy had seen his eyes slide sideways towards Lady Beaufort, who hadn't quite been able to hide a discreet little snort of laughter.

'I *was* talking about fish,' Mrs. Howell snapped. 'In any case, the vicar couldn't come, so I invited Dr. Tenby instead. But the fish has gone off and there's none for dinner.'

'Where's it gone off to?' Having got into a facetious vein, he continued to mine it.

'Don't be ridiculous. You know perfectly well what I mean. It's high.'

'Flying fish? I don't believe I've ever seen them at the fishmonger.'

'Brin!'

'Well, what do you want me to do about your flipping fish? Take a rod out to the grotto pool? No, a net would be best, I don't think there's anything bigger than minnows in it.'

His sister-in-law shot him a glance of pure loathing.

'With such splendid dinners as you give us, Mrs. Howell,' said Lady Beaufort, 'I'm sure we shan't feel the want of fish.'

Owen Howell brought his mother a glass of sherry, and he and Lady Beaufort set themselves to smooth her ruffled feathers.

Daisy looked at Rhino to see how he was taking the prospect of no fish course. He was staring after Julia, who had drifted quietly away to speak to a young man who must have entered the room in the wake of Mrs. Howell. The stranger was nothing out of the ordinary – sandy-haired, slightly snub-nosed, no more than a couple of inches taller than Julia – his evening clothes respectable, but clearly not from

Savile Row. He was puffing at a pipe. His chief attraction appeared to be that he was not Rhino.

The earl might have been glowering at them, but his usual expression was so like a scowl that Daisy wouldn't have sworn to it.

His attention was distracted by the entrance of another couple, followed by a sleek, blond young man. Owen Howell instantly abandoned his mother and hurried to greet them.

'Lady Ottaline, Sir Desmond, welcome to Appsworth Hall.'

Sir Desmond apologised for the lateness of their arrival. ' – unavoidably detained by my wife's loss of a glove just as we were leaving.' His words were sarcastic, but his tone was indifferent.

Lady Ottaline, Sir Desmond. Where had Daisy heard those names recently? Ah, the Wandersleys, at whose house the Beauforts had made the acquaintance of the Managing Director of Pritchard's Plumbing Products. Wandersley was a civil servant, she recalled, and the two had business together.

Sir Desmond Wandersley looked like a senior civil servant, suave – not to say bland – impeccably turned out, his impressive girth evidence of decades of good living, but he had the height and the tailoring to carry it off. A well-barbered mane of white hair and gold-rimmed eyeglasses added to his distinguished air.

Daisy was more interested in his wife. Lucy and Julia agreed that she was an aging vamp, and her appearance did nothing to contradict their description.

Lady Ottaline wore a slinky grasshopper-green frock, with a long, gauzy, spangled scarf draped over her pointed elbows. Her angular arms emerged with insect-like effect. Her collarbones and face were all sharp angles, pointed chin, pointed nose, even pointed lobes to her ears, exaggerated by long, dangling, glittering earrings, faceted like an insect's eyes. Her face was powdered white, with a touch of rouge on high, sharp cheekbones, loads of eyeblack, and blood-red lipstick to match her fingernails.

A cross between a mosquito and a praying mantis, Daisy thought fancifully. She was quite surprised when Lady Ottaline's voice turned out to be not a high, thin whine, but low and husky.

Howell introduced his mother and his uncle to the Wandersleys and their follower. Sir Desmond turned out to be a Principal Deputy Secretary at the Ministry of Health, and the sleek young man was Carlin, his Private Secretary.

As Owen Howell provided the newcomers with drinks, Daisy, still standing next to Rhino, was aware of his lordship's tension. And when Lady Ottaline glanced round the room and caught sight of him, Daisy was perfectly placed to see that she was unsurprised – and pleased. Her crimson mouth curved in a small, smug smile, but she made no other move to acknowledge him.

He turned away to fuss with lighting yet another cigarette.

'Are you acquainted with the Wandersleys, Lord Rydal?' Daisy asked.

He didn't respond. Though it could have been just another example of his rudeness, Daisy was convinced there was more to it. He and Lady Ottaline knew each other, but he didn't want to admit it. Rhino, being who he was, had probably irredeemably offended her. Judging by her smile on seeing him, she had either revenged the insult or had immediate plans to do so. Of course, Rhino, being who he was, probably didn't realise he had offended, or didn't care, and he might well not recognise the revenge for what it was.

Dying to expound her theory to Lucy, Daisy decided she had complied with the requirements of civility where Rhino was concerned and deserted him. Before she had a chance to talk to Lucy, the doctor and his wife arrived, and a few minutes later they all went in to dinner.

CHAPTER 6

Daisy found herself seated between Sir Desmond and the doctor. The latter, a tall, gaunt, melancholy man, and a silent one, proved more interested in his food than his neighbours. When Daisy asked him politely whether he was a native of Wiltshire, his answer was an unpromising, 'No.'

'I don't know it well, but it seems to be a beautiful county.' This, phrased as a comment rather than a question, received no response whatsoever. Daisy made one more attempt. 'Do you enjoy living here?'

'Not particularly,' he said in a low, despondent voice.

Daisy gave up. Fortunately, Sir Desmond was less inclined to taciturnity than the medical man, or just more socially adept.

'I gather you're not a local resident, Mrs. Fletcher? What brings you to Appsworth Hall?' Implicit in the question was an inference that she did not belong in the world of plumbers. Hearing her speak a few words to somebody else had been enough to make him place her on his side of the fence.

'I'm a writer,' she told him.

A fleeting spasm of distaste crossed his face, quickly hidden. 'Ah, one of these modern clever young women.'

'I don't claim to be clever,' Daisy said coldly. 'I'm a journalist; I don't write literary novels, or blank verse, or anything like that. Mostly just articles for magazines, about places and history, but Lucy – Lady Gerald – and I are doing a book about follies.'

' "When lovely women stoop to follies . . ." ' he misquoted.

'Stoop! Most of them are on hills and we have to climb. But obviously you're ignorant of the existence of the Appsworth grotto. "Where ignorance lends wit, 'tis folly to be wise." '

'Wise after the event, I'm afraid! You and Lady Gerald are writing a book about the follies of eighteenth-century landowners, not of mankind in general, or lovely women in particular.'

'Strictly speaking, I'm doing the writing. Lucy is a photographer.'

'Tell me about the Appsworth grotto.'

'We haven't seen it yet. We arrived too late this afternoon. According to what we've heard, though, it's the best in the country. There never were very many, and most are in a shocking state of dilapidation, but when Mr. Pritchard bought Appsworth Hall, he repaired this one. Practically rebuilt it, in fact. They say he did an excellent job of it.'

'I expect he did, as far as the physical fabric is concerned, at least. The firm is noted for good, solid workmanship. Aesthetically – '

Daisy laughed. 'Aesthetically, grottoes are noted for a mishmash of Romantic sentimentality, Gothic grotesquerie, and Classical pretensions.'

'Indeed! I shall have to make sure to visit the place while I'm here.'

'I understand you're at Appsworth to do business with the firm.'

'Not on my own account,' Sir Desmond said quickly, as if Daisy had accused him of robbing a bank.

'Of course not.'

'You're laughing at me, Mrs. Fletcher. Your generation may find it quaint, but I assure you, it's not so long since being personally involved with a manufacturing business could get one blackballed.'

'How fortunate that you're involved only on behalf of the government – or so I hear? And in the building business, rather than manufacturing.'

His eyes narrowed, though on the surface his manner remained urbane. 'You seem to know a great deal about my business. You're a journalist – but this isn't the place or the time. I'd like a word with you after dinner, if you please.'

'I'm not a reporter. And even if I were in the habit of regaling the scandal sheets with tidbits, which I'm not, I rather doubt they'd be interested in this particular snippet of news. But if you need further reassurance, I'll be happy to give it to you later.'

He gave an abrupt nod, and turned away to respond to Mrs. Howell's anxious twitterings on the subject of the lack of fish.

While sparring with him, Daisy had overheard Rhino, seated on Mrs. Howell's other side, ragging her about the bad soles. Lucy now distracted him with a question about some mutual acquaintance on the London social scene. She had been chatting quite happily with her other neighbour, the sandy young man, who had a Canadian accent. His name was apparently Armitage, but Daisy hadn't been able to hear enough of their conversation to work out what his place was in the scheme of things. His attention, in turn, was captured by the doctor's wife, as loquacious as her husband was taciturn. Perhaps, Daisy thought, her loquacity accounted for his taciturnity.

At least his silence left her free to study the rest of the diners. Armitage, though attending to the doctor's wife sufficiently to make the proper noises in the proper places, was gazing diagonally across the table at Julia, with a besotted expression on his face.

Oh dear, Daisy thought, another victim, and by the look of him one who was not likely to win Lady Beaufort's approval even if he earned Julia's.

Julia was on friendly terms with Owen Howell, as far as Daisy could tell, though they were on her side of the table, beyond the doctor, so she couldn't see them properly. A pleasant chat at the dinner-table was hardly significant, but what a turn-up if Julia were to fall for the plumber! It seemed at least as likely as that she should accept the abominable Rhino.

At the far end of the table, the unlikely quartet of Mr. Pritchard, Lady Ottaline, Lady Beaufort, and the young bureaucrat were getting on like a house on fire. Daisy decided Pritchard must be a brilliant diplomat, wasted on the world of plumbing.

A couple of maids removed the soup dishes. Sir Desmond turned to Daisy and said in a low voice, 'Why all this fishy business?'

'Much ado about nothing. I'll tell you later if you really want to know.'

The maids reappeared. An astonished silence fell as they placed in front of each diner a small plate with a couple of sardines, decorated with croutons and parsley.

Daisy looked at Lucy. Lucy looked at Julia. All three burst into fits of laughter. The infectious sound made most of the others smile, but Mrs. Howell looked ready to weep. Rhino didn't help by saying disdainfully, 'Fish! This might just possibly be adequate as a savoury.'

'I told Cook to do the best she could.'

'Very ingenious of her,' said Daisy. 'I'm sorry, Mrs. Howell. We were just laughing at a private joke. Nothing to do with your cook, or your excellent dinner.'

'Are you going to share it with us?' Pritchard enquired with a grin.

'Certainly not,' said Lucy, simultaneously with Julia's, 'Oh, we couldn't possibly, I'm afraid.'

'Just a bit of juvenile schoolgirlish nonsense,' Daisy explained. 'Not at all funny to anyone else.'

'Well, Lord Rydal, at least your obsession has given us all a bit of a laugh. If this isn't enough fish for you, you're welcome to mine, too. Winifred, you know I don't like fish.' Ignoring her resentful look, he beckoned to his butler. 'Barker, present this to Lord Rydal, with my compliments.'

Rhino looked askance at such a brazen departure from ordinary etiquette, but to insult his host at his own table would be an even worse breach of decorum. He was apparently conversant with the rules of good manners, even if the guiding principles escaped him. Daisy noticed that he ate all four sardines.

Dinner continued without further untoward events. Mrs. Howell managed to eat with her lips pursed. Daisy wondered whether she was contemplating revenge, perhaps in the form of offering her brother-in-law nothing but kippers and kedgeree for breakfast. Silent, she made no demands on Sir Desmond's attention. He apparently forgave Daisy for being a journalist and entertained her with a smooth flow of small talk. He had an endless fund of anecdotes, no doubt very useful to a civil servant, and some of them were even quite amusing.

At the end of the meal, Mrs. Howell was still lost in a brown study. She made no move to lead the ladies from the dining room. Daisy disliked the practice except insofar as it allowed her to escape cigar smoke – it was bad enough that Rhino had lighted a fresh cigarette after each course. She wondered whether the plumber's household had abandoned the custom of the ladies' withdrawal, or had never followed it. Then she realised that Lady Beaufort was staring at her with a slightly desperate fixed look. When her ladyship saw that she had Daisy's attention, she nodded towards their hostess.

Daisy leant forwards and said gently, 'Mrs. Howell, shall we leave the gentlemen to their port and cigars?'

She came to with a start and a shudder. 'Cigars? Horrible things.' She stood up. 'He *will* smoke them, though he knows I hate the smell.'

Daisy didn't believe it was the thought of cigars that had made her shudder.

The host went to the door and politely held it as the ladies departed. Daisy hung back so she was last to reach him. 'Would you mind awfully if I used your telephone, Mr. Pritchard?' she asked. 'It's a trunk call, I'm afraid, but of course I'll reverse the charges.'

'Of course you won't, my dear. Make as many calls as you want.'

'Thanks, one will do! I promised my husband I'd ring to let him know I arrived safely.'

'That's the ticket. But don't hang about waiting for the connection. Barker can fetch you to the telephone when the call goes through. I'll tell you what, how's this for a notion? Why don't you ask Mr. Fletcher to join us at the weekend? I don't know why I didn't think of it before. He'd be very welcome.'

Daisy beamed at him. 'That's frightfully kind of you. I'm not sure whether he's going to be free, but I'll pass on the invitation.'

'And ... I don't suppose ... Do you think Lord Gerald might like to come down as well?'

'I've no idea what his plans are, but I'll tell Alec to ring him up and ask.'

'Better check with Lady Gerald first.'

'She won't mind. If he comes, either she'll be glad to see him, or she'll be too busy taking photos to notice. We're both so much looking forward to exploring the grotto tomorrow.'

'No need to wait if you'd like to take a look later this evening. I had gaslights put in, you know.'

'Did you really? I'd like to see it.'

'I think you'll find the effect quite ... interesting.' Pritchard's tone had suddenly become mysterious, even creepy. 'I'll have it prepared.'

'Thank you.' Daisy went after the rest of the ladies.

How odd, she thought. Could anything be more prosaic than plumbing? Or manufacturing? A creepy manufacturer of plumbing supplies seemed like a contradiction in terms. All the same, she was jolly well going to drag Lucy out into the frosty night to accompany her to the grotto, like it or not.

CHAPTER 7

Daisy's call came through quite quickly. Barker summoned her before the men rejoined the ladies in the drawing room. He led the way across the front hall.

'The master said to use the apparatus in his den, madam,' he said, opening a door.

'Thank you, Barker.' Pritchard's den, at a glance, resembled any country gentleman's private retreat. Somewhat to her disappointment, she saw no obvious reminders of plumbing, historical or modern, just a large leather-topped desk, leather-covered chairs by the fireplace, several bookcases. She promised herself a quick look at the books after her call. It wasn't nosiness, she assured herself, just her usual inability to resist satisfying her curiosity about people. Reading a few titles wasn't snooping.

She sat down at the desk.

'If madam would be so kind as to hang up the receiver when the call is finished . . .'

'Of course,' said Daisy, surprised.

'I beg madam's pardon for mentioning the matter, but the fact is, one of our present guests never does so.'

'Lord Rydal? It would be just like him!'

'Far be it from me to contradict madam. Will that be all, madam?'

'Yes, thank you, Barker.' Daisy picked up the phone. 'Alec? Darling, we arrived safely.'

'So I gather.'

'You do sound grumpy. Bad day at work?'

'So-so. I got home early enough to play with the twins, for once. It would have been nice if you'd been there, too. Mrs. Gilpin was at her most difficult.'

'She always is when I'm away.'

'What's more, I'm going to have the weekend free, barring trouble, and you're off in the wilds of Wiltshire.'

'Do come down, darling. Mr. Pritchard's invited you, without my saying a word on the subject. He's rather a nice little man.' Daisy remembered the creepy feeling and added, 'I think.'

'You think? What does that mean?'

'I don't know exactly. I can't explain, not on the phone. It's nothing really.'

'I'm coming down, as soon as I can get away.' Alec's tone said, *I'm a policeman, don't argue with me.*

'Oh, good!'

'Ring me every evening till I arrive. Not before Saturday afternoon, I'm afraid. And if I find you're making a mystery just to get me to come – '

'Darling, I wouldn't! Oh, by the way, the invitation is for Gerald as well. Could you ring him, and if he can manage it, you could drive down together.'

'I can't see squeezing him into the Austin.'

'Why not? If you can fit Tom Tring in, you can fit Gerald.'

'I was thinking more of his dignity than his size.'

'Gerald's not that fussy! But let him drive.'

'Then the Bincombes would have two cars there, and we'd have none.'

'That's all right. I'll go back to town in luxury in Gerald's Daimler, and you can have the grand adventure of being driven by Lucy.'

'Not on your life! I'm too fond of mine. I'll ring him and we'll work it out one way or – '

'Caller, your three minutes are up. Do you want another three minutes?'

'No, thanks,' Alec said. 'Don't forget to ring tomorrow, love.'

'I won't. 'Night, darling. Give the babies a kiss from Mama.'

She wasn't sure how much of that he'd heard before they were cut off, but the babies were young enough not to notice if they didn't get a proxy kiss from Mama. In fact, they'd long since be in bed and asleep anyway. She missed them already.

Hanging up, she took extra care to make sure the receiver was securely in its hook. She didn't want the butler thinking she was as careless as Rhino of other people's convenience.

Beside the desk was a deep cabinet that appeared to hold wide but shallow drawers. Blueprints, Daisy guessed vaguely. She wasn't absolutely sure what a blueprint was, but something to do with technical designs, she thought. Resisting the temptation to peek, which really would be prying, she turned to the nearest bookcase.

The titles left her not much the wiser. There were books on hydraulics, hydrology, metallurgy, geology, and a couple more 'ologies she'd never heard of. Her school had not considered it necessary, or indeed advisable, for young ladies to study the sciences. Ceramics wasn't much more comprehensible, and how could anyone find enough to say about coal-gas to write a whole book on the subject? But others included pottery, porcelain, earthenware, and tile-making. Bathtubs and lavatories and wash-basins, sewer pipes and drainage tiles, Daisy assumed. As a landowner's daughter she had at least heard of these last. At Fairacres, the watermeadows by the Severn had flooded every winter and the drain tiles were constantly in need of upkeep.

Plumbing was a much more technical and scientific occupation than she had realised. And then there was the financial side of creating and running a large and successful business, successful enough to enable Mr. Pritchard to buy the estate from the impoverished Appsworth family. He must be a much cleverer man than he appeared on first acquaintance.

Daisy returned to the drawing room. During her absence, the men had gone in, but as she entered, the doctor said to his wife, 'Time to go, Maud.'

'Yes, dear.' She went on talking to Lady Beaufort.

'Maud!'

'Coming, coming. So you see, Lady Beaufort, I had absolutely no choice. I told her there was no question . . .'

Giving his babbling wife a look more likely to kill than cure, the doctor sat down in a corner and brooded.

Mr. Pritchard saw Daisy come in and came over to her. 'Call go through all right?' he asked.

'Yes, thank you. Alec will be happy to come down on Saturday if he can get away – he can never be absolutely sure till the last moment, I'm afraid. And he's going to ring Lord Gerald to see if he's free.'

'Excellent, excellent. And the children, how are they getting along without you? Lady Beaufort mentioned that you have twins.'

Daisy warmed to him again. No one who enquired after her babies could really be creepy. 'They have a very good and trustworthy nanny, or I wouldn't leave them.'

'Glenys and I always wanted children,' he said regretfully, 'but it was not to be. Her nephew Owen is like a son to me. He'll have everything when I go, the house as well as the firm. But let's not think of such gloomy things. Have a liqueur to warm you and then I'll take you to the grotto. I recommend a Drambuie. Those Scots know a thing or two about keeping out the cold.'

Having accepted his offer, glass in hand, she looked for Sir Desmond, intending to reassure him about her lack of interest in writing about council house bathrooms. She wondered why he was so anxious about it. Was there some sort of shenanigans going on? Bribery and corruption, she thought vaguely, but she didn't know enough about any aspect of the subject to have a clue whether he was in a position to sign a contract in favour of Pritchard's, or anything of the kind. Perhaps Alec would be able to enlighten her, though she wasn't at all sure she really wanted to be enlightened.

The Principal Deputy Secretary was talking to Julia and Rhino, so Daisy joined Lucy, who was chatting vivaciously with the Principal Deputy Secretary's Private Secretary.

'Daisy, did you meet Mr. Carlin?'

'Not properly. How do you do?'

'How do you do, Mrs. Fletcher.' Carlin was very young, scarcely down from Oxford, at a guess. His family must have influence for him to be a Private Secretary rather than a common or garden secretary or a mere clerk; not sufficient influence to get him into the more prestigious Foreign Office, however.

'I've told him Alec is a civil servant, too,' said Lucy, her eyes sparkling with mischief. She knew that was Daisy's usual evasive description. Most people equated bureaucrats with dullness so it generally served to head off further enquiries.

But to young Carlin, not yet jaded, the civil service that had recently swallowed his life without a hiccup was still a subject of absorbing interest. 'Which office is Mr. Fletcher in?' he asked eagerly. 'What's his line?'

'Oh, this and that.' Daisy gave a vague wave intended to signify that she'd never bothered to find out what Alec did every day. 'Lucy, Mr. Pritchard has offered to show us the grotto tonight. You will come along with us, won't you, Mr. Carlin?'

'I say, of course! Only too delighted.'

'Darling, you can't be serious,' Lucy protested. 'At this time of night? It's freezing cold outside, and I wouldn't be able to take any photos. You can write about the grotto by night if you want, but I'm not wasting plates and flash-powder when I can't even see what I'm photographing.'

'Mr. Pritchard has put in lighting. He says the effect is worth seeing so you're jolly well going to come and see it, photos or no. You won't be cold if you wear your motoring coat.'

Between them, Daisy and Mr. Pritchard rounded up most of the party for the expedition. Lady Ottaline wasn't keen, but when she realised it was the older ladies – Lady Beaufort, Mrs. Howell, and the doctor's wife – who were staying behind, she obviously didn't want to be counted among them.

Daisy noticed that it wasn't till Lady Ottaline committed herself that her husband agreed to go. However, as they all set out across the gardens behind the house, Sir Desmond offered the support of his arm not to his wife, but to Daisy.

The only person unaccounted for was the mysterious Mr. Armitage. He hadn't joined the others in the drawing room. Daisy resolved to interrogate Lucy about him. After sitting next to him at dinner, she surely must have learnt something about him.

The gravel path was well-lit by wrought-iron gas lamp-posts of an old-fashioned appearance though no doubt the workings had been refurbished to modern standards. The light was bright enough to be helpful without being garish. On either side of the path, the ghosts of trees, bushes, and hedges loomed ahead, to vanish behind as they passed.

'One might almost suppose oneself in Hyde Park,' said Sir Desmond derisively.

'It may not be according to Repton or Capability Brown,' Daisy retorted, 'but the lights seem to me extremely sensible if one has an attraction in the gardens that is worth seeing at night and one doesn't want one's guests to break their necks.'

'I hope it actually is worth seeing at night.'

'You should have waited to hear from the rest of us before going to see it.'

He glanced back at those of the party following them – in front were Julia, young Carlin, and Pritchard. Daisy thought Sir Desmond frowned, but they were halfway between lamps and the light wasn't bright enough to be sure. All he said was, 'I'd rather see for myself.'

She, too, looked back, turning slightly and using the movement as an excuse to let go his arm. She didn't need his assistance on the smooth path, and she was not altogether comfortable with him. Lucy was a little way behind them. Like Daisy, she had changed into walking shoes. She was with Owen Howell and was being polite, as far as Daisy could tell.

At the rear came Lady Ottaline and Lord Rydal. She was clinging to his arm, tottering along on her high heels, which were most unsuitable for a night-time excursion in the garden, or any time, come to that. Daisy heard a giggle that certainly didn't come from Lucy. Odd, she thought, considering the looks they had exchanged on meeting earlier. And why hadn't Rhino stuck to Julia's side as usual?

Looking away from the lights, Daisy saw a glint of hoarfrost on the grass. The air was crisp. Above, the floor of heaven was 'thick inlaid with patines of bright gold,' as Lorenzo put it with the aid of the Bard, millions of stars seldom seen in England's cloudy climate and never in the smoky skies of the metropolis. Ahead, against the backdrop of the Milky Way and its attendant swarms, swirls, and clusters, loomed a black hill, smoothly rounded, with a spinney at the summit looking ridiculously like a poodle's topknot.

The path started to ascend, with short flights of steps every now and then.

'Aren't you glad now to have the lamplight?' Daisy asked teasingly.

'One might certainly come quite a cropper without,' Sir Desmond admitted. 'Especially on the way down.'

They crossed a wooden bridge over a gurgling brook. Daisy leant for a moment against the stout wooden rail, looking down at the ripples.

'I doubt that it's very deep,' said Sir Desmond, 'but there, I concede, you have another good reason for the lights. I wouldn't want to take a dip in this weather. I'll have to give you best, Mrs. Fletcher.'

'Give it to Mr. Pritchard,' Daisy suggested.

'Yes, I can see Pritchard is above all a practical man.'

'I wouldn't go so far. Rebuilding a ruined grotto is hardly a practical act. If you ask me, it shows he has a distinctly romantic streak.'

'A romantic plumber! Dreadful thought.'

'It does rather boggle the mind,' Daisy agreed, laughing. 'But there's really no reason even the most practical person shouldn't have his romantic moments.'

CHAPTER 8

Beyond the bridge the path followed the stream's meanders, rising higher and higher above the water. Ahead of Daisy and Sir Desmond, Pritchard, Julia, and Carlin passed a lamppost and disappeared round a limestone bluff.

'Oh!' Julia's exclamation rang out above a low, sonorous hum almost like the buzzing of a swarm of bees. 'How marvellous!'

'I say, sir, splendid!'

'Do let's go in.'

'If you don't mind, Miss Beaufort, let's wait for the others,' Pritchard suggested.

'I can't think why you haven't showed it off to Mother and me before. We've been here nearly a week.'

'I was saving it till Mrs. Fletcher and Lady Gerald arrived.'

Daisy hurried forward to see the cause of all the enthusiasm. Her foot landed on something large, hard, and unstable, and her ankle gave way. Luckily Sir Desmond had kept pace with her. Her desperate clutch found his arm. 'Ouch!'

'Steady! What happened?'

'I twisted my ankle. I think I've just ricked it. Yes, it's better already. Thank you for catching me. I stepped on something . . .' She glanced back at the path. 'Yes, look, a big stone. It must have fallen from the cliff.'

'I'd better chuck it in the stream before someone else trips and lands in the water.' He suited action to the words and fastidiously dusted his gloved hands together. 'There, one hazard the less. Gas lamps or no gas lamps, you'd better slow down, Mrs. Fletcher.'

They proceeded round the bend at a more decorous pace, joining the first arrivals on a sort of paved landing.

'Oh!' Daisy echoed Julia in the only possible reaction to the spectacle before her.

A waterfall plunged twenty feet or so into a dark pool. The cascade itself was anything but dark, because the ingenious plumber had somehow placed lamps in niches behind it. The sheet of falling water glowed, flinging out droplets that flashed and glinted as they caught the light.

'Isn't it wonderful, Daisy?'

'It is. How very clever, Mr. Pritchard. I wish Lucy could take a photo of it.'

'Of what?' Lucy came round the bluff, with Owen Howell. 'Mr. Howell refuses to tell me – ' She fell silent, contemplating the luminous cascade. 'That's quite a sight, Mr. Pritchard,' she said with a sigh.

'I could go back to the house and fetch your camera, Lady Gerald,' Howell offered.

'Believe me, if I thought I could do it, I'd fetch the camera myself. But I'm afraid a photograph simply wouldn't do it justice.'

'Why not?'

Lucy started to explain about long exposure times and moving subjects. Meanwhile Daisy, who had heard it all before, looked up at the source of the waterfall. Issuing from a dimly lit cavern, the stream was split in two by a plinth on which posed a marble female in Greek draperies, rather like the statue in the fountain at home. Instead of water streaming from her urn, however, she poured forth a marble river. She had small wings on her head and the lower part of her gown was decorated with a relief of bulrushes. Daisy racked her brain.

'Tethys!' she said triumphantly, and scribbled a few descriptive words in the notebook she had, of course, brought with her. Her version of Pitman's shorthand was at the best of times rather hit and miss. She hoped she'd remember what she'd written.

'You know your Greek mythology,' said Pritchard. 'Most people ask me why not Poseidon.'

'Tethys?' Sir Desmond mused aloud. 'Wasn't she a goddess of the sea? So why not Poseidon?'

'She was the mother of rivers, sir,' Carlin said eagerly. 'A minor figure. I'm not surprised you don't remember her.'

'Hmph.' His superior was not pleased to be reminded of the gulf of years separating him from his education. 'You've studied the classics, Mrs. Fletcher?'

'We read the myths at school, in English. I expect you concentrated on the gods, but I, at least, was always more interested in the goddesses.'

Julia giggled. 'Wasn't Tethys the one who had an incredible number of children? As well as the rivers, I mean.'

'Circe among them,' Carlin chortled, 'if I'm not mistaken.'

'Miss Harrison passed rather rapidly over Circe, d'you remember, Julia? I expect we missed a lot, reading the expurgated translations.'

'I wonder where my wife's got to?' Sir Desmond said abruptly. 'I hope she didn't turn her ankle, like Mrs. Fletcher. In those ridiculous shoes of hers, she'd certainly sprain if not break it. Perhaps I'd better go back and see. Don't wait for us.' He turned on his heel and was gone.

'Dear me,' said Pritchard, 'did you wrench your ankle, Mrs. Fletcher? I'm so sorry. The gardeners rake the path regularly, but I'm afraid bits and pieces keep rolling down the slopes.'

'No harm done. I can't even feel it any longer. Do say we can go up to the grotto now.'

'Perhaps I ought to make sure Lady Ottaline is all right . . . '

'Sir Desmond and Lord Rydal can take care of Lady Ottaline between them,' Lucy said impatiently, 'if in fact she's come to any harm.'

'Which I haven't.' The lady in question came into view, swathed in furs, leaning heavily on her husband's arm. 'You didn't tell me it was such a long way,' she said reproachfully to Pritchard.

'It's not really very far, Lady Ottaline. I'm afraid I didn't notice your footwear.'

'You didn't?' Pouting, she held out one slender – not to say bony – ankle and green glacé shoe with a diamanté clasp and very high, narrow heels. She turned it this way and that. 'They're intended to be noticed.'

'Charming,' said Sir Desmond dryly, 'but not intended for a walk through a garden at night.'

Rhino had arrived close behind them, the smoke from his inevitable cigarette curling up into the still air. He made straight for Julia's side. He murmured in her ear while Lady

Ottaline was complaining, then said to Pritchard, 'Well, are we going into your dashed grotto or not?'

'There are steps. I don't know if Lady Ottaline will be able to – '

'I'm freezing, standing here. I'm going up.' Lucy started the climb.

The steps, cut into the limestone cliff surrounding the mouth of the grotto, ascended steeply for about ten feet. Daisy was glad to see a stout-looking iron railing. She set off after Lucy, whose fashionably tubular frock didn't appear to impede her much, one of the advantages of a knee-length hemline.

Each step was worn, the centre lower than the sides. Daisy deduced that the flight had been cut by the original creators of the grotto and trodden since by generation after generation.

Lucy, plodding upwards ahead of her, glanced back. 'Darling, this had jolly well be worth the effort.'

'You must admit it looks intriguing from below.'

'I wouldn't be up here else. I hope Pritchard's going to lend me a gardener to carry my stuff tomorrow.'

'Has he given you any reason to suppose he might not?'

'No,' Lucy admitted grudgingly. 'He seems quite a decent little man.'

Dismayed, Daisy looked behind her to make sure the 'decent little man' was not close at her heels. He was not, but his nephew was a few steps below her. The roar of the waterfall had covered the sound of his footsteps, and she hoped it had also covered the sound of Lucy's condescending words. Unlike Lady Ottaline's husky contralto, Lucy possessed a penetrating soprano.

Owen Howell showed no sign of having heard, or perhaps he didn't care a hoot about Lucy's opinion of his uncle. Looking up at Daisy, he said something she couldn't make out.

'Sorry?'

He raised his voice. 'My uncle would like you to wait till he gets there to explore.'

'Of course.' Why? Because he wanted to see their initial reactions at firsthand? Because parts were dangerous – falling ceilings, perhaps? Daisy wondered, glancing up a trifle nervously as she followed Lucy from the steps onto the floor of the grotto. Surely not! Pritchard would never permit such inefficiency, and if the hazard was a recent occurrence, Howell was there to keep them away from it. Or was the request to wait related to their host's mysterious and some-what sinister eagerness to show them the grotto at night?

'Hold on,' she called to Lucy, who was heading for the rear of the cave. 'Mr. Pritchard doesn't want us wandering about before he comes up.'

'Why not? I can't see that he'd be much help if one of us fell into the Styx.'

'Lucy!'

'I just want to . . . Oh, all right! I probably can't tell in the dark, anyway.'

Though murky, it wasn't really dark in the grotto. Just above head-height on the walls gas lamps burnt, the mantles shielded by translucent shells that diffused the light. Among the thousands of shells encrusting the rugged walls, here and there mother-of-pearl gleamed and crystals glittered. The floor was polished limestone, five or six yards in breadth, ending at a low stone parapet beyond which the stream flowed swift and smooth, satiny black, to its drop into the pool beneath.

One couldn't walk into the stream unaware, Daisy thought, but it wouldn't be difficult to fall over the low wall.

'At least it's warmer in here,' said Lucy with a shiver.

'That's partly the gas lights,' Howell told her, 'and partly the insulating effect of the tons of rock around us.'

'Don't remind me!' With another shiver, Lucy looked up.

The upper part of the walls sloped inwards and gradually converged on either side. Their meeting point was beyond the reach of the lights.

'Are there stalactites?' Daisy asked. 'And stalagmites? I can never remember which is which, but this is the right kind of rock for them, isn't it?'

'Yes, the same stuff that furs pipes and kettles. There are some knobs and protuberances up there that may grow into stalactites in a few centuries. My uncle considered bringing some in from elsewhere or having some manufactured, but he decided against it.'

'Are the shells real?' Lucy sounded suspicious.

'Oh yes. Most of them were already here when Uncle Brin bought Appsworth, though many had fallen off the walls. He brought in more to fill the gaps. In fact, some are where nature put them. Limestone and chalk are made up of ancient shells, you know. There are fossils, too.'

'I'd like to see those.' Julia joined them.

'I'll be happy to show you tomorrow, Miss Beaufort, if I get home in time. I'm afraid the light's not good enough now to see them properly.'

'It's not good enough to see anything much,' grumbled Rhino, lighting a cigarette as he appeared on the heels of his beloved. 'What a waste of time!'

Daisy had to suppress an urge to shove him backwards down the steps. Someone else was probably behind him.

'Rhino, darling,' came Lady Ottaline's plaintive voice, 'do get a move on. I can't balance on this step forever.'

'I'm right here, my dear,' said Sir Desmond soothingly. 'You can't possibly fall.'

Rhino lumbered forwards. The Wandersleys entered the grotto, then Carlin, and bringing up the rear, Mr. Pritchard.

'Well, here we all are,' said their host, with a sigh of relief at having safely shepherded his unruly flock to their destination. 'It's as close to the way it used to look as I could make it, but the old pictures and descriptions aren't too clear.'

'Don't tell me the Appsworths had gas lighting put in,' Rhino said aggressively.

'No, it would have cost much too much if I wasn't in the business. Don't worry, you can't see them in daylight.'

'No good for photography,' Lucy grumbled.

'It's wonderful, but a bit spooky, isn't it?' said Julia.

'Don't!' Lady Ottaline's shudder combined the delicate with the theatrical.

'Grottoes were originally intended to be eerie.' Daisy had done her preliminary homework. 'That is, *originally* originally they were caves where hermits lived, the religious kind. But in English parks and gardens, they were supposed to be both picturesque and grotesque, and in general frightfully Gothic and romantic. The owners – '

'It's haunted!' shrieked Lady Ottaline, pointing towards the rear of the cave.

Everyone swung round. A cowled figure lurked in the dim depths. On silent feet, it glided to one side, started to withdraw, then suddenly vanished.

CHAPTER 9

'By Jove, an intruder!' exclaimed Carlin. 'Tally-ho! Don't worry, I'll nab him! Hey, you, stop!' He sprang after the monkish shape.

'Yoicks, tally-ho!' Rhino, too, rumbled into motion. Like his namesake, he was slow to get going but once under way would be very hard to stop.

But Daisy, as she turned, had seen Pritchard and Howell exchanging a conspiratorial glance of glee. Remembering Pritchard's mysterious eagerness to show her the grotto by night, she caught Carlin's arm as he passed her.

'Hold on! Something tells me our host is quite well acquainted with this particular ghost.'

'What?' asked the bemused young man. 'Let go, he'll get away!'

Uncle and nephew had managed to grab Rhino before he got up steam.

Pritchard chuckled. 'We are,' he confessed.

'Mr. Armitage,' said Julia.

'Exactly, Miss Beaufort. I should have realised Mrs. Fletcher was too knowledgeable to be fooled.'

'I was just about to say, the owners of grottoes in the eighteenth century often had an aged and infirm retainer in residence playing the hermit to give visitors a thrill.'

'He certainly gave me a thrill,' Lucy admitted dryly. 'Not that I believe in ghosts, but – '

'I do.' Lady Ottaline played the fragile damsel to the hilt. 'Are you sure that wasn't . . . ?'

'Quite sure,' Howell assured her. 'Come back to his lair and see.' He offered his arm, but she chose Rhino's.

Julia had already set off in pursuit of Armitage. Rhino followed her, Lady Ottaline attached to him at the elbow. The others went after them.

'I wonder if a photo of the hermit in daylight would look silly?' Lucy said to Daisy. She started muttering to herself about exposure and focus and filters.

Sir Desmond was on Daisy's other side. 'Quite a surprise,' he murmured. 'I'd never have credited Pritchard with sufficient imagination.' He sounded slightly amused, but Daisy got the impression that underneath, well hidden by his shell of imperturbability, was a different sentiment. Anger? Surely he couldn't be seriously annoyed by the apparition's having given his wife a shock.

Lady Ottaline was much easier to read than Sir Desmond. She had been startled but not, Daisy was sure, genuinely frightened. Was her husband unable to see through her penchant for melodrama? He hadn't rushed to her side to comfort her. Something else must have provoked him, or Daisy had mistaken his emotions.

The latter was probably the case, she decided. She wasn't well acquainted with him, and she couldn't even see his face clearly. In fact, she was indulging in pure speculation, as Alec would undoubtedly have pointed out to her.

As she pondered, they penetrated deeper into the grotto, passing a number of statues on the way. Most stood in niches in the walls, impossible to identify in the pre-vailing gloom. Ahead however, a stalwart Neptune barred the way. From the navel down, as a change from the usual scanty drapery about the loins, he was modestly clad in stylised marble waves with the heads of horses in place of whitecaps. From this frozen sea emerged a naked torso, a head adorned with the usual wildly curling hair and beard, and two muscular arms, one wielding a trident.

Lucy stopped to contemplate the water-god. 'I wonder if it's always being wet that makes his hair curl. Rain plays havoc with mine.'

Daisy laughed. 'I bet you're the first person in history who's posed that particular question!'

'What about the original artist who depicted him that way? Back in Rome or Ancient Greece or wherever it was?'

'Neptune or Poseidon. Sir Desmond, which do you – ? Oh, he's disappeared.'

'He went round behind the statue. Everyone must have gone that way.'

'Yes, I can hear them. Come on.'

Poseidon stood sentry to one side of a low arch. His wife Amphitrite guarded the other side, crowned with shells and crab-claws, dolphins frolicking about her legs. Beyond the arch was a short tunnel.

'It's much lighter at the end,' Lucy said thankfully. 'I'm getting tired of groping through the dark.'

'Hush a minute. I heard Rhino say something about a second monk.'

'Here's a stone one,' Lord Rydal cawed as Daisy and Lucy emerged from the tunnel. 'Much to be preferred to the real thing, what?'

'St. Vincent Ferrer,' said Pritchard, 'the patron saint of plumbers.'

'Popish nonsense!'

'What makes you think you have the right to disparage anyone's religion?' Pritchard demanded angrily. He had put up with a lot from the earl, but apparently this was the last straw. 'I happen to be a Methodist, and as you can see, I've put St. Vincent out here with a lot of pagan gods, not in a shrine in the house, but I don't hold with disrespecting other people's beliefs.'

His outburst stunned Rhino. 'Hold on, hold on! No offence meant. I just say what I think.'

'It's about time you started thinking before you say.'

'Gosh,' Lucy whispered in Daisy's ear, 'I thought Pritchard was a bit of a milksop, but Rhino is positively cowering.'

'A milksop wouldn't have risen to be Bathroom King. Though I wouldn't exactly say Rhino is cowering.'

'Perhaps not quite, but I've never seen him even slightly taken aback before. It must have been a severe shock to the system. I bet he's seething.'

'He wouldn't try to . . .'

'Try to what?'

'Oh, you know, get his own back.'

'Do him in, you mean? Don't be silly, of course not. You've got murder on the brain, my girl. That's what comes of marrying a detective. I'm going to see what excuse Mr. Armitage has for playing the fool in a monk's robe.'

'You were talking to him at dinner,' Daisy said, trying to keep an eye on Pritchard and Rhino as they went towards the hermit. His cowl thrown back to reveal Armitage's roundish, snub-nosed, sandy-haired, altogether un-ascetic countenance, he was chatting with Carlin and Julia. 'Who is he?'

'Some sort of colonial,' Lucy said vaguely. 'Canadian? Yes, Canadian. Quite amusing. Mr. Armitage, I do think you might have warned me you were planning to scare us all to death.'

'Would you have been scared to death if I'd warned you, eh, Lady Gerald?' he asked with a grin.

'I must say,' Carlin put in, 'you ladies don't look as if you turned a hair.'

'Hairdressers can work wonders these days,' said Daisy.

'Naturally, I wouldn't have risked making your hair stand on end if I hadn't known modern hairdressing methods could put it right in a trice.'

'I, for one,' said Julia grandly, 'am quite capable of brushing my own hair. Lucy, Daisy, Mr. Armitage has been telling us that Mr. Pritchard employs him to play the hermit.'

'Not exactly "employs," eh? He doesn't usually bother with a hermit at this time of year, but I wanted to take a look at some old papers he has in the house, and he offered me access and room-and-board in exchange for playing hermit now and then. He'd already heard from you, Lady Gerald, and Mrs. Fletcher, about putting the grotto in your book. In the summer, when he has constant requests to see it, he hires an actor full-time. He's even built in quite a decent sort of bed-sitting-room through there.' He pointed at another archway.

'Gas and water laid on, I assume,' Lucy drawled.

'But of course. All the same, I'm glad he doesn't expect me to live there at this time of year. In the summer it would be OK.'

Pritchard came over to them. Daisy looked to see if Rhino was pouting in a corner, but he had joined the Wandersleys and Howell. He was lighting a cigarette yet again, and his expression was no more bad-tempered than usual. No doubt Pritchard's rebuke had disconcerted him for only a moment. In fact, if anyone was pouting, it was Lady Ottaline.

Daisy wondered momentarily what irked her. However, what little she had seen of the lady had not inspired any desire to become better acquainted. Curiosity might be her besetting sin, but she simply didn't much care what her ladyship's troubles were.

'Mr. Pritchard,' Julia greeted him gaily, 'how could you play such a trick on us? If my mother had come, she'd have been startled out of her wits.'

'No she wouldn't. I consulted Lady Beaufort first. I wanted to be sure she had no objection. Besides, she has too many wits ever to be startled out of them.' He patted Armitage's shoulder. 'How do you like my hermit?'

'He's quite the best hermit I've ever seen,' said Daisy.

'The only one, I expect,' he said, laughing.

'Unless you count hermit crabs. They'd have a wonderful time in here with all the shells.' She glanced about. In his shell-walled sanctuary, St. Vincent dwelt among Oceanids, Nereids, and Naiads, all scantily draped.

'Do tell,' said Lucy, 'is the hermit's lair decorated in the same style? Mr. Armitage says you've provided living quarters here in the grotto.'

'No, creosote to keep the place dry, and plain white distemper. You can have too much of a good thing. Would you like to see it?'

Lucy started to deny any desire to do so, but Daisy forestalled her. 'Yes, please. I doubt I'll use it for the follies book, but I've been meaning to ask if you'd mind if I wrote a magazine article about Appsworth . . . ?'

'As well? Delighted. I'm sure Armitage'll be able to help you with family history, the way he's been poring over all those fusty old papers the Appsworths left behind.'

Armitage muttered something, looking as if he could think of approximately fifty-thousand ways he'd rather spend his time. He dug his pipe-and-tobacco pouch out of the depths of his robe and started stuffing the fragrant shreds into the bowl.

'Did you light the gas in the back room?' Pritchard asked him.

'Yes, sir. Both the lights and the fire.'

'Good, good. This way, anyone who'd like to come.'

As Julia took Pritchard's arm and moved towards the next arch, Daisy hung back and said to the Canadian, 'I don't want to bother you if you'd rather not.'

'That's all right. Mr Pritchard's been very accommodating. I guess if he wants me to give you a hand . . . ' He struck a match and started that desperate puffing that eventually results in a lit pipe. Sometimes. Pausing in mid-puff, he asked, 'What sort of information are you looking for? What sort of articles do you write?' He sounded annoyed and a trifle defensive.

Why defensive? Not that she was after scandal, but in any case, if the Appsworths had wasted their last pennies in riotous living, it was no skin off his nose, nor Pritchard's. What exactly was his interest in the Appsworths' history?

The only explanation she could think of was that he'd

found a really good story and wanted to keep it for a scoop of his own. But what had brought him to Appsworth Hall in the first place? All the way from Canada!

Curiouser and curiouser.

Armitage struck a fourth match as he and Daisy followed the others into a surprisingly spacious room. At last the tobacco caught and blue smoke wafted up. Alec smoked a pipe and Daisy didn't mind the smell as much as cigarette smoke, or worst of all, cigars.

They were followed in turn by the Wandersleys, Rhino, and Howell. They were all smoking, Rhino waving his cigarette holder as he made some vehement remark Daisy didn't catch. She hoped the hermit's lair was well ventilated.

'Well,' said Armitage, 'what about this article of yours?'

'I'll tell you later. Hush, I want to hear what Mr. Pritchard has to say.' She moved closer, notebook in hand. Armitage went over to a small wardrobe – brought in in pieces, presumably, given the hazards of the path – and shrugged out of his habit. Emerging in his dinner jacket, he hung up the robe and headed towards Julia like a moth to a woolly jumper.

Pritchard, meanwhile, said with pride, 'You wouldn't guess it started as another natural cave, would you? The workmen broke through into it by accident when we were dolling up the second cave.'

He turned out to be a good storyteller. He made finding the cave and exploring it sound almost like a Rider Haggard adventure. Even Rhino listened. Daisy took a few notes, on both the original discovery and the resulting room.

With ten people in it, the room felt crowded, but for its intended solitary inhabitant it was more than adequate. Apart from the lack of a window, it could have been anywhere. Though there was no natural light, the plain white walls made it bright, and rush matting gave it an air of comfort. Against one wall was a divan bed covered with a counterpane in a jazzy blue-and-green pattern. Two Windsor chairs flanked a deal table. A gas fire dispelled the subterranean chill.

'As you see,' Pritchard continued, 'we've laid on gas. There's good natural ventilation, luckily.' With the flourish of a conjuror, he drew aside a curtain to reveal a wash-basin and a copper geyser. 'And hot and cold running water. This is one of the same new-style safety geysers as we have in the house. Unless the water supply is turned on, the gas won't turn on, so it's not likely to blow up from steam pressure and practically impossible for it to get hot enough to melt down.'

His nephew started to explain the technical details. Daisy's mind wandered.

A row of paperback books on a shelf nearby made her squint to read the titles. Thrillers and detective stories! It was all very well Lucy saying she was obsessed with murder. Not only was it untrue, she wasn't the only one by a long chalk.

Carlin asked about the ventilation. He seemed to be the only person still concentrating on what Pritchard and Howell had to say. Julia, Lucy, and the hermit were chatting in low voices. Armitage's pipe appeared to be giving him trouble; he was striking match after match, and puffing away without apparent effect. Daisy decided one reason she didn't mind pipe smoke was that pipe-smokers so rarely actually managed to keep their tobacco alight for long.

Lady Ottaline had sat down on one of the chairs. She had her husband and Lord Rydal in attendance. As Daisy glanced that way, Rhino was staring hungrily at Julia. He started towards her, only to be called back by Lady Ottaline.

'Rhino, darling, you'll take me back to the house, won't you? I'm getting frightfully cold. I do believe my toes are frost-bitten.'

With obvious reluctance, Rhino turned.

'Those shoes!' Sir Desmond said testily. 'You'll be colder outside. Just wait till everyone's ready to leave.'

Pritchard couldn't help but have heard Lady Ottaline's complaint. Fortunately, he seemed to be amused, rather than justifiably affronted. 'Owen, we've got carried away by our hobby-horses again. Time we were heading back to the house.'

Howell took out a gold pocket-watch. 'Good lord, yes, Uncle. Mother will be worrying about when to serve coffee. I'll show you the rest later,' he added to Carlin. 'We've the same machine in the house, and I already promised to demonstrate it to Mrs. Fletcher.'

'Thank you, sir,' the young civil servant said with every appearance of delight. He should rise high in his chosen profession.

Daisy, however, had decided against an article on modern inventions.

'Coffee!' exclaimed Lady Ottaline. 'Bliss! Anything hot. I'd even drink cocoa. Rhino!' She grabbed his arm as he once again drifted towards Julia, who was on the way out with Armitage, heads together. 'I'll need your support on those dreadful steps.'

'You can take my arm, Ottaline,' said Sir Desmond. 'It sufficed on the way up.'

'But darling, these ridiculous shoes! I shan't feel safe without a *strong* arm.'

The three of them followed Julia and Armitage, who had retrieved a lamplighter's pole from the niche behind one of the naiads. Lucy, Daisy, Carlin, and Pritchard went next, with Howell bringing up the rear, making sure all the gas fixtures were safely turned off.

Carlin went first down the steps. 'I'll catch you if you slip,' he told Lucy and Daisy.

Pritchard was close behind Daisy. One hand on the railing, she looked back to say to him, speaking loudly, over the sound of falling water, 'Such a good idea to illuminate the cascade. I'm glad you persuaded us to come out in the dark.'

'So am I,' he said with a grin, 'even though you spoilt my little surprise.'

'I shan't spoil the surprise when I write about your ghostly hermit,' she promised. 'Unless you'd rather I gave away the secret so that you don't get too many people coming to see the ghost for themselves?'

'I enjoy visitors. Make it as mysterious as you like.' As they reached the bottom of the steps, Pritchard stopped and said, 'Put your fingers in your ears, Mrs. Fletcher. I have to signal to Owen that we're all down and he can turn off the waterfall lights.'

'Oh, of course, you won't want them burning all night.'

Even with her fingers in her ears, Daisy heard his piercing whistle. One by one the lights went out. The tumbling water still caught some light from the cave mouth above, then that too was extinguished. The only light was from the lamp where the path curved round the bluff.

Daisy's eyes took a moment to adjust to the lower level of light. In that moment, cutting through the waterfall's hypnotic roar, someone screamed.

Daisy had a confused impression of flailing arms and legs tumbling off the path towards the stream below.

CHAPTER 10

Just ahead of Daisy and Pritchard, Carlin started to run forwards, shrugging out of his overcoat and ripping off his dinner jacket as he went. He stooped to lever off his shoes, at the same time peering over the edge, then straightened, pinched his nose between finger and thumb, and jumped.

'Good job he didn't dive,' Howell commented, coming down the last steps. 'There's only three or four feet of water there. Who went in?'

'Lady Ottaline,' Daisy told him.

'Those ridiculous shoes!'

'Owen,' his uncle said sharply, 'get back to the house, quickly, and tell Barker what's happened. They'll need hot drinks, hot water bottles, dry clothes – he'll know what to do.'

Howell departed at a trot.

In the meantime, Armitage had dashed back round the bend, stripping as he ran, and followed Carlin over the edge.

Julia appeared with her arms full of Armitage's discarded coat and jacket. 'He said there's an electric torch in the pocket of his coat. Hold on.' She dropped the jacket and delved into the coat-pocket. 'Here.' She switched it on and directed the beam down at the stream, but it was too weak to show anything but a reflective gleam from black waters.

Pritchard call down through cupped hands, 'Anyone hurt?'

Armitage's voice echoed back: 'No. But we're bloody freezing.'

'You'll have to go downstream. You can't climb out here. We'll meet you.'

'Right-oh!'

'Rhino!' Julia said in a surprised voice, 'I thought you'd have been the first in. But I suppose you *are* a bit elderly to go rushing to the rescue.'

Rhino stood a prudent foot back from the brink, peering into the darkness below. He had got as far as unbuttoning his coat, and no further. Sir Desmond, at his side, hadn't even gone that far, though it was his wife who'd fallen in. Still, he did have the excuse of being a couple of decades older.

Sir Desmond didn't appear to hear Julia's words, but Rhino said indignantly, 'Elderly!' With obvious reluctance he shrugged out of his coat and next moment he was on his way downwards.

'He was pushed!' Lucy hissed in Daisy's ear.

Daisy had no chance to question this extraordinary assertion, as Pritchard herded his remaining flock down the path. 'We'll have to give them a hand down by the bridge,' he explained, anxious and apologetic. 'The water's not deep but the bank is a couple of feet up. They shouldn't come to much harm. I can't think how it happened. It's never happened before!'

'Those ridiculous shoes,' Daisy, Lucy, and Julia chorussed.

'I certainly don't hold you to blame, Pritchard,' Sir Desmond agreed. He sounded more amused than anything. 'My wife will always put fashion above common sense. It's entirely her own fault.'

By the time they reached the stretch of low bank just before the bridge, a sodden trio had appeared round the bend. Carlin and Armitage, knee-deep, supported Lady Ottaline between them. She had lost or abandoned her coat and hat, and her hair hung in rats' tails round a face blotched and striped like an Indian brave on the warpath.

'*Escob annwyl*! Her face!'

'No need to go all Welsh,' said Lucy. 'Her make-up's run, that's all.'

'Oh, well done!' Julia cried encouragingly. 'Just a little farther.'

Sir Desmond and Mr. Pritchard hauled Lady Ottaline out, streaming with water and shivering convulsively. Between chattering teeth, she spat out, 'My m-mink! They m-made me leave it!'

'Too heavy,' said Armitage, taking the hand Julia held out to steady him as he climbed onto the bank.

'We couldn't have got Lady Ottaline out of there in her coat, sir,' Carlin agreed. Daisy and Lucy lugged him out. 'It weighed a ton, wet.'

'So do you,' said Lucy.

'No matter,' said Sir Desmond. 'I must thank you, gentlemen, for retrieving my wife. Her coat can wait until tomorrow.'

'It'll be ruined,' Lady Ottaline wailed.

'I daresay. I told you it was unsuitable for a country weekend. Here, wrap yourself in mine.'

'I can't walk back to the house with no shoes!'

'You couldn't walk *with* shoes. Come along, you don't think you could manage in mine, do you? And I'm not carrying you.'

'Rhino will!'

Everyone turned back to the stream. Unnoticed, Lord Rydal had arrived and stood glowering. 'I most certainly will not. Get me out of here!'

Pritchard stepped forwards, but Carlin and Armitage were ahead of him. Each grabbed one of Rhino's outstretched hands.

'On your marks . . .' said Sir Desmond, 'get set . . . heave!'

For a moment it looked as if Carlin and Armitage were going to join Rhino in the water. Then they did. They landed face down and Rhino went over backwards with a tremendous splash that showered those on the bank.

Though Daisy's coat protected most of her, the water that hit her legs and face was icy enough to make her gasp. She realised how cold Lady Ottaline must be, even with her husband's coat over her wet things.

'Mr. Pritchard,' she said, 'Lady Ottaline needs to get dry and warm, and she shouldn't walk back to the house alone.'

'I can't walk,' Lady Ottaline moaned.

'Bosh,' said Lucy, 'it'll warm you up.'

'My shoes are squelching,' Daisy put in hurriedly, if not quite accurately. 'I'll take them off and walk on the grass with you. It won't be as uncomfortable as the gravel.'

'All you young ladies had better go,' said Pritchard cheerfully. 'Sir Desmond, that leaves you and me to help the others out.'

'I ought to go with my wife.'

Julia scotched his escape. 'Don't worry, Sir Desmond, we'll take good care of her.'

'We'll send out a search party,' Lucy promised satirically, 'if you don't catch us up by the time we reach the house.'

Lady Ottaline complained constantly as she and Daisy crunched across the frosty grass. Daisy didn't want to sound equally whiny, so she held her tongue though she was sure her toes must be getting frost-bitten. Lucy and Julia crunched along the gravel path beside them, Julia making encouraging remarks.

Halfway to the house, they met Howell returning with three menservants to the rescue. A practical man, he had brought several pairs of wellingtons.

'Rubber boots!' exclaimed Lady Ottaline. 'I've never worn rubber boots in my life. I wouldn't be seen dead wearing those hideous things.'

'I would,' said Daisy. 'Thanks, Mr. Howell, just what I need.' She hung on to Lucy's arm and thrust her feet into the smallest pair. 'They're better than nothing, Lady Ottaline, honestly.'

'Don't be asinine, Lady Ottaline,' Lucy said sharply, adding with more truth than tact, 'No one's going to see you whose opinion you care a fig about. Do you want to catch pneumonia?'

'The others will need your help, I'm sure, Mr. Howell,' Julia suggested.

As soon as Howell and the servants went on, Lady Ottaline gave in. She might not care a fig for his opinion, but he was male – and she couldn't see the figure she already cut in a man's overcoat that could have gone round her three times, with her hair dripping in lank rats' tails and her face streaked in clownish red, white, and black.

Clomping along with numb feet in boots two sizes too large, Daisy tottered. Lucy propped her up and supported her the rest of the way. Just behind them came Julia and Lady Ottaline, the latter complaining constantly.

'All I want,' Daisy said when they reached the terrace behind the house, 'is a hot bath.'

'You won't be the only one. I wouldn't mind it myself.'

'At least we won't run out of hot water, thanks to Pritchard's Plumbing.'

'I never said plumbers aren't a good thing in their place. Oh lord, the old biddies are waiting to hear all about it.'

Mrs. Howell and Lady Beaufort were peering out of the French windows of the drawing room.

'This is where my t-t-t-teeth start chat-t-tering uncontrollably,' said Daisy. 'Can you get us past them without stopping to chat?'

'Of course, darling. In any case, we can't go in that way dripping, in gumboots.'

'Well, find a way in quickly, or my teeth really will start chattering uncontrollably.'

'Serves you right for that nonsense about your shoes squelching!'

'I had to do something, or we'd still be standing there trying to persuade her to budge.'

'*I* wouldn't.'

'No, I don't suppose you would, darling.' Daisy sighed. 'You always were much more strong-minded than I am.'

Julia caught up with them and was pointing out a side-door when it opened and the butler appeared. Barker showed his mettle. Not turning a hair at the sight of four aristocratic ladies in varying states of disarray, he quickly ushered them in. Relieving them of wet shoes, rubber boots, and other impedimenta, he assured them that maids had been alerted, baths were being drawn, and hot drinks prepared. He would take it upon himself to make their excuses to Mrs. Howell and Lady Beaufort.

A few minutes later, Daisy was wallowing in hot water, murmuring to herself, 'A butler is a lovesome thing, God wot,' and beginning to believe she might thaw out someday. Twice she turned on the hot tap with her toes, without any diminution in the blissful warmth.

'A plumber is a lovesome thing, too, God wot,' she told herself as she reluctantly heaved herself out of the water and wrapped herself in a vast towel, warm from the heated towel rail.

Beside her bed, she found a thermos flask of cocoa and a plate of Marie biscuits. Clearly she was not expected to put in an appearance downstairs if she chose not to. She chose not to, but she did want to talk to Lucy. She reached for the bell to summon a maid, intending to ask whether Lady Gerald was up and about. Just before she rang, she heard a tap on the door.

'Come in?' To her relief, Lucy appeared, elegant as ever in a silk kimono of her favourite peacock blue. 'Oh, it's you, darling. Come in and sit down. I was afraid it might be Mrs. Howell come to fuss.'

'It might have been, but I persuaded her if you didn't come down you'd rather be left in peace.'

'Thanks!'

'She sent all sorts of anxious messages, which I can't

remember. Actually, I think she's too busy fussing over Lady Ottaline to be frightfully concerned about lesser beings.'

'Is Lady Ottaline all right? She bore the brunt of the whole thing.'

'Sir Desmond insists she's healthy as a horse. I doubt she'd be pleased to hear it.'

'She does rather cultivate the fragile look, though it's very much the brittle kind of fragility. Lucy, what on earth made you say Rhino was pushed? Did you see someone give him a shove?'

'Heavens no! Nothing Alec would call evidence. It was too dark to see much, anyway, but that's what made it seem so opportune. You can't say he was exactly keen to jump in and help the other fellows rescue Lady O.'

'Rather the reverse.'

'So there he stood balking on the edge with someone on each side who had good reason to wish him ill. And in he went.'

Daisy thought back to the scene. 'Julia and Sir Desmond. He'd been pestering Julia to death, but I can't see her resorting to such drastic means, especially as all she has to do is keep saying no. As for Sir Desmond, his wife was flirting with Rhino – strange tastes some people have! – but if anything, Rhino was trying to deter her. At least that's what it looked like to me.'

'What you don't know, darling, because you retired from the world, is that they've been having a torrid affair for months.'

'Are you serious? There really is no accounting for tastes! But that's hearsay, of course.'

'If you mean did I see them come out of a hotel bedroom together at dawn and draw my own conclusions, no, I didn't. But it's not gossip I went digging for. I'm not turning into a second Great-Aunt Eva. It's been common knowledge among people one meets everywhere.'

'Does Julia know?'

'I think not. As a matter of fact, I've been wondering whether I ought to put her in the picture.'

'She must have seen that there's something between them. This evening, I mean. I should let sleeping dogs lie, if I were you. It's not as if she's fallen madly in love with him and you have to prevent her making a terrible mistake.'

'That's a good point. My lips are sealed. Actually, it'd be more to the point to tell Lady Beaufort.'

'Why don't you?'

'Catch me!' said Lucy, in a rare descent into vulgarity. 'You do it.'

'Not likely! What about Sir Desmond, did he know?'

'Oh, Daisy, what does it matter? No one was hurt, and in any case, I told you, I was joking when I said Rhino was pushed. Though I must say, if I'd been close enough, I'd have been awfully tempted.'

CHAPTER 11

Bright sun streamed through the window of Daisy's bed-room when Lucy flung back the curtains next morning.

'Get up. It's a glorious day.'

'What time is it?' Daisy mumbled, screwing her eyes tight shut.

'Breakfast-time. Come on, darling, we daren't miss a moment of this sunshine. It could be snowing by midday.'

'I can write perfectly well in snow.'

'But I can't take photos, as you know very well. Besides, you wouldn't want to walk along that path in snow, would you?'

'Nor in rain, come to that, which is much more likely.'

'In any case, even if it's shining the sun will be all wrong later.'

'Right-oh, I'm on my way.'

'Fifteen minutes, or I'll be back to fetch you,' Lucy threatened.

'Have a heart! Twenty. Now buzz off and let me get dressed in peace.'

When Daisy went down, she encountered Barker crossing the entrance hall with a silver coffee-pot on a tray.

'The breakfast parlour is that way, madam, second door on

the left. May I venture to enquire as to whether madam has suffered any ill-effects from last night's – ah – adventures?'

'Not at all, thank you, Barker. The hot bath and cocoa were just what was required. Do you know how Lady Ottaline is faring? She had the worst of it.'

'I understand her ladyship desires to remain abed this morning, madam, but Sir Desmond does not consider it necessary to send for a medical attendant.'

'Thank you, Barker.'

'Does madam prefer anything in particular for breakfast? Tea or coffee?'

'Tea, please. Indian. For the rest, I'll take what's going.'

'Very good, madam.'

In the breakfast parlour, Daisy found Lucy with Pritchard, Howell, and Armitage. None of the other ladies had yet put in an appearance. Pritchard bustled about seating her, helping her from the buffet.

'Will you try a little Welsh ham, Mrs. Fletcher? You've likely not eaten it before. We cure a leg of mutton instead of pork, you know, Wales having the most flavoursome mutton in the world. I believe you'll find it tasty.'

'Thank you, do give me a slice.' Daisy glanced at Lucy to see if she was indulging in Welsh ham, but she was sticking to her usual coffee and toast. 'You're very patriotic, Mr. Pritchard. I'm surprised you ever left Wales to come and live in England.'

'That was my father's doing. He started the firm in Wales, just when people were beginning to want indoor plumbing. As it grew, he found most of his sales were in England and it was more practical to have the factory here. That's when Owen's father, my wife's brother-in-law, invested in the company, which made the move to Swindon possible. My da made the right choice. We've continued to prosper. Then Appsworth Hall came on the market just when I was thinking of leaving the day-to-day business to Owen. Glenys wanted to move out of the town, so here we are – or rather,' he said sadly, 'here I am.'

'I hope your wife had a chance to enjoy living here.'

'We had a couple of good years before I lost her, thank you kindly.'

Daisy was itching to find out what had become of the Appsworth family. However, she didn't think it proper to ask the man who had profited, however legitimately, from their misfortunes.

Absently consuming the Welsh ham, she turned her gaze on Armitage. He was said to be 'taking a look at' old papers left at the Hall by the Appsworths. What his work involved and for whose benefit he was doing it had not been mentioned. He was the obvious person to ask, all the same.

Lucy was telling him about the photos she had taken of the front of the house in the evening light the day before.

'Would you be willing to sell me a print?' he asked. 'I've taken a few snaps with my Kodak, but I'd like to have a good professional picture of the old place.'

'By all means, if they come out well after the way Rhino was chucking my stuff about.'

'Chucking your stuff about?' Howell demanded in outrage, temporarily forsaking his methodical attack on his breakfast. 'Your photographic apparatus, you mean? Chucking it about? Why was he chucking it about? Did he damage anything?' Clearly the thought of machinery being abused was anathema to him.

'I don't think so,' said Lucy, 'but I can't be sure till I develop the plates.'

'He fetched Lucy's tripod for her,' Daisy explained, 'then dropped it on top of the camera and bag of plates.'

'How on earth did he come to do anything so halfway helpful?' Armitage exclaimed.

Lucy exchanged a glance with Daisy and they both laughed.

'My car was in the middle of the drive and he couldn't get past,' Lucy said dryly.

'Of course, *force majeure*. The only possible explanation.'

Pritchard said a trifle fretfully, 'I don't see why an earl can't be as polite as the next man. If it was up to me, he'd be long gone, but Winifred won't hear of me asking him to leave.'

'You don't need Mother's permission to kick him out, Uncle Brin.'

'Ah well, my boy, it's her home, too, now, and it doesn't do to cross a woman in her own home. It just makes everyone uncomfortable. Be thankful Lord Rydal is a late riser and won't be here forever.'

'I am, Uncle, I am.'

Presumably Rhino would stay until the Beauforts departed, so Owen Howell's heartfelt retort suggested that his heart was not preoccupied with passionate love for Julia. On the other hand, he was not a demonstrative man. Could his outward calm hide a passionate heart? Daisy wondered.

He had returned to his pigs-in-blankets, unconcerned or oblivious of Daisy's scrutiny. She was still watching him when Julia came in. He looked up from the bacon-wrapped sausages to say good-morning, and his expression was definitely admiring. Still, Julia in a tweed skirt, silk blouse, and cardigan was just as ravishing as Julia in an evening frock. No man under eighty could possibly look at her without admiration. Only in this mercenary age could she have failed to find a suitor acceptable to both her mother and herself.

Though to be fair, Daisy thought with an internal sigh, one had to make allowances for the fact that so very many altogether eligible young men had died in the War.

Pritchard bustled about again to get Julia settled with her breakfast. Sir Desmond and Carlin came in and helped themselves to hearty platefuls. Howell took out his watch and checked the time with a frown. But the civil service could not be expected to keep business hours. Daisy had more than once heard Alec animadvert upon the slothful habits of bureaucrats.

Lucy, on the contrary, was all business this morning. 'As soon as you're ready, Daisy,' she said crisply. 'I left my equipment in the hall.'

Daisy swallowed a last gulp of tea. 'I'm right with you.'

'Would you mind if I came with you?' Armitage asked. 'I'd like to see how you work, and I can be your packhorse, eh. And being well acquainted with the grotto, from a hermit's point of view, of course, I may have helpful information.'

Lucy looked dubious, but Daisy said firmly, 'We could definitely do with a packhorse. Those photographic plates weigh a ton.'

He grinned. 'I'm wholly at your disposal.' As he stood up, he exchanged a glance with Julia and she smiled.

'I may drop by later,' she said, 'if it won't disturb you, Lucy.'

'Why not? I might as well invite the whole world.'

'Don't be snappish, darling,' Daisy admonished her. 'I'll herd them out of your way if they encroach.'

'A packhorse and a sheepdog,' said Pritchard with a chuckle. 'That's the ticket.'

The walk to the grotto was very different on that bright morning. Urns on the terrace spilled cascades of aubretia with a few purple flowers already opening here and there. The gardens were sheltered to the north by the house and to the east by a high beech hedge still thick with last year's leaves. Daffodils, narcissus, and crocuses already bloomed in great sheets of colour, mostly yellow, as if reflecting and intensifying the sunlight.

'The Victorian gas lamp standards add a delightful touch of whimsy to the landscape,' Daisy remarked, and pleased with the phrase she whipped out her notebook to write it down.

'You may want to save the word *whimsy* for the grotto,' Armitage suggested. The heavy satchel of plates didn't appear to discommode him in the slightest. He carried it over one shoulder and the tripod over the other.

'Since follies are whimsical by their very nature,' said Lucy, 'Daisy's trying to avoid overuse of the word.'

'This is for my article about the house, darling, not the grotto book. I can be as whimsical as I like.'

'You still intend to write that, eh?'

'Definitely. I'm sure my American editor will be interested, even if *Town and Country* isn't. I don't want to bother you with my questions, though. I expect I can get enough information at the British Museum library. Victorian vicars were forever writing dim little volumes about the history of local notables.'

'I've read a few, but I haven't been able to trace any from this parish. No, I said I'd help you, and I will. But you never told me what sort of articles you write.'

'Oh, I just describe interesting country houses, with little tidbits of the history of the family thrown in. I don't write about the present residents – well, just a bit about "gracious permission" and so on – nor any of the skeletons in cupboards if they don't want me to. Most don't mind as long as none of those concerned are still living.'

'You may write about dead skeletons, but not living ones, eh? That sounds reasonable. All right, you can ask, though I can't promise to answer.'

'Fair enough. The best stories usually come from members of the family, who've grown up hearing them. What –'

'Not now, Daisy,' Lucy interrupted. 'Wait till we've finished what we're doing. Let's concentrate on the grotto for the moment.'

They came to the first set of three shallow steps. The path was now leading them up the lower slopes of the downs. The lawns on either side gave way to rough tussocks. Ahead, sheep-cropped grass rose steeply to the rounded summit, crowned with a spinney. More steps, then they reached the bridge over the stream.

Here Armitage paused. 'You may not want to mention this,' he said, 'as it somewhat detracts from the picturesqueness, but the channel is lined with some sort of tile. Otherwise, I'm told, the creek would often dry up in the summer.'

'It tends to happen in chalk and limestone country,' Daisy said.

'You grew up in this sort of country?'

'No, quite different. The valley of the Severn, in Worcestershire. It's just one of those useless bits of general knowledge one remembers from school.'

'Knowledge is seldom useless, especially for a writer, though its usefulness isn't always immediately apparent.'

'That must be why Daisy's such a successful writer,' said Lucy, impatiently moving onward. 'She has a vast fund of apparently useless information.'

'Whereas you, Lady Gerald, have a vast fund of specific technical information.'

'I wouldn't say *vast*,' Lucy demurred, but she looked pleased.

Amused, Daisy realised he was buttering them up, in a rather roundabout and subtle fashion. Doubtless he wanted them on his side if Julia asked what they thought of him. She was sure by now that they were attracted to one another, though to what degree the attraction was acknowledged she couldn't guess.

The stream was below them now, though the gorge was by no means the fearsome chasm it had seemed last night. On the far side, here and there, small plants clung to the whitish cliff. They turned the corner of the bluff. The sun, still quite low in the southeast, shone directly into the mouth of the grotto. Sparkling, the waterfall flung itself down into a pretty pool fringed with reeds and watermint. It was a delightful scene, but Daisy was glad she had seen its dramatic aspect the previous evening.

Lucy called a halt. Armitage put down his burdens and started setting up the tripod at her direction.

'I'm going up,' Daisy said. 'I'll make a list of things I want to write about, and then you can decide which will make good photos.'

'Right-oh. Stop at the top, though, while I get a couple of shots. A human figure gives an idea of the scale,' Lucy explained to Armitage.

Gazing back the way they had come, he made some indistinct reply. Daisy grinned. Lucy shrugged, shook her head, and rolled her eyes.

Daisy went up the steps, much less steep and narrow by daylight. At the top, she went over to the the stream. As it approached the lip of the cave, the low wall confining it to its bed sloped down from eighteen inches high to no more than six, so that it wasn't noticeable from below.

She moved forwards, stopping a prudent couple of feet from the edge, and waved to Lucy, who was peering through her viewfinder. Lucy motioned her to come closer. Daisy shook her head.

Lucy turned to Armitage, who by now had returned at least part of his attention to what she was doing. (Another part was on filling his pipe.) Pointing up at Daisy, she said something. As he replied, he glanced back down the path again. Lucy looked at her wristwatch, tapped it, and shook her head vigorously. Daisy guessed what she was saying: 'Julia won't be here for ages. She was just starting breakfast and she may seem ethereal but she has a healthy appetite.'

Armitage blushed, cast one last longing look backwards, then headed for the steps, his unlit pipe clenched in his teeth. Lucy generally got her way when she was being forceful.

'Besides,' said Daisy as the lovelorn swain arrived in the grotto, 'she won't want people to think she's chasing after you.'

'How did you know . . . ? What people?'

'Pritchard, Howell, Sir Desmond, Carlin, for a start. Anyone else who goes down to breakfast. Barker – he was just coming in with fresh coffee when she said she'd join us. Then there's her mother, who'd be bound to wonder where she was if she got up and found her missing. She'll probably go up to her and tell her we – Lucy and I, that is – are working in the grotto and she's going to pop along to see how we're doing.'

'You don't think she'll mention me to Lady Beaufort?' Armitage asked wistfully.

'I wouldn't. But then, my mother is much more daunting than Lady Beaufort. Come on, Lucy's getting impatient, and she can be almost as daunting as Mother when she tries.'

Armitage moved into position to be the requisite figure in Lucy's composition, leaving Daisy to explore.

She found herself making reams of notes on everything from the fossils visible in the polished marble of the floor to the curious formations dependent from the roof, which she thought might be incipient stalactites. Armitage would know. She turned towards the cave mouth to ask him.

He wasn't there.

Appalled, Daisy dropped her notebook and rushed to the edge. With one hand on the statue of Tethys, how far over dared she lean – ?

'Daisy,' Lucy cried behind her, 'for pity's sake take care!'

Startled, she lost her balance and tottered . . .

CHAPTER 12

A tug on Daisy's coat made her fall backwards, instead of forwards and down. She staggered back. About to sit down, hard, she found herself clasped in Armitage's arms.

'My plates!' Lucy yelped.

In hindsight – or rather hind-hearing if there was such a word – Daisy realised she had heard a crash just before she felt the jerk on her coat that had saved her. Lucy was on her knees, feverishly unbuckling the straps of her satchel.

'Sorry, Lady Gerald, but better your plates than Mrs. Fletcher.'

'Of course, but – . Daisy what on earth were you doing?'

'Charles!' Julia had appeared at the top of the steps. She looked at Armitage with heartbreak in her eyes. 'I mean, Mr. Armitage!'

He whipped one arm away from Daisy's person. 'Can you stand alone?'

'Yes, thank you. He saved me from a wetting, or worse, Julia. I thought *he'd* fallen in – '

'Oh, Charles!'

'Thank heaven, nothing seems to be broken. Darling, why on earth should you think *he'd* fallen?'

'One minute he was there, posing for your pictures. The next minute I turned round and he was gone.'

'It's ten or fifteen minutes since he came down to help me carry the stuff up. It's sheer luck that the plates are all right. Of all the idiotic – !'

'I was being careful. If you hadn't shouted in my ear – !'

'Lucy, Daisy!' With obvious reluctance Julia disentangled herself from Armitage's arms. 'You're only shouting at each other because Daisy had a shock and Lucy's relieved – '

'*I* wasn't shouting,' said Lucy at her most dignified.

Armitage grinned. 'That's what it sounded like to me.' He'd moved several paces from Julia and was smoothing his hair, though it was cut too short to be ruffled by any amount of exertion. Extracting a box of matches from his waistcoat pocket, he set about trying to light his pipe.

'I was,' Daisy admitted. 'I really thought I was in for a ducking.'

'I ought to have told you I was going down,' Armitage said, 'but you were so busy taking notes I didn't like to interrupt.'

'Oh, where's my notebook?'

'I hope you didn't drop it over the edge,' said Armitage, making for said edge.

Lucy, Daisy, and Julia spread out and moved towards the back of the cave, searching.

'Darling,' Lucy said to Julia in a low voice, 'you've only known the man three days. Should you be throwing yourself into his arms?'

'Actually, we first met in town several weeks ago. Mother thinks it was her idea to get us invited here, but I inveigled her into it. You won't give me away, will you?'

'Of course not,' said Daisy.

'Having Rhino drive us down was entirely her own idea however.'

'And a rotten one!' Lucy exclaimed. 'Look, here's your notebook, Daisy. Heavens, you've got masses of notes. No wonder you didn't notice when Mr. Armitage – '

'Guess who's on his way here,' Armitage said in tones of doom, retreating rapidly from the mouth of the cave. 'His ruddy lordship.'

'Rhino? Oh no!' Julia was equally dismayed.

'Let's go into the second cave,' Daisy proposed. 'With any luck he'll think we've left and go away.'

'I think he saw me, but we can try it. I'll go first, shall I? It's darkish in the tunnel even on such a bright day. Perhaps I'd better light the lamps in the inner grotto. There's a little natural light, from a rift in the roof, but not enough for Mrs. Fletcher's serious studies.'

He took a small electric lantern from the niche behind a naiad and led the way between Neptune and Amphitrite. After lighting the first shell-shaded gas lamp, he continued striking match after match and applying them alternately to his pipe and the rest of the lamps.

Daisy studied the statue of St. Vincent Ferrer. He was interesting if only because he was an anomaly among the Classical figures and natural adornments of the grotto. He was dressed in a monkish robe and cowl, like Armitage playing the hermit, and like Armitage now he carried a flame in one hand. Patron saint of plumbers, Pritchard had said. The statue was definitely noteworthy, but she couldn't decide whether she should write about it or not.

She turned to consult Lucy. Lucy wasn't there.

'I do wish people wouldn't keep disappearing! Where's Lucy got to now?'

'Isn't she here?' Julia looked round vaguely. 'She must have stayed behind. I'll go and see, shall I?'

'That's all right, I'll go. You two enjoy a moment's privacy – it's liable to be brief enough. But behave yourselves.'

Lucy was feverishly setting up her tripod and camera before Neptune. 'Oh, there you are, Daisy! Come and lend a hand. The sun will have moved too far round in a few minutes and flash photos never come out as well. Get out the exposure meter, would you?'

Daisy had helped Lucy with her photography in the days before she started to make money with her writing, so she knew what she was looking for and where to look. She was taking it from the inner pocket of the satchel when an all too familiar grating voice behind her said, 'What are you doing here? They told me Julia – Miss Beaufort – was coming here.'

'Go away, Rhino, we're working.'

'Julia has no particular interest in the grotto, Lord Rydal,' Daisy pointed out.

'What she's interested in is that damn colonial counter-jumper. And he lives here.'

'Not at this time of year.'

'Rhino, come here,' Lucy commanded.

'What? Why?'

'Because I need your help moving this.'

'Why should I?'

'Are you saying you're not strong enough to move a tripod with a camera attached? Sorry, I shouldn't have put you in such an embarrassing position, where you had to admit it.'

'Darling, don't torment the poor man. He can't help it if he's let himself get a bit – ' Daisy eyed him up and down – 'flabby.'

'Flabby! Of course I'm strong enough,' Rhino snarled. He strode over to Lucy and reached out to grasp two legs of the tripod.

'Stop! Half a sec.' Lucy made a big fuss about peering through the viewfinder. 'Let's see, I think three inches to the left should do it.'

'Three inches? And you can't manage that yourself?'

'Not after carrying my stuff from the house.' Lucy pronounced this taradiddle without a blink, and without any attempt to look limp and exhausted.

'What difference does three inches make anyway?'

'All the difference in the world. I can see you don't know the first thing about photography. Make it four inches to the left.'

'Show me, exactly. I'm not moving it twice.'

'This leg here,' Lucy said patiently in the sort of voice one uses to a two-year-old – a not very bright two-year-old. 'And this leg here. Hold on, just let me check.' She squinted at Neptune through the viewfinder again. 'It's not quite straight. Rotate it just the tiniest bit to the right.'

Rhino looked daggers at her but obeyed. She managed to keep him busy for several minutes, but he was about to go past Neptune in search of Julia when another distraction arrived.

'There you are, Rhino darling,' cooed Lady Ottaline, hurrying to him and clutching his arm, which fortunately was not supporting any vital bit of photographic equipment at that moment. 'Look, I'm wearing sensible shoes today.'

She held out one silk-clad leg. Her 'sensible' shoes were not proper walking shoes, but at least they had comparatively low Cuban heels. Though she seemed not to have suffered any lasting ill effects from her unexpected midnight swim, she was not eager to repeat it for the sake of fashion.

'Look out!' said Lucy. 'If you knock against the tripod I'll have to start again.'

Still standing on one foot, Lady Ottaline turned the other this way and that. 'What do you think, darling?'

'Very sensible,' Rhino said woodenly.

Lady Ottaline pouted. 'Oh, I'm going to fall!' With an unconvincing wobble, she flung her arms round his neck.

'If you *must* stand on one foot,' Lucy snapped, 'please go and do it somewhere else. I'm trying to get some work done here.'

'Poor you, having to work still even though you managed to get married at last.'

'Poor you,' Lucy retorted, 'having no interests beyond the pursuit of men after donkey's years of marriage.'

Lady Ottaline shot her a venomous look, but Rhino had escaped from her toils during this exchange and was rapidly heading for the inner cave. She sped after him.

'I hope they didn't wreck that exposure, the silly asses.' Lucy slid a plate out of the camera. 'It's a pity she drove Rhino away, but I couldn't keep him occupied much longer.'

'I'm amazed that you succeeded in keeping him so long. Or in getting him to do anything at all, come to that.'

'It's just a matter of being firm. It's a pity more people don't try it on him.'

'You could say Lady Ottaline's being firm, I suppose. Or perhaps tenacious is the word. He looked positively hunted.'

'Yes,' Lucy said thoughtfully. 'I suppose he really is in love with Julia, as far as he's capable of it, and he's afraid Lady Ottaline will turn her against him if he doesn't surrender to her wiles.'

'I doubt anyone or anything could turn Julia more against him.'

'No, but you can't expect him to realise that. In his own eyes he's as close to perfection as a man can be.'

'I can't see why Lady Ottaline should be so desperate to hang on to him if he doesn't want her. But then, I can't see what she wanted with him in the first place.'

'Darling, that's obvious. She has to have a lover at her beck and call, and she's getting beyond hooking a new one.'

Daisy shook her head. 'The great advantage of never having been beautiful is that one doesn't have to worry about growing older and losing one's looks.'

'Would you mind going after those beautiful people and stopping them coming back till I've finished this shot? I don't want another one ruined. Besides, you may be needed to help prevent Rhino massacring Armitage.'

'I thought you didn't approve of "the colonial counter-jumper" for Julia.'

'I don't. But I approve still less of Rhino. The man's a menace to civilisation.'

'Perhaps Armitage will massacre Rhino.'

'Not likely. He's outweighed two to one. Rhino's both an irresistible force *and* an immovable object. He'll do the massacring.'

'Oh dear! I don't think it counts as a massacre, though, if it's just one person.'

'Then perhaps Rhino will oblige and massacre Lady Ottaline, too,' Lucy said dryly.

With great reluctance, Daisy went round Neptune and through the short tunnel. Approaching the end, she heard raised voices.

Armitage and Rhino were shouting at each other, Armitage sounding more Canadian than ever and Rhino's caw raised to roc-like proportions. Since they were both shouting at once, Daisy caught only the odd word here and there. Judging by those, it was just as well she missed the rest. Lord Rydal had the vocabulary of a coalheaver. Armitage seemed to prefer more esoteric imprecations, including a phrase or two that had a Shakespearian ring.

Daisy emerged from the tunnel. Armitage and Rhino faced each other a few feet apart. Both had clenched their fists. Neither pipe nor cigarette holder was in evidence.

Beyond them she saw Julia's aghast face. Lady Ottaline looked excited. Could she so far have misunderstood the situation as to believe the men were fighting over her? Or was it sheer bloodlust?

'Oh, don't!' Julia begged.

Daisy took out her notebook. 'This will make a wonderful story for the scandal sheets! The noble earl of Rydal attacks a man half his size, in the presence of horrified ladies. I can just see the headlines. But hold off a minute, won't you, please? Lucy will want to see this so that she can give an accurate report to Lord Gerald to spread in the clubs. I expect he'll be able to dine out on the story for weeks.'

The would-be combatants looked at her. Armitage appeared both annoyed and amused. Rhino glared, his face turning from red to purple.

'It'll make an even better story if Rhino has a stroke. For the papers, I mean. Gerald wouldn't care to – '

'Daisy!' Julia objected uncertainly.

'Not that I'd want Rhino to make himself ill, of course. Or worse. People do die from strokes, and you look awfully overwrought, Rhino. If you could see the way your eyes are bulging . . . Perhaps you ought to sit down.'

'I'll fetch you a glass of water from the back room,' Armitage offered. He hurried off, just in time – Daisy thought – to avoid laughing in his antagonist's face. Julia followed him.

'I expect you ought to cut down on the cigarettes,' Daisy said to Rhino. 'They're frightfully bad for you.'

'I am perfectly well,' he said through gritted teeth. Then he parted them just far enough to stick his cigarette holder between, stuck a cigarette in the holder, and struck a match as he strode back to the outer cave.

Lady Ottaline gave Daisy a look of pure loathing and went after him.

Lucy's anguished wail was audible in the inner cave. 'Rhino, you blithering idiot! You've ruined another shot!'

CHAPTER 13

Under the circumstances, lunch was bound to be an uncomfortable meal. Business having taken the rest of the men to the works in Swindon, Rhino and Armitage were the only two present, and they, of course, were not on speaking terms.

As well as the strained relations between several of those who had visited the grotto that morning, Mrs. Howell was irritated because the soup was already growing cold when Lady Ottaline at last came down after refreshing her make-up. And Lady Beaufort was annoyed with Julia for leaving it to their maid to inform her as to her daughter's whereabouts.

'Mother, I'm twenty-eight!'

'Past old enough to have better manners!' snapped the usually equable lady.

'I thought you were probably still asleep, so I left a message with Willett. It was very early, but when I came down to breakfast, Daisy and Lucy were just about to leave, because Lucy had to catch the best light for her photographs. I wanted to see what they were doing.'

'It's about time I had a look at this grotto everyone is making such a fuss about. I hope you can spare the time to show me this afternoon, Julia?'

'Of course, Mother.'

'I don't know why you want to see it,' Mrs. Howell grumbled. 'Brin's spent an absolute fortune on it, but when all's said and done, it's just a fancy hole in the ground.'

'I suppose Mr. Pritchard may spend his money as he chooses,' Lady Beaufort said sharply.

'He might spare a thought for my Owen trying to make ends meet after he's gone.'

After the strenuous activity of the morning, Daisy was too hungry to pay their sniping much heed at the time. Later, when they went out to the hall after lunch, she said to Lucy, 'Mrs. Howell's certainly changed her tune, hasn't she!'

'Has she?'

'Didn't you notice? Yesterday she was all deference to Lady Beaufort. At lunch she contradicted her practically every time she opened her mouth.'

'I wasn't listening.'

'But don't you think it's odd? Perhaps she's realising that a title isn't all it's cracked up to be. I must say, Lady Beaufort gave as good as she got.'

'I have to go back and take some more flash photos,' said the single-minded Lucy. 'Will you come and lend a hand?'

'I can't, darling. I'm going to be interrogating Armitage for my article.'

'Blast! Then I can't have him to help with the flash.'

'Try Rhino.'

'Not something likely!'

'Mrs. Howell might lend you a servant. But considering the mood she's in, I'd ask Barker instead, if I were you. Or Julia might do it. She has to escort her mother there anyway. There's nothing to carry, remember. You left all your stuff in the hermit's lair.'

'Yes, Armitage swore it would be safe. Everything will have to be carried back here, though.'

'I'm sure you'll work something out. If you're not back by tea-time, I'll send a rescue party. I've got to fetch a new notebook and meet Armitage in the muniments room. Toodle-oo.'

'Pritchard has a muniments room? That's a bit grandiose for a plumber!'

'I suppose title deeds and other legal documents relate to the property itself as well as to the family that used to own it. I'm hoping Armitage will tell me what became of the Appsworths. I must go. Good luck with the photos. At least Lady Beaufort should be easier to keep out of the pictures than Rhino!'

Following the directions of the ever-efficient Barker, Daisy found the muniments room without difficulty, though it was tucked away in an odd corner of the ground floor near the servants' wing. Armitage was already there, standing at the window, gazing out at a small paved courtyard. A pretty housemaid was crossing it, carrying a basket. By the slump of his shoulders, Armitage did not find the sight cheering.

Daisy hesitated on the threshold, then tapped on the door. He swung round.

'Mrs. Fletcher! Sorry, I was a long way away.'

'In Canada?'

'Well, yes.'

'Whereabouts?'

'Toronto. That's where I live.'

'It's quite a big city, isn't it?'

'Part of your vast fund of apparently useless information? Not by London standards, but yes, it's over half a million, and growing fast.' Abruptly he changed the subject. 'What is it you want to know about the house?'

'Anything that might appeal to the average reader of magazines.'

'The average reader?'

'Do I detect a "tone of intellectual snobbery"?'

'What?' he asked, startled.

'Shaw. George Bernard. At least, I'm pretty sure he's responsible.'

He laughed. 'Now who's using a tone of intellectual snobbery! I've no idea of the intellectual capacities of the average reader of magazines.'

'Well, they're literate,' Daisy explained kindly. 'I'm not writing for the *Illustrated London News*. Let's start with basic facts such as when the house was built and who the architect was. I take it you know?'

He was in fact extremely knowledgeable about the building and quite willing to talk about it.

After scribbling down a couple of pages of notes, Daisy stemmed the flow. 'Hold on! This is far more information than any of my readers, however literate, are likely to want to know. Unless they're students of architecture, which seems unlikely. Is that what you are?'

'Pritchard knows far more about it than I do. You should ask him to give you a tour, as he did me.'

'Really? I didn't know he was interested in anything but the plumbing.'

'He bought the Hall because he'd visited it in his professional capacity and fell in love with it. They consulted him, hoping to modernise the plumbing, but they couldn't afford more than minor updates.'

'They?'

'The Appsworths.' His terseness contrasted with his previous loquacity.

'You've been studying the family papers. What's your interest in Appsworth Hall?'

'I hardly think that's relevant to your article, Mrs. Fletcher.'

'Not at all. I'm just curious. Nosy, if you prefer.'

His lips twitched. 'As a matter of fact, I'm a historian.'

'How very respectable. Why make such a mystery of it?'

'I haven't made a mystery of it.'

'Oh yes you have. Why else would Lucy and I be seething with curiosity? Well, actually, Lucy hasn't been thinking about anything much beyond her photography. But I've been seething like billy-oh. It's one of the perils of my profession. Does Julia know?'

'Yes. Not that it's any of your business.'

'But Lady Beaufort doesn't. Why on earth don't you tell her?'

'She wants Julia to marry wealth and a title. Who can blame her? Julia deserves the best of everything.'

'Don't be soppy. Julia deserves a chance to be happy. Titles don't bring happiness.'

'All right! Forget the title. I can't see much in it myself.'

'Being rich isn't much more to the point. I've known dozens of rich people who weren't happy.'

'Dozens?' Armitage asked sceptically.

'Plenty, anyway. As long as she doesn't have to live on sardines... Are you a professional historian, or is it a hobby? Or are you going to write an article about the Appsworths? That would explain why you don't want to tell me about them. You want to scoop me!'

'Bosh! I may write an article, or even a book, but it'll be the scholarly kind with lots of footnotes, no competition for you.'

'Well, talk about intellectual snobbery!'

'Sorry. But you must agree we have different aims and audiences. As a matter of fact, I'm a lecturer in history at the University of Toronto.'

'What are you doing here in the middle of term-time?'

'I took the term off – what they call a "sabbatical" in the States – to come over and do some research into – some historical research.'

Daisy was sure he'd been going to say something else, but it really wasn't her business, she decided regretfully. 'A lecturer . . . Surely you can afford to support a wife in reasonable comfort? Things can't be so different in Canada. Or – don't tell me they still insist on dons being celibate?'

'Good lord, no! Even Oxford and Cambridge gave that up decades ago. If I were an Oxbridge don I might conceivably be acceptable to Lady Beaufort. Though I doubt it,' he added gloomily. 'Not with that fellow Rydal hanging about.'

'For pity's sake, you don't think Julia would agree to marry Rhino just to please her mother? Talk about a fate worse than death! If all you're worried about is living with a disapproving mother-in-law, I can give you a few tips. Not that Lady Beaufort could possibly hold a candle to Alec's mother in that respect. Nor to my mother, from Alec's point of view. And you'd have the Atlantic between you.'

'What if she wanted to go with us?'

'You do like to borrow trouble, don't you? I shouldn't think it's likely. Isn't Toronto in the Arctic?'

'Not quite! It does get pretty cold in the winter, though. Another reason for Lady Beaufort not to want Julia to marry me.'

'Do stop being such a defeatist! Faint heart never won fair lady. Think of all the Englishwomen who go off to India and Africa with their menfolk to rule the Empire. They put up with much worse than a bit of snow.'

'Undeniable. Toronto is really a very pleasant city, even under several feet of snow. Mrs. Fletcher, have you ever considered setting up as an agony aunt?'

'An agony aunt? You mean one of those columnists who dishes out advice to people who write letters to the popular papers?'

'Yes. I believe you'd be very good at it.'

Daisy gave him a suspicious look. 'I'm sorry if you think I'm being officious, interfering in your affairs.'

'Well, you are, you know. But kindly meant, I know. And you're making awfully good sense. I'm sure you'd be good at it professionally. I promise I shan't dismiss your words of wisdom out of hand. I need time to think.'

'I'll give you time to think when you give me some information about the Appsworths.'

Armitage sighed. 'Tenacious, aren't you? What sort of stuff are you after?'

Once he'd made up his mind to it, Armitage provided Daisy with several stories of a sort she could use in her article. One she particularly liked was about an eighteenth-century daughter of the house who had eloped with a handsome groom. Unlike most of its kind, the tale had a happy ending. The couple had been welcomed back into the bosom of the family because the groom was the only person capable of managing her papa's favourite stallion.

'Perfect! I suppose they wrote reams of letters about it? And someone saved them all? Being a historian is going to get much more difficult, don't you think, now that people send telegrams and ring each other up on the phone. No one saves telegrams.'

'That's an interesting point, Mrs. Fletcher. When it comes to consideration of our times, future historians will have the newspapers, with everything they consider worthy of being printed, and I don't suppose the bureaucracy will ever cease to produce rivers of paper. But social historians won't have so much in the way of personal papers to delve into, I guess.'

'Still, most of those personal papers were always produced by a very small section of the population, weren't they? So history's been biased towards the rich and literate. Now most people are literate but most can't afford phones and cables, so they write letters, so history will be biased towards them. Does that make sense?'

'Very much so.'

'I'm never sure whether my logic is leading me round in circles. I'll tell you what else they'll have to delve into: gossip columns for the rich and famous, and for the others, the columns of agony aunts!'

'With a good deal more truth in the latter than the former, no doubt!' Armitage said, laughing. 'I hope you have all you need for your article, Mrs. Fletcher. You've just about wrung me dry.'

Daisy still wanted to know what had led to the Appsworths losing their family estate. However, she probably wouldn't be able to use it in the article, and she didn't want to try his patience too far. 'Yes, thanks,' she said. 'You've been frightfully helpful. Now I just have to ask Mr. Pritchard to give me a tour of the house. I wonder whether he'll be going into Swindon tomorrow.'

'I can't help you there. It depends on Wandersley, I guess.'

'You don't know exactly what he's here for, do you?'

He shrugged. 'Only that it involves considerable prestige as well as profit for Pritchard's Plumbing Products. I hope the old boy gets it. He's a good chap. My apologies, by the way, for the excessive alliteration. It's difficult to avoid.'

'Perhaps,' Daisy suggested, 'you should take up writing advertising slogans.'

Not until she was in the middle of transcribing her shorthand into something more readable did she realise that, by chance or deliberately, he had never actually explained his interest in the Appsworths' papers. It was all very well saying he was a historian. The Appsworths had been an obscure country family with no claim to fame, a very minor barony who rarely made an appearance in the public life of the country, and never notably. So what was it about them that had drawn the attention of a Canadian academic?

CHAPTER 14

Of the Swindon contingent only Mr. Pritchard returned to Appsworth Hall in time for tea, as befitted his semi-retired status. He came in a little late, fetched himself a cup of tea from Mrs. Howell, and went to sit by Lady Beaufort.

'I hear you visited my grotto,' he said. 'How did you like it?'

'Sheer folly,' said her ladyship, 'but a most amusing folly.'

He laughed. Daisy caught only snatches of their conversation thereafter, because Lucy was intent on describing every photo she had taken that afternoon. She explained which shots she expected to come out best, and wanted Daisy's opinion as to whether she should take any more.

'I was thinking, I might be able to get something worthwhile of the monk. Sort of blurry and atmospheric.'

'Ghostly.'

'Yes. Too silly, do you think? It's just that this is the first folly we've tackled that deserves more than a couple of illustrations, at most.'

'Nothing venture, nothing gain. We don't have to use it if it doesn't work.'

'I'll have to persuade Armitage to pose for me again.'

'Not on the edge!'

'No, by St. Whatsit, I think.' Lucy fell silent, pondering ways and means.

Pritchard was urging Lady Beaufort, 'You should really see it by night.'

'Julia tells me it's beautifully illuminated. But I don't know . . . It's quite a walk up that hill. You should put in some sort of seats for us elderly folk.'

'Elderly? Not you, Lady Beaufort! But that's an excellent notion. I can't imagine why I didn't think of it before. This evening – if you'd like to go up this evening? – I could have chairs carried up.'

'Let's try it,' said Lucy, emerging from her abstraction. 'Where's – ? Oh, he's talking to Mrs. Howell. Blast.'

'I think it's more a case of Mrs. Howell talking to him, or *at* him. I expect he'd be glad to be rescued. I'll leave you to it. I'm going to ask Mr. Pritchard if he'll give me a tour of the house tomorrow. And then I'd better rescue Julia from Rhino and Lady Ottaline.'

'Right-oh, but for pity's sake don't breathe a word about going back to the grotto. The last thing I need is that blundering jackass ruining any more shots. I should charge him for the wasted plates.'

'Try sending him a bill. You never know.'

Of course, Lucy's hope of returning to the grotto without a flock of companions hadn't a chance. Lady Beaufort expressed a preference for going there after tea rather than waiting until after dinner. Lucy promptly told Armitage that after dinner would suit her best – she had preparations to make, she said vaguely – and he agreed. Then Lady Beaufort said that of course Julia would go with her; she didn't propose to walk that path in the dark without her daughter's support. Armitage promptly changed his mind.

'Lady Beaufort would like to see the hermit, I expect,' he said, while Lucy simmered. 'I'll go ahead and light the lamps, sir, shall I?'

'Certainly, my boy. I'm sure Lord Rydal will help to carry your equipment, Lady Gerald.'

'Me? What the deuce d'you think I am, a packhorse?'

'A gentleman?' Pritchard hazarded, a glint in his eye.

Rhino had no answer to that.

'Daisy,' Lucy hissed, 'you've got to come, too, and *please* do a better job this time of keeping everyone out of sight.'

In the end everyone went except Mrs. Howell. Daisy was surprised that Lady Ottaline wanted to venture back to the scene of her accident, especially as Rhino was too laden for her to cling to him. He was too laden even to smoke. Somehow Pritchard seemed to have gained the upper hand.

While Lady Beaufort was exclaiming in delight at the illuminated cascade, Lucy chivvied Rhino up the steps. Daisy couldn't decide whether she ought to follow them to keep him out of Lucy's way or stand guard at the bottom to stop Lady Ottaline chasing after him.

Then Lady Beaufort asked Lady Ottaline how she had come to fall. 'The path is perfectly adequate,' she said magisterially, 'whatever shoes you were so ill-advised as to wear.'

As Lady Ottaline replied, Daisy left them and hurried upwards. The moment Rhino reached the grotto he put down his burdens and lit a cigarette. 'Enough is enough,' he snorted. 'I can't see why you don't use a Brownie.'

Lucy was speechless with fury. Ruthlessly sacrificing Julia's comfort for the sake of Lucy's blood-pressure, Daisy shooed Rhino back down. 'Thank you, we'll manage now. Come on, darling, before they all arrive.'

The hermit came from the rear, robed but uncowled. 'Let me give you a hand. You'll have to explain exactly what you want me to do, Lady Gerald.'

'I'm not absolutely certain myself yet. Do call me Lucy, won't you?'

'Sure. I'm Chuck back home, but Julia doesn't like it, so let's stick to Charles.'

'And I'm Daisy, Charles. Lucy, I think I'd better go back and try to fend off the others.'

From the top step, holding tight to the rail, Daisy saw Rhino go straight to Julia. The noise of the waterfall prevented Daisy's hearing what was said, but it looked to her as if he interrupted whatever Julia was saying to her mother. To Daisy's astonishment, Lady Beaufort turned to him and said something sharp enough to make him take a step backwards.

Fortunately he was facing the stream – not that Daisy would have been averse to seeing him topple in again.

Could it be, she wondered, that a few days in the same house as the rich Lord Rydal had made Lady Beaufort reassess his desirability as a son-in-law? For Julia's sake, she hoped so.

Rhino might conceivably be doing some reassessment, too. Lady Beaufort, the widow of a mere knight even if he had been a general, was not the first person at Appsworth to fail to kowtow before his hitherto invincible complacency. Julia persisted in refusing to marry him, yet at her bidding he did such menial tasks as fetching luggage from the station. Lucy ordered him about. Even Pritchard had made him back down.

On the other hand, Rhino was so conceited, he probably managed to convert these incidents in his mind into further proof of his superiority to the rest of mankind.

'Daisy!' Lucy called from the back of the grotto.

Daisy moved away from the waterfall's roar. 'Yes?'

'Didn't you hear me? We're ready to shoot, but I don't want to start if everyone's about to barge in. Are you on guard?'

'Horatio on the bridge was nothing to me, darling,' Daisy said resolutely.

'Well, don't go plunging into the Tiber if they do overwhelm you, but do your best.' She disappeared behind Neptune.

To carry out the parallel to Horatio, Daisy ought to stand at the most defensible point, the bottom of the steps. However, she couldn't see herself barring Lady Beaufort and Pritchard from his grotto. She glanced around. A couple of basket chairs had been brought in and placed to one side, with a good view of Neptune and the spot where the river emerged from the rock through the gaping mouth of a sea serpent. They were reasonable people and, given a place to rest their bones, would certainly comply with a request not to go through to the second cave to disturb Lucy. So would Julia.

Neither Rhino nor Lady Ottaline could by any stretch of the imagination be described as reasonable. But Rhino would stay with Julia and Lady Ottaline would cling to Rhino.

Or so Daisy hoped.

Julia arrived first, looking harried.

'Hold up the monster till I have a chance to hide!' she begged.

'Sorry, no can do. He'd only come looking for you, and Lucy and I are counting on you to keep him out here till she's finished shooting Charles.'

'Shooting – ! Oh, shooting. But – '

'A small sacrifice for the sake of Art,' Daisy urged, 'with a capital *A*. Not to mention for *my* sake. Lucy will never forgive me if he ruins another picture, and I was counting on you to act as my barricade.'

'Oh, all right. But if it makes him think I'm softening towards him, *I* may never forgive you.'

Lady Beaufort reached the top of the steps, panting a little. Pritchard was close behind her.

'You see, Lady Beaufort,' he said triumphantly, 'I had chairs brought up, just as I promised. Do come and sit down.'

'How kind!' Her ladyship beamed. 'Julia, my love, you were quite right to insist on my seeing the grotto at night. It's like something out of the *Arabian Nights*. Daisy, I hope you and Lucy will do it justice in your book.'

'We'll do our best, though I doubt that it's possible. People will have to come and see for themselves.'

'The more the merrier,' said Mr. Pritchard.

'Well, I've seen it before.' Lady Ottaline arrived complaining. 'I don't know why you made me come, Rhino.'

'Made you come! I tried to persuade you to stay behind. I don't know why you insisted on tagging along.'

'I thought I ought to face it,' she said bravely. 'Don't they say one should climb straight back on a horse after falling? But now . . . I'm afraid it's too much for me . . .' And she fainted gracefully into Rhino's unwelcoming arms.

He didn't exactly drop her, but he deposited her none too gently on the cold stone floor and stepped away. 'Mrs. Fletcher, could you – '

'I don't know the first thing about nursing,' Daisy said firmly, giving Julia a nudge. As far as she knew, Julia had no more expertise than she did, but while she was succouring Lady Ottaline, Rhino would be stymied.

Julia moved forwards hesitantly.

'I believe it's a hysterical fit,' Lady Beaufort said in robust tones. 'The most efficacious treatment to attempt is a slap on the face.'

Lady Ottaline made a miraculous recovery. She sat up, saying, 'Oh, where am I?'

'There, just as I suspected,' said Lady Beaufort. 'It's an old-fashioned remedy, but it frequently works even before it's applied.'

The light was far from bright, but Daisy thought she saw Pritchard smother a grin. He came over and helped Lady Ottaline up, saying, 'I'm so sorry your accident last night has had such a lasting ill-effect. I can't abandon Lady Beaufort, but I'm sure Lord Rydal will be happy to support you back to the house. Sir Desmond should be back from the works by now. He'll know what to do to make you comfortable.'

Her husband's name brought a sour-lemon look to Lady Ottaline's crimson lips. It was momentary, outweighed by the prospect of getting Rhino to herself.

Rhino had no such counterbalance to his bile. 'I don't see why she can't go and lie down for a bit on the hermit's bed till she's recovered,' he said mutinously.

'No one may go through the inner cave till Lucy's finished!' Daisy declared, taking up a militant position in front of Neptune.

'I can't believe my ears!' said Julia in a shocked voice. 'Rhino, surely you aren't so ungallant as to make a lady in distress walk alone through the night, especially along that dangerous pathway.'

Rhino was neither capable of looking abashed, nor of giving in graciously, but he did give in.

Just as he and Lady Ottaline departed, Lucy came through from the inner grotto. Looking after them, she asked, 'Where are they going?'

'Lord Rydal is escorting Lady Ottaline back to the house,' Pritchard told her.

'Are you finished, darling?' Daisy asked. 'That was quick.'

'No, Julia! You can't go through. He'll move if he sees you and he has to stand absolutely still for another minute and a half. You must be mad to let Rhino take her back alone after she fell in last time. Got to go. If this works, it's going to be ripping!' And she whisked back round Neptune.

Pritchard frowned. 'What does Lady Gerald mean? Surely she's not suggesting Lord Rydal was responsible for Lady Ottaline's fall? I thought they seemed – quite fond of each other.'

'Say rather, on terms of considerable intimacy!' Lady Beaufort said severely.

'In the recent past, perhaps.' Daisy was hesitant, Alec having frequently reminded her not to mistake speculation for fact. 'We've wondered, Lucy and I, whether he hasn't been trying to convince her it's over.'

'Well, I won't have a guest pushed over,' Pritchard declared, 'not into my stream. I'm going to keep an eye on them.'

'I hardly think he'd do anything drastic when we all know he's alone with her,' said Daisy, but Pritchard was already on his way to the front of the grotto.

'Perhaps Lady Ottaline will push Rhino in,' Julia said hopefully, and followed Pritchard.

'Oh dear,' said Lady Beaufort, 'the earl won't do for Julia, will he? I'm quite disillusioned. He's not at all the sort of gentleman I wish her to marry.'

'Gentleman he's not,' said Daisy, 'for all his wealth and rank.'

'Which doesn't mean I shall allow her to marry a penniless colonial nobody! So don't go giving her any ideas, Daisy.'

Daisy was baffled. Why on earth didn't Julia tell her mother that while Armitage was not rich and titled, he was perfectly respectable and able to support her in better style than she had managed to survive these past several years? Surely his ridiculous qualms weren't holding her back. The weather, forsooth!

He must have told her to keep it secret. Could he be afraid Lady Beaufort might write to the University of Toronto and discover he didn't exist – so to speak? Or he did exist, and was peacefully going about his business teaching history to a lot of young Canadians while an impostor paraded under his name in England?

Pure speculation, Daisy reminded herself. All the same, something was rotten in the province of Ontario. She must get Julia alone and ask her what was going on.

'He hasn't done anything terrible.' Pritchard returned from the waterfall lookout looking cheerful. He was talking about Rhino, of course, not Armitage. 'They're round the bend,' he went on. 'It's much shallower there, so she couldn't come to any harm if she did fall in. And I must be round the bend to let Lady Gerald make me think for a moment that the earl would do anything so wicked.'

CHAPTER 15

In spite of Pritchard's half-joking words, Daisy noticed that on the way back to the house he kept casting anxious glances at the stream. Nothing untoward was visible. When they reached the house, Barker informed them that the Swindon party had returned and everyone had gone up to dress for dinner.

'Including Lady Ottaline?' Pritchard asked.

'Certainly, sir. I myself saw Lady Ottaline go upstairs with Sir Desmond.' The butler addressed his employer in indulgent, slightly condescending, almost fatherly tones, although he looked twenty years younger than Pritchard. Daisy realised she'd heard him speak the same way before.

'As though he used to work for an irascible duke,' she said later to Lucy, when she went to her room to see if she was ready to go down. 'And Pritchard is much pleasanter to work for, besides paying much better, but nonetheless the duke was infinitely superior.'

'For heaven's sake, Daisy, of course he was. If he exists outside your imagination. What a lot of rot you talk! What does it matter?'

'I was thinking I might interview Barker for my Servant Problem article.'

'You've been working on that for three years.'

'You never know, I might finish it before servants go the way of the dinosaurs. Are you ready at last? Let's go. That frock is much more suitable than last night's.'

'Well, I can't compete with Julia, whatever I wear, and to try to outshine Lady Ottaline would be pathetic.'

'The poor thing's rather pathetic all round, isn't she?'

'Darling, if I ever get like that, you will stop me, won't you?' Lucy studied her face in the looking glass. 'I'm not too old and too *married* to care about fashion, am I? Like all those frightful fat matrons who buy the latest frock from Paris straight off the mannequin, expecting to look like her?'

'It'll be a few years yet, darling, and no one could call you fat. I'll tell you when the moment comes, but I expect you won't want to hear. Come on. A single dab of powder more would be gilding the lily.'

Everyone except Lady Ottaline was already in the drawing room. Howell gave Daisy a glass of Cinzano and soda and she glanced around.

Sir Desmond, bland and sleek as ever, was talking to Pritchard. Lady Beaufort had captured Armitage and Carlin and was listening to the former with an assessing look in her eye. Rhino shared a sofa with Julia – how could she have been so careless as to sit down on an otherwise unoccupied sofa? – and was holding forth. Julia's expression of polite interest suggested she was enduring excruciating boredom. Mrs. Howell, in a chair on Rhino's other side, received no share of his attention. She looked disgruntled. She ought, in Daisy's opinion, to be grateful.

Howell handed Lucy her gin and It. 'I hear you had a successful photography session in the grotto,' he said.

'I hope so,' Lucy said cautiously. 'One can never be sure till the plates are developed.'

They went on to technical talk. Daisy drifted over to Pritchard and Sir Desmond.

'I hope I'm not interrupting business,' she said.

'All work and no play makes Jack a dull boy,' Pritchard assured her.

'Oh dear, I'm afraid it's work I wanted to talk to you about, but mine, of course, not yours.'

'How is your "work" going?' Sir Desmond's eyebrows put jocular quotation marks round *work*, making an otherwise innocuous question patronising.

Daisy considered giving him one of her mother's grande-dame looks, but she decided he wasn't the sort to be impressed. Or even to notice. 'Very well indeed, thank you. Mr. Pritchard and Mr. Armitage have been extremely helpful. Mr. Pritchard, I wondered whether you'd be so kind as to give me a tour of the house tomorrow, if you don't have to go to Swindon. Mr. Armitage told me you're a wonderful guide.'

'I'd be happy to, my dear. Owen will complete your business, Sir Desmond. I have every faith in his abilities. You won't really need me there. Excuse me, here's Lady Ottaline. I'll just make sure she gets her cocktail as Owen's busy discussing photography with Lady Gerald.'

Watching him go, Sir Desmond swigged down half a tumbler of whisky. 'There goes a happy man.' He sounded more cynical than admiring or envious. 'Wealth, no wife, no children, no worries.'

Daisy ignored most of this and said, 'Have you children, Sir Desmond?'

'I do, Mrs. Fletcher. For my sins, I do. A son who believes he's a poet, and a daughter addicted to good works.'

Daisy wondered just how much whisky he'd put away. To her relief, Barker came in and announced that dinner was served.

In the hall, he discreetly beckoned her aside. 'A telephone message, madam, from the local exchange. Mr. Fletcher wired to say he and Lord Gerald Bincombe will arrive tomorrow afternoon. About four o'clock, he hopes.'

'Spiffing! Have you told Lucy – Lady Gerald? Mr. Pritchard? Mrs. Howell?'

'Since the message was for you, madam, I have not.'

'I hope Mr. Pritchard informed Mrs. Howell that he'd invited them.'

'I believe so, madam. The housekeeper was aware that further guests might arrive.'

'Thank you, Barker.' Daisy was much relieved. She had no faith whatever that Mrs. Howell would welcome unexpected guests, even if one of them came with a title attached. 'Please pass the word to Mrs. Howell and the housekeeper that they're definitely coming.'

'Certainly, madam.'

Daisy caught up with Lucy. 'A message from Alec, darling. They're coming.'

'Gerald's coming with Alec?' Lucy's face lit up at Daisy's nod. 'Oh, good.'

Seated on Pritchard's left, opposite Lady Beaufort, Daisy told him at once about Alec and Gerald's proposed arrival. He was delighted.

So was Lady Beaufort. 'I'm looking forward to meeting your husband, Daisy.'

Blast! Daisy thought. She remembered Lucy saying the Beauforts knew Alec was a copper, and she hadn't asked Julia to suggest to her mother that the fact was best kept quiet. In her experience people, however honest, tended to act oddly if they knew there was a policeman in the house, however off-duty. She took a spoonful of soup, trying to decide how to carry it off.

But Lady Beaufort was a woman of discretion. She said to Pritchard, 'We met Lord Gerald in London. I know you will like him. He plays rugger, and you Welshmen are all devotees of rugger, aren't you?'

'Naturally. We're the best players.'

'Tell that to Gerald,' Daisy said. 'He played for his university, though I can't remember whether he's light or dark blue.'

'I've no doubt he'll agree with me, Mrs. Fletcher. Half the varsity players are Welshmen, if not more.'

Lady Beaufort laughed. 'I'll have to ask Lord Gerald.'

At the far end of the table, Mrs. Howell said belligerently, 'Well, Brin, Barker tells me we are to expect two more guests. I hope they don't expect fish for dinner. I've taken it off the menu. For good.' And she glared at Lord Rydal.

'Thank you, Winifred. I'm much obliged.'

Daisy was careful not to look towards Lucy or Julia lest they all disgrace themselves again. 'Alec won't mind. His hours are so irregular we don't go in for five-course dinners. Our cook is an expert at casseroles and things that won't spoil keeping hot in the oven.' She suddenly realised she had laid herself open to the question of what exactly Alec did, just what she wanted to avoid. 'What about Gerald, Lucy?' she asked hastily.

'The only kind of fish Gerald really enjoys,' Lucy said dryly, 'is the kind that comes in batter, with chipped potatoes, wrapped in newspaper. Frightfully plebeian, but he says nothing's better after a game of Rugby and a few beers.'

'And beer after the game,' said Pritchard, 'is of course an essential part of Rugby football!'

Throughout this exchange, Rhino had stared in disbelief at Mrs. Howell. 'Well! I thought you'd be grateful for a hint or two about how things are done in the best houses. But it's obviously a waste of time trying to raise people above their natural level.'

'I should certainly never attempt it with *you*, Rhino,' said Lucy.

Mrs. Howell, taking not the slightest notice, continued to drink her soup.

Lady Beaufort said softly, 'My dear Mr. Pritchard, I can't express how sorry I am we ever brought the man down upon you. If the only way to induce him to leave is for us to go, we'll take our departure tomorrow.'

'Nonsense! I won't allow a boor to upset our arrangements. You were to stay till Monday and till Monday you shall stay. But next time I invite you, I shall send my own car to fetch you from London.'

'How kind!' She patted his hand – not the one holding the soup spoon, fortunately, as he was left-handed. 'I should like to see the gardens in summer, I must admit.'

'So you shall.'

Everyone started talking about gardens. Rhino's contribution was a rant against his head gardener, who never seemed able to supply the required vegetables for his kitchens.

'No doubt he expects French beans in February and asparagus in August,' Daisy said, but she spoke in a low voice, not wanting to reignite the embers.

Only Pritchard heard her. He responded, 'Let's hope no one brings up the subject of fishponds.'

The rest of the evening passed reasonably smoothly. In the morning Daisy got up quite early again, although Lucy wasn't hurrying her to catch the sunlight. In fact, the sun was rising behind a haze of high, thin cloud. Rain before nightfall, she thought.

She had forgotten last night to ask Pritchard what time would be convenient for him to show her the house. She didn't want to keep him waiting. Hence the early rising.

This time only Carlin and Armitage were down before her. They were talking about fly-fishing.

'An innocuous subject, one would think,' said Carlin.

'But to be approached with caution in this house at present,' Armitage added.

'Definitely!' Daisy agreed, helping herself to a couple of rashers of bacon and a muffin.

'Before we ventured into such deep waters, we were wondering if we ought to offer to throw the rhinoceros out. He's big and stubborn, but between the two of us we ought to be able to manage it. What do you think, Mrs. Fletcher?'

'Should we tell our esteemed host that we're not merely willing but anxious to go big game hunting?'

Armitage grinned. 'It'd make a change from angling.'

'No,' said Daisy.

'No?' Carlin was disappointed. 'Expound, pray.'

'If you ask me, Mr. Pritchard is perfectly capable of routing Rhino if he chooses. If he lets him stay till Monday, which is when he's supposed to leave, it's for his own reasons. Better not to interfere.'

'By Jove, wheels within wheels we wot not of!' Carlin exclaimed facetiously.

'Not at all. Just better to let sleeping rhinoceroses lie,' Daisy advised.

'If only he *would* sleep,' Armitage sighed.

'He hasn't come down yet,' Daisy pointed out. 'Enjoy the peace and quiet while you may. Don't let me interrupt the fishing. You must strike while the fish are biting.'

They took her at her word. She was able to add her own mite to the discussion as her brother Gervaise had occasionally condescended to take her fishing with him on the Severn in her youth, in another world. Gervaise, had he survived the trenches, would not have approved of this world where his sister consorted on the friendliest of terms with a plumber, she thought sadly.

Howell came in next. 'Glad to see you're up and about,' he said to Carlin. 'What do you suppose is the earliest we can expect your lord and master to be ready to go into Swindon?'

'Eleven. At the very earliest. He has to have his after-breakfast stroll alone with his cigar and his thoughts or his digestion goes wonky. You saw him strolling up and down the terrace yesterday, remember.'

'Pity it's not raining,' said Howell, glancing at the window.

'Believe me, you wouldn't want to try to work with him when his digestion's wonky. It's a concession to work at all today. He doesn't usually come in to the office on Saturdays, though I'm junior enough to have to put in a brief appearance. It's a good job there's not much left to be done. I shouldn't think you'll be able to keep him at it for very long, and he'll expect at least an hour's lunch break.'

'I don't want to hold it over till Monday.' Howell frowned. 'I have other business scheduled. If we don't leave till eleven, I doubt we'll be home before five.'

Carlin shrugged. 'Sorry, old chap, nothing I can do about it.'

'"The customer is always right,"' Howell said with a sigh. 'I sometimes think it's a pity Selfridge ever coined the phrase.'

'I'm supposed to be playing golf tomorrow, myself, in Essex. It's a tournament. I was hoping to catch a train back to town tonight.'

'That shouldn't be difficult. Swindon being a junction on the Bristol line, there are plenty of fast trains.'

'Good! I'll pack my bag and take it with me. But first, another sausage or two. May I bring you something, Mrs. Fletcher?'

Daisy was munching a second muffin when Pritchard, Julia, and Lucy came in.

'I'm going to tour the house with you, Daisy,' said Lucy. 'I have two unused plates left, and plenty of magnesium, so I'll take a couple of photos for you if you see anything you'd like for your article.'

'You're all finished with the grotto, are you?' Armitage asked.

'Yes. A good job I caught the sun yesterday. It looks like rain.'

'The grotto's a bit dank in wet weather,' Pritchard conceded, 'though the hermit's lair is cosy with the fire lit.'

'I know Alec will want to see it,' said Daisy. 'How about Gerald, Lucy? Do you think he's interested?'

'I haven't the slightest, but if so he can go with you and Alec. I've had enough of tramping that path. What time did you say they're arriving?'

'Barker told me four o'clock. Good morning, Rhino.'

Rhino produced a morose grunt and waved a sort of greeting with his cigarette holder, already sending up a tendril of smoke. Without further acknowledgement of the company, he headed for the food.

'It'll still be light enough to see the grotto in daylight, then,' Lucy said. 'Or were you going to show Alec the night spectacle?'

'Depends what the weather looks like. I wouldn't want to tackle the path at night in the rain.'

'Just let me know if you want to go after dark,' said Pritchard, 'and I'll have the lamps lit for you.'

'I'll do it,' Armitage volunteered. He smiled at Julia as he spoke. No doubt she would join the tour.

Pritchard got up. 'I've one or two things to see to in my den, Mrs. Fletcher. If you wouldn't mind, you and Lady Gerald, coming there in half an hour or so, I'll give you the grand tour.'

Having eaten all she wanted, if not more, Daisy sat on with another cup of tea, chatting. Eventually Sir Desmond put in an appearance. Howell and Carlin watched in dismay as the Principal Deputy Secretary helped himself to a huge plateful.

Daisy heard Howell mutter to Carlin, 'We'll be lucky to finish our business before dinner! Never mind, lad, there's a good late train.'

Unfortunately, Rhino also overheard. 'Anxious to get away early, are you?' he said with a sneer. 'All you bureaucrats are bone-lazy slackers. Take the taxpayer's money and do as little work as possible.'

Carlin turned scarlet. 'Sir Desmond, Mr. Howell, I'll be in my room when you're ready to leave,' he said with quiet dignity. 'Excuse me, ladies.'

Sir Desmond turned a long, considering look on Rhino, but sat down without saying anything and began his breakfast.

It was left to Julia to utter what everyone was thinking. 'Rhino, you really are irredeemably vulgar.'

Rhino stared at her with blank incomprehension. 'You must be thinking of some other fellow,' he said. 'My shield has more quarterings than nine out of ten peers. Hasn't been a commoner in the family in three centuries.'

CHAPTER 16

Daisy was a bit disappointed with the house. The trouble was that it was such a perfect example of its kind that there wasn't really much to say about it. Houses with quirks and oddities were much easier to write about. With the grotto to describe and Armitage's stories about the Appsworths, however, she reckoned she had enough for an article of reasonable length.

One noticeable difference from the general run of stately homes was the lack of family portraits and knicknacks. Pritchard told Daisy and Lucy that he had bought almost all the Appsworths' furniture, all except the few pieces the last remaining family members chose to take with them.

'But I didn't think it was right to keep portraits that had nothing to do with my own ancestors,' he explained.

Lucy looked a trifle self-conscious. Her own family's rise was recent enough to provide no portraits older than Victorian. The walls of their huge entrance hall were hung with other people's ancestors.

'As for bits and bobs of precious porcelain on every surface,' Pritchard continued, 'I'd be afraid to move for fear of breaking something priceless.'

'Some of the ewers in your entrance hall must be valuable,' said Daisy.

'I daresay, but they're tucked up safe in those niches and Winifred insists on dusting the finest herself for fear the maids might break 'em.' He laughed. 'The girls are allowed to do the common china ones. Winifred keeps trying to persuade me to get rid of those, but they're *my* family's history.'

Daisy and Lucy settled on what photographs Lucy would take. Daisy helped with the flash apparatus, as usual ending up covered in whitish powder. She went to wash, then sought a place to transcribe her notes in peace.

Given the constraints of Lucy's car, she hadn't brought her portable typewriter, but the sooner she copied out her shorthand in longhand, the easier to remember what her erratic symbols were intended to represent. She tried the muniments room, but Julia was there with Charles Armitage. Though they insisted she was welcome to stay, she didn't want to disturb them. The library should be free. This was not a bookish household.

In the library, lined with tier after tier of leatherbound volumes most of which appeared never to have been opened since their purchase a century or two ago, Daisy found – of all people! – Rhino and Lady Ottaline, the latter in canary yellow this morning. They were standing by a window looking out onto the gravel drive at the front. Both gave her hostile glares. She would have preferred to leave them in peace, but she couldn't think of anywhere else to go. Her bedroom had no suitable table, and she really must unscramble her notes while they were fresh in her memory.

'Don't mind me,' she said brightly. 'I have some work to do. I'll be quiet as a mouse.'

'That's all right, Mrs. Fletcher,' said Lady Ottaline with equally spurious brightness. Unlike Rhino she had manners if not morals. 'We were just going. You're working on your magazine article? Sometimes I wish I had something useful to occupy my time.'

Daisy doubted a suggestion that ladies of her generation often took up charitable causes would be appreciated. Especially as, she now remembered Sir Desmond mentioning, their daughter was addicted to good works. She murmured something vague, sat down at a writing table, and opened her notebook.

They passed her on their way to the door, polluting the air with the inevitable cigarette smoke as they went. Daisy wasn't listening, but she couldn't help hearing Lady Ottaline saying to Rhino, 'I told you, nowhere in the house is really private. That's why we – ' The closing door cut her off.

Why they what. Daisy wondered. The weather was not conducive to canoodling out of doors. Surely Lady Ottaline hadn't had the bright idea of seeking privacy in the hermit's lair?

Daisy quickly forgot about them, becoming absorbed in trying to decide whether she had intended one particular scribble to represent *marble* or *marquetry*. Perhaps she ought to take a refresher course in shorthand.

She finished transcribing just in time for lunch. Lady Ottaline arrived late for the meal, causing their hostess to sit throughout in tight-lipped silence, no great loss to the conversation. Afterwards, Mrs. Howell led the way through to the drawing room for coffee. She sat down and started pouring, while Armitage went to her to hand round the demitasse cups.

'There, that's for Lady Ottaline. Black without sugar, isn't that right Lady –. Where is Lady Ottaline?'

'I expect she went to powder her nose, Winifred.'

'Well, I do think she might have said a word to me. Some people never spare a thought for other people's convenience. Now her coffee's going to get cold and be wasted.'

'We can't have that,' Pritchard said jovially. 'Give it to me.'

'You like yours half milk.'

'I'll be a martyr.'

'No need for martyrdom,' Lucy drawled. 'I drink it black, no sugar. I'll take it, Charles.'

'Lord Rydal isn't here either,' Mrs. Howell complained. 'Not that I expect better manners of him.'

Just as Lucy took her first sip, Lady Ottaline came in from the hall. Her make-up failed to hide flushed cheeks, and her eyes glittered.

'Ah, coffee! I don't suppose, dear Mr. Pritchard, I could have a drop of brandy in mine?'

'Of course, Lady Ottaline. Anyone else fancy a drop?'

No one else did. Mrs. Howell poured coffee; Armitage took it to the Welsh dresser, where he added brandy. He handed it to Lady Ottaline, who had followed, and she drifted over to the French windows. She stood gazing out, her back to the room.

Conversation, halted by her entrance, resumed. Lady Beaufort asked Daisy about her progress with her article. Daisy was trying to explain the difficulties of writing about a perfect house without it sounding like a lecture on architecture when Barker came in to announce that Lord Gerald Bincombe and Mr. Fletcher had arrived.

Pritchard popped up. 'Excellent, excellent! They've beaten the rain. You'll be able to show them the grotto, Mrs. Fletcher, without having to brave the path when it's wet.'

He hurried out to the hall. Daisy and Lucy went after him.

Daisy hadn't seen Gerald in a few months. He was the big, solid kind of rugger player, not the little wiry kind. Though Alec was tall and broad-shouldered, he looked barely average in size beside Gerald. He also looked considerably slimmer. Sitting in City boardrooms and consuming City lunches had added a few inches round Gerald's waist. By now the occasional game of Rugby football was probably a ritual more honoured in the breach than the observance.

Alec, on the other hand, though he did more sitting behind desks than he would have preferred, also did a fair amount of foot-slogging when he was on a case. Not infrequently his lunchtimes were a ritual more honoured in the breach than the observance.

Once all the greetings and introductions were out of the way, Daisy said, 'You're much earlier than we expected, darling.'

'We did manage to leave a bit early. But it's mostly because when I estimated the length of the journey, I failed to allow for Gerald's style of driving.'

Gerald grinned. 'Knew I was safe with a copper in the car. Fletcher kept his eyes peeled for peelers all the way. Would have spotted one half a mile off. Plenty of time to slow down.'

'It would have been very embarrassing to be stopped by a bobby who recognised me, even though I wasn't at the wheel.'

Pritchard turned to Alec. 'So you're a policeman, are you, Mr. Fletcher?'

'You let the cat out of the bag, darling,' Lucy said acidly to her husband.

'My own fault,' said Alec. 'Bincombe's usually such a taciturn chap, I didn't think to mention I prefer not to have it known. My apologies, Mr. Pritchard, if you feel I'm here under false pretences.'

'Not at all, not at all, my dear fellow. I daresay the reaction you get is a bit different, but there are times and places when I don't mention I'm a plumber by trade. No need to tell my sister-in-law, though,' he added hastily. He offered them something to eat, but they had stopped at a pub for a bite.

'Good,' said Daisy. 'I want to show you the grotto before it starts raining.'

'Give me time to catch my breath,' Alec begged.

'Coffee for the gentlemen, Barker,' Pritchard ordered.

'Darling, did you see the babies before you left?' Daisy asked on the way to the drawing room. 'How are they?'

'Blooming.'

'I wish they missed me,' she said mournfully.

In the drawing room, Pritchard introduced Alec and Gerald to Mrs. Howell, the Beauforts, and Charles Armitage. Predictably, Mrs. Howell gushed over Gerald and practically ignored Alec. Gerald let her gush. The Beauforts, having met Gerald in town, were more interested in Alec. They both managed not to reveal their knowledge of his profession, so Mrs. Howell and Armitage were the only two present to be left in ignorance. Unless, Daisy thought, Julia had told her beloved, in which case he was equally discreet.

An elderly parlour maid brought in fresh coffee. Daisy went to the window to look at the sky. The high, thin haze had thickened and lowered.

'Do drink up, darling,' she said. 'We'll have to go now to miss the downpour.'

'How badly do I want to see this grotto?'

'You mustn't feel obliged, Mr. Fletcher,' said Pritchard.

'Yes, you must,' said Daisy. 'Come on. Are you coming, Gerald?'

'Right-oh,' said Gerald, always obliging.

Turning away from the window, Daisy caught a glimpse of someone moving in the garden below the terrace, just disappearing behind a yew hedge. Lady Ottaline? Surely not. But she was missing from the drawing room, Daisy realised. When had she left, before or after Alec and Gerald's arrival?

'Better take your umbrella, love,' said Alec.

'Lucy, coming?'

'Not me. Run along, children.'

'I'll go with you,' said Armitage. 'The more the merrier.'

'Julia, you'll come, won't you?' Daisy asked helpfully.

'Yes, I'd like to get some fresh air before the rain starts. Are you sure you won't come, Lucy?'

Lucy sighed and said, 'Oh, very well. I'll bring my Kodak and take a snap or two if there's enough light.'

Daisy was afraid Lady Beaufort would veto Julia's going with them now that the party looked so like three couples, rather than simply a mixed group. Perhaps her ladyship failed to hear their plans. A smile on her plump face, she was listening to Pritchard, who leant with one hand on the back of her armchair, bending towards her and speaking in a low voice.

'Sheer folly!' snapped Mrs. Howell. 'You'll all be soaked to the skin and my servants will be put to the trouble of drying all your things again.'

'*My* servants, Winifred,' Pritchard reminded her. '*My* guests, going to admire *my* folly. At least, I hope you will admire the grotto, gentlemen, and let's hope the rain will hold off till you return.'

He shepherded them out to the hall, where the omni-provident Barker had enough umbrellas waiting for all.

'Just in case it starts raining before you return,' he said.

'Barker,' said Lucy, 'do you know how to work a Kodak? It's very simple. I can show you in a minute. Would you come out to the terrace and take a snap of all of us in our expedition gear?'

Barker didn't bat an eyelid. 'Certainly, my lady.'

Five minutes later the six were posed on the flagged terrace, with the butler peering gravely at them through the viewfinder. 'Say "cheese,"' he instructed them.

It was so unexpected that they all laughed as he pressed the button.

At that very moment, as if caused by the action, came a huge *boom*. Behind them, windows rattled. All heads swung to stare towards the source of the explosion. The bare, grassy hillside to the southwest erupted in a shower of rocks. Daisy clutched Alec's arm.

And then, before her horrified eyes, a patch of the slope subsided into a sudden sink-hole. But a sink-hole surely wouldn't throw up boulders, nor sound like a bomb?

'What the deuce was that?' Gerald demanded.

'The grotto,' Armitage said grimly. 'It's blown up.'

'How could a cave blow up?' Alec asked in what Daisy

called his 'policeman voice.' 'Pritchard surely didn't store munitions there. An unexploded German bomb?'

'Gas. Coal gas laid on for light and heating.'

'Gas doesn't ignite itself. Someone must be there. Daisy, ring for police and a doctor, and send able-bodied help. Come along, you two.'

The men set off at a run.

CHAPTER 17

Alec let Armitage take the lead. He hadn't yet had a chance to take the measure of the young Canadian, but at least he knew the way to the grotto.

'How far?' Alec asked as the three men crunched along the gravel path like a herd of stampeding buffalo.

Armitage slowed his pace a trifle. 'Half a mile? Thereabouts. Uphill.'

They passed a yew hedge. The path curved to the right. Ahead were three stone steps going up. Armitage took them at a single leap. Mounting more conservatively one at a time, Alec hoped he'd never have to chase the man with intent to arrest him.

The slope grew steeper. Bincombe, less fit, was already falling behind. Alec was glad he'd resisted the temptation to give up exercising when the twins were born.

He summoned enough breath to ask Armitage, 'Any ideas?'

'Lord Rydal. Went off right after lunch. Smokes like a chimney. Doesn't explain, though, sufficient accumulation of gas. That was a big bang.'

'It was indeed.'

No explanation for the accumulation of sufficient gas to cause a huge explosion? A leak was always possible, but in an open cave it should have quickly diluted to comparatively safe proportions. Rydal – or anyone else – ought to have smelt it as he approached. No explanation, either, of why Lord Rydal should have decided to go off, apparently alone, for a quiet postprandial smoke in the grotto, of all places. But perhaps there were perfectly obvious answers. Alec just didn't have enough knowledge of the situation to begin to formulate theories.

They galloped up more steps and thundered onto a wooden bridge. Armitage slowed to stare down at the brook below.

'The water's draining away! The stream must be blocked.' He came to a halt. 'I don't like the look of this.'

Bincombe arrived, panting. 'What's the matter?'

'The stream is drying up.' Alec looked at Armitage. 'What does it mean?'

'Its source is in the grotto.' His face was white, freckles standing out starkly. He took off his hat and wiped cold sweat from his brow. 'The whole roof must have come down.'

'Wasn't that pretty obvious from what we saw from the terrace?' Bincombe asked.

'I hoped . . . The thing is, anyone who was in there must be dead.'

'No hurry then. May I stop running?'

'No,' said Alec. 'People survive cave-ins. But not for long, if they're injured or trapped in an airless space. Let's go.'

He started running again, taking the lead as the path rose above the dying stream. The footing was solid chalky lime-stone now instead of gravel – at least, he hoped it was solid. Cautiously he slowed as he rounded a steep bluff.

He was concentrating on the path's surface, here littered

with rocks. For a moment the whimpering sound didn't penetrate his consciousness, then he heard it and looked up. Ahead of him, a greyish-white figure slumped in a heap against the cliff wall.

It stirred. Alive!

'Great Scott –'

'That's not Rydal,' observed Bincombe, coming up behind Alec.

Armitage arrived last. 'Lady Ottaline!'

'Lady Ottaline,' said Daisy. 'I'm sure I saw her going after Rhino, down through the garden. I think I ought to go with them.'

'I shall telephone the doctor and the police, madam.' Barker handed the camera to Lucy as he spoke. 'I'll inform Mr. Pritchard of this unfortunate occurrence – though he must certainly have heard the explosion – and send the gardeners and the chauffeur to help.'

'Thanks.' Daisy hesitated. 'I suppose you'd better tell the police Detective Chief Inspector Fletcher of Scotland Yard is on the spot. Though not in his official capacity!'

'Very good, madam.' Not by so much as a flicker of an eyelash did the butler betray whether this was news to him. He went off with his usual stately mien.

'Coming, you two?'

Lucy and Julia looked at each other.

'Daisy, shouldn't you leave it to the men?' Julia suggested. 'It's not as if you have any nursing experience, darling.'

'No, but I know if I were hurt and frightened I'd want a woman with me. I'm going.'

'She may be dead,' said Lucy bluntly.

'She may not. Why don't you go and make sure Mrs. Howell gets everything ready in case she's alive and injured.'

'Right-oh. That I can manage.'

'I'll come with you, Daisy,' said Julia.

The men were long gone by then. Daisy and Julia hurried after them along the familiar path. Daisy was vaguely surprised that the trees and shrubbery and sheets of daffodils looked no different from last time she had passed that way.

'Do you think it's dangerous?' Julia said worriedly. 'I hope Charles will take care. And your husband and Lord Gerald, too, of course.'

'I haven't the foggiest. I suppose it depends just what they find there. It seems to me the roof, or whatever you want to call it, can't have been very thick or it wouldn't have blown bits and pieces up in the air, just collapsed. Don't you think so?'

'I suppose so. Then Rhino may not be buried very deep.'

'You think it must be Rhino, too?'

'Well, he didn't turn up for coffee, which he usually does, and you said Lady Ottaline went after him.'

'I didn't actually see him go, and I couldn't swear it was her I saw. It was only a glimpse. Alec's always accusing me of speculating wildly.'

'Not really wildly. Everyone else was in the drawing room, except the three who went to Swindon. Daisy, the awful thing is I have a beastly urge to tell them not to try to rescue Rhino.'

'I know what you mean. But you wouldn't dream of actually saying it, and if you did they'd take no notice, so you needn't feel guilty. I – ' She cut herself off as a strange figure appeared where the path curved round a large bush. 'Good gracious, what on earth?'

'It's Charles! What's he carrying?'

Armitage had a large, grey burden slung over his shoulder in a fireman's lift.

'Lady Ottaline,' said Daisy, hurrying towards him. 'She can't be dead or he'd have left her and gone on to help the others look for Rhino.'

'Charles, where did you find her?'

'Just outside the grotto.'

'Is the entrance blocked?' Daisy asked.

'Not as far in as we could see.'

'They're going in, then,' she said resignedly. The thought made her feel nauseated, but nothing she could say or do would change matters. *Stiff upper lip*, she exhorted herself.

'Yes. I've got to get Lady Ottaline to the house. Fletcher thinks she may be concussed. Something about her eyes not reacting properly to light.'

'We'll manage her, won't we, Julia? Lay her down and get back to Alec and Gerald.'

Armitage hesitated. Then, with obvious reluctance, he let Julia and Daisy shift Lady Ottaline from his shoulders and lay her on her back on the grass. She was not heavy. Daisy knelt beside her and started to wipe chalk dust from her face.

'We can manage her, Charles,' said Julia, squeezing his hand. 'Take care, won't you?'

He gave her a strained smile. 'Don't you think I should carry her?'

'People will be coming. The gardeners and the chauffeur.'

Still he didn't leave. Daisy was puzzled. She wouldn't have thought him so callous as to abandon even such an unlovely specimen as Rhino when there might be a chance of saving him.

Lady Ottaline moaned, blinked eyelashes clogged with eyeblack and chalk, and made a premonitory sound in her throat that reminded Daisy all too clearly of Nana about to be sick in the car.

'Quick, Julia, help me turn her over.'

While they were coping with ensuing events, Armitage departed. Daisy would have been more than happy to go with him.

Inside the cave, the chalk dust was as thick as a London pea-souper. Alec coughed in spite of having tied a handkerchief over his nose and mouth. Peering forwards, he wished he'd taken the time to get hold of a torch, not that it would have helped much in this murk. He didn't dare breathe deeply enough to try to detect gas.

The floor crunched beneath his feet. He didn't know whether he was stepping on debris or irreplaceable artifacts.

'Fletcher?'

Bincombe hadn't wanted to stay outside, but he had sense enough to realise, without a long argument, that they mustn't put all their eggs in one basket. If the roof came down . . .

Better not to think about it, or only to remind himself that a shout might be enough to trigger collapse.

Turning his head – mustn't lose his sense of direction – he called in a low voice, 'All right so far. I can't see much.' He stood absolutely still for a moment, listening. No ominous creaking from the roof, nor clatter of falling rubble. No calls for help, no screams, no groans.

Slowly he moved on, hands held out before him.

'Ouch!' he exclaimed involuntarily as his knuckles met stone.

He wished he could have sent Bincombe back with the woman, and kept Armitage, who knew the place. But it was no use asking the poor chap to come in here. He'd been willing to try, but he'd have been more of a liability than an asset.

While these thoughts passed through Alec's mind, he had been running his hands over the obstacle in front of him. It was not a disordered heap of broken stone but carved marble, smooth except for a few nicks and a groove gouged by some hard object hitting it from above. He glanced up, uselessly. As well as the dust in the air, it was darker here.

The statue was large and surely would have told him where he was if he were familiar with the grotto. Three linked caves, Armitage had said. Was Alec near the end of the first, or had he already passed unknowing into the second, or had he scarcely begun to penetrate the depths?

He felt his way round the statue. Beyond, empty space began again, but he had taken no more than three tentative steps when once again his knuckles hit a solid mass. A rough wall, a more or less right-angled protruding corner – he reached up and felt the curve of an arch. The way through to the second cave, he guessed.

Behind him stone clunked on stone. He stiffened, arms raised to protect his head.

'Fletcher?' Bincombe's voice was nearby, but muffled, as if he, too, had masked mouth and nose with a handkerchief.

And his feet must have knocked the loose stones on the floor against one another, Alec hoped.

'I told you to stay outside.'

'I'm not one of your bobbies, old man. Armitage came back. Met Daisy and Miss Beaufort, left Lady Ottaline with them.'

'Daisy!'

'She's not one of your bobbies, either.' He sounded as if he was grinning. Though laconic, he seemed to have lost his customary taciturnity. 'Lady O will keep 'em busy. I told Armitage to stay outside, poor devil.'

'Poor devil – assuming his story's the truth.'

'You don't believe him? He's in a real funk, I'd swear.'

'Has it occurred to you that he may be responsible for this mess? Inadvertently, or on purpose. He wouldn't want to find Rydal, alive or dead.'

'If Rhino's in here.'

'If he's in here,' Alec agreed. 'I'm afraid we could easily pass him by without noticing. We need more men. But not Armitage. At least he's more likely to obey you than you are to obey me. Right-oh, now you're here, stay here, *please*! I'm going ahead. I wish we had a rope.'

'Hold on a moment.' He sneezed. 'Phew, dust up my nose. Here, Lucy makes me wear one of these new-fangled belts. Catch hold of the buckle and I'll hang on to the end. Dammit, where are you? It's not very long, though, in spite of my adding a pound or two.'

'Got it. Tell Lucy braces would have been much more useful. We could have tied yours and mine together.'

'And both lost our trousers.'

'You won't lose yours, will you? Fat lot of help you'll be if you trip over your turn-ups at every other step.'

'My tailor's lost a customer if I do. Ties!' Bincombe exclaimed, inspired. 'Yours and mine. Tie them together.'

'Good idea.' A bit miffed that he hadn't thought of this expedient first, Alec pulled off his tie and knotted it to Bincombe's. The tight knot wasn't going to do either much good. He was glad he hadn't worn his Royal Flying Corps tie. 'Here, tie your end through the buckle of your belt. That'll make it even longer. Not that it's going to be strong enough to pull me out with if something happens, but at least we'll be able to find each other.'

'Hope so. I'd hate to have to face Daisy if I lost you. Keep one hand on the wall.'

'Here goes.' He took a tentative step under the arch, and a second. The wall here was masonry, hewn stone with mortared joints, not the natural sides of a cave. There seemed to be much less rubble underfoot. On the other hand, it was dark. Not that visibility had been much better in the first cave, but the diffuse daylight had given an illusion of sight, of belonging to the outer world.

Another step, and another. With one hand on the wall and the other clutching the necktie, he wished for a third to feel ahead for obstacles. He took his hand from the wall and reached forward. Nothing. Fingers found the wall again. Another step –

'Damn!'

'Fletcher, what's wrong? Are you all right?'

'Yes. Overconfident. I stepped on something and . . . But I'm all right. Half a mo –' Alec's next step met an immovable obstacle. 'I'm going to have to let go of my umbilical cord. I'll lay the end right by the wall so I should be able to find it if you don't pull on it.'

'Right-oh. What – '

'Hang on. I think this is the end.'

With care, Alec went down on one knee on the rubble. His best suit must be past praying for by now, he reckoned. Crouched there, feeling blindly, he could find no way round or through the barrier. He stood up. Stretching upwards, he could touch all but the topmost curve of the arch, but the slope of the rock fall made it impossible to reach to find out whether it met the ceiling.

He lowered his handkerchief mask. Either there was less dust in here or it was settling. He sniffed.

No stink of gas.

'Bincombe, can you smell gas?'

A brief silence, then, 'No,' followed by a sneeze. 'But I can't claim my nose is reliable just now.'

Alec put his hands round his mouth like a megaphone and made a hooting noise towards the top of the obstruction. The sound returning to his ears seemed to him to have bounced off a solid wall.

'What the deuce? Was that you, Fletcher?'

'Yes. I'm pretending to be an owl. It's impossible to be sure without light, but I don't think there's any way through. I'm coming back.'

CHAPTER 18

Over Lady Ottaline's limp body, Daisy and Julia exchanged a glance.

Julia giggled. 'I don't know what she'd say if she knew you were using spit to clean her face.'

'Not couth,' Daisy agreed, 'but I had to do something after she was sick. She's a mess. It's a good job she passed out again.'

'I'll go and wet my hanky in the stream.'

'Here, take my scarf, too, and hurry. I'm running out of spit.'

Julia returned in a couple of minutes. 'Daisy, the stream has practically disappeared! The source must be blocked.' She knelt opposite and started to dab with a dripping handkerchief at the cashmere jacket the victim was wearing in default of her soaked furs. 'Do you think they're all right? Suppose it breaks through while they're up there?'

'Your Charles must have noticed the drop in water level. He'll have warned them and they'll watch out for any changes.'

'But – '

'Julia, stop it! I know you're not used to having a sweetheart to worry about, but if you carry on like that you'll give me the jitters, too.'

'Sorry. After so many years of one day being just like the day before, I don't know how to cope with the unexpected.'

'You'd soon learn if you married a police detective. I don't suppose it's a skill much required of the wife of a university lecturer, though. Oh, blast, it's beginning to rain! She shouldn't lie here in the cold, getting wet again. I wonder whether she does have concussion.' Eyes dilated by drug use didn't react properly to light. Unequal pupils were a symptom of concussion, she vaguely recalled, but she didn't feel like messing about with Lady Ottaline's eyelids to take a look. 'She must be in shock, at least.' Would that, or the drug wearing off, account for the vomiting?

'I wish someone would come.'

'Do you think we can carry her between us?'

'We can but try,' Julia said with determination. She stood up. 'Oh, thank heaven, here comes a man. It's Pritchard's chauffeur.'

The chauffeur, Madison, like his employer, was a small man, but he was wiry. 'You help me get 'er ladyship up on me shoulders, madam, and I'll get 'er to the house all right. Little bit of a thing like 'er. What 'appened to 'er?'

'I don't know exactly,' said Daisy. 'I should think she must have been outside the grotto when the explosion happened and got blown down. But that's pure guesswork.'

As she spoke, she and Julia lifted Lady Ottaline by shoulders and ankles. Madison ducked underneath and they deposited her face down across his shoulders. He grabbed her skinny legs round the knees on one side, and one brittle wrist on the other, and set off back down the path. Very undignified, Daisy thought, thankful again that Lady Ottaline wasn't aware of the pickle she was in.

When they came to steps, Daisy and Julia had to steady Madison in his descent, but he never faltered beneath the weight.

'I suppose there are other advantages than fashion to being slim,' Daisy remarked to Julia with a sigh. 'Carrying me would be another story altogether.'

'The possibility of being blown up is hardly a good reason to go on a Banting diet.'

'Oh, I don't know. After what Howell said about the new safety features of the hot water geyser, if it can blow up, anything might blow up any minute.'

'I don't think that can have been what did it,' Julia said doubtfully. 'He was talking about a steam explosion. That would happen if the gas was lit and the water wasn't running through. It would be dangerous to anyone nearby, and it would cause some damage, but would it be so huge? There could only be a very limited amount of steam, I'd have thought, just from the water left in the machine after the last time it was used.'

'I'm afraid I sort of lost track of his explanation in the middle. These safety thingummies wouldn't prevent a gas explosion, then?'

'Not if I understood correctly.'

'I expect you did. Technical things tend to muddle me. Or at least to make my mind wander. It must have been a leak in a gas pipe, and poor old Rhino wandered into it waving his cigarette about as usual.'

'But what on earth was he doing there? He wasn't any more interested in the grotto than you were in the workings of the geyser.'

That was a question to which Daisy considered the answer

obvious, given Lady Ottaline's presence following Rhino. However, she'd much prefer to save the elucidation for Alec. To her relief, the chauffeur had reached the last steps and called to them. They had fallen behind, not wanting him to hear their discussion.

'Madam, miss, I c'd do with a hand 'ere, if you'd oblige. Don't want to drop 'er, do we.'

As they came up with him, a horde of gardeners – at least, a head gardener, an undergardener, and two gardener's boys – appeared on the scene. Each had a spade on his shoulder. In addition, one carried a pickaxe, one a crowbar, and one a coil of rope.

'Good,' grunted Madison. To the younger boy, small but wiry, he said, ''Ere, Fred, or whatever your name is, you can carry 'er ladyship to the house.'

'I'll thank you not to give orders to my lads, Mr. Madison,' said the head gardener icily.

'You planning to stand there all night argufying while the pore lady freezes to death?'

'That will do,' said Daisy, who was quite capable of putting even more ice into her voice than the head gardener. The 'servant problem' was between servants almost as often as between servant and employer, she reflected. 'Mr. Madison has already carried Lady Ottaline a considerable distance. Fred –. Is your name Fred?'

'Billy, miss.' Billy was clearly delighted by the row between his superiors.

'With your permission, Mr . . . ?'

'Simmons, madam,' the head gardener sulkily. He gestured at the undergardener and the other boy. 'You two lift her ladyship onto Billy's shoulders. Careful there, you oafs!'

Billy's face fell. He obviously wanted to go with the others to the scene of the disaster.

'You can go after them as soon as we get Lady Ottaline to the house,' Daisy consoled him as the others went on up the slope, Simmons and Madison stiff with indignation.

'She'm a real lady? 'Er don't seem like nuthen but a bit o' bone and hair. Fair dicky, ben't en? 'Er ben't dead, be en?'

'No, but she soon will be if you don't take more care.'

'Oi bain't agoing to flump, missus,' the boy said, injured, 'nor yet drop the lady. This yere rain, 'er'll be shrammed for sure ifn Oi don't peg it.'

Daisy gave up. She and Julia hurried to keep up with him.

Rain drifted down, soft, gentle, but persistent, seeping insidiously into every crack and crevice. Daisy hoped it would not hinder the rescue effort and make it more dangerous.

Towards the mouth of the grotto, a Scotch mist drifted in, permeating the air and beginning to clear the dust. Alec and Bincombe took off their handkerchief masks.

'Whew, bliss to breathe!' Bincombe exclaimed, then issued a final sneeze and blew his nose.

'Bliss to see,' Alec retorted. 'Even though you look like a ghost. A pretty substantial ghost.'

'So do you.'

They were both powdered from head to foot with grey dust. The all-pervading dampness was rapidly turning it into splotches of plaster, but there wasn't much they could do about it at present.

Alec approached the open edge of the cave and looked down. To his right water trickled over a lip of inset granite and down a vertical rock wall into a small pool. Mud and stranded reeds round the margin showed that it had very recently been larger. A slight overflow still gave a semblance of life to the stream, shrunken in its bed at the bottom of the steep-sided gorge.

To his left, perhaps a third of the distance down from the grotto to the pool, he saw the platform where he had found Lady Ottaline. Backed by a solid cliff, it faced the grotto and the defunct waterfall. Armitage stood there, looking up.

'What do you think happened to Lady Ottaline?' Bincombe asked.

'I'd guess that, when the inner cave blew up, the blast was funnelled out through that archway, through the grotto, and threw her against the cliff.'

'Hmm.'

'I doubt it would have been strong enough by then to do you or me much damage, but she's a scrawny little thing. I think she was down there. If she'd been up here she'd have had the fall as well as the impact. She'd probably be dead. All the same, she must have been heading up here. Why?'

Under the blotchy coating of damp chalk, Bincombe's face turned red. 'Hmm, well, none of my business, don't you know.'

Gentlemanly reticence added to natural taciturnity was a strong mix. Alec forbore to press him. Time enough for that if he couldn't get the information – or rumours – from Daisy.

'Right-oh. We'll have to try and get to the site of the collapse. I hope Armitage can direct us.'

He started down the steps, treading carefully on the rain-slick stone.

'Here come the troops,' said Bincombe.

Four men loaded with digging implements came tramping along the path. Pritchard's servants, Alec assumed. One carried a rope he could have done with a few minutes ago. He considered sending a couple to try to break through the barrier.

No, too dangerous. It would be better to have everyone working at the site of the hillside's collapse. He had little hope of pulling anyone out alive, but it had to be tried. It was always possible that Lord Rydal had found shelter in some crack or cranny.

Rhino, Bincombe had called him. An odd sort of a nickname, but this was not the time to ask about it. Alec reached the bottom of the steps and faced a barrage of questions from Armitage, while the others waited to be told what to do.

'Nothing doing there,' he said briefly to the former.

Armitage looked relieved. 'Fletcher, this is Simmons, the head gardener, and a couple of his chaps. And Madison, chauffeur. He took over carrying Lady Ottaline from me.' He turned to the men. 'Mr. Fletcher is in charge.' He looked a bit puzzled, as if he hadn't considered the question before and couldn't quite work out why Alec should be so definitely and obviously in charge.

'Thank you for helping Lady Ottaline, Madison.'

'My second lad's carrying her ladyship now, sir,' Simmons said with inexplicable belligerence.

'Only because Mrs. Fletcher – '

'I'm glad to see you've brought spades, Simmons.' Alec cut short their wrangling, wondering how on earth Daisy came into the matter. 'Good thinking. Now we need to make for the spot where the hillside subsided. I hope you can lead us there, quickly.'

CHAPTER 19

As Daisy and Julia and Billy, with his burden, reached the terrace, Pritchard hurried out of the drawing room, hatless in the rain, and Barker swung open the side door. They had obviously been watching out anxiously.

'Lady Ottaline?' said Pritchard, very upset. 'Bring her in! Lay her on the sofa.'

'She'll ruin the sofa!' objected Mrs. Howell, standing at the open French window. 'And look at the boy's boots!'

'It's my sofa, Winifred. What's more, it's my fault the poor lady is in this condition. Though leaks will happen, you know, no matter how careful you are. Come in, come in.'

'I'm no nurse,' said Daisy, 'but I think she ought to be taken straight to her bed. Billy, you'd better go with Barker. Is a doctor on the way?'

'Yes, madam,' Barker assured her. 'Her ladyship's maid and the housekeeper are making preparations upstairs to receive her ladyship. Not that we expected anything quite so . . .' At a loss for words, he looked with some dismay at Billy's boots, but ushered him in through the side door.

Regardless of the rain, Lady Beaufort came out, stately as a galleon in her brown tweed skirt and white blouse. She laid her hand on Pritchard's arm and said, 'Don't distress yourself. I'll go up and make sure everything that can be done is done properly.'

'Would you? How can I thank you!'

'I expect I'll think of a way,' Lady Beaufort promised. 'Julia, go inside at once, before you catch your death of cold.' She sailed off in Barker's wake.

Daisy and Julia, conscious of their muddy shoes and knees, were all for going in through the side door, but Pritchard insisted on taking them into the drawing room.

Mrs. Howell glared at their feet.

'Darlings, you *are* a mess,' Lucy greeted them.

'Aren't you glad you didn't come?' said Daisy, gravitating to a radiator.

Lucy shuddered. 'Very. What happened to Lady Ottaline?'

'We don't know,' said Julia. 'We met Charles carrying her and he left her with us, to go back to the others.'

'Then the chauffeur arrived and carried her until we met the gardeners and Billy took over.'

'This is beginning to sound like one of those endless fairy tales,' Lucy complained.

'It did seem endless at the time,' Julia agreed.

Meanwhile, a maid came in to light a fire in the fireplace.

'I didn't order a fire,' Mrs. Howell told her.

'Mr. Barker said to, ma'am.'

'Who's orders do you obey, mine or the butler's?'

The maid looked nonplussed, the butler clearly as great a figure in her eyes as the lady of the house.

'I think we might have a fire, Winifred,' said Pritchard mildly. 'Mrs. Fletcher and Miss Beaufort are damp and chilled.'

'Oh, well, if Barker is more important – '

'Barker is doing an excellent job under unusual and difficult circumstances.'

Emboldened, the maid said, 'If you please, sir, Mr. Barker said as how he'd 'preciate a word with Mrs. Fletcher.'

'I ought to change, so I'll go and find him.' Daisy reluctantly abandoned the radiator. 'It'll be marvellous to come down to a real fire.'

'I'd better change, too,' said Julia.

'Mrs. Fletcher,' Pritchard begged, 'isn't there something else I can do to help? I'm afraid I'd only be in the way out on the hill.'

Daisy hesitated. There was one thing she felt should be done as soon as possible, which no one else seemed to have thought of yet. The trouble was, she suspected Alec would prefer to do it himself, in person. She reminded herself that gas leaks happened all the time. She had absolutely no reason to suppose the explosion was anything but an accident – nothing, at least, beyond the character of the apparent victim. But she didn't even know that Rhino *was* a victim.

She made up her mind. 'Someone's going to have to tell Sir Desmond that his wife's been hurt. As their host, I'd say you're probably the proper person. Can you telephone him at the factory?'

Pritchard paled. 'How could I have forgotten? Yes, of course, I'll do it right away.' He squared his shoulders and followed Daisy and Julia out to the hall.

Lucy was left with Mrs. Howell. Her manners were too good to desert their hostess, though whether she'd bestir herself to make conversation was another matter. Daisy wished she could watch and listen invisibly.

The butler was waiting in the hall.

'You wanted to see me, Barker?'

'Thank you, madam, yes. I merely wished to inform you that I fear I did not follow your instructions to the letter when I telephoned the police. There was not time to advise you, but being acquainted with the constable in the village, I could not feel it desirable to notify him of Mr. Fletcher's profession and rank.'

'Oh?'

'A man easily flustered, madam, by matters outside his usual purview. Very competent, I understand, where poachers, tramps, boys scrumping apples, and Saturday night fights outside the Spotted Dog are concerned, but apt to lose his head in more complex circumstances.'

'Oh dear. Yes, I quite see your point. A Scotland Yard detective added to an explosion might be altogether too much for the poor man. Thank you, Barker.'

'Thank *you*, madam.'

'Did you tell the doctor? About my husband, I mean.'

'No, madam. As I recall, you suggested telling the police only. I should perhaps also inform you that, after consulting Mr. Pritchard, I telephoned the landlord at the Spotted Dog and asked him to round up a few able-bodied men and bring them to assist in the digging if required.'

'Barker, you're a regular Jeeves,' Daisy said warmly.

'Thank you, madam. Excuse me, madam,' he added as the doorbell rang. 'I expect that's Dr. Tenby.'

'Jeeves?' asked Julia.

'A fictional butler who's a genius at dealing with extraordinary circumstances. Your reading has been altogether too serious.'

'Jeeves sounds like the Admirable Crichton. You can't say that's too serious. Come on, what are we waiting for? I'm dying to get out of these wet clothes.'

'You go on up. I want to have a word with Dr. Tenby. I'll take him up to Lady Ottaline.'

'Surely Barker ... Oh, you're going to tell the doctor about Alec?'

'I think I'd better. It was almost certainly only an accident, but as long as there's the least chance of hanky-panky being involved –. Well, the doctor will examine Lady Ottaline with a different eye if he might have to testify in court.'

'Daisy, aren't you rather putting the cart before the horse? I mean, just because Alec happens to be on the spot, it doesn't mean a crime's been committed.'

'I know. But just think about it, a man who manages to make himself thoroughly disliked by –. Here's Dr. Tenby.'

'I'm off.' Julia disappeared in the direction of the stairs.

Heading in the opposite direction, Daisy heard Barker remind the doctor of her name before bearing away his top-coat.

'Good afternoon, Dr. Tenby.' As he merely bowed silently, she went on, 'I'll take you up to Lady Ottaline.'

He gave her an enquiring look. She realised that Barker had not known, when he rang up, who the patient would be, or indeed whether there would be a patient at all.

'Lady Ottaline is your patient.' She started towards the stairs and he followed, black bag in hand. 'Lady Ottaline Wandersley. You must have met her the other evening.'

He grunted assent.

'Did Barker tell you what happened?'

'An explosion.'

'Yes, we don't know exactly how it happened, but it was probably a gas leak. Out in the grotto. Have you seen the grotto?'

'Yes.'

'It blew up. My husband is leading a rescue party, in case there are other victims.'

'Burns?'

'What? Oh, Lady Ottaline. No, she's not burnt. I don't exactly know, but my husband thinks she may have a concussion. Something about the eyes.'

'Medical man?'

'Alec? No, but he's a police officer and he's had to deal with a lot of injuries. As a matter of fact, he's a detective chief inspector at Scotland Yard. Not that he's here on business, just as a visitor, but I thought you ought to know. In case he finds out it wasn't an accident and you're asked to testify to an inquest, or even in court.'

He gave an abrupt nod.

'When you've finished with Lady Ottaline, he'd like you to go out to the grotto in case they find another victim.' Alec hadn't actually stated as much, but he'd sent for the doctor before he knew anyone at all was injured.

'Someone missing?'

'Lord Rydal.'

Another grunt. No doubt taciturnity had its admirers, but it made conversation very difficult.

They reached the Wandersleys' bedroom and Daisy knocked. A lady's maid opened the door.

'Dr. Tenby,' Daisy introduced him. She went straight off to change, despite her interest in Lady Ottaline's condition.

She was quite sure that her chance of learning anything from the doctor was nil.

A quarter of an hour's tramp brought Alec and his troop to their goal. They stood on the short turf on the edge of a pit some ten or twelve feet deep. A certain amount of debris was scattered about the rim, but most of what the explosion had thrown up had landed back in the hole. After hurrying uphill to get here, all except the gardener's remaining boy were silent, catching their breath as they stared down at the jumbled mess.

The boy said, 'Me mum'll take on something turrible if 'er finds out Oi bin down that 'ole.'

'You'll do what you're told,' snapped Madison.

'I'll not order *my* men into yon death-trap,' Simmons snapped back.

'Volunteers only,' said Alec.

'Oi won't tell me mum,' the boy assured him.

'Death-trap,' mused Armitage. 'I hope he isn't really down there.'

'Friend of yours?' Alec asked.

'What? No, on the contrary. But it sort of spoils one's abhorrence if it's diluted with pity. A nasty end. I've been thinking. Assuming this was caused by a gas leak and not some natural occurrence, gas in the middle cave wouldn't collect in great concentration because of the tunnel to the outer grotto. There's – or there was – also a rift in the roof which let in a certain amount of light and plenty of air.'

'Yes?' Alec encouraged him.

'So if Rydal walked in with a lit cigarette, and he

practically always had a lit cigarette in his holder, it might singe his eyebrows but I doubt it would create a disaster of this magnitude. The hermit's lair on the other hand – '

'The *what*?'

'Mrs. Fletcher hasn't told you? I suppose she hasn't had the opportunity.' He explained Pritchard's fancy of keeping a tame hermit in his grotto. 'The room had some sort of natural ventilation, but no source of natural light. It also had a door. It seems to me, the most likely thing to have happened is that Rydal opened the door on a room full of gas. In that case, he'd have been blown backwards, I imagine. He'd be somewhere over there.' Armitage gestured to the left. On that side, the hole sloped up to become a depression that could easily have been a natural part of the hillside.

'We should start digging in that dip?'

'I'm a historian, not a geologist or an explosives expert. But my guess is, the confined explosion blew out the roof of the lair, which then collapsed. It also blew Rydal back into the middle cave, but quite likely didn't do much direct damage to the cave itself. It would be the ground tremors from the blast that brought parts of that one down, leaving some of it undamaged.'

'So he could quite well be alive in there, and it's going to be devilish difficult to get him out.'

Armitage, who had been pink from exertion, turned pale as a ghost and looked down at his feet. 'I c-can't dig in these shoes,' he stammered unhappily. He was wearing house-shoes, not having changed after lunch before the impromptu expedition to the grotto. 'I have hiking boots back at the house – been tramping the downs to take a look at barrows and the ancient camps, you know – '

'You'd better go and get them.' Alec, like Bincombe, had donned sturdy walking shoes for their drive into the country. One could never be certain even a Daimler would not throw a rod in the middle of nowhere. 'More to the point, someone must explain to Mr. Pritchard what appears to have happened, and what we're going to try. Knowing the territory, you have the best grasp of the situation. You'd better wait till the police and the doctor arrive and bring them back with you.'

'Right you are, sir.' The colour began to return to Armitage's cheeks as he turned to leave.

'But first, old man,' Bincombe put in, 'if Pritchard hasn't yet had the gas turned off at the mains, make sure it's done, pronto.' He reached out a long arm and twitched away a packet of Woodbines the undergardener had just pulled out of his pocket.

While Simmons berated his underling for idiocy, Alec, Bincombe, Armitage, and Madison leant over the edge of the crater and sniffed. Alec caught no whiff of gas. Bincombe and Armitage both shook their heads. Madison thought he could smell it, but Alec suspected it was his imagination. As a man who spent much of his life breathing petrol fumes, he was not likely to have a sensitive nose.

In the meantime, the youth had wandered off round the rim of the hole, poking and prying. He now came back, carrying something in a grubby handkerchief, which he showed to Simmons.

The head gardener snorted. 'A bit o' copper pipe's not going to make you rich, me lad!'

'This 'ere's a *clue*, Mr. Simmons. I bet it's got dabs on it. That's what they call fingerprints in the books.'

'I'll give you dabs!'

'And it ben't just a scrap o' pipe. En's got a gas tap – '

'Chuck it away and – '

'Let me see that!' Alec interrupted urgently.

He took the trophy from its eager finder, careful to keep the indescribable handkerchief round it. A few inches of twisted pipe protruded from either end of the tap fitting. The tap itself was parallel to the pipe. Turned on.

Frowning at the damning object in Alec's hands, Bincombe shook his head and said, 'I can't believe even Rhino would be such a fool as to turn on the gas while holding a lit cigarette.'

CHAPTER 20

Daisy was brushing her hair when she heard a tap at the door.

'Come in!'

It was a very young housemaid, her eyes bright with excitement and a touch of apprehension. 'Mr. Pritchard says can you come down, madam. He wants to talk to you. Mr. Endicott's here. He's the p'liceman from the village, madam. It's about her ladyship – Lady Ottaline that is – and the 'splosion. He's ever so upset, madam, Mr. Endicott is.' She chattered on.

Daisy wondered if Pritchard considered that being married to a policeman must make her an expert at soothing members of that profession. On the contrary, she recalled numerous episodes tending to confirm the reverse. Not that she intended to tell Pritchard that she was more likely to exacerbate Constable Endicott's annoyance than to calm it.

'Please tell Mr. Pritchard I'll be down in a minute.'

The girl left. Daisy gave her curls a final whisk of the brush and put on lipstick to give herself courage. Her experience of past battles with Superintendent Crane of the Metropolitan Police, some won, some lost, were no help when it came to facing an irate village bobby.

But when she reached the hall, she found PC Endicott bewildered, not angry. The round-faced young man, helmet in hand, was saying piteously to Pritchard, 'You see, Mr. Pritchard, sir, there ben't nuthen in the handbook about explosions.'

'So you've already told me, Constable.' More than once, to judge by Pritchard's face. 'Ah, Mrs. Fletcher! This is PC Endicott. His sergeant is down with pleurisy, and he can't make up his mind whether he ought to notify his superiors in Swindon or not.'

Daisy tried to decide what Alec would prefer. Bringing in the Swindon brass hats without telling them he was from the Met was out of the question, certain to cause trouble. Honesty, though not always the best policy, was advisable in this case.

On second thoughts, not just yet. 'I should think, Mr. Endicott, your best course would be to go out to the scene of the disaster and find out exactly what happened. Then you can decide whether it should be reported or not.'

The harried look lifted from Endicott's face. 'Aye, thet'll be best. Thank 'ee kindly, ma'am.'

'If you hurry, you can catch up with the lads from the village,' Pritchard suggested.

Barker was miraculously on hand to show the constable to the back door.

'Just what I would have suggested, Mrs. Fletcher,' said Pritchard. 'Masterly inaction.'

'Why didn't you, then?'

'I wanted to be sure you concurred. I didn't want to make trouble for your husband by either giving information unnecessarily or witholding it. Now it's up to him to make the decisions.'

'Usually the best course.' Daisy sighed. 'Don't they say it's a sign of growing old when policemen start to look like schoolboys?'

Pritchard's eyes twinkled. 'I'd always heard the same of doctors.'

'Oh, that's all right then. Dr. Tenby doesn't look at all like a schoolboy to me.'

'More like an undertaker,' he said in a conspiratorial whisper. 'But hush, here he comes. How is your patient doing, Tenby?'

'Bad bruising. No concussion. Fainted from pain. Still considerable discomfort. I've left some powders.'

'Should I send for a nurse?'

'No, no, quite unnecessary. Lady Beaufort seems competent – '

'Very competent.'

'And her ladyship's maid can do whatever is required. Where's my other patient?'

'We're not certain there is one.'

'But Lord Rydal is still missing,' Daisy put in. 'Possibly blown up with the grotto. Oh, hello, Charles. What's up?'

Armitage squelched in. 'Fletcher sent me to get my hiking boots,' he said, looking down apologetically at his sodden, mucky footwear. 'I just met the copper already on his way, but I'm to escort you back, Dr. Tenby – '

'Galoshes, sir.' Barker rematerialised at the doctor's side, proffering the said objects. 'The weather is inclement, I fear.'

Tenby's gloom deepened, but he didn't protest. Perhaps it would have required the utterance of too many words.

'If you wouldn't mind waiting just a moment while I fetch my boots, Doctor.'

'I shall send a maid for them, sir,' Barker told Armitage, departing once more.

'Thanks!' Armitage turned to Pritchard. 'And most important, sir, Fletcher wants to know whether you've had the gas supply to the grotto turned off.'

'Yes, yes, immediately after the explosion. I take it there's no sign of Lord Rydal?'

'No. There's a dangerous blockage between the outer and inner grottoes – trying to move it could cause further collapse – so the job has to be tackled from the other end.' He hesitated. 'Fletcher didn't say – I think I should tell you three, but for pity's sake don't tell anyone else.'

'My lips are sealed,' Pritchard promised. Dr. Tenby's lips were practically always sealed anyway.

Daisy wasn't prepared to promise the same, but Armitage apparently assumed that as Alec's wife she was entitled to know all. Not that she hadn't already guessed what he was about to reveal with so much premonitory palaver.

'We've found what appears to be evidence that the explosion was not an accident.'

'Hmph,' said the doctor, unimpressed or uninterested. 'Pritchard, a stretcher.'

'I'll see what I can arrange and send it after you. Barker,' he said as the butler silently returned, 'can we provide anything in the way of a stretcher for Dr. Tenby?'

'Certainly, sir.'

'Mrs. Fletcher,' said Pritchard, 'ought I to ring up the Swindon police, now that it looks as if – '

'Not unless Alec said to.' Daisy turned to Armitage.

'He didn't. He told me to bring Dr. Tenby and the police –. Oh, do you suppose he expected the bobby's superiors to be on their way already? Are they?'

Pritchard shook his head. 'PC Endicott didn't report the explosion to them. He wanted my advice as to whether he should.'

'And I said no,' Daisy admitted. 'I think Alec would want to speak to the constable before anyone sends for anyone else. If he wants them to come, he can send you back again, Charles.'

'That's all right, eh, as long as I have my boots.'

'Here they come.'

A maid arrived with the boots and Armitage put them on. He and Dr. Tenby went out into the rain. It was coming down quite heavily now, Daisy saw. She hoped it wouldn't make the excavations more dangerous. At least Alec had plenty of assistants now – the gardeners, the villagers, Pritchard's chauffeur . . . And while on the subject of chauffeurs –

The butler was back, no doubt having instructed his subordinates to construct a stretcher.

'Barker, did Lord Rydal's man go to help?'

'No, madam. I am given to understand that Gregg failed to give satisfaction. His lordship informed him that his services would no longer be required after their return to London, but he chose to leave immediately.'

'And who can blame him!' Pritchard muttered.

'When was this?'

'This morning, madam.'

'And he actually did leave? How?'

'Madam?'

'I mean, did someone take him to the station, or was he seen trudging off down the drive with his bag in his hand and his box on his shoulder?'

For once Barker was at a loss. 'I'm afraid I don't know, madam. Gregg not being one of the household . . . Madison didn't take him, that's for sure. But he could have cadged a lift with Mr. Howell, or even with Sir Desmond's chauffeur.'

'They both took cars?'

'I believe so, madam.'

'Thank you, Barker.'

'If you'll excuse me, sir, I must ensure that work on the stretcher is proceeding according to plan.'

As Pritchard waved the butler away, Julia came down the stairs.

'Mother's still with Lady Ottaline.'

'Your mother is a saint, Miss Beaufort,' Pritchard said warmly.

Julia looked startled. 'The old dear is being rather a brick,' she conceded.

'My sister-in-law ought to be at Lady Ottaline's bed-side,' he acknowledged, 'but I'm afraid she would not be a soothing companion.'

Daisy and Julia exchanged looks, but tactfully held their tongues. His comment reminded Daisy that Lucy had been left alone with Mrs. Howell for far longer than was advisable. But he had appeared puzzled by her questions about the chauffeur, Gregg, and she owed it to him, if not to satisfy his curiosity, at least to hear him out. He might even contribute something useful. Also, she had questions for him.

'Julia, be an angel and tell Lucy I'm on my way,' she said. 'There's a couple of things I must discuss with Mr. Pritchard.'

'Right-oh, but first tell me, have you heard anything more about the grotto?'

'Charles came to fetch Dr. Tenby. You just missed him.'

'Bother! He's all right?'

'Yes, perfectly, apart from wet feet. He came for his boots, too. He said they can't get through the grotto itself so they've all gone to dig in the hole in the hill.'

'That'll be fun, in this weather.' Wistfully, Julia added, 'I suppose I'd be in the way.'

'Definitely.'

'You mustn't dream of going out there, Miss Beaufort,' said Pritchard. 'Mr. Fletcher has plenty of men to help him.'

Julia nodded, sighed, and went off to the drawing room to rescue Lucy from Mrs. Howell – or vice versa.

'Will you come into my study, Mrs. Fletcher? I must ring Sir Desmond again, to tell him Lady Ottaline is in no danger, though I expect he's left the works by now.'

'How did he take it?' Daisy asked, preceding Pritchard along the passage.

'I was afraid you were going to ask me that. It's very difficult to say. Do sit down.' With a little sigh, he sank into the chair behind his desk, looking tired. 'He didn't explode with anger – in the circumstances that's a bad way to put it, but you know what I mean. He didn't sound desperately worried, though I told him I didn't know how badly she was injured.'

'I doubt if Sir Desmond ever sounds desperately anything. Either he's naturally detached or he cultivates detachment.' Even, or perhaps especially, with regard to his wife.

'Yes. There was something in his voice . . . But I may have imagined it. You know what the telephone lines are like.'

'What sort of something?'

'I just suspected he wasn't quite as indifferent as he wanted to sound. I couldn't pin it down to anything specific. But I hate to believe a man could be so unmoved by his wife being injured, so maybe it's wishful thinking.'

'Perhaps. Or a bad connection. He said he'd come straight back, though?'

'Hmm, not exactly. He said the business was nearly finished and he'd be back shortly. But we can't guess what was in his mind from a brief telephone conversation over a bad wire. What was in your mind when you wanted to know how Lord Rydal's chauffeur left the house?'

'Not so much *how* as *whether*.'

'Ah, yes, a different question altogether, now we know the explosion wasn't an accident.'

Daisy hadn't expected him to catch on so quickly. She should have. He impressed her more and more with his astuteness. She hoped Alec wasn't going to be annoyed with her for letting Pritchard see her suspicion of the chauffeur. To distract him, she said, 'You looked relieved when Charles Armitage said it looked like murder.'

Prichard was dismayed. 'Oh dear, was it obvious? I'm afraid relief was my first reaction. After all, if the explosion had been caused by a gas leak, I'd have been to some degree responsible; whereas, though it may be unpleasant to have a murder on the premises, I can hardly be blamed if some idiot chose my grotto as a suitable place to blow up Lord Rydal.'

CHAPTER 21

Leaving Pritchard to try to reach Sir Desmond on the phone, Daisy went to the drawing room. She was halfway across the hall when Mrs. Howell came out. She was muttering to herself, distracted, and didn't notice Daisy. She hurried away and Daisy went on in.

'Darling!' Lucy greeted her. 'I thought you'd quite abandoned me to that madwoman.'

'Lucy thinks Mrs. Howell's gone completely off her rocker,' said Julia.

'Why?'

'She never was completely normal, if you ask me,' said Lucy. 'All that fuss about fish.'

'No more fuss than Rhino made.'

'Would you call Rhino completely normal?'

'Well, no. But not *crazy*.'

'He seems crazy to me,' said Julia. 'Swearing he adores me and will do anything in the world for me, and then going off for an assignation with Lady Ottaline.'

'That's men for you,' Lucy averred. 'Though he could at least have waited till you accepted him! But to be fair, it was she who made the running.'

'You knew he had an assignation, Julia?' Daisy asked.

'Lady Ottaline could just have followed him to see where he was going.'

'Why on earth should he go to the grotto,' Lucy demanded, 'if not to meet her? That divan bed is quite comfortable – I sat down on it. And much more private than anywhere in the house.'

'Willett told me.'

'I knew I should have brought my maid,' said Lucy. 'We'd have known all about it, too.'

'Did Willett tell your mother?'

Julia gave a very Gallic shrug. 'I've no idea. Probably. She's on my side, though she's only been with us a few weeks, so she'd pass on anything that might change Mother's mind about him.'

Daisy wondered why Lady Beaufort hadn't already told her daughter she had changed her mind about Lord Rydal. 'If Willett knew, probably all the servants did, too, at least the upper servants. Hmm.'

'Daisy, are you sleuthing?' Lucy said suspiciously.

'As far as we know it was an accident,' Julia reminded her.

'That I could believe of anyone else, but not of Rhino. Besides, I recognise that look of Daisy's.'

'What look! I don't have a special "sleuthing" look.'

'Yes, you do. You know it wasn't an accident, don't you?' Lucy accused.

Lucy wouldn't believe her if she denied it. 'You won't tell Alec I told you, will you,' Daisy begged.

'You didn't tell us, darling. I guessed, all by my little self.'

'Well, don't breathe a word to anyone else, for pity's sake.'

'Our lips are sealed, aren't they, Julia?'

'Of course. Who do you think did it, Daisy?'

'The obvious person is Sir Desmond.'

'But he was in Swindon,' said Julia.

'Lady Ottaline was right on the spot,' Lucy mused. 'Perhaps she was hoist by her own petard? I've always wondered what a "petard" is.'

'Some sort of bomb,' said Daisy.

'It's in Shakespeare,' Julia elaborated. '*Hamlet*, isn't it, Daisy?'

'I wouldn't like to swear to it. Why should Lady Ottaline want to blow up Rhino? He came to heel very nicely, for a rhinoceros.'

The picture this conjured up made them all laugh for a moment. Then Lucy returned doggedly to the subject.

'He came to heel, yes, but unwillingly. You could see that, Daisy, or you wouldn't have used the phrase. I could see it. So it's not likely Lady Ottaline didn't realise, too. She must have been furious to be supplanted by a beautiful younger woman. That's you, Julia.'

'I didn't want him!'

'No, so she had no cause to be angry with you. All her fury – what's that thing about "hell hath no fury"?'

'Hell hath no fury like a woman scorned,' said Daisy.

' "Nor Hell a Fury, like a Woman scorn'd," ' said Julia.

'Whichever, that's Lady Ottaline to a T, isn't it? It's Rhino she had it in for. All the same, Julia, when she's recovered enough to get out of bed, you'd better watch your back.'

'You're assuming she set up the explosion,' Julia protested, 'but she was caught up in it herself.'

'She wanted to see him blown up,' Lucy said as if it were obvious. 'She miscalculated and got too close.'

'It's possible,' Daisy said reluctantly. 'I suppose we'd better keep an eye on you when Lady Ottaline comes down, unless Alec arrests someone before then.'

'I hope he does, though I can't believe you're serious!'

'Well, it wasn't necessarily Lady Ottaline. Lucy, what were you saying about Mrs. Howell having a screw loose?'

'Religious mania. She told me Rhino was evil and deserved to be blown up, but it was all her brother-in-law's fault for putting pagan statues in the grotto. They're bound to attract evil people – and I'm telling you, the look she gave me was enough to make one believe in the evil eye!'

'You're the ones who were attracted by the grotto,' said Julia, not without satisfaction. 'So while I'm waiting for Lady Ottaline to stab me in the back you two will be waiting for Mrs. Howell to stab *you* in the back. But I still can't see how Lady Ottaline could have forced Rhino to go to meet her in the grotto, if he was really unwilling.'

Daisy looked at Lucy. The gossip about the unlikely couple's long-standing affair was her story, and it was up to her to decide whether to enlighten Julia.

Lucy didn't hesitate. 'People have been talking about them for months. We wondered whether she threatened to tell you about their affair if he didn't cooperate.'

'Did you know about it before she arrived here at Appsworth?' Daisy asked.

'No. But I gather you did.'

'Not me. Lucy did.'

'I do think you might have told me, Lucy.'

'I would have, if there'd been the slightest sign you might accept him. Or if I'd had the slightest idea she was going to turn up here. When she arrived, I did consult Daisy. She said as I wasn't an eyewitness and the evidence wouldn't hold up in court – '

'I never did!'

'Near as makes no difference. Anyway, the way Lady Ottaline was behaving, you'd have had to be blind not to notice.'

'But Rhino,' said Daisy, 'being completely oblivious to everyone else's feelings, could easily be brought to believe you remained unaware. Even he, though, could hardly hope that he'd still stand a chance with you if she told you he was her lover.'

'Yes, I see. You almost make me feel sorry for him.'

'No!' said Lucy, revolted.

'I said "almost."'

'It's all speculation,' Daisy pointed out. 'Perhaps he had some other deep dark secret she was holding over him. It would have to be very deep and dark for him to deserve to be blown up. You're allowed to feel a bit sorry for him.'

Lucy shook her head. 'Not yet. We don't even know yet if he actually was blown up, or if so, whether he was killed.'

'Stone dead,' said Alec, 'and I use the word *stone* with due deliberation.'

He was in Pritchard's den, sitting in front of the big mahogany leather-topped desk, instead of in his accustomed place of power on the other side. This was not his only disadvantage. The detective inspector from Swindon had arrived just as Alec and his crew returned from the excavation. Alec had judged it best not to linger to take a bath before speaking to the local police. His hair, his nostrils, his fingernails, and his clothes were clogged with grey-white dust that, dampened by rain, took on the consistency of partly set plaster of Paris.

The butler had been swift to provide a dust sheet for him to sit on.

In response to DI Boyle's raised eyebrows, Alec elaborated. 'He was buried in a pile of chunks of limestone and pieces of marble statuary. One hit him on the temple and appears to have despatched him pretty nearly instantaneously. Just as well, perhaps, as he was badly burnt, probably prior to death. The doctor is a GP, not a police surgeon, and unfamiliar with having to make such determinations.'

'You didn't call in a police surgeon? Sir?'

'At the time I was in a position to send for help, I had no reason to suppose a crime had been committed. The explosion could have been caused by a gas leak.'

'But now, you say, you have evidence of intent. Are you telling me,' said Inspector Boyle sceptically, 'you're here on the spot purely by chance?' Boyle had the sort of face that is naturally inexpressive and a flat voice to match. Nonetheless he managed, when he chose, to make his feelings perfectly plain.

'It happens to be the truth,' Alec insisted. 'My wife is down here to write about the grotto – '

'The one that got blown up.'

'It's the only one, to my knowledge. Look here, man, I'm as unhappy about this as you are.'

'Oh, I doubt it, sir. I doubt it very much.'

'All you have to do is treat my wife and me as ordinary witnesses. In fact, you're in luck. She was here for a few days before the incident, so she knows the people concerned, including the victim. I arrived just as it happened, but I went straight to the scene and I was there when the body was discovered, so I can tell you all about it. You could do worse than to . . . Sorry.'

'You see my difficulty, sir.' There was a glint of what might have been humour in Boyle's small, pale eyes.

'Yes. I beg your pardon. I'm already telling you the best way to start the investigation, and that Daisy and I are your best witnesses.'

'I'm not saying you're wrong, mind,' Boyle conceded.

A muffled snort came from his detective sergeant, a pale, plump young man in a green bow-tie and wire-rimmed glasses. Boyle turned on him a stare worthy of a basilisk. He coughed and fidgeted with his pencil.

'Unfortunately,' said Alec, 'it's already too dark for you to see much out there.'

'It might have been helpful if Constable Endicott had seen fit to notify us somewhat earlier.'

'Endicott's not to blame. He didn't know until he joined us at the site that the explosion was no accident, and then I discouraged him from leaving to telephone before we knew for certain there were victims. He's a good man with a shovel, your PC Endicott.'

'Is he indeed! I'll have to remember that.'

Alec sent a mental apology winging towards Endicott. In defending him, he'd probably let him in for all sorts of unpleasant jobs in the future. 'We needed every man available. Wait till you see the mess. And we couldn't be too aggressive about clearing it for fear of causing further injuries, or further collapse.'

Boyle looked him up and down, sighed, and said, 'Perhaps

I should be grateful to have arrived late. You'd better tell me the whole thing from the beginning, if you'd be so kind, sir.'

'My part started when I arrived here. My wife was eager to show me the grotto before it started raining. We had just gone out to the terrace at the rear of the house when the explosion occurred.'

'It was heard this far, then?'

'Believe me,' Alec said dryly, 'it was not only heard, it was seen and felt.'

Concisely, he described finding Lady Ottaline and exploring the outer grotto. He explained his decision that digging in the tunnel was too difficult and too dangerous.

'Just a minute, sir. You haven't mentioned why you considered it necessary to dig. That is, what made you suppose someone might be underneath.'

'In the first place, gas doesn't explode by itself. There has to be a spark to ignite it, which suggested someone was there. Lady Ottaline was nowhere near the scene of the actual explosion. She was obviously caught in the blast, and she must have been outside the grotto or she'd have fallen twenty or thirty feet and probably be dead. So she hadn't provided the spark.'

'So someone else had.'

'Exactly. Never having been near Appsworth Hall before, I didn't know the lay-out of the grotto. Mr. Armitage explained it and sketched a plan.'

'Armitage? Who's he?'

'For that, I'll have to refer you to my wife. Or, of course, any of the residents of the house.'

'Right. Go on. Please, sir.'

'With Armitage's sketch as guide, we started digging in what seemed the most likely spot. I can explain my reasoning, but I'd prefer to postpone it until I've had a bath.'

Another muffled snort came from the sergeant.

'It can wait,' Boyle agreed.

'We were trying to get into the central cave of the grotto, which was only partly collapsed. We hadn't been at it long when one of the men heard a tapping noise. That made us both more determined and more cautious.'

The inspector nodded his understanding.

'To cut a long and painstaking story short, we found Lord Rydal's chauffeur, Gregg, bruised but essentially unhurt. The roof was more or less intact where he happened to be, over by one wall. A toppled statue pinned him down but also protected him from flying debris. He was able to point out to us more or less where he had last seen his employer. Lord Rydal was less fortunate. From the look of it, he was blown backwards against another statue and knocked it down, and then that part of the roof collapsed, killing him.'

'Lord Rydal's chauffeur,' said DI Boyle. 'What the devil was he doing there?'

'I decided I'd better not ask,' Alec told him. 'After all, officially, it's none of my business.'

CHAPTER 22

'So he wants me to help him unofficially,' Alec said grumpily, sitting on his dust-sheet on the bed. 'The worst of all possible worlds.'

'No, it's not, darling.' Daisy, in the adjacent bathroom, raised her voice to be heard over the rush of tap-water. 'You'd hate to be treated like an ordinary witness. This way, you can poke your nose in without being actually responsible for finding out who did it.'

'Poke my nose in!'

'What about me?'

'I'm quite sure he doesn't want you poking your nose in. Isn't that bath full yet? I hope the hot water isn't going to run out.'

'The house belongs to a plumber, remember. No stingy boiler; Mr. Pritchard put modern gas geysers in every bathroom. Endless hot water, regulated by thermostat.'

'Gas. You did light the thing, didn't you?'

'Of course. I'd be dead from the fumes by now if I hadn't. Can't you see steam billowing?' She turned off the tap. 'There you are. Be careful, it's really hot. I hope the stuff you wash off doesn't solidify to cement in the pipes.'

'It's plaster, not cement.' Alec picked his way across the

carpet, trying to keep the sheet wrapped round him so as to deposit as little debris as possible on the floor.

'Same difference. They both go solid.'

'My coat of plaster is as solid as it's going to get. This house belongs to a plumber. I'm sure he can deal with blocked pipes.'

'Do you want me to stay and scrub your back?'

'No, that's all right, if that's a loofah I see through the steam. I'm certain you're dying to go and poke your nose in.'

'I'll take that as permission,' Daisy retorted, and left before he could deny it.

She was halfway down the stairs when a maid caught up with her. 'Madam!' It was the same young girl who had summoned her to speak to Pritchard earlier, still – or again – both excited and anxious. 'The inspector wants to see you. In the den, madam, right away, he said.'

'Thank you. It's Rita, isn't it? Who else has the inspector talked to so far, Rita?'

'Just Mr. Fletcher and Mr. Pritchard, madam.'

'Really! Are you sure?'

'Yes, 'm. 'Lessn you count Len Endicott, our bobby from the village.'

Clearly Rita did not count PC Endicott.

'Is Constable Endicott still with the inspector?'

'No, 'm. He was sent out to guard the 'splosion.' This was said with such satisfaction that Daisy gathered Endicott was not merely of no account, but had somehow offended Rita. 'There's just 'Tective Inspector Boyle and 'Tective Sergeant Thomkin. Sir Desmond wanted to see them, madam, but Mr. Boyle said he'd have to wait his turn.'

'Odd! I wonder why he wants to see me first.' Daisy didn't expect an answer, far less the one she got.

'It was Mr. Pritchard, madam. He told the inspector he ought to talk to you before anyone else.'

Daisy didn't know whether to be flattered, affronted, or dismayed. She felt rather as if Pritchard had thrown her to the wolves, but why?

She thanked the girl and proceeded to the den, wishing it was interrogation by Alec she was going to face.

Without knocking, she went straight in and announced baldly, 'I'm Mrs. Fletcher. You wanted to see me?'

'Ah, yes, Mrs Fletcher.' The man behind the desk rose and came round to offer her a chair. His face gave away nothing of his thoughts, neither irritation at having been told by Pritchard what to do, nor gratitude for her compliance, but he said, 'Thank you for coming. I'm Detective Inspector Boyle of the Wiltshire police, and this is Detective Sergeant Thomkin.'

'How do you do?' Daisy sat down. 'What exactly makes you think I'm the best person to help you get started?'

'Mr. Pritchard told me you're a straightforward sort of person, madam. I'd say his judgement in that is already borne out. He also said he believes you to be observant, clear-sighted and unbiassed.'

Even as Daisy stored up these compliments to relay to Alec, she felt herself blushing as she made a couple of mental reservations: She was not so unbiassed as to credit for a moment that Lucy or Julia could have anything to do with the explosion. 'That's a lot to live up to,' she said guardedly.

'We shan't hold his words against you, if he was – ah – exaggerating a little,' said Boyle with apparent solemnity.

'I should hope not! What is it you want to know?'

'I gather you and Lady Gerald have been here several days. Tell me about the people who were here when you arrived. Let's keep it simple: make it in order as you encountered them. I'll probably interrupt with questions.'

'Right-oh. The first person we met was Lord Rydal, the victim. He had fetched our suitcases from the station, as no one else was available.'

'He was a friend of yours?'

'Lucy – Lady Gerald – knew him slightly, just because they both move in the same circles of society. I'd never met him before. I'd heard of him, but only because my brother was at school with him.'

'A friend of your brother's, then.'

'I don't think he ever was, but in any case, not for the past several years. Gervaise was killed in the War. I rather doubt Lord Rydal had any real friends. One way or another, he managed to insult practically everyone.'

'Including you, Mrs. Fletcher?'

Daisy frowned in thought. 'To tell the truth, I can't remember any specific incident. He was just so generally objectionable, there was no point in taking it personally. Half the time he didn't even realise he was upsetting people, perhaps didn't realise other people have feelings to be hurt. I think – I have children, you know. Do you, Inspector?' Boyle nodded, and she went on, 'I think little children have to be taught to consider the feelings of others, and perhaps Rhino never was. He went through life like a blind bull – or rhinoceros – in a china shop, never noticing the destruction he wreaked.'

Boyle nodded again, but gave no other sign that he understood what she had tried to explain. 'Rhino was his nickname?'

'Thick-skinned, and pots of money.'

'Who's his heir?'

'Good heavens, I haven't the foggiest! Do you suppose his heir could have followed him here and somehow found out he was going to – '

'I don't know enough yet to suppose anything. He made enemies of everyone in the house?'

'"Enemies" is a bit strong. Umm . . .' She reflected on the past couple of days. 'I can't actually name anyone he wasn't rude to at some point,' she confessed. 'But people don't go about murdering people just because they were rude.'

'It's not unknown,' Boyle said dryly. 'Let's continue with your arrival. What induced Lord Rydal, not a personal friend and so generally disobliging, to fetch your and Lady Gerald's bags for you?'

Daisy hesitated. But if she didn't tell him, plenty of others would. 'Julia. Miss Beaufort. He believed himself madly in love with her.' No need to explain that Julia had more or less invented the errand to get rid of him for a while.

'Miss Beaufort told you Lord Rydal was in love with her?'

'Gosh, no. Julia isn't the sort to boast of something like that.'

'Boast?'

'Well, however appalling he is – was – there's no denying he was an earl and a very well off one. She would have been a rich countess.'

'So Miss Beaufort was eager to marry Lord Rydal?'

'On the contrary, she couldn't stick him at any price. It was her mother who thought he was a great catch.'

'Her mother.' Boyle consulted a list. 'Lady Beaufort was

pressing Miss Beaufort to accept the suitor she hated, and lo and behold! The suitor is murdered.'

'Bosh! Nowadays girls don't let their mothers choose husbands for them. Besides, Lady Beaufort changed her mind. I heard her say so.'

'To her daughter?'

'Who else would she tell?' Daisy hoped he wouldn't notice the evasion, but his next question suggested he was well aware of it.

'Miss Beaufort is an old – let me rephrase that – a friend of yours of long standing.'

'She was at school with Lucy and me, but I hadn't seen her in years before we came here. Let's see, who did we meet next? It must have been Barker, the butler. A very superior sort of butler. And then Mr. Pritchard.'

'How long have you known *him*?'

'Neither of us had ever met him before. He invited us because he liked the idea of his grotto being in our book.'

'I can't say I've ever had much to do with house-parties,' the inspector said severely, 'but this seems to me a very odd one.'

'It is,' Daisy agreed. 'You have to remember that Lucy and I are here on business, and Sir Desmond, too, and our being here is the only reason Alec and Gerald and Lady Ottaline came.'

'Business?'

'Sir Desmond's on government business. Something to do with slum clearance, I believe, but you'll have to ask him.'

'And you and – uh – Lady Gerald? What's your business?'

'I told you, our book. Nothing to do with plumbing or gas or explosions. It's about follies and –. Oh, gosh, I've just thought. Perhaps our publisher won't want to include the Appsworth grotto now it's in ruins and someone's been killed in it! I wonder if Lucy – '

'Mrs. Fletcher, could we please get back to *my* business?'

'Do you want to go back to the order in which I met people? Because Sir Desmond didn't come into it till much later.'

'He didn't?'

'No, he and Lady Ottaline – '

'Never mind! We'll get to them in their proper place. Let's see, you'd reached Mr. Pritchard, who you'd never met before.'

'That's right. He came out to the hall to greet us. He took us into the drawing room, where Lady Beaufort and Julia – '

'Half a mo. Didn't you tell me about them already?'

'Only because you asked about the baggage.' Daisy was beginning to feel as confused as Boyle sounded. 'This always happens when Alec wants everything in order from the beginning. It's all interconnected, but more like a web than a chain.'

'Always?'

'Always?'

'You said "This always happens . . ."'

Daisy felt the blood suffuse her cheeks. Twenty-eight years old and still blushing like a schoolgirl! It was downright humiliating. 'I've . . .' Assisted? Better not, Alec might deny it. 'I've been involved in a couple of his cases.'

Boyle's face went blanker than ever. 'No doubt that would explain why he . . .' He didn't voice the remainder of his thought, so Daisy was sure it must be uncomplimentary, but whether to Alec or herself she couldn't be sure. Which was probably just as well.

'I'll keep going with our arrival,' she said hurriedly. 'It was tea-time. Lady Beaufort and Julia – Miss Beaufort – were in the drawing room. So was Mrs. Howell. She's Mr. Pritchard's sister-in-law and she lives here, though they don't seem to get on very well together. Let's see, I think Mr. Howell had come home by then. He's her son, Mr. Pritchard's nephew, or rather his late wife's, if you want to be precise. He runs their factory. Fortyish, and a confirmed bachelor to all appearances, but I haven't talked much to either of the Howells. I think that's all –. No, Mr. Armitage was there, too. And Lord Rydal came in after us.'

'Armitage? Who's this Armitage?'

'He's staying here, but for a while, not just visiting for a few days as we are.'

'For a while?'

'I don't know exactly how long he's been here or how long he intends to stay. You'll have to ask him, or Mr. Pritchard. I don't know much about him except that he's Canadian.' And madly in love with Julia, but let Boyle find that out for himself. 'Oh, and he's a historian. He was very helpful in giving me information for my article.' After a still unexplained initial reluctance.

'Article? I thought you and Lady Gerald were writing a book.'

'I'm writing and she's taking photographs for a book. I'm also writing an article.'

DI Boyle's inexpressive face actually contrived to brighten. 'Lady Gerald has taken photographs of the grotto?'

'Of the two outer caves, at least. I don't think she took any of the bit that blew up. It wasn't very interesting. But they're not snapshots, they're plates, and she'll want to develop them herself.'

'I would remind you, Mrs. Fletcher, that this is a murder investigation.'

'You don't need to remind *me*. It's Lucy you'll have to convince that your investigation is more important than her art. Irreplaceable art, what's more. We need those pictures. Lucy – '

'Do I hear my name being taken in vain?' Lucy drawled from the doorway. 'Rumour reached us, darling, that you were all on your lonesome being interrogated. Julia thought we'd better come and make sure you're holding your own.' She sauntered into the room.

Her words implied that Lucy herself was not at all concerned about Daisy's ability to stand up to a policeman or two. As usual, she was cool, calm, and collected, unlike Julia, who followed her in.

But of course, whichever way you looked at it, Julia had a great deal more to worry about. Not that Lucy's calm was destined to last very long.

Inspector Boyle stood up. Daisy introduced him. 'Darling,' she continued, 'Mr. Boyle is sure your photos of the grotto are going to prove very useful to him.' She sat back to enjoy the fireworks.

'My photos?' Lucy sounded as if she couldn't believe her ears. '*My* photos? The ones I've spent the last three days getting absolutely perfect? You can't be serious!'

'Absolutely serious, Lady Gerald. All I have is a rough sketch plan. Your photographs may be vital in working out exactly what happened.'

'What happened is that some benefactor of humanity turned on the gas and let Rhino blow himself up. You don't need my plates to work that out. And you're not getting them.'

'Lady Gerald, you are obstructing the – '

'I've obstructed the police in the course of their duties before, and no doubt I'll do it again!'

'Well, now, what have we here?' Alec came in, looking much more himself, though either his dark hair had greyed a bit while Daisy wasn't watching or he still had chalk dust in it. 'Three little girls from school. I do beg your pardon, Miss Beaufort. We're not well enough acquainted for me to – '

'Really, Alec!' said Lucy in disgust. 'That is not at all helpful. This person wants me to hand my photography plates over for some incompetent nincompoop to ruin, after I – '

'I'll get a warrant if I have to, sir. They may – '

'Now just calm down, both of you. No, Lucy.' He held up his hand. 'Hear me out. Boyle, is there any reason Lady Gerald should not develop her own plates and provide you with prints?'

'I suppose not,' Boyle admitted grudgingly. 'But we don't have our own darkroom in Swindon. I'll have to make arrangements.'

'Saturday evening,' Daisy pointed out. 'You won't find a commercial photographer open till Monday.'

'It seems to me,' Lucy said, a waspish note in her voice, 'if I have to do it, it'll be quickest and easiest if I dash back to town and use my own darkroom. I don't know how Gerald's going to like leaving a couple of hours after he arrived, having spent the interim digging.'

'I haven't had a chance to talk to Lord Gerald yet,' the inspector said doggedly. 'I need him to stay, as a witness to finding the victim. Or victims.'

'I'm quite sure my husband will have nothing to add to what Detective *Chief* Inspector Fletcher can tell you.'

'Nonetheless, I need to hear his description. And if you were thinking of staying in London, I'll be needing you to come back as soon as the photos are ready. I'll send Detective Sergeant Thomkin with you,' he added with a reckless air. 'Leave your notes with me, sergeant.'

Thomkin looked alarmed – even though he was ignorant as yet of Lucy's driving habits.

Lucy was furious. 'For pity's sake, Inspector! You expect me to drive off into the night with that . . .' She glanced for the first time at Thomkin. '. . . With such a dashing young man? My husband would definitely not approve.'

Daisy and Alec exchanged a glance. Gerald might be a rugger Blue and a financial wizard, but he'd never had a determining influence on Lucy's actions.

The sergeant protested incoherently, whether at being sent to London with Lady Gerald or at her imputation of dashingness was impossible to disentangle.

'On the other hand,' said Lucy, amusement abruptly taking the place of annoyance, 'did you want prints of all the pictures, Inspector? Every single one?'

'Certainly. It's for me to decide which are important.'

Lucy heaved a deep, dramatic, and undoubtedly spurious sigh. 'If you insist, I suppose I have no choice. Come along, what's your name, no time to waste. You can carry the plates down to the car for me.'

'Yes, your ladyship. Thomkin, your ladyship.' He gave

his superior a reproachful look and his notebook, then followed Lucy out.

Inspector Boyle turned to Julia. While he explained to her that he would take her statement later and she had no need to stay at present, Alec said to Daisy in a low voice, 'What the deuce is Lucy up to?'

Daisy had an inkling of what was in Lucy's mind, but she gave him a wide-eyed, misleadingly ingenuous look as spurious as Lucy's sigh. 'Up to, darling? What makes you think she's up to something?'

'I know Lucy,' said Alec grimly.

CHAPTER 23

'Now I have no one to take notes,' said Detective Inspector Boyle gloomily. 'I've got some men coming over from Devizes, but it'll take them a couple of hours to get here. Swindon can't spare anyone on a Saturday night, what with the railway works and all.'

'I'm very good at taking notes,' Daisy said at once. 'Aren't I, Alec?'

'I've known worse.'

'You write shorthand?'

'Yes,' she said firmly.

'If you don't mind that she's the only person who can read it.'

'Darling, must you be so damping?'

'It's only fair that Mr. Boyle should know what he's getting himself into, if he decides to get.'

'Am I to assume, sir, that Mrs. Fletcher has taken notes for you in the past? In a police investigation?'

'Often,' said Daisy.

'Occasionally. She has never to my knowledge suppressed information she has written down in the course of an interview.'

Daisy was about to protest against his 'to my knowledge,'

when Boyle, passing over that derogatory caveat, pounced on the rest.

'Are you saying Mrs. Fletcher is liable to suppress information otherwise acquired, sir?'

'I've been told so often that hearsay isn't evidence,' Daisy told Boyle, 'that I don't report it, or gossip, unless it's of vital importance.'

'And just who decides what's of vital importance?'

'Who decides what's hearsay?' Alec put in. 'You must admit, love, that you're not altogether certain of the definition.'

'Even the courts don't seem able to decide on that,' said Boyle. 'All right, Mrs. Fletcher, I'll accept your kind offer to take notes, but I'd appreciate it if you'd allow me or the chief inspector to determine what's allowable evidence and what's not. Come to that, even inadmissible evidence can lead us in the right direction. Now, where were we when we were interrupted?' He opened Thomkin's notebook, turned to the last written-on page, and stared at it blankly.

'May I?' Daisy asked, reaching for it. 'Perhaps I don't write the clearest shorthand in the world but I'm an expert at deciphering it. Besides, what he wrote is what I told you.'

Reluctantly Boyle handed the notebook over. 'You'd better read it out loud from the beginning. Mr. Fletcher missed it.'

Daisy had no difficulty reading the detective sergeant's shorthand. She found her description of residents and guests at Appsworth transformed into indigestible officialese, so she transformed it back, in the process glossing over certain aspects. After all, her worry about the publisher refusing to include the scene of a murder in the folly book was not relevant. Alec wouldn't want to hear her philosophising about

Rhino's upbringing and the twins. And she had exaggerated Julia's dislike of Rhino, giving Boyle the false impression that it could have led to murder. No need to repeat his words to Alec, who would much prefer to draw his own conclusions.

Reaching Lucy's interruption of proceedings, she rushed on before Boyle had a chance to question the thoroughness of her report. 'Actually, now I come to think of it, Armitage and Howell weren't at tea, I didn't meet them till just before dinner. That was when the Wandersleys arrived, too. I already told you about Sir Desmond Wandersley. He's from the Ministry of Health, here on business.'

'I don't suppose you happen to know his rank?' Alec asked.

Daisy pondered. 'Principal Deputy Secretary, I'm pretty sure. Unless it's Deputy Principal Secretary . . .'

'No such thing. Lower level of the upper tier,' Alec informed Boyle. 'It behoves us to tread with care. What's he like, Daisy?'

'Expert at presenting a façade to the world.'

'That's what it takes to rise in the bureaucracy.'

'Good at small talk, fund of entertaining anecdotes – '

'Also prerequisites,' Alec said cynically. 'You said he's here on business? What's that all about?'

'Well, I haven't been privy to their discussions – '

'You surprise me.'

She frowned at him. ' – Which were held at the Pritchard Plumbing plant in Swindon. But I gather he's in charge of some sort of contract for plumbing supplies for slum clearance. I did wonder –. But that's not even hearsay, just pure speculation.'

'What did you wonder, Mrs. Fletcher?' Boyle demanded.

'If you get her going on her wild theories,' Alec warned, 'we'll be here all night.'

'Likely we will anyway. Sir. Mrs. Fletcher?'

'Oh, it's just that in spite of the façade, I could tell he wasn't at all pleased to find out I'm a journalist, and I wondered whether there might be something fishy about the contract.'

'Payments under the table?'

'I've no idea. His reaction wasn't necessarily anything to do with plumbing. Some people have an aversion to journalists as others do to policemen. After I assured him I was neither an investigative reporter nor a gossip-column tattler, he was quite friendly.'

Alec asked, 'Can you pinpoint whether one or the other was more responsible for his change in attitude?'

Daisy tried to remember. 'No, not really. Though subsequent events have made me wonder – '

'I see what you mean, sir,' said Boyle. 'Mrs. Fletcher is much given to wondering.'

'Is this material, Daisy?'

'Absolutely. But the best way to explain will be to go back to Mr. Boyle's method of telling you about each person in turn as I met them.'

'Not,' Boyle muttered, 'that you have been doing anything of the sort.'

Treating this observation with the silent disdain it merited, Daisy continued, 'Lady Ottaline Wandersley came in with Sir Desmond. I'd never met her, but Julia and Lucy told me –. No, that's definitely hearsay. Isn't it, darling?'

'I expect so,' Alec admitted with a sigh. 'If it seems necessary, we'll ask them what they told you.'

'Not that it wasn't pretty obvious. She's one of those women who . . .' Daisy hesitated, not wanting to sound catty. 'You know the sort. She must once have been truly beautiful and she can't accept the fact that she's growing older and is no longer irresistible to men. She dresses to the nines, and she's still attractive – '

'When not covered in chalk dust!'

'You weren't terribly attractive yourself in the same condition,' she retorted. 'The important thing is that Lady Ottaline was pleased to see Rhino – Lord Rydal – and he wasn't at all pleased to see her.'

'What made you think that?' Boyle asked sharply.

'I was standing beside Rhino, having recently suffered what passed for a conversation with him. When Lady Ottaline came in, he came over all tense and wary and made no move to greet the Wandersleys, although as later became apparent he was acquainted with both of them. And it wasn't at all like Rhino to be put out by anyone or anything.'

'And her ladyship?'

'She looked like the cat that stole the cream. A sort of self-satisfied smirk.'

'Sounds to me as if we should be arresting Lord Rydal for the murder of Lady Ottaline,' Boyle complained.

Daisy decided against trying to describe, let alone explain, her subsequent observation of Rhino and Lady Ottaline's behaviour and attitude towards each other. It was all hearsay and guesswork. She didn't mind expounding her theories to Alec and being told they were pure speculation, but she was getting tired of Boyle's quibbling. She was just plain getting tired, come to that. The day seemed to have gone on forever.

'Mr. Carlin arrived with the Wandersleys,' she said. 'He's Sir Desmond's Private Secretary, capital *P* capital *S* as in civil service rank. He was talking at breakfast today about getting back to town this evening for a golf match tomorrow. He went to Swindon with Sir Desmond and Howell. I gathered he didn't intend to come back to Appsworth Hall.'

Boyle consulted a couple of sheets of paper on the desk in front of him. 'No doubt that's why Carlin is on the butler's list but not Mr. Pritchard's. I assumed he must be a servant. We'll have to get hold of him.' The inspector jumped up and rang the bell. 'I hope Thomkin hasn't left yet.'

'I'm sure Lucy's still packing up her stuff.'

'Undoubtedly,' Alec agreed. 'Speaking of servants, Daisy, I don't suppose you know anything about this Gregg chap, Lord Rydal's chauffeur-valet or whatever he was?'

'I never saw him, to my knowledge, but I heard about him shortly after meeting Rhino. Not by name, though. He was furious with him because when Julia asked him to fetch our bags, mine and Lucy's, from the station, he said he had to remove a grease spot from his dinner jacket so he couldn't go.'

Boyle blinked. 'Have I got this straight, Mrs. Fletcher: Miss Beaufort asked the chauffeur Gregg to fetch – '

'No, no, she asked Rhino – Lord Rydal – and he wanted to send his servant, but Gregg said he had to clean the jacket – Rhino's, that is, of course – so he couldn't go. He was acting as valet as well as chauffeur. Rhino told us he – the servant – was a lazy good-for-nothing, or something similar, and should have done it the night before. Gregg apparently claimed he hadn't been able to see it by artificial light. But that's hearsay,' Daisy added hurriedly.

'There was already bad blood between them, then,' said Boyle, 'before Lord Rydal gave him the sack. What do you reckon he was doing in the cave, Mr. Fletcher?'

'I can't believe he'd be stupid enough to set up the explosion and then stay around to watch. Nor can I believe he was up to any good.'

'He might have seen whoever did set it up,' Daisy suggested, 'and hoped to return to Rhino's good graces by warning him. Not that Rhino had any good graces. Nor that anyone in their senses would want the job back.'

'And the doctor's sedated both him and Lady Ottaline,' the inspector said, morose now, 'so we can't ask any questions.'

'Tomorrow. Neither's badly injured. Daisy, you don't happen to have any other ideas about what Gregg might have been up to?'

'It would be the wildest speculation,' Daisy said virtuously.

A parlourmaid came in. Boyle told her to find his sergeant and say he was wanted double-quick.

'He's in the hall, sir, waiting for Lady Gerald.'

'Good. Send him in. Mrs. Fletcher, do you know this Carlin's Christian name? Anything else about him?'

'Only that he's a civil servant. Ministry of Health, like Sir Desmond.'

DS Thomkin came in. Boyle explained about Carlin's departure. 'You'd better try and bring him back with you,' he said. 'Find out what you can about his likely whereabouts from Wandersley before you leave and see if you can track him down while Lady Gerald is working on those photographs.'

'Yes, sir,' said the sergeant despondently.

'Here.' Alec handed him a bit of paper on which he had just written a name. 'Call the Yard and ask for this chap.

Tell him to give you a hand, as a purely unofficial favour to me.'

'Yes, sir!' said Thomkin, looking a trifle more hopeful.

'All right, get on with it. Let's hear your wild speculation now, Mrs. Fletcher.'

'What –. Oh, yes, about Rhino's servant. Well, Barker didn't mention it, but I bet Rhino refused to give Gregg a letter of reference. It wouldn't surprise me if Gregg followed him in hopes of doing a little blackmail, not for money but for a good recommendation.'

'Blackmail?' Boyle said in surprise. 'On what grounds?'

'Sorry!' said Alec. 'I thought someone would have told you by now. It seems to be common knowledge that Lord Rydal and Lady Ottaline had an assignation in the grotto.'

Boyle glared at Daisy. 'Somehow that vital detail failed to reach me. But "common knowledge" is hardly meat for blackmail.'

'It depends how common it is,' Daisy argued. 'I expect Rhino would have given a good deal to conceal his liaison from two people in particular. Or possibly three.'

'Who?'

'Well, Julia, obviously, since he adored her. Insofar as he was capable of adoration. And her mother, Lady Beaufort, who had been supporting his suit, but would more than likely change her tune if she found out he was consorting with his mistress while courting Julia. And Sir Desmond, of course. Except that I doubt he was still in ignorance, or, come to that, whether Rhino cared whether he knew.'

'When you say it was common knowledge, Daisy, what exactly do you mean? How common?'

'Umm. Actually, I just guessed. I put together the way they behaved, something I overheard – '

'What?'

'Isn't that hearsay?'

'Not if they were speaking of their own actions,' Alec said patiently.

'Oh, really? Lady Ottaline said they'd never manage to find privacy in the house, which was why . . . And then the door closed so I didn't hear why what. But when Lord Rydal missed coffee after lunch and then I saw Lady Ottaline sneaking off through the garden, I put two and two together. Lucy guessed, too, and the Beauforts's maid told Julia, so I presume most if not all of the household servants knew. Goodness only knows whom they told.'

Boyle pounced. 'Miss Beaufort told you she knew?'

'This afternoon.' Daisy attempted to sound as if she was clarifying her statement, though her intent was to obfuscate. She didn't know when Julia had found out, and she shouldn't have mentioned her in justifying the statement that the rendezvous was common knowledge. 'But once Lucy was aware that Lady Ottaline had been injured and Rhino was missing, she said it was obvious what they'd been up to.'

'The first thing is to talk to the servants,' Boyle proposed to Alec, 'see what they know, how they know it, and who they've told. They'll probably know more than most about people's movements, too.'

'A good place to start,' Alec agreed smoothly. 'If you want to get going on that, I'll just get the details from my wife as to exactly when and where she overheard Lord Rydal and Lady Ottaline.'

'Right you are, sir. I'll go and talk to them in the servants' hall. I'll take my own notes.' With a pointed look at Daisy's blank notebook, he departed.

'Oh dear,' said Daisy, 'I didn't take any notes after all. It would have seemed rather odd taking notes of my own interrogation.'

'Never mind notes. You may have pulled the wool over DI Boyle's eyes, though I wouldn't count on it, but you can't distract me so easily. When did the maid tell your friend Julia about that pretty pair making their assignation?'

'What does it matter? Julia had no reason to blow Rhino up. She just had to keep saying no.'

'Daisy, you know I can't let it go at that. I agree that there are others who would appear to have better motives, but Julia Beaufort is definitely on my list. Now tell me about your eavesdropping.'

'Eavesdropping! They knew I was there.'

Before she could explain, the door swung open. Mrs. Howell marched in. In a shrill voice, she announced, 'I know who did it!'

CHAPTER 24

As Alec sprang to his feet to offer Mrs. Howell his chair, Daisy scribbled on her pad: *Don't believe a word she says*! Certain that he'd move to his preferred position behind the desk, she tore off the leaf and slid it across the leather top.

He glanced at it, then at her with a frown, then continued seating Mrs. Howell with his best soothing manner.

Daisy had no idea what Mrs. Howell was going to say, whom she was going to accuse. But the woman was full of rancour and didn't seem to care about anyone except her son. Even there, it was a case of care *about*, not care *for*. Daisy had seen no signs of affection between them. If Mrs. Howell promoted Owen's interests, it was, to all appearances, only because they meshed with her own.

Besides, Lucy had said their hostess seemed to be developing some sort of religious mania. None of that had seemed relevant when Daisy was telling DI Boyle about the Howells, but if she was going to go round accusing people, her state of mind could not be ignored.

Alec sat down behind the desk. Reading the note without touching it, he leant forward. 'Please go on, Mrs. Howell.'

Since her dramatic entrance, Mrs. Howell hadn't said a word. She didn't seem to notice Daisy sitting there with her notebook at the ready. She stared wild-eyed at Alec, her mouth opening and closing silently. Even if she happened to be telling the truth, she didn't at present look in the least like a credible witness.

'You say you know who blew up the grotto?' Alec prompted.

'An evil place! Full of pagan idols and popery! *He* built it and *he* destroyed it.'

'Mr. Pritchard?' His tone was so neutral as to express incredulity. 'Why should he destroy his own creation?'

'I told him.' She was triumphant. 'I convinced Brin of the wickedness, the shame of it.'

'How do you know he acted on his conviction?'

'I saw him.' Mrs. Howell looked away from Alec and started to fidget with her skirt. 'I saw him going to that place this morning, after breakfast. I didn't go down to breakfast and I happened to glance out of my bedroom window, and I saw him.'

'You're certain it was Mr. Pritchard?'

'Of course,' she asserted, gaining confidence. 'I've known him since my poor sister married him forty years ago. I couldn't possibly be mistaken.'

'What time did you see him?'

'I can't say for sure. I didn't think anything of it then. Why should I? He's obsessed with his horrible grotto! He's so eager to show it off, he lets complete strangers come and stay in the house if they express the slightest interest, without any regard for my convenience. He even lets that man live here, just because he wants someone to play hermit now and then. What does Mr. Armitage want, poking about in dusty old papers that should have been cleared out years ago? Up to no good, if you ask me, and carrying on with that girl, into the bargain. But Brin won't hear a word against him.'

Alec responded to this tirade with a mild 'How long have you lived in Mr. Pritchard's house?'

'What does that have to do with anything? We're not living on his charity, I assure you! My husband left me plenty of money, and half the firm to Owen. Brin only invited us to live here so as to have someone to entertain his guests and so he can keep his thumb on Owen.'

'Oh?'

'He's supposed to have retired, but Owen can't do a thing without consulting his uncle. I don't know why Owen doesn't let him get on with it. My son could live like a gentleman if he sold off his half of the business. But no, all he cares about is Pritchard's Plumbing. He hasn't even got his own name on it! I should never have let him visit the plant when he was a boy. My husband never went near the place.'

'Could we get back to what you saw this morning, Mrs. Howell? Where exactly was Mr. Pritchard, and what was he doing?'

She blinked at Alec vaguely, as if she'd forgotten the purpose of this interview. Perhaps Lucy was right, Daisy thought, and she had developed a mania, though it seemed to be more concerned with her brother-in-law than religion. Why had she turned against him?

'He was walking along the path towards the grotto,' she said at last. 'Almost running. And he kept looking behind him as if he was afraid of being seen. I knew he was up to something terrible. He's an evil man. You must arrest him at once and take him away.'

'I'm afraid I can't do that, you know, not simply on your word. Especially as he doesn't seem to have done anything dreadful while you were actually watching him.'

Mrs. Howell deflated. Rubbing her forehead, she complained, 'I have a frightful headache. I'd better go and lie down till dinnertime.'

'We'll talk again later, when you're feeling well enough.' Alec went to open the door for her. Closing it behind her, he ran his hand through his hair. The crisp crop shed a dusting of chalk and became one shade nearer its usual dark hue. 'Whew!' he exclaimed, returning to the desk. 'What a virago. I hope you're going to explain what that was all about.'

'She seems to have gone completely dotty!'

'She's got it in for Pritchard all right. But at a guess there's method to her madness. When one gets a wild accusation like that, it's often an attempt to cover up guilt, either her own or her son's.'

'Pure speculation, darling, and I doubt it. Rhino was rude to her but no more so than to everyone else. She forgave him because of his title.'

'She seems to have a genuine hatred of that wretched grotto. Perhaps she wanted to blow it up and didn't consider that someone was bound to get hurt in the process.'

'It's possible, I suppose, but I don't believe she's that dimwitted. In any case, it wouldn't surprise me if she hadn't the slightest idea how to do it, or even that turning on the gas could cause an explosion. *That* dim-witted she is.'

'What about protecting her son?'

'Owen Howell – well, I just can't imagine him blowing up perfectly good machinery, if that's the right word. Technical equipment. He got quite indignant over Rhino being careless with Lucy's camera stuff.'

'Indignant at Rhino?'

'Yes, but not violently. In general he's cool, calm, and collected. He rejoices in what you might call an orderly brain. In fact, he's one of the most rational people I've ever met. I can think of much more likely motives for Mrs. Howell to try to get Pritchard arrested.'

'Such as?'

'It boils down to simply getting rid of him. She may have enough money to be independent of him, but she likes being chatelaine of Appsworth House. I've heard him talk about letting women have their own way in the house, for the sake of peace, but in actual fact, as far as I can see, everything is run his way. He invites whomever he chooses, his favourite food is served – and his unfavourite not served – '

'What do you mean by that?'

'It's a fishy tale, darling, that's completely irrelevant. I'll tell you sometime. Suffice it to say, they don't get on at all well. He teases her and she carps at him – . Oho, more fish! I'll have to tell Lucy and Julia.'

'Daisy!'

'Sorry. The important thing is that Owen inherits the house, I gather, as well as everything else, including Pritchard's interest in the company. He doesn't seem to be in any hurry, but obviously if Appsworth was his, his mother's position would be much enhanced. She could even consider herself safely ensconced for life, because he's not the marrying kind.'

'How on earth do you know?'

'For a start, he's forty and unmarried. And he appears to appreciate Julia's looks, but doesn't follow her about with his tongue hanging out, like Rhino and . . .' Bother! She didn't want to draw attention to Charles Armitage's passion for Julia.

'And?'

'And I've never seen him show the least sign of jealousy. He's far more interested in explaining the latest technological improvements in the safety of water heaters than in Julia being beautiful and in need of a wealthy husband.'

'The safety of water heaters? Was it a water heater that blew up out there?'

'Probably. But, if I've got this right, it couldn't have been a steam explosion because – let's see – because the gas can't be turned on before the water is. Or something of the sort.'

'I'm going to have to talk to Howell and Pritchard about the technical aspect of the explosion. Or rather, Boyle is. I suppose I'd better bring him up to date on Mrs. Howell's rant.'

'You don't believe her, do you?'

'Great Scott, no! Too many inconsistencies in her story, not to mention her manner. But all the same, as you're well aware, I don't know nearly enough to cross Pritchard off the list.'

Daisy sighed. 'I like him. I can't believe he'd destroy his beloved grotto just to get rid of an irritating guest who was leaving soon anyway. But I know you and your precious list.'

' "You know my methods, Watson." Can you spare a sheet from your notebook, or shall I pinch some of Pritchard's paper?'

'He wouldn't mind, but if you feel it's inappropriate for a policeman to misappropriate his host's stationery, here you are.' She tore off a blank page and handed it over. 'What's it for?'

'Just a note for Boyle. I don't want to send a verbal message and have it published to the world before it reaches him. Ring for a servant, would you, love?'

The little maid Rita scurried in a very short time later, as flustered as ever.

'Have you been promoted to parlourmaid, Rita?' Daisy asked her.

'Oh no'm. That Mr. Boyle's asking Lily questions, and Mr. Barker said I was to come.' She scurried off again with Alec's note, but some time passed before Boyle appeared. While they waited, Alec asked Daisy what she had really been going to say when she'd stopped herself after comparing Lord Rydal's pursuit of Julia with Howell's lack of interest. She should have known he wouldn't miss her hesitation. She managed to fob him off with the fish story, which made him laugh, but she knew the reprieve was temporary.

Boyle arrived before he could press her. 'Sorry to have kept you waiting. The girl only just gave me your note. She didn't want to interrupt. What's up?'

'The lady of the house has accused her brother-in-law of blowing up the grotto.'

'Wonderful!' the inspector said acidly. 'I can't possibly get a warrant at this time on a Saturday evening.'

'Not so fast. Wait till you've heard what she said. Daisy?'

Daisy read her notes aloud. She had written them recently enough to be able to decipher them without difficulty.

Mrs. Howell's ranting didn't sound quite as mad in her own prosaic voice, but it was still pretty mad.

'Well now,' Boyle said doubtfully, 'that's not good enough for a warrant, agreed, but Mr. Pritchard's going to have to account for himself. What was he doing trotting off through the gardens towards the grotto at that time in the morning?'

'I think it's pure fabrication,' said Daisy. 'He told me he had a few things to do in here before he gave me a tour of the house, and I bet he was right here the whole time.'

'Why should Mrs. Howell fabricate a story to incriminate her brother-in-law?'

'You'll have to explain, Daisy.'

'But it's all speculation, darling. With a bit of hearsay mixed in, I shouldn't be surprised.'

In spite of his naturally inexpressive features, Boyle's look spoke louder than words. 'If you recall, Mrs. Fletcher, I told you I want to hear *everything*.'

So Daisy repeated the arguments she had already given to Alec.

'Sounds reasonable,' Boyle conceded. 'All the same, sir, we'll have to ask him about it.'

'Of course. I didn't mean to suggest otherwise. However, I don't consider it urgent. But it's your case,' Alec apologised.

'Maybe we'd better change that, put it on a formal footing. In the morning I'll ring up my super and ask him to put it to the Chief Constable – '

'Great Scott, no! The more informal we can keep it, the happier I'll be. You may have to remind me now and then, though, Inspector, that I have no standing whatsoever in this case. I am merely a consultant.'

'Well, sir, if you insist. For the present at least. Suppose I was to want to consult you right this minute. What'd you say's the most urgent item on the agenda?'

'First, did you get anywhere with the servants? I'm sorry I interrupted you, but it seemed to me that, being in charge, you'd have had every right to be annoyed if I hadn't let you know immediately about Mrs. Howell's claim.'

'Even though you don't think it's important. I would've been. I found out what we wanted to know. The parlour-maid, Lily Inskip, she overheard Lord Rydal and Lady Ottaline last evening, arranging a rendyvoo. She was in the drawing room, seeing everything was put straight after Mrs. Howell went up to change for dinner, when those two came in from the grotto. That right, Mrs. Fletcher?'

'Yes, most of us went to the grotto after tea. Lady Beaufort hadn't seen it yet. Lady Ottaline said she was getting cold and Pritchard suggested Lord Rydal should escort her back to the house. He didn't want to but Julia made some remark about being ungallant so he went. We were all glad to see the back of both of them.'

Boyle nodded. 'Miss Inskip, she says they looked like they'd been arguing. They didn't see her at first. As Lady Ottaline stepped in through the French window, she turned and said to him, "The grotto, at two tomorrow, if you know what's good for you. No one will be there then." His lordship muttered something the maid didn't hear. Then they saw her and shut up. Then – and this is the most interesting bit, to my mind – Sir Desmond came in. Miss Inskip had left the door to the hall open to make it easier to carry out ashtrays for cleaning, so she didn't hear him arrive and can't say if he heard what Lady Ottaline said.'

Alec nodded. 'Sir Desmond has by far the most obvious motive.'

'But he's a bigwig, and if he didn't do it, we don't want to have given him cause to bring a hornet's nest about our ears.'

'Very true. Did you find out who else knew about the planned meeting?'

'Miss Inskip went straight off to have a good gossip with the housekeeper and the cook, and one way or another all the indoor servants got to hear about it. The visitors' servants, too. Miss Willett told Lady Beaufort and Miss Beaufort when she went to dress them for dinner – not this afternoon, like you said, Mrs. Fletcher.'

'I didn't! I said Julia told us this afternoon that Willett had told her. I didn't know when.'

'You gave me the impression – '

Alec intervened. 'Who else among the household and guests was told?'

'Most of 'em,' Boyle said morosely, 'one way or another. There's not a one I can say for sure didn't know.'

'You obviously didn't have much difficulty getting them to talk.'

'The butler, Barker, said right off he wasn't going to gab about anything he hadn't seen for himself, and for a moment I thought they were all going to go bolshie on me. But most of 'em were dying to talk, and the housekeeper said it was their duty to help the police, so after that it was plain sailing. Barker never did come round though. Said it wasn't his business to gossip about his employer's household or guests. Very high and mighty, is Barker,' he said with considerable resentment.

'A cross between Jeeves and the Admirable Crichton,' Daisy observed. 'Even Rhino, though he was forever moaning about the failings of servants in general and his own in particular, never complained about Barker. You'd almost think Barker had a hold on him, like Lady Ottaline.'

Boyle stared at her, mouth open, as if struck by a *coup de foudre*. 'What if Lord Rydal – him being a ladies' man – what if he once seduced Barker's daughter, or sweetheart, or even his wife? What if the butler did it?'

CHAPTER 25

'No,' said Daisy.

As though summoned by the monosyllable, Barker entered in his stately manner. He didn't look at all like a man who had just taken violent revenge on the noble ravisher of his beloved.

He addressed Alec. 'I beg your pardon for interrupting, sir, but Mr. Pritchard wishes to know whether you will be free to dine with the company.'

Alec turned to Boyle. 'What do you think?'

Boyle glanced at Daisy, then said firmly, 'Yes, you'd better.'

'Then I shall.'

'Thank you, sir. Dress will be informal.' The butler turned to Boyle. 'A tray will be brought to you here,' he said with severity and no 'sir.'

Bland and impassive, Boyle said. 'That'll do me nicely, thank you. All you servants working on those timetables I asked for, are you?'

'Insofar as it is compatible with preparations for dinner.' He bowed to Daisy and departed in good order.

'Snooty, bloody-minded s –. If you'll excuse the expression, Mrs. Fletcher. What did you mean by "No"?'

'I can't believe the butler did it.'

'It's hard to see Barker as an explosive sort of chap,' Alec agreed, 'though I'm sure he'd do it very efficiently if he set his mind to it. But something less violent, poisoning for instance, would be more his line, I'd say.'

Daisy agreed. 'But it's not only that. My impression of Rhino is that it's dashing ladies of the smart set who appeal to him, not ruining innocent servants and shop girls. Lucy would know if there are any rumours to the contrary.'

'And Lucy's in London. Still, I wouldn't put Barker high on my list. You know, Inspector, while timetables are going to be useful, we're not going to get far until we have some idea at what o'clock the trap must have been set. If I remember correctly, a certain proportion of gas in the air is a necessary condition for an explosion.'

'How the deuce are we going to work that out? Wouldn't we need to know the volume of the room for a start? Well, it hasn't got a volume any longer.'

'No,' said Daisy, 'but I bet Mr. Pritchard knows, or could work it out. Look at that cabinet, darling. Aren't those deep, shallow drawers meant for plans and technical drawings? Blueprints? I can't see why he'd have stuff from Pritchard's Plumbing at home. It's far more likely to be the plans for the grotto.'

Boyle jumped up and went to open the top drawer. 'Yes! Appsworth Grotto it says. Good thinking, Mrs. Fletcher.'

Daisy preened. 'I have my uses on occasion,' she said modestly.

'I can't read 'em, can you, sir?'

'Not me. There's gas pressure to be considered, too. We'd better have Pritchard in and ask him to explain the whole thing.'

'Howell at the same time, d'you think? He must know a lot about gas, if not the grotto itself.'

'At the same time? What do you think, Daisy, if Pritchard tried to mislead us, would Howell back him?'

'How would I know? But no, I don't think so. He has too much respect for matters technical. He came back from Swindon, I take it?'

'Yes, he and Sir Desmond, while I was talking to the servants.'

'Well, I don't suppose Howell would outright contradict his uncle, but he'd probably argue.'

'That's my feeling,' Boyle agreed. 'These engineering types can't stand it if everything's not spot on.'

'Let's get them in here, then,' said Alec, 'and get that sorted out before we – you – start asking them questions that will upset them.'

'I'll ring for Barker.' Boyle reached for the bell.

'Don't bother,' said Daisy. 'If you can spare me, I'm off. It's no good asking me to take notes of what they say. Technical stuff sends me to sleep. I'll tell them you want to see them.'

'Thank you, Mrs. Fletcher. Don't tell them what we want them for, please. Would you mind writing up what notes you've already taken so that they're . . . available when my men arrive?'

'Legible, you mean. Right-oh.'

Daisy went to the drawing room. There she found Pritchard and Howell, as well as Julia and Lady Beaufort, Charles Armitage, and Gerald. Pritchard and Howell had their heads together. When Daisy gave them the message, Howell said, his tone congratulatory, 'You were right, Uncle.

Good job we've got it straight in our heads. Won't take half a moment to look up the numbers for them.'

'Now don't you go giving them the impression we can provide an exact answer,' Pritchard said as they headed for the door. 'There's too many variables. We don't know how many gas taps were – ' The door cut him off.

So much for not telling them what they were to be asked, Daisy thought. No doubt Boyle would blame her, though he had seemed to be softening a little.

'Daisy, what the deuce is going on?' Gerald asked. 'Miss Beaufort says Lucy's dashed off back to town with a copper in tow, to develop some photos the police need. It's not like Lucy to go out of her way to help the police, not even Fletcher. What does she have up her sleeve?'

Daisy was in a quandary. It seemed only fair for Gerald to know what his wife was up to, but it wouldn't be fair to Lucy to spoil her surprise. She glanced at Julia and Armitage, who both looked amused, so they had presumably worked out what was going on.

'They want her pictures of the grotto,' she said at last, 'and she doesn't trust them not to spoil her plates. Neither Alec nor the inspector saw it before the explosion so they don't really have an idea of what it was like.' She turned to Lady Beaufort. 'How is Lady Ottaline?'

'Uncomfortable. Her back is considerably bruised and she has a headache from a knock on the head, but no concussion, the doctor says, and no broken bones. He's given her some powders. He says she should be up and about in a couple of days, though moving stiffly.'

'No! Don't tell me Dr. Tenby actually managed to utter so many consecutive words.'

'Far from it. The information was conveyed in a series of grunts. After living so long in France, I'm quite good at interpreting incomprehensible utterances.'

'Mother, your French is as good as mine.'

'More than one of the Dinard tradesmen spoke in grunts, you must admit, my pet, and French grunts at that. But I shouldn't be joking when poor Lord Rydal is lying dead and Lady Ottaline in great discomfort.'

'Is Sir Desmond with her?' Daisy wondered aloud.

'Yes. He's very much shocked at what happened in his absence. One must hope,' Lady Beaufort said doubtfully, 'that the disaster will bring them closer together.'

'Should've put a stop to her nonsense years ago,' Gerald muttered.

Lord Gerald Bincombe being almost as devoted to taciturnity as Dr. Tenby, Daisy hadn't considered him as a source of information. 'You know Sir Desmond, Gerald?' she asked.

'Only to nod to at the club.'

'But you've known about Lady Ottaline's . . . activities for years?'

'M'father warned me to steer clear when I first went up to town,' he said uncomfortably.

'You're older than Gervaise, though younger than Alec, so she was already notorious before the War. Sir Desmond *must* have known she was apt to stray. The only question is, did he know specifically about Rhino?'

'Look here, Daisy, it's not the sort of thing a chap likes to talk about in the drawing room!' He glanced at Lady Beaufort.

'Let's go somewhere else, then.'

'Don't mind me,' said her ladyship robustly. 'I lived with the Army too long to pay any heed to what's fit to discuss in a drawing room. If there's someone else with a better motive for doing Rydal in than Charles Armitage, I want to know about it.'

Julia gaped at her. 'Mother!'

'I'm not blind.'

'But you don't want me to marry him, so why should you care – '

'I changed my mind when I discovered Lord Rydal's character. A woman is permitted to change her mind, I believe.'

'Why on earth didn't you tell me?'

'That's my business.'

'It may not remain your business,' Daisy warned. 'I don't know along what lines Boyle is thinking, but the police are liable to ferret out absolutely everything.'

'Let them try,' said Lady Beaufort. 'Now, Lord Gerald, did Sir Desmond know about his wife's . . . connection with Lord Rydal, or did he not?'

'He didn't confide in me,' Gerald said stiffly, 'but it was common talk. I doubt he could fail to be aware of it.'

'Quite apart from her behaviour here,' Armitage put in, tearing his bemused gaze from Julia's glowing face. They were now openly holding hands.

Daisy looked pointedly at the clasped hands. 'The police may ferret out everything, but there's no need to make it too easy for them.'

Armitage dropped Julia's hand as if it were a smoking gun.

Julia frowned. 'You think it's best to pretend we aren't . . . um . . .'

'On second thought, no. They'll find out anyway and it'd just look fishy. At least, I'm not sure of Inspector Boyle's abilities, but Alec will find out.'

'Fletcher's in on the investigation?' Gerald asked.

'Sort of. He's caught between two stools. He doesn't really want to get involved, but he already is, having seen the explosion and found the body. Boyle's in the same position: He doesn't want Scotland Yard taking over his case, but having an expert on the scene and already mixed up in it, how can he avoid asking for help? So they're trying to keep their collaboration informal. The trouble is, Alec finds it frightfully difficult not to take charge.'

'Is it a good thing for us if he takes charge?' Julia asked.

'He won't let my opinions influence him,' Daisy said, 'if that's what you mean. But he'll get at the truth with the least disruption possible, and he'll rein in the inspector if he gets any wild ideas into his head. At least, he'll try,' she amended.

Lady Beaufort looked alarmed. 'Wild ideas?'

'Well, Boyle's already proposed applying for a warrant to arrest – a certain person, on very slim grounds. Alec dissuaded him, but there's no knowing what direction he'll go off in next.'

'What it boils down to,' Boyle grumbled, 'is that you can't give us an answer.'

'Not unless you find all the gas taps,' said Pritchard.

'Even then, we couldn't be precise, Uncle,' Howell objected, 'not with the ventilation being natural and its flow never measured.'

'Close enough for these gentlemen, I daresay.'

'What beats me is how *he* worked out how long it would take for the gas to build up to explosive proportions.'

Boyle pounced. '*He?*'

'The murderer,' said Howell patiently.

'You think it was a man?'

'Stands to reason, doesn't it? Ladies aren't really interested in the technical details. Mrs. Fletcher asked for a demonstration of the new safety features on the hot water geysers, but I could see, her attention soon wandered. None of the rest even expressed an interest.'

'Did any of the men?' Alec asked.

'Er, well, no.'

'So you two are the only ones with the necessary knowledge,' said Boyle, darting a significant look at Alec.

'Except that even we couldn't be precise,' Howell repeated, in the tone of one prepared to reiterate the point as often as necessary.

'It seems to me,' said Alec, 'that everything points to someone who in fact had no expert knowledge. Someone who had heard of coal-gas explosions, but had no idea they only occur if the proportion of gas to air is between five and fifteen percent.'

'Roughly,' Howell insisted. 'It depends to some degree on the local distribution of the various components of the gas. Some are heavier than air, some lighter, so – '

'I think Mr. Fletcher has grasped that point, Owen.'

'In your discourse on the geyser, Mr. Howell, did you happen to mention that explosive fraction?'

'Certainly not. I was talking about the new safety feature that prevents a steam explosion. I'm not at all sure all my audience grasped the difference, but I didn't touch on gas explosions at all. They are much more difficult, if not impossible, to prevent, but considerably less likely to occur.'

'What happens if the concentration's too high and someone walks in?' Boyle asked.

'They smell the gas and walk out,' said Pritchard. 'In a hurry. Unless there's a spark or flame entering with them.'

'As was presumably the case with Rydal,' Alec put in.

'He always had a lit cigarette, or was in the process of lighting one. If there was too much gas to explode, there would almost certainly be a fire, which could well have killed Lord Rydal equally effectively.'

'*Almost* certainly.' Boyle groaned. 'You're right, Mr. Fletcher, it looks as if he was killed by someone who had no idea what he was doing. And that means *she* is just as likely as *he*.'

CHAPTER 26

Even with the addition of Alec and Gerald, a diminished company sat down to dinner. Lucy had left for London and her studio; Carlin for London and his golf match; Lady Ottaline and Mrs. Howell had both taken bromides and stayed abed; and Rhino's absence made itself felt in a curious combination of lightened spirits and wariness.

Sir Desmond had come down at the last minute. He responded to queries about his wife's condition with his usual suave courtesy – 'resting as comfortably as can be expected' – but, not unnaturally, he looked harried.

Mr. Pritchard invited Lady Beaufort to take Mrs. Howell's place at the end of the table. With six men to only three women, seating was necessarily informal, though Daisy suspected Mrs. Howell had in any case been responsible for previous attempts at formality. Sir Desmond, of course, had a proper appreciation of hierarchy. He appropriated the place to Lady Beaufort's left, leaving that on her right to Gerald, but Gerald chose familiarity over precedence. He sat down next to Daisy, who had found herself on Pritchard's right, opposite Julia.

Lady Beaufort beckoned Alec to the empty chair beside her. Howell beat Charles Armitage to Julia's side – or perhaps

Charles was being discreet. He took the one remaining seat, between Sir Desmond and Gerald.

Daisy was amazed at how much one could guess about people simply from where they chose to sit at an informal dinner.

As Barker and the parlourmaid started serving the leek and potato soup, Lady Beaufort said to Alec, 'Well, Mr. Fletcher, were you able to pin down the time to your satifaction?'

'The time, Lady Beaufort?' Alec asked cautiously.

'The time the trap was set. The time someone was out in the grotto turning on the gas.'

'Not exactly.'

'Anything but exactly,' said Howell. 'There are just too many variables.'

'The best we could do,' Pritchard confirmed, 'was to place it somewhere between eight in the morning and noon.'

'Is that helpful to you, Mr. Fletcher?' Lady Beaufort enquired.

'Better than nothing.'

Armitage said, 'I assume you'll be asking us all to account for our time between eight and noon. It's a long period to account for.'

'Not really. It was just this morning, and unless you're an early riser – '

'Which I am not,' Lady Beaufort declared. 'I walked all the way to the grotto and back yesterday afternoon and again in the evening – all those steps! – and I was quite exhausted.'

'Exhausting,' Alec murmured, a trifle ironically. Daisy could tell he hadn't intended to ask any questions during dinner, but he wasn't displeased to have the subject raised.

Lady Beaufort gave him a shrewd look. 'I know you've been there all afternoon, and digging besides, but I'm an elderly lady.'

'Not at all!' Pritchard protested.

'Do go on, Lady Beaufort,' Alec suggested.

'I slept until nine o'clock and then I had breakfast in bed, so it must have been quite half past eleven before I came down. I hadn't been in the drawing room more than a minute or two when Mrs. Howell came in. We sat together until lunchtime. So there you are, time all accounted for. And I can assure you that had I risen early, I should not have ventured to the grotto without an escort, for any purpose.'

Pritchard sighed. 'I'm afraid it'll be a long time before I shall have the pleasure of escorting you there again. When I think of all the . . . But it's no use crying over spilt milk. Now let me see, what time did I get up?'

They all started discussing their movements and trying to work out times. Daisy hoped Alec was succeeding in keeping it all straight, because she soon found herself losing track.

Her mind wandered. No one seemed to be taking the exercise seriously, perhaps because no one was really mourning Rhino. Though she had disliked him, Daisy wondered sadly whether anyone, anywhere, would mourn Rhino. That brought her to his family, if any, and consideration of his family led to Boyle's question about his heir.

Greed was a common motive for premeditated murder, perhaps the commonest, Daisy wasn't sure. It would be comforting to presume that the unknown heir to the earldom and pots of money had sneaked into the grounds of Appsworth Hall and turned on the gas. Unfortunately, she couldn't imagine how a stranger could be sufficiently familiar with the grotto, let alone have known about Rhino and Lady Ottaline's assignation.

If she wanted to cling to the money motive theory, only one among the assembled company could possibly be a long-lost heir: Charles Armitage. He would have had a double motive, greed and jealousy, and he obviously had some mysterious secret in his past, something he didn't want to talk about. But Daisy didn't want to believe he was a murderer. In fact, she refused to believe it.

Her unbelief did not dispose of his motive of jealousy – and a secret.

Lady Beaufort had a secret, too. Why did she refuse to discuss her reason for having delayed disclosure of her change of heart about Rhino's suitability as a son-in-law? The delay was a great pity. With Rhino no longer a rival, Charles would have had little cause for jealousy.

Of course the motive of jealousy applied equally to Sir Desmond, in fact even more so. Apparently unruffled, he was now tucking into roast pork with apple sauce and broad beans (no fish course!), having briefly mentioned his simple movements of the morning. He had risen from his bed – he could not name the hour, but no doubt his valet would know – and after breakfast had been driven into Swindon to the Pritchard plant. Howell and the missing Carlin could vouch for his presence there.

Carlin. He'd skedaddled in rather a hurry, but Daisy couldn't think of any reason for him to have murdered Rhino. The only insults flung his way had been general animadversions on the bureaucracy, nothing to take personally. He hadn't shown any particular interest in Julia, either. Probably he considered her to be an 'older woman,' Daisy decided gloomily, just as she and Lucy and Julia had pigeon-holed Lady Ottaline.

What had Lady Ottaline been doing this morning? She wasn't present to speak for herself. She hadn't come down to breakfast, either. That was hardly surprising. Women *d'un certain âge* (how much kinder the French phrase) often breakfasted in bed at country-house parties.

Daisy's attention was drawn back to present company as Julia said, 'Mr. Armitage wanted me to see Barbury Castle. He is a historian, after all.'

'I wasn't aware of that,' Alec said mildly. 'And I'm afraid I've never heard of Barbury Castle. Tell me about it.'

'It's an Iron Age...' She glanced at Charles and he nodded. '...An Iron Age fort. There are barrows, too. Those are ancient burial places. There's supposed to have been a battle nearby, as well, in five hundred and something A.D., between the Britons and the Saxons.'

'Who won?'

'I can't... Oh, the Saxons, I suppose. They drove the Britons out, to Cornwall and Wales. Do you remember, Daisy? The Angles, Saxons, and Jutes?'

'How could I forget? Lucy used to complain that the Angles belonged in geometry and the Jutes in geography. The exports of India or somewhere.'

'How far from here is Barbury Castle?'

Charles answered. 'It's a couple of miles as the crow flies, on the ordnance survey map. Farther walking, of course, and quite rough country in places. We went on beyond for a bit, too, hoping to get within sight of one of these white horses carved in the chalk – I expect you know about them.'

'I've seen the Pewsey White Horse. I didn't know there were others. Why didn't you get as far as this one?'

'Julia – Miss Beaufort was afraid we'd be late for lunch, so we turned back.'

'It was quarter to one when we got back, just time enough to tidy up before lunch.'

'Which direction is Barbury Castle from here?' Alec asked.

After a painful pause, Armitage said, 'More or less south.'

'Beyond the grotto.'

'Yes.'

'It sounds like an interesting place.' Pritchard seemed to have decided his guests had been interrogated sufficiently at his dinner table. 'I'd like to see it. You must take me there when the weather improves, Armitage.'

'Certainly, sir. You won't have to tramp as far as Miss Beaufort and I did. There's a lane goes quite close.'

Lady Beaufort, whose obvious anxiety had eased at Pritchard's words, turned to Alec and asked, 'Are you interested in history, Mr. Fletcher?'

'Yes, as a matter of fact. My degree is in history, but I specialised in the Georgian period, not the Ancient Britons.'

'Darling,' said Daisy, 'I've just had a brilliant idea. We should collaborate on a book about the early history of the police and call it *From Beadles to Bobbies*.'

Everyone laughed.

'A catchy title,' Armitage remarked. 'If you ever write it, I'll certainly recommend it to my students.'

'Students!' Lady Beaufort exclaimed. 'You're a teacher?'

'University lecturer, actually.'

'Why – ?' She had been going to ask why she hadn't been informed, Daisy was sure. But that would imply she had a reason for expecting to be informed, and that in turn might lead the police to question the relationship between Julia and Charles. Though Alec's face gave nothing away, Daisy could have told her he had already drawn his own all too obvious conclusions. 'How interesting,' her ladyship said weakly instead.

'In Canada?' asked Gerald. He had been ploughing silently through the meal, no alibi being required of him. Now Barker and the maid, Inskip, were clearing the dishes in preparation for serving pudding, so momentarily Gerald had no excuse for failing to do his conversational duty.

The arrival of plum tart and a pitcher of thick cream put an end to his participation, but he had diverted the stream. Life in Canada, life in France, relations between France and Canada, relations between French Canadians and British Canadians – there was plenty to keep everyone going. Daisy would have liked to ask about the Royal Canadian Mounted Police, but in the circumstances, she decided, the less said about any kind of police the better.

All too soon they'd have to face once more the unpleasant demands of the murder investigation.

'Good grub,' said Boyle as Alec returned to Pritchard's den. He put a spoonful of plum tart in his mouth and chewed.

'You were right, I learnt quite a bit at dinner. They were actually keen for me to ask them where they were this morning.'

'All of them?' Boyle grunted sceptically.

'Some were keener than others. But I got stories from all of them, for what they're worth.'

'What are they worth, d'you think, then?'

'Some more than others. Let me write it all down – I couldn't very well at table – and we'll go over it.'

While the inspector finished his dinner, Alec made notes. They'd have to ask each person the same question all over again, but how they answered the second time was often more significant than the first. Omissions and additions, alterations, or repetitions in the same words, suggesting rehearsal, might all be clues to the truthfulness of the speaker.

Boyle heard him out, then said, 'I still haven't got a real grasp of who all these people are, or why they're at Appsworth Hall. Not that Mrs. Fletcher wasn't helpful, but I'd like to hear from Pritchard what they're doing here in his house. If you've no objection, sir, we'll have him back first.'

'Do you regard him as a suspect?'

Boyle frowned. 'Not on such information as I've got already. But, of course, there's no knowing what I'll – we'll dig up. Nor there's no knowing what'll set some people off, and Mrs. Fletcher did say Rydal insulted Pritchard, along with everyone else.'

CHAPTER 27

Boyle was about to summon Pritchard – or rather invite him to step into his own study – when the troops from Devizes arrived at last. They consisted of a detective sergeant, a detective constable, and two uniformed constables, all damp. The rain was coming down in torrents by now.

The inspector wanted to send one of the uniformed pair to relieve PC Endicott who was still out there on the hillside in the storm, guarding the site of the explosion. 'And the other to the grotto entrance, don't you think?' he asked Alec. 'You said you couldn't see for dust, but when that's settled, and in daylight, it ought to be searched, as well as the hole.'

Alec nodded, forbearing to point out in the presence of Boyle's subordinates that all the suspects had visited the cave in the past few days, so any evidence of their presence was unlikely to be meaningful.

The two men stood stolidly waiting for instructions. After a moment of thought, Boyle said gloomily, 'The only thing is, how the devil are they going to find their posts in the dark? One of the outdoor servants'll have to guide them.'

'Ask Barker,' Alec suggested.

'Mr. Barker's eating his supper, sir,' protested the maid who had shown the policemen into the room.

'Can't be helped,' said Boyle curtly. 'Take these fellows along, and tell Mr. Barker there'll be a detective following in a minute or two to collect the timetables you should all have made out. When he arrives, take my compliments to Mr. Pritchard and tell him we'd like to have a word with him in here.'

With a doubtful shake of her head, the girl took the constables away.

The junior detectives were eyeing Alec askance.

'This is Mr. Fletcher. He's a guest here. As he's . . . connected with the police, he's lending a hand. Unofficially.' Boyle went on to explain to DS Gaskell that he wanted him to go over with the servants their statements about the household's movements that morning. He was to make sure they not only made sense but didn't contradict each other. 'And see what they can tell you about the victim's chauffeur, the bloke that was caught in the collapse,' he added.

'Pity we can't talk to him yet,' Alec said as Gaskell departed.

'That doctor's a bit quick with the sedatives, if you ask me! It'll be interesting to see if the servants agree with what the nobs told you about what they were doing and when,' Boyle remarked to Alec. To the detective constable, he said, 'I hope your shorthand is up to scratch. I want a verbatim record of the interviews I'm going to be doing. Got plenty of pencils and an extra notebook?'

Alec thought regretfully of DC Piper, his usual notetaker, who was never caught without a supply of well sharpened pencils. He could only hope Gaskell got on half as well with servants as Tom Tring, the massive and superlatively competent detective sergeant who was his right arm.

Pritchard came in. He moved more slowly than earlier and looked tired, but he asked with unabated courtesy, 'What can I do for you now, gentlemen?'

'First,' said Boyle, 'I'm looking for a bit more information about all these people you've got together in your house. It's what you might call a mixed bunch, if you don't mind me saying so, and I don't properly understand how they fit together, so to speak, or what they're doing here.'

'I'm not surprised you're confused,' Pritchard said with a weary smile. 'I'm none so clear on the subject myself. But let's see if I can help. It all starts with my sister-in-law, I suppose.'

'Mrs. Howell. She's been living with you for a long time?'

'Several years. Her husband, my partner, died soon after my wife and I moved to Appsworth Hall, and naturally Glenys invited her to stay while she decided what she was going to do next. Daffyd left his half of the business to Owen, his only son, but Winifred got their house and a good deal of money.'

'She told us she wasn't living on your charity.'

'Well, not from necessity. But after she sold the house for a pretty penny, she couldn't decide where she wanted to live so she stayed on. Then Glenys died – and Winifred stayed on.' He shrugged wearily. 'I like having Owen about the place, and his mother's a capable manager, so . . .'

Alec wondered how much the inestimable Barker had to do with Mrs. Howell's capable management.

Boyle finished Pritchard's incomplete sentence. 'So Mrs. Howell is what you might call a permanent resident? You're on good terms?'

'Good enough. Most of the time. The reason I've gone into all this is that she's responsible for the presence of some of my guests. Not that she'd invite anyone without consulting me.' His tone suggested a sudden doubt as to whether it was just a matter of time before his sister-in-law overstepped this particular boundary. 'Owen went up to London over this government contract business, meetings at the Ministry of Health and so on. Sir Desmond kindly invited him to dine at his house, and there he met Lady Ottaline, of course. Lady Beaufort and Miss Beaufort were also dinner guests. He wrote to Winifred about them. She was all agog to meet them – '

'Why was that, sir?'

'She's a bit of a . . . She fancied the notion of entertaining titled people. In the normal way, she has to make do with the vicar, the doctor, our solicitor, business associates, a few old biddies from the village – that sort of people. Of course I wouldn't have presumed to invite them to stay just because Owen had casually made their acquaintance. Then it turned out that Sir Desmond had to come down to take a look at the works. It seemed easiest to keep Winifred happy by saying we'd be delighted if he brought his wife. To tell the truth, I was surprised when she accepted. I suppose she just happened to be at a loose end this weekend.'

Boyle grunted.

Alec thought it more likely that Lady Ottaline had heard about Lord Rydal's pursuing Miss Beaufort to Appsworth. 'What about the Beauforts?' he asked.

'I'm not entirely clear about them, though I'm very glad they're here. Delightful guests. As is Mrs. Fletcher,' he added, with a nod to Alec, who noted with amusement the omission of Lucy. Lady Gerald Bincombe could be a prickly companion. 'I only wish Lord Rydal hadn't offered to drive them down. Once he was here, I felt I had to offer hospitality for the night – it was a foggy evening – and he seemed to assume he'd been invited to stay as long as they did.'

'Mrs. Howell didn't kick up a fuss about an unexpected guest?' Boyle asked, possibly with memories of Mrs. Boyle's feelings in like circumstances.

'What, with a genuine earl under her roof? Even if it's actually my roof . . . No, she was thrilled. So thrilled she put up with rudeness –. Well, if the Czar of Russia treated his peasants and workers like that, I for one don't blame 'em for having a revolution. I can tell you, if I spoke to my factory hands that way, I'd have 'em out on strike within the hour.'

'Bad language?'

'No, not that. It was more as if he'd learnt by heart all the rules about acting the gentleman but didn't really grasp what it was all about. I can't explain properly. Maybe Mrs. Fletcher, being a writer, can describe what he was like. I'd've kicked him out – asked him to leave – a dozen times if it wasn't that Winifred wouldn't have it.'

'She didn't mind how he behaved?'

'Far as she was concerned, he was a lordship so whatever he did was all right by her, right up until it came to meeting his fancy woman in the grotto. That she wouldn't stand for. I'll say this for Winifred: She's a snob, but she was brought up Chapel, and she's never turned her back on it, no matter that all the nobs go to Church. She'll have the vicar to dinner, but that's as far as it goes.'

'Not . . .' Alec hesitated, trying to word his question tactfully, then decided there really wasn't a tactful way to put it. 'You wouldn't say there was a touch of religious mania?'

'Certainly not.' Inevitably Pritchard took affront. 'I'm Chapel myself.'

Boyle made no attempt at tact. 'Yet you put pagan statues in your grotto, and some Papist idol Mrs. Howell was carrying on about. An evil place, she called it.' He glanced for confirmation at Alec, who nodded.

'Evil?' Pritchard was startled and worried. 'She never liked it, but she's never said anything like that before. It does sound as if she's got some sort of bee in her bonnet. Sounds to me as if the explosion and Lord Rydal's death have been too much for her nerves. I wonder if I should call the doctor to her?'

'Couldn't hurt,' said Boyle, 'unless she takes it into her head that you're conspiring against her.'

'Conspiring?' Now he seemed bewildered.

'To get her out of the way. She made a serious accusation – '

'Against me? Surely she can't imagine I blew up my own grotto! If you knew the time and effort I put into restoring it – to say nothing of the money – and the fun I had, the fun I've had showing it off, too! All those years of perfecting and peddling plumbing – not that I regret a moment, plumbing's important, but the grotto was . . . artistic. I don't suppose any real artist would think much of it, but it was my own creation. And Winifred claims I blew it up? She *must*'ve gone round the bend!'

'Unless she was trying to protect her son,' Boyle proposed, his face more than usually blank.

'No, that's going too far! I'd as soon believe I did it myself, walking in my sleep, as Owen. He helped me build it, and he'd no cause to want to murder Lord Rydal, neither. If that's what Winifred thinks, she's even madder –. But she wouldn't have told you that. You've made it up out of your own head.' He gave Alec a reproachful look. 'Heads.'

'We have to explore every possibility, Mr. Pritchard, especially when an allegation has been made.'

'Well, if Winifred's suddenly convinced herself the grotto's evil, and on top of that it was being used for immoral purposes, maybe she did it herself!'

'That's another possibility we have to explore.'

'Come to think of it, she never did like the hermit business. She never could see it was just a bit of fun. If it wasn't popery, she'd say, it was sacrilege. I never could persuade her it was either both or neither.'

'That's another thing I haven't quite got the hang of,' said Boyle. 'This hermit business. You hired the Canadian just to play hermit in your grotto?'

'Not exactly.' Pritchard showed a sudden unexpected touch of shiftiness. 'In the summer I hire someone from the village to play the part. You'd be surprised how many visitors we get. I don't usually bother before Easter, but when … Armitage wrote to ask permission to take a look at the old documents in the muniments room, I told him he could come and stay and pay for his keep by dressing up as the hermit in the grotto if anyone happened to turn up to see it.'

'There's the curious coincidence of his name, too,' said Alec.

'What? Oh, yes, quite a coincidence, isn't it?'

'The name?' Boyle asked, genuinely blank this time.

Pritchard seemed disinclined to answer, so Alec explained, 'The name Armitage is derived from the word hermitage, I believe.'

No police detective could let such a fishy coincidence pass without question. 'I hope you asked him for references,' Boyle said.

'Certainly.' Pritchard recovered his composure. 'I'm a businessman, Inspector. He showed me his passport and a letter from his university. Perfectly satisfactory, I assure you. He's been here for several weeks, apart from occasional trips to London to look things up in the big libraries.'

'Could he have met Lord Rydal in London?'

'He wasn't interested in high society. "A great waste of time," he told me more than once. Frankly, I should've thought Rydal had much the same opinion of libraries. It doesn't seem likely they'd meet, but they might've run into each other somewhere.'

'Neither of them acknowledged having met before when Lord Rydal arrived here?'

'Not by a flicker of an eyebrow.'

'Was Lord Rydal ever insulting to Mr. Armitage?'

'What you have to understand,' Pritchard said patiently, 'is that he insulted everyone, though I must say Lady Gerald gave as good as she got. Except I never heard him being rude to Lady Beaufort. After all, he wanted to marry her daughter.'

'What about Miss Beaufort herself? Surely he wasn't rude to her!'

'But he was. Very odd I thought it, when he was courting her.'

'Odd! I'd call it downright peculiar. Are you sure?

'Yes. The young ladies were giggling about it.'

'Oh, then they were just joking about,' Boyle said large-mindedly. 'The nobs have their ways.'

'I don't think so.' Alec remembered what Daisy had said. He hadn't taken it very seriously at the time, but he was once again reminded that dismissing her theories was frequently a mistake. 'My wife told me Rydal simply didn't realise how offensive he was.'

Boyle nodded. 'Mrs. Fletcher said to me she thought he had never been taught to consider anyone else's feelings. I don't suppose you know anything about his childhood, Mr. Pritchard?'

'Not a thing.'

'If he acceded to the earldom at an early age,' said Alec, 'it could be that he was brought up by servants and perhaps dependent relatives, who were afraid to cross him.'

The inspector was scornful. 'Sounds like something one of those psycho-doctors would say. I can't see it makes any difference one way or the other. If someone goes around offending people, they're not going to worry about whether he's doing it on purpose or can't tell the difference.' He reached for Alec's notes on the dinner-table alibis. 'Let's see here. You claim you were alone in here for half an hour this morning.'

'That's right. I had some accounts to make up. I came straight here after breakfast and was here when Mrs. Fletcher and Lady Gerald came to fetch me to give them a tour of the house.'

'Mrs. Howell said she was alone in her bedroom all morning and saw you walking towards the grotto.'

Pritchard sighed. 'Then I don't know whether to hope she was hallucinating or making it up. Either way, it's a sad state of affairs.' He sat there with his hands on his knees, looking tired and worried. 'I don't know what I'm going to say to Owen.'

'I'd rather you didn't discuss this with anyone for the moment, sir.' Boyle glanced at Alec. 'Any more questions, sir?'

'Not for the moment. Thank you for your cooperation, Mr. Pritchard. I hope this will prove a momentary aberration on the part of your sister-in-law.'

The moment the door closed behind Pritchard, Boyle said, 'I don't think he did it, do you? But this Mrs. Howell's another kettle of fish. Sane or not, she had it in for both Mr. Pritchard and Lord Rydal, not to mention the grotto itself. Then there's this Armitage fellow. Something dodgy about him being here in the first place, if you ask me. All the way from Canada to look at some fusty old papers! Out walking with Miss Beaufort, he claims. Walking out, more like, I shouldn't wonder. After her money.'

'Miss Beaufort is an extraordinarily beautiful young woman,' Alec informed him, 'and I have a vague memory of my wife mentioning that she and her mother are far from well off.'

'Oh,' said Boyle, disconcerted. He rallied. 'At any rate, Armitage wanting to marry her, him a professor – if he's telling the truth about that! – and her courted by a rich lord. Stands to reason he'd want to get his rival out of the way.'

'But Miss Beaufort also says they were walking the entire time. Why would she back his story if he'd destroyed her chance of an excellent marriage?'

'Because Lord Rydal insulted her. Strange, that. What do you reckon to this theory of Mrs. Fletcher's, sir?'

'About Lord Rydal's upbringing? I think she may well be right, and you may well be right that it doesn't make any difference to us. Except insofar as it's always useful to understand the victim.'

'I daresay.' Boyle sounded unconvinced. 'Seems to me it's more important to know he was rude to everyone than why. It gives us a lot of people with reason to dislike him, but the ones with the best motive *and* opportunity are Armitage, with or without Miss Beaufort as accessory; Mrs. Howell, assuming she's batty; and Lady Ottaline Wandersley, that he wanted to throw over for Miss Beaufort, as your good lady told us.'

The door opened, and Alec's 'good lady' appeared.

'Darling, I've been thinking,' she announced.

CHAPTER 28

Daisy shut the door and advanced into the room. She didn't recognise one of the three men who rose to their feet. He must be a new arrival.

Perhaps his presence explained why she didn't hear the groan with which Alec usually greeted any declaration of hers that she had been thinking. It was too much to hope he at last realised the value of her thoughts.

'Is this urgent, Daisy? We've got a lot of people to interview this evening.'

She sat down, and they followed suit. 'It might be urgent. I was thinking about Lady Ottaline. I assume she's near the top of your list of suspects?'

DI Boyle answered. 'She seems to have had a strong motive, though we've not got much to go on yet besides your word for it, Mrs. Fletcher. Same goes for opportunity. I'm waiting for DS Gaskell to bring me the servants' reports on that. He and DC Potter here arrived at long last from Devizes.'

Daisy smiled at the large young man. 'It's a good job you're here. You're the very person to guard Lady Ottaline.'

'What?' Alec and Boyle exclaimed together.

'The thing is, it's all very well – in a manner of speaking – if Lady Ottaline blew up Rhino. But supposing she didn't?

Whoever did probably intended to blow her up, too. Isn't it quite likely they'd have another go? Possible, at least. There she is, alone and helpless under the influence of whatever powders Dr. Tenby gave her – '

'Daisy, do you know something you haven't told us?'

'No, of course not. At least, not consciously. I have a feeling there's something I've missed. Oh, and I heard Sir Desmond ask Barker to move him to a separate room, because he's a noisy sleeper – presumably he snores – and he doesn't want to wake his wife. They have separate rooms at home, I expect. He'll have to have Rhino's room. It's the only good room unoccupied. Either he doesn't realise, or he's not afraid of ghosts!'

'Daisy!'

'Well, it means she'll be alone all night. Unless you've found out enough to be sure she's safe, I really do think she ought to have a guard, just overnight.'

'You're right,' said Boyle, clearly pained him to have to admit it. 'We can't risk it, and you're the only one we can spare, Potter. Off you go. Ask the butler which is her room. If there's a connecting bathroom with another door, make sure it's bolted from the inside.'

'But sir, I can't do that without going through the lady's room!'

'Use your initiative, man. Take her maid with you or something. And give me your notebook before you go. Mrs. Fletcher,' he went on sourly, 'I'm going to have to ask you to stay and take notes again, until Gaskell finishes with the servants. He shouldn't be much longer.'

Daisy sighed. Though Alec wouldn't be deceived, with luck Boyle would believe she was doing him a favour. 'Oh, all right. Devizes didn't send you enough men. I haven't brought my notebook, though. May I use DC Potter's?' Perhaps she'd have time to skim Potter's notes of the interview with Mr. Pritchard. She hoped his writing was easily legible.

'If you have no preference, Mr. Boyle,' said Alec, 'I like to clear what you might call the dead wood out of the way. That is, to question the least likely suspects first.'

Foiled! Daisy naturally was much more interested in what the most likely had to say for themselves.

Luckily, so was Boyle. 'That's a good idea, sir. It's getting late, and it'll speed things up no end if we split the load, though Lady Ottaline won't be available till the morning, I suppose. Do you want to stay in here? I'm sure the butler can find one of us another suitable room for interviews.'

For once outmanoeuvred, deliberately or inadvertently, Alec gave in gracefully. 'You stay. I take it you want Armitage first? I'll send him to you.'

'Thank you, sir.'

They both looked at Daisy, and then at each other. Daisy wasn't sure whether each wanted to shuffle her off on the other, or each hoped to retain her services. Whoever kept her would have better notes for the other to read later. She knew where she wanted to be.

'Mr. Boyle has more need of me, darling,' she said. 'You'll want a verbatim report of what the chief suspects say, won't you?'

'I'm just lending a hand,' he reminded her, 'not officially a part of this investigation. But yes, you'll be more useful here. I'll ask Armitage to bring his passport and letter of recommendation, shall I, Boyle?'

'Er . . . yes. Yes, I'd better take a look at them. You really think that's not his real name?'

'I think we ought to have evidence to settle the question. Right-oh, I'm off. The one I really want to see is Lucy – Lady Gerald – whose view of things, I'm sure, is very different from Daisy's. In her absence, Lady Beaufort first, I think.'

'If you see my sergeant, tell him to buck up. When he comes, I won't have to trouble Mrs. Fletcher any longer. She can give you a hand.'

'Right-oh.' Alec went out.

Boyle looked glumly at Daisy, then suggested, 'You'd better read through Mr. Pritchard's interview, I suppose.'

DC Potter's shorthand was much better than Daisy's. It took her only a couple of minutes to read his notes. 'I see why you're suspicious of Charles Armitage,' she had to admit. 'It's odd about his name, but I'm sure there's an innocent explanation. Such as it really being his name. Coincidences do happen. I *would* like to know what drew his interest to the papers here at Appsworth Hall, though.'

'I hardly think that's relevant to the enquiry into the death of Lord Rydal.'

'You can't be sure. Alec always insists that any detail may turn out to be significant. And you yourself said you wanted to know absolutely everything I know, hearsay and all, so that you can decide for yourself if it's important.'

Armitage came in so quietly they didn't hear him until he said, 'Fletcher told me you wanted to see me?'

The inspector waved him to a seat and held out his hand. 'Your passport, please.'

'I'm afraid I don't have it on me.'

'Didn't Mr. Fletcher tell you I want to see it?'

'Oh yes, but you see, I don't have it here. I keep a room in London, and I leave it there while I'm travelling. I don't need it. I've never been asked for it before.'

'I daresay. But you do need to keep your introduction from your university to hand, surely. That will do to be going on with.'

'It's upstairs, in my bedroom, yes,' Armitage acknowledged reluctantly. 'But I can't see how it's going to help you, Inspector. It doesn't have a photograph attached, eh, so there's no proof I'm the person referred to, assuming you suspect I'm not.'

Boyle leant forwards, his eagerness obvious. 'Are you admitting that you're here under false pretences? A con-man, is that it? Lord Rydal was onto you, so you had to put him away?'

Daisy was too horrified to remember she was supposed to be taking notes.

Armitage shook his head wearily. 'Nothing so dramatic. I told Mr. Pritchard it was bound to come out. I was willing to help him avoid embarrassment – myself, too, really, but not to the point of being arrested for murder.'

'What the deuce are you talking about? I warn you, everything you say will be taken down and may be used in evidence in a court of law.'

Hastily Daisy started scribbling.

'I told you, I didn't kill Rydal. But you're obviously not going to believe me. I'd better fetch that letter.' He started to stand up.

'No! You just stay here under my eye if you please.' Boyle looked at Daisy, irritated. 'You're going to have to go and get it, Mrs. Fletcher. Mr. Armitage – or whoever you are – tell her where to find it.'

'In my chest of drawers.' Armitage grinned at Daisy. 'Top left, under my socks and . . . other things, an ivory envelope with the university crest embossed on the flap.'

His underwear, no doubt, Daisy thought indignantly, but Boyle didn't seem to have drawn the inference. She could hardly inform him she objected to rummaging through Charles's pants and vests, especially in search of an incriminating letter she'd prefer not to find. Yet if she refused to go without giving a reason, he might use her unhelpfulness as an excuse to bar her from the investigation altogether.

On her way out of the room, she wondered momentarily whether she ought, for Julia's sake, to steel herself to the distasteful task and then to destroy the letter. However, its disappearance would probably cause Charles more trouble than whatever it revealed. She decided to ask Barker to send one of the staff. Then she reconsidered. The envelope must be unsealed, because Charles had made use of the letter. If the servant yielded to temptation and peeked, the entire household would have the information in no time.

Daisy resigned herself to carrying out the job.

She had just reached the foot of the stairs when she heard footsteps behind her and turned. A man – to Daisy's practised eye obviously a policeman – was crossing the hall, carrying a wodge of scraps of paper, all sizes and shapes and of varying degrees of cleanliness.

'Hello, are you DS Gaskell?'

He looked a bit surprised by her glad greeting. 'Yes, madam?'

'I'm Mrs. Fletcher, DCI Fletcher's wife. Mr. Boyle's been wondering when you'd be finished with the servants' timetables.' True. 'He needs a letter from Mr. Armitage's chest-of-drawers.' True. 'Top left, in an ivory-coloured envelope with a crest on the back.' All perfectly true, if somewhat misleading. But Boyle would undoubtedly have sent the sergeant if he'd been available. 'Shall I take those to him?' She indicated the papers in Gaskell's hands.

He handed them over like a lamb. 'They're a bit confusing. That's what took me so long, working out what they were trying to say, and then checking the times and places to make sure they didn't contradict each other. Er . . . Can you tell me where this bloke's room is? So's I don't have to ask that snooty butler?'

Daisy gave him directions and watched him hurry up the stairs. So far so good. Now all she had to do was to present the *fait accompli* to Boyle in such a way that he wouldn't be annoyed with either her or Gaskell.

She riffled through the papers, but she couldn't make head or tail of them at a glance and she didn't dare delay to study them. They couldn't help Armitage, in any case. His opportunity to turn on the gas in the grotto had already been established by his own admission.

In Pritchard's den, Charles Armitage was staring at the floor in gloomy silence, while Boyle read through the papers on the desk. Both looked up and started to rise as Daisy entered. She waved them down.

'I've brought the servants' timetables, Inspector.' She set them before him. 'I met DS Gaskell on his way with them. It seemed best that he should go for Mr. Armitage's letter. Being a police officer, I mean.'

Boyle grunted what might conceivably be approval, or possibly thanks, and started to sort out the heap of scraps: used envelopes; the backs of shopping lists, receipted bills, and notes for the milkman; and even a torn triangle of butcher's paper. Daisy, realising that her presence would be superfluous as soon as Gaskell arrived, found an inconspicuous seat against the wall, in an ill-lit corner, well to one side and slightly to the rear of the desk.

She gave Charles (if Charles was actually his name) an encouraging smile and he smiled back. Insofar as it was possible to judge his mood, he seemed more exasperated than worried. This, Daisy thought, was a good sign, suggesting that his deception had innocent roots.

Nothing to do with murder, at least. What secret could he and Pritchard share that would embarrass both? She was baffled.

CHAPTER 29

Alec ushered Lady Beaufort into the breakfast parlour, pointed out to him as a suitable location by the butler. He held a chair for her, and she sat down with a sigh. She was a handsome woman still, though a little inclined to embonpoint.

'My dear man, you are a lesson to me.'

Alec opened his mouth, closed it again, then said cautiously, 'I am?'

'A lesson already learnt,' she went on, confusing him still further, 'but too late, alas. I'm afraid I'm responsible for the shocking occurrences of today.'

Doubtless Boyle would have applied for an arrest warrant instantly. Alec merely blinked and was glad he'd ended up interviewing her on his own. He didn't for a moment suppose she was physically responsible for turning on the gas taps in the grotto.

'Would you please elucidate, Lady Beaufort? Explain,' he explained, when she looked uncertain.

'Of course. Where shall I start?'

'At the start of the events that led to the murder of Lord Rydal.'

'Oh dear, I suppose it all began in my girlhood – '

'Perhaps not quite that far!' Alec said quickly.

'That's when I was taught to believe in the importance of a girl marrying well, and *well* meant money and if possible a title. I don't know how much Daisy has told you about our circumstances?'

'Very little. Nothing, really, except that she and Lucy were at school with Miss Beaufort and you have been living in France.'

'My late husband was a younger son of a baronet, and everyone said he would do brilliantly in the Army, as indeed he did.' Lady Beaufort declaimed somewhat in the style of a Victorian melodrama. Alec suspected she was quite enjoying herself. 'He was made a general while still in his forties, and knighted.'

'Admirable,' Alec murmured.

'But the Beauforts, though aristocratic and all too numerous, were not wealthy. George had a little money of his own, but army life is expensive. When he was killed in the War . . .' She paused to dab her eyes with a lace-trimmed but substantial handkerchief. '. . . I found it had all been spent. Julia and I were left in straitened circumstances.'

'So after the War you went to live on the Continent.'

'Yes. And then I came into a small inheritance and decided to use it to make sure Julia never had to suffer such deprivation.'

'Hence Lord Rydal.'

'He was everything I'd been brought up to think was necessary in a husband. Rich, an earl, and he loved her madly into the bargain. He would do anything for her. Almost. I managed to overlook his faults for far too long.'

'I still don't quite understand how he and the two of you ended up at Appsworth Hall.'

'I'm not surprised,' Lady Beaufort said frankly. 'I'm not at all sure Julia didn't outwit me. We met Mr. Howell at a dinner party at the Wandersleys'. Not that we knew them well. If I'd known then what I know now, we shouldn't have known them at all, I assure you!'

Accustomed to Daisy's sometimes convoluted sentences, Alec had no difficulty disentangling this. 'But you didn't expect to meet them here?'

'Not in the least. Julia seemed to get on well with Mr. Howell, so ... Well, I suppose I had two possibilities in mind, besides the fact that I found London quite tiring. Endless shopping and parties and theatres ... I expected a week in the country to be restful, to set me up to tackle the rest of the season. Little did I know!'

He brought her back to the subject: 'And your two possibilities?'

'Possibilities? Oh, either Julia would see the difference between a manufacturer and a nobleman and come to her senses, or else she'd captivate Mr. Howell and be rich if not titled. At the time, she had recently told me about making the acquaintance of a Canadian in some library or other. It's quite shocking the way young people fall into conversation these days without waiting to be properly introduced. How did you and Daisy meet?'

'She felt obliged to draw to my attention a murder which was about to be passed off as an accident.'

'No!' Lady Beaufort laughed. 'I don't suppose Lady Dalrymple –. But I mustn't waste your time in idle gossip. Where were we?'

'Miss Beaufort met Armitage in a library.'

'Yes, well, she's always been what we used to call bookish.'

She sighed. 'I daresay a professor will do very well for her. But at the time I didn't think so. In fact, I didn't even know he was anything so respectable as a professor. I seized what seemed to be an opportunity to get her out of town and away from him. I cajoled Mr. Howell into inviting us – '

'How?'

'As it has nothing to do with your investigation, Mr. Fletcher, I'm not prepared to reveal my methods. But I will say that I'm quite an expert cajoler when I put my mind to it. It's a skill necessary to the wife of a general.'

'I can imagine,' Alec said with a grin. 'And then you cajoled Rydal into driving you down?'

'That wasn't necessary. I didn't expect that it would be. He really doted on Julia, you know, a most determined pursuit. He offered his services as soon as he heard she was going to the country for a week, though not without some grumbling about the idiocy of leaving town at the height of the season. Julia never breathed a word about her Canadian being a temporary resident of Appsworth Hall, the sly thing!'

'When did you come to the conclusion that Armitage is preferable to Rydal?'

'In the grotto, yesterday afternoon. I'm not a great walker. Brin – Mr. Pritchard was keen for me to see it, and I gave in yesterday. Fortunately as it turns out. Not that I did decide in favour of Mr. Armitage, mind you. Merely against Lord Rydal. His behaviour was outrageous.'

'And when did you inform your daughter of your changed opinion?'

'Good heavens, I can't remember. With all that's been happening, it's a wonder that I remember to bring my head with me!'

'Not immediately, though. Why was that?'

'It wasn't convenient just then. Other people were about. Besides, I was in no more hurry than the next person to admit I was wrong.'

It was reasonable. Still, she didn't quite meet Alec's eyes and he was sure she was not telling the truth. Not the whole truth, at least. Odd, but probably not significant, he decided. At this stage in the investigation he couldn't afford the time to stray down every enticing by-way. Later, too, he might have to try to pin her down as to exactly when she had told Julia of her change of heart. He'd wait and see what Julia had to say on the subject.

He wanted to see Julia next, but Boyle probably considered her a major suspect and therefore wanted to question her himself. With dismay, Alec recognised in himself a disposition to regard her as innocent simply because she was Daisy's friend.

Julia Beaufort had been out on the downs with Armitage. If he had gone to the grotto, she could hardly have failed to know. She might not have had the slightest idea what he was doing there at the time, but since the explosion she could no longer plead ignorance. If he was guilty, she was concealing evidence, and that made her an accessory after the fact.

She didn't have much of a motive for killing Rydal, but despite Daisy's glossing over the relationship, she had the best of motives for protecting the man she loved.

Not for the first time, Alec was going to have to perform a delicate balancing act, between leniency because of Julia's friendship with Daisy and undue harshness because he was afraid of being lenient. He reminded himself with gratitude that this was not his case.

Lady Beaufort was fidgeting under his blank gaze. 'Well?' she asked, a challenge in her voice. 'Are you always in a hurry to admit when you've made a mistake?'

Alec smiled and shook his head. 'It depends on the circumstances. In general, I don't claim to be any more eager than the rest of the world. But if I've arrested someone and discover I shouldn't have, the sooner it's put right the better for all concerned, including me.'

'Fair enough.'

He liked the lady. He could only hope he wouldn't have to assist in the arrest of her daughter.

He stood up. 'Thank you for your cooperation, Lady Beaufort. That will be all for the moment.'

'For the moment! Next time it will be the local inspector, I suppose. It's too much to expect that he, too, is a gentleman.'

'More to the point,' said Alec, absorbing the implied compliment without a blink, 'Inspector Boyle appears to be a competent officer.'

He escorted her back to the drawing room, thinly populated by Pritchard, Howell, Wandersley, and Bincombe, all with glasses in hand. Wandersley was standing with his back to the fire, apparently holding forth. The other three rose as Lady Beaufort entered. Pritchard and Bincombe in particular looked delighted to see her.

Pritchard came to meet them. 'Let me get you a liqueur, dear lady. Crème de menthe, as usual? And a whisky for you, Mr. Fletcher?'

Lady Beaufort sank into a chair. 'I think I'll take something a little stronger tonight, Mr. Pritchard. Brandy and soda would do nicely.'

What the hell, Alec thought. He was unofficial, after all.

'Yes, please. With plenty of soda. Mr. Howell, I've a couple of questions for you, if you please.'

'Or if I don't please?' But he spoke mildly, a comment, not a hostile protest. 'I was in Swindon most of the day. I doubt I have anything useful to tell you.'

'That's what we'll find out.' He took the glass Pritchard proffered. 'Thank you, sir.'

Howell was already at the door. As they walked towards the breakfast parlour, he said, 'You've saved yourself some work. Much longer stuck with Sir Desmond's funny stories about politicians and I'd have up and strangled him. You'd have had another murder on your hands.'

'On DI Boyle's hands, not mine. You'd have done his arrest statistics a bit of good. I take it Wandersley is better to do business with than to entertain, if that's the right word.'

'If only he wouldn't insist on being entertaining. In the circumstances, it's a bit much.' Entering the room ahead of Alec, he sat down at the table. Alec took a chair opposite him. He continued, 'As for business, I can't complain. He's going to recommend that we get the contract. Contracts, rather. It's for local governments to make the purchasing decisions, but with a recommendation from the ministry, most are not likely to want to spend the time and money to vet other companies.'

'Congratulations. What is it you would complain about otherwise?'

'Oh, just that he's wasted a good deal of my time. These bureaucrats keep very short working hours. It's incredible that they ever get anything done. I'm a businessman. If I made a habit of starting work at eleven o'clock, the firm would be bankrupt by now.'

'You didn't get going till eleven this morning?'

'Nearer quarter past. Wandersley came down late to breakfast for a start. We still could have left for Swindon at a reasonable hour if he wasn't such a – a hearty eater.'

'Pig?' Alec proposed with a grin.

'You said it, not me. I got tired of watching him stuff his face and left him in here.'

'Alone?'

'No, several other people were still here.'

'Do you recall who?'

'Let me see. My uncle had already gone. Mrs. Fletcher and Lady Gerald left with me. Lady Gerald said something about sorting out her unused photographic plates. She was going to take some interior pictures of the house for Mrs. Fletcher, I gathered. That would leave Miss Beaufort, Armitage, and the abominable Rhino.'

'Where did you go?'

'To Uncle Brin's den, to have a word with him about – '

'How long after he left this room was that?'

'Quarter of an hour. Perhaps twenty minutes.'

'And how long were you with him?'

'No more than five minutes, I'd say.'

The exact length of time didn't matter. Pritchard had had at most half an hour or so to get to the grotto, turn on the gas taps, and return to the house to be waiting in his den for Daisy and Lucy. That was the bare minimum necessary. If Owen Howell had spoken with him during that period, he was out of the picture.

Except that Alec was pretty sure Howell would lie for his uncle, especially in what he might consider a good cause. He'd do it well, too. Men of business, like policemen, were on the whole adept at hiding their thoughts and emotions.

'The *abominable* Rhino, you called him.'

Howell shrugged. 'I can't think of a better word for him. He was abominably rude to my mother. There was no point having it out with him, though. He just didn't seem to understand why people got upset with him. I put up with it, in the certain knowledge that he wouldn't be here forever. I'm a peaceable sort of chap. More important matters on my mind than squabbling with an aristocratic ass.'

'A very sensible attitude. But how did your mother feel about it?'

He hesitated. 'I'm afraid Mother was dazzled at first by having a living, breathing earl under her roof. Well, under Uncle Brin's roof, but she tends to regard it as her own. All the same, I can't see how she can go on living here after what she's said about him.'

'He told you? Or she did?'

'He told me Mother went to the police – to you and the inspector both, was it? – and accused him of blowing up the grotto.'

'So you expect him to ask her to leave Appsworth Hall.' Alec felt for him. He had twice had to ask his mother to move out, because of clashes with both his first wife and Daisy.

'Uncle Brin? Good lord no! He wouldn't do a thing like that. I'm trying to work out what's best for all concerned. For a start, I think when she's well enough to travel, she must go away for a rest cure – Bournemouth, or Harrogate, Switzerland even.'

He didn't sound like someone with a guilty secret, whether his own or Pritchard's. He didn't seem very interested in Rydal's demise at all. Mrs. Howell's behaviour was monopolising his thoughts. That his mother herself might have been responsible for the explosion didn't appear to have crossed his mind.

'I'm afraid she won't be allowed to go abroad until Inspector Boyle has cleared up this case.'

'It's probably better if she stays in England, in any case. Less agitating than foreign travel . . . and fewer Papists,' he added with a wry grin. 'How long – ? No, that's a stupid question. I suppose you'll want to interview her tomorrow.'

'I'm sure Boyle has a few questions for her.'

'I don't want to teach the inspector his job, but you'd upset her less than he would. And get more answers from her.'

'I'll see what I can do, but it's his call. Just one more point: What did you do this morning after leaving Mr. Pritchard in his study?'

'I went to my room to check some figures, to save time when we got to the works. One of the maids came to tell me when Sir Desmond was ready to leave. That must have been about half past ten. By then I was fretting and fuming, I can tell you! Half the morning gone.'

'It often amazes me that the Empire survives, run by bureaucrats,' Alec agreed dryly. 'That will be all for now, thank you, Mr. Howell. Would you mind asking Sir Desmond to come and see me?'

'Running shy, are you?'

'I suspect he'll kick up less of a dust if the request comes through you, rather than directly from me.'

'We won't have any data for comparison, but all right, I'll do your dirty work for you!'

As with Lady Beaufort, Alec didn't think Howell was Rydal's murderer and he hoped not to see the man's nearest and dearest arrested. The hope was not as strong as in the lady's case, however. If Julia Beaufort was guilty of anything it was because she had fallen in love with a jealous young man, whereas Mrs. Howell had bitten the hand that fed her.

An enormous yawn caught Alec by surprise. He was very tired, he realised. He had got up early to finish reading and writing reports at the Yard, so as to be able to join Daisy for a couple of lazy days in the country. Instead he'd spent several hours digging in the rain, a level of physical exertion he wasn't accustomed to these days. Here he was enmeshed in a case that wasn't even his own, that could bring him no kudos yet might very well get him into trouble if his informal part in the investigation ever came to official ears.

For once he couldn't even blame it on Daisy. It was entirely his own fault.

Ah well, involved he was, so he'd better see that it came to a satisfactory conclusion. With a sigh, he extricated from a pocket the sheets of writing paper he'd filched from Pritchard's desk and scrawled a few details of his interviews with Lady Beaufort and Howell.

CHAPTER 30

DS Gaskell entered Pritchard's den with an ivory-coloured envelope held by one corner between finger and thumb, as if he expected it to be covered with useful fingerprints.

'Mrs. Fletcher said – '

'Yes, yes, put it down here.' Boyle gestured at a bare spot on the desktop, and then at the scatter of notes covering most of the rest. 'I hope you can explain all this muddle to me.'

'Yes, sir. Like I told Mrs. Fletcher, that's what took me so long, sorting it all out with them so's it makes sense.'

'Good. You can write it all out neatly for me later, but first, tell me what they had to say about whatsisname, Lord Rydal's chauffeur.'

'Gregg, sir. Not strictly speaking a chauffeur, more of a valet. His lordship preferred to drive himself, but required his manservant to be able – '

'All right, all right, I don't need to know the details. Not yet, at least. What were his relations with his employer?'

'For a start, he'd only been with him a couple of months and wasn't planning on staying, from what he told the others. The fellow before him wasn't there more than six months, neither. Gregg told them he never kept servants long. If you done something wrong and get sworn at, that's one thing, he said, and par for the job, but getting blasted all the time for what can't be helped is more than flesh and blood can stand.'

'Did anyone know he hadn't left Appsworth?'

Daisy stopped listening. She wasn't interested in the hapless Gregg. She didn't believe for a moment that he had anything to do with the explosion, apart from getting caught in it. No one could be so stupid as to set a trap of such magnitude and then hang about to see what happened. Whatever he had been up to, it wasn't turning on gas taps.

Nor did she believe Boyle was so stupid as to suspect Gregg of murder. The inspector was trying to rattle Charles Armitage, who so far was far too blasé about his fateful secret. The envelope lay there on the desk between them, an innocent rectangle of ivory paper, waiting to explode.

Or was it fateful? More likely, as he had claimed, merely embarrassing. Nonetheless, Daisy was dying to know what the contents would reveal.

Armitage took his tobacco pouch and pipe from his pocket and started to stuff the bowl. Getting a pipe going was a wonderful cover for nervousness – or irritation. Daisy thought he was more irritated than nervous as he tamped down the tobacco and took out matches.

He was striking the third when Julia marched into the room. Armitage leapt to his feet.

'What's going on?' she demanded militantly. 'Charles has been in here for hours.'

'Darling, it's quite all right. They're not giving me the "third degree."'

'What's the *third degree*?'

'Strong-arm methods the American police are known to use sometimes in interrogating suspects.'

'Strong-arm . . . You mean hitting?' Julia was appalled.

'Not the English police,' the inspector protested, scarlet with indignation.

'I should hope not! But you're not a suspect, Charles. You were with me the whole time this morning. I know you didn't go into the grotto.'

'*I* don't,' Boyle pointed out.

'You're saying I'm lying about it? Why should I tell a lie?'

Boyle looked significantly at Armitage, whose arm Julia was holding, and back at her. She wilted into the nearest chair.

'Perhaps you're not aware, miss, that it's a felony to conceal evidence from the police.'

'I haven't! We didn't go anywhere near the grotto entrance, just walked over the hills.'

'That's for you to know and me to find out.' The inspector picked up the envelope and tapped with it on the desk, looking again at Armitage.

'Julia, you'd better go back to your mother and let Mr. Boyle get on with his finding out. He can't find out that I was responsible for the explosion, because I wasn't.'

'I'm staying,' Julia declared, no longer militant, but determined. Glancing from Boyle to DS Gaskell, she caught sight of Daisy. Her eyes widened.

Daisy frantically but fractionally shook her head. If Julia addressed her, she was sure to be sent out. It was touch and go for a moment whether Julia herself would be expelled, whether by the police or her beloved, but both subsided.

Julia watched, obviously puzzled, as Boyle untucked the flap of the envelope, pulled out the letter, and opened it. He started reading.

His jaw dropped and he said incredulously, '*Appsworth*?'

For a moment, Daisy felt as blank as Julia looked. Then she had to bite her lip, hard, to stop herself laughing aloud. *Appsworth*! Was Charles a long-lost son of the family?

'What do you mean, *Appsworth*?' Julia said crossly.

Boyle gestured at Armitage/Appsworth. 'Ask him.'

'It's my name,' Charles explained, rather flushed. 'That's why I'm interested in the old family papers. It's – or more accurately, it was – my family. Mr. Pritchard asked me not to use the name down here. He was afraid it would start all sorts of rumours flying, people saying there was something fishy about his buying the house and I ought to have inherited it.'

'And is there something fishy?' Boyle enquired. 'Should the place be yours?'

'Good lord no! My great-grandfather was a fourth son. He emigrated to Canada and lost touch with the family. To tell you the truth, I think he started out as a bit of a ne'er-do-well, but he made good. My grandfather made a fortune in wheat, in Alberta. So we're a junior branch at best. I suspect the senior branches have died out, though I haven't finished tracking down the details. There have been a number of distractions.' He smiled at Julia, who was still looking somewhat bemused.

'So you may be the Appsworth heir,' the inspector persisted.

Daisy couldn't see why he was interested. After all, it was Rhino who had been blown up, not the usurping Pritchard, who might conceivably have been a target to Charles. But she wanted to know the whole story – and she didn't want to draw attention to herself – so she didn't interrupt.

'Good lord no! I'm not even an eldest son of an eldest son. If any of my immediate family were the heir, it would be my uncle, and since all my cousins are girls, my father after him, followed by my older brother. But the entail was broken long ago. My uncle may be able to call himself Lord Appsworth, but he has no rights in the estate whatsoever. It was left jointly to the two daughters of the then holder of the title, failing male heirs-of-the-body. When the younger died, the elder was perfectly at liberty to sell the place lock, stock, and barrel. She retired to a cottage in Dorset, I believe.'

'We must look her up, darling,' said Julia, 'and make sure she's all right.'

'Yes, I'd intended to, before I go home. Before *we* go home.'

They gazed into each other's eyes.

Boyle broke up this picture of love's young dream with a loud cough. 'Yes, that's all very well, but it's got nothing to do with my investigation.'

'At least you know now that my presence at Appsworth Hall isn't a long-laid plan to do away with Lord Rydal.'

'That's as may be. I've got plenty more questions for you, Mr. Arm – Appsworth, so – '

'Inspector, as long as you're not about to arrest me immediately and need my right name to do so, would you mind continuing the fiction? The possibility of embarrassing Mr. Pritchard continues.'

'I suppose it doesn't make much odds,' Boyle grumbled. 'Gaskell, you're to write down Appsworth, though, whatever

I say. In the meantime, I'll thank Miss Beaufort to take herself off until I send for her. I promise not to engage in any strong-arm tactics.'

At this point, an enormous yawn overcame Daisy. It drew the attention of both Julia and Charles, and Boyle turned his head to see what they were looking at.

'Mrs. Fletcher,' he said, his tone resigned. 'All right, I don't need you, either, now Gaskell's here to take notes. Perhaps Mr. Fletcher can avail himself of your services.'

'Right-oh.' Daisy was actually quite willing to leave now that she knew Charles's secret.

Julia was not. 'But I don't see why I shouldn't – '

'Come on, darling,' said Daisy. 'It's no good arguing with a copper in full cry. You'll get your turn, never fear.'

'But what am I going to tell Mother about who you really are, Charles?'

'Don't tell her anything until you've warned Pritchard that my alias is blown. See what he says, but I should think he'll want to keep quiet about it as long as possible – with your cooperation, Mrs. Fletcher? Inspector?'

Daisy nodded. 'Of course. Except Alec.'

'I was going to say,' Boyle said, 'except Mr. Fletcher. It's all the same to me. At present, at least. I can't see your name has anything to do with your committing murder.'

'Thank you,' Charles said ironically.

'Though it does show a talent for deceit.'

Julia wasn't going to let that pass. 'For Mr. Pritchard's sake!'

'Don't worry, Julia. Just think what a story we'll have to tell our grandchildren when we're old and grey.'

Daisy managed to get her friend out of the room without

any further outbursts. 'Darling,' she said, 'you really must stop showing yourself so partisan. You make it less and less likely that Boyle will believe anything you say about Charles.'

'It's already too late. He thinks Charles turned on the gas when we went out, and I'm aiding and abetting him. After all, apart from Pritchard and Howell, Charles knows about the gas supply in the hermitage better than anyone.'

'Bosh! Anyone who's been in there knows about all the lights and the fire. I expect there'd have been enough gas to blow up without using the geyser, but anyway, we were all there when Pritchard was talking about it. Most of us. Let's see, who was actually there?'

'Charles and I,' Julia said gloomily. 'And Rhino.'

'Lady Ottaline and Sir Desmond. Carlin. Lucy and I. And Pritchard and Howell, of course, but the gas was no news to them. Mrs. Howell didn't come, nor your mother.'

'Nor the doctor and his wife. They came to dinner, remember? But I think they'd gone home by the time we got back to the house. It all seems so long ago. Whatever became of Carlin? Oh, Daisy, you don't think he's out there under the rubble?'

'Heavens no! Didn't you hear him at breakfast? He was engaged to play in a golf tournament tomorrow so he went back to town by train. Does – did Rhino play golf?'

'No. He called it a footling occupation for fools who had nothing better to do with their time. Why?'

'I was just thinking it was a bit fishy the way Carlin disappeared so promptly. Pritchard telephoned Sir Desmond in Swindon when we got Lady Ottaline back to the house, so the three men were still there, so Carlin must have known about the explosion before he caught his train. It's a bit cool, if you ask me, his just going off like that.'

'What's that got to do with Rhino and golf?'

'Well, suppose he and Rhino had quarrelled over a game sometime in the past. Men get frightfully worked up about it. Rhino might forget, but Carlin brooded about it and – '

'But Rhino didn't play.'

Daisy sighed. 'No. Pity.'

'All the same, I don't think the inspector should let Carlin off without being interrogated.'

'He told his sergeant to find him in London and bring him back. I hope Lucy took the Daimler or poor DS Thomkin will be stuck in the dickey all the way down. Always supposing he manages to find Carlin and persuade him to abandon his match.'

'It sounds like a tall order.'

'Alec gave him the name of an inspector at the Yard who'll help him. I just hope it doesn't get Alec into trouble.'

They had been standing talking just outside the drawing room. Now Julia said, 'Are you coming with me to warn Mr. Pritchard about Charles having to reveal his alias to the police?'

'Not me. I'll leave that to you. I'm just going to find out where Alec is, then I'll go and see if – '

'Madam!' It was the little housemaid, Rita. Twisting a corner of her apron in nervous fingers, she was obviously upset. 'Oh, if you please, madam!'

'What is it, Rita?' Daisy asked.

'Oh, madam! Mr. Barker said I got to tell you.'

Daisy envisioned her best evening frock ruined by over-enthusiastic application of the smoothing iron. She gave

Julia a little push towards the drawing-room door, and taking the hint, her friend went in alone.

'What do you have to tell me?' she asked.

'Oh, madam!' Rita glanced wildly round the hall.

'Would you like to go somewhere private? How about the dining room?' Daisy led the way. 'Now sit down and spit it out. I won't eat you, you know.'

'Mr. Barker said you was the best one to tell. I'm sure I couldn't say a word to that inspector, but you'll know what to do, madam. Oh, madam, I never thought he meant it.' The girl flung her apron over her face and started crying.

'Who? Who meant what?'

'Mr. Gregg, madam.' Her voice was muffled by the cloth and interrupted by sobs and hiccups. 'His lordship's man, madam. And I'm sure I wish he'd never said a word to me!'

'Oh dear!' said Daisy and set about coaxing the story from the frightened maid.

CHAPTER 31

When Howell left him, Alec folded his arms on the table and laid his head on them for a moment's respite. Feeling his eyes inexorably closing, he changed his mind, stood up, and went to one of the windows. He parted the curtains and looked out at belting rain, illuminated by electric lamps at the front door, under the portico. The window faced the carriage sweep. The room was at the northeast corner of the house. Thinking back to his arrival with Gerald that afternoon – could it possibly have been this very day? – he reckoned the view from the other window must be across a narrower drive to the service entrance and a group of out-buildings, including garages, partly concealed by shrubbery.

At any rate, it was impossible for breakfasters in here to see anyone heading for the grotto.

Alec rested his forehead against a windowpane. The cold glass revived him a little and the sound of heavy footsteps approaching the door, which Howell had left ajar, completed the process. Given a villain to track down, he could stay awake all night.

Sir Desmond Wandersley was still an enigma to him. They had been introduced just before dinner and sat opposite each other at the dinner-table, on either side of

Lady Beaufort. When everyone had started to discuss their whereabouts during the morning, Sir Desmond had said briefly that after breakfast he had gone into Swindon, to the Pritchard works. Apart from that, he had made little effort to converse, preoccupied, presumably, by his wife's accident. Yet Howell had said he produced an endless supply of funny stories later, in the drawing room. Curious. Still, Daisy described him as being an expert at presenting a façade to the world.

Alec waved him to a chair and sat down, saying, 'How is Lady Ottaline, Sir Desmond?'

'Sleeping soundly. She wasn't seriously injured, you know, just considerably shaken.'

He didn't sound at all concerned. Alec assumed he hadn't actually been to see how his wife was doing. He surely would have commented on the presence of DC Potter guarding her door.

When dealing with bureaucrats, it was safest to make sure all *t*'s were crossed and *i*'s dotted. 'You're aware that I'm a Scotland Yard CID officer, giving Inspector Boyle of Swindon a hand quite informally with preliminary questioning? I have no official standing in the investigation. If you prefer to speak to Mr. Boyle –'

'No, no, my dear fellow. I'm sure I can count on your tact, your understanding, as a man of the world, so to speak. A matter of some delicacy . . .' He hesitated. Though a pause of that sort was usually a sign of uncertainty, Sir Desmond's urbane manner never faltered. 'I'll let you decide whether it's worthy of being passed on to the inspector.'

Alec waited. When nothing further ensued, he prompted: 'Yes?'

'Do you know, I find this deuced difficult.' Yet he was still cool, calm, and collected.

'Perhaps we should start with your movements this morning. I couldn't take notes at dinner, obviously. Would you mind telling me again, for the record?' He smiled. 'We coppers like to have a solid foundation for further enquiries.'

'It's quite simple. I came down to breakfast – doubtless my valet will be able to tell you the precise time – and after breakfast I drove to Swindon, to the plumbing works. That is, my chauffeur drove me and Carlin, my Private Secretary. Howell took his own motor-car. I was at the factory, apart from a break for luncheon, until Pritchard telephoned to tell me Ottaline was hurt.'

'Thank you. Now, what about this delicate matter you want to talk to me about?'

'Dammit, man, it's not easy. If it weren't that – ' Sir Desmond took off his gold-rimmed glasses and fixed Alec with eyes like blackcurrant wine-gums, dark and opaque but with a slight sheen. 'You realise that in my position, any breath of scandal can be fatal.'

'Sir Desmond, until I know what you have to tell me, I can't give you any assurances, except that the police do not disclose information unless it becomes necessary in the prosecution of a court case.'

'Which I'm terribly afraid . . . If only I knew what to do!'

'If you are aware of facts that could materially affect police enquiries, it is your duty as a citizen – and especially, surely, as a servant of the Crown – to pass them on.'

'My duty! Yes, it's my duty, however painful.' He shaded his eyes with one hand. 'I fancy you must already have heard certain . . . rumours about my wife and Lord Rydal?'

'We have.'

'The inspector, too? I suppose I should have expected it. Ottaline was obsessed with the fellow, couldn't leave him alone. You didn't have the doubtful pleasure of meeting him, I gather, but your wife must have told you what an unpleasant specimen he was. I can only believe that Ottaline was . . . unbalanced. It's dangerous to thwart a woman in such a condition.'

'You didn't consider consulting a psychiatrist?'

'No. I didn't realise until recently to what extent her mind was affected. And I must admit, it was abhorrent to me to have her – and, I confess, myself – exposed to the talk that would surely have arisen. These things get about. I felt certain it would blow over in time, so I didn't kick up a fuss. Then I heard that he was pursuing a young lady with a view to marriage. She – I'm speaking of Miss Beaufort, of course – was badly off and not at all likely to refuse a rich peer. I assumed his . . . connection with Ottaline would come to a natural end. A reasonable assumption, don't you agree?'

'Certainly.'

'When she said she'd like to come into the country with me, I was sure it was over. I didn't know Rydal was here, although, as I found out too late, she did. I could see right away that she still wanted him, and if she couldn't have him, she'd have her revenge. She's a vengeful, grudge-holding person. But I was thinking in terms of petty revenge, and I guessed wrongly that Miss Beaufort would be her target. If I'd had the slightest inkling of what she planned . . .'

Alec let the silence hang for a moment. Then he said impassively, 'You'd have warned Lord Rydal? Warned your host? Somehow prevented Lady Ottaline from blowing up the grotto? That is what you're telling me, isn't it? Your wife killed her lover.'

Momentarily, Sir Desmond slumped. Then he stiffened and stood up. He leant forwards with both fists on the table. 'I've said enough. I have no proof. But I couldn't let you arrest someone who may perhaps be innocent because you hadn't considered all possibilities.'

'Oh? Whom do you think DI Boyle is about to arrest?'

'Why, the Canadian, of course. Lady Beaufort favoured Rydal, who was pestering the girl. Obviously Armitage was jealous. At one blow he rid himself of his rival and freed her from harassment. But I shan't try to teach you your job. Good night, Mr. Fletcher. No doubt I shall see you in the morning. I must warn you, however, that I must leave for London tomorrow, or early Monday without fail. Perhaps you will be so good as to point out to the inspector that the nation's business cannot wait on the convenience of the provincial police.'

'I'll let him know.' But a trifle more tactfully. Not that he could hold anyone against his will, government business or no government business. 'Good night, Sir Desmond.'

A slight scuffling sound out in the passage was muffled by Sir Desmond's heavy footsteps. Alec wouldn't have heard it had he not been listening for it. In the middle of the interview, he had seen the door handle turn and the door open an inch. He hadn't wanted to stop Sir Desmond in full flow, though he would have done so if he hadn't been all but certain the eavesdropper was Daisy.

Sir Desmond's weighty tread receded down the hall. A moment later Daisy came in.

'He didn't see me, the snake!'

'Snake?'

'All those nasty insinuations about Lady Ottaline, and he admitted he had no evidence whatsoever. He's trying to get rid of her. Well, one can't help but sympathise a bit, but still . . . Darling, you don't believe him, do you?'

'There isn't anything to believe or disbelieve, since he didn't make any direct accusations. Snake, yes. I was thinking rat. You shouldn't have been listening.'

'I had to see you, and I didn't want to interrupt. Oh dear, more insinuations, I'm afraid, but without malice.'

'Daisy, what are you blithering about?'

In response, she stuck her head out of the door and called, 'Rita, come along now.'

Rita?

'Come on, he doesn't bite, I promise.' She ushered in a very young housemaid. 'Rita has something to tell you.'

'Oh, madam, cou'n't you tell for me?'

'Right-oh.' Nothing loath, Daisy sat down at the table. 'But he or the inspector is going to want to ask you some questions. You know, I told you they would. Alec, Rita is the third housemaid, so she does the senior and visiting staff bedrooms. That's how she came to chat with Gregg, Lord Rydal's manservant. And perhaps to flirt a little?' She gave the nervous girl an encouraging smile.

'We didn't do nuthen wrong!'

'Of course you didn't. I'm just telling him that so he understands how it came about that Gregg told you things he didn't tell anyone else.'

'I never thought he'd really go and do it,' the maid said tearfully.

'Brace up. Perhaps he didn't. It's for the police – '

'Daisy!'

'Sorry, darling. This morning, when Rita went in to make Gregg's bed and dust around, as usual, he was in his room packing his belongings. He was in a "state," and he told her he'd been sacked.'

'For nuthen!' Indignation overcame fright. 'Just his lordship wanted to wear a tie Mr. Gregg'd left behind in Lunnon.'

Daisy continued. 'He said he'd put up with enough and he was going to get his own back. He told Rita about a neighbour of his aunt's who had tried to commit suicide with gas. She'd turned on the oven and put her head in, then grew uncomfortable and impatient and decided to have a last cup of tea. She struck a match to light the burner. The gas exploded and burnt off her eyebrows. Gregg decided it would be a good idea to burn off Rhino's eyebrows. I must say, I agree, only he did it rather too thoroughly. If he did it.'

'I never thought he would,' Rita wailed. 'I thought it were just talk.'

'You couldn't possibly have guessed,' Alec said soothingly. 'He knew about Lord Rydal and Lady Ottaline's plan to meet in the grotto, did he?'

'Oh yes, sir, everyone knew. Wicked, I call it.'

'Thank you for telling Mrs. Fletcher about Gregg's threat. Does anyone else know?'

'Just Mr. Barker, 'cause I didn't know what to do.'

'Good. Don't tell anyone else, there's a good girl.'

'What about that inspector, sir? Will I have to tell him?'

'I'll tell him. I expect he'll want to ask you some questions, as Mrs. Fletcher warned you. You can run along now. Remember, not a word to anyone else.'

'I'll keep mum, sir. Oh, madam, thank you ever so. I'd never 've done it without you.' Departing, the maid cast a dubious backward glance at Alec and added, 'Not but what he's not as scary as you might expect.'

Daisy managed to shut the door before she collapsed in laughter. 'Darling, what a come-down! The great Scotland Yard detective can't even scare a third housemaid!'

'I could an I would,' Alec said darkly. 'What do you think of her story?'

'I'm sure it's true. What it means is another matter. The fact that Gregg was on the spot when the place blew up suggests he wasn't expecting anything half so dramatic.'

'Which need mean no more than that he simply didn't know much about the properties of coal-gas.'

'What do you mean?'

Alec explained what Pritchard and Howell had said about the necessary concentration to cause an explosion. 'Now I come to think about it, whoever was responsible probably didn't realise how uncertain the outcome was. Even those two experts couldn't predict a specific result, taking into account how many taps were turned on for how long.'

'I don't believe Gregg did it. I can't imagine him going to the grotto, turning on the gas, then waiting right there for long enough for enough gas to escape to cause an explosion, expected or unexpected. If you ask me – which I suppose you won't – he'd have hung about the house or garage or somewhere until half an hour or so before the assignation. When he got to the grotto, he would have opened the door at the back and smelt gas and promptly closed it again, thinking someone had got there before him.'

'And waited to watch Rhino get his come-uppance?'

'Yes. To be charitable, he may also have intended to warn off Lady Ottaline if she arrived first. He had no quarrel with her, did he?'

'Not as far as I know. But I know very little. If he really meant to release only a small amount of gas, as much as he expected to be enough to burn off Rhino's eyebrows, what made him think Rhino wouldn't smell the gas too soon for his purposes and depart in haste, or at least put out his cigarette? In fact, that seems to me a flaw in the scheme whoever did it, and whatever they hoped for the outcome to be. As far as I know, the door of the hermitage wasn't airtight. A certain amount of gas must have seeped under it.'

'Darling, if you'd seen the way Rhino smoked, you wouldn't wonder. I very much doubt whether he'd had any sense of smell for years.'

CHAPTER 32

'If I tell him, he's bound to complain that it's nothing but hearsay,' Daisy grumbled as she and Alec approached Pritchard's den. 'Why can't you?'

'Because from me it would be at third hand.'

'He'll want to talk to Rita himself, anyway.'

'Yes, but with luck not until tomorrow. You can explain better than I can that she's an extremely reluctant witness, and I doubt he'll have any desire to tackle her at this time of night.'

'Oh, all right.'

The door opened just as Daisy reached for the handle, startling her. Julia came storming out, startled in her turn as she nearly ran into Daisy.

'Oh, the beast!' she cried, tears in her eyes. 'He absolutely refuses to believe me!'

'It's his job to be sceptical, Miss Beaufort.'

'Call me Julia, for heaven's sake, or I'll think you don't believe me, either.'

'I don't.'

'Oh! Well, call me Julia anyway. But I'm telling the truth, and so is Charles.'

'If it's any comfort, I don't actually disbelieve you. I have to keep an open mind.'

'Boyle had Charles's ordnance survey map. He made me look at it and tell him exactly where we went, to see if I agreed with Charles, but I've never had to read one before and I had no idea.'

'You win!' Alec said out of the corner of his mouth to Daisy. 'I'll tell him.' He made a shooing motion.

Daisy took Julia's arm and urged her drawing-roomward. 'Come along, darling, you need a drink.'

'He obviously thinks Charles killed Rhino out of jealousy. I told him Charles had no reason to be jealous because I loathed Rhino and swore I'd never marry him, but he seemed to think Mother could stop me marrying Charles. Did you ever hear anything so Victorian? I wish Mother had decided sooner that she didn't approve of Rhino!'

'So do I,' said Daisy. 'And I can't help wondering why she didn't tell you right away.'

Julia wasn't listening. 'And he said – *soooo* sympathetically – it was quite natural that I'd lie for Charles because I loathed Rhino and was glad to be rid of him. He twists whatever you say to fit his beastly theories.'

They reached the drawing room. Pritchard and Lady Beaufort, on a sofa by the fireplace, were so deep in their conversation that they didn't notice Daisy and Julia's entrance. Charles, Howell, and Gerald sat in reasonable proximity to each other, but not quite in a group, all smoking, all looking slightly uncomfortable. Daisy guessed they had probably been exchanging occasional remarks, probably on the weather, for some time. All three jumped up when she and Julia appeared.

'Drinks?' Howell offered.

'Think I'll go and telephone Lucy's studio, make sure she's arrived safely,' Gerald muttered. 'All right, Howell?'

'Of course, but with the inspector in my uncle's den, you'll have to use the phone in the hall.'

'If Lucy's in the middle of some delicate process, she won't thank you,' Daisy warned.

'She won't answer,' Gerald responded.

Daisy forbore to point out that in that case he wouldn't know whether or not she had arrived safely.

By that time, Julia and Charles had retreated to a far corner of the room.

'Like a drink, Mrs. Fletcher?' Howell said.

'Yes, please.' Daisy almost asked for cocoa, but she didn't know how much longer this dreadful evening was going to last, so she could do with a bracer. 'Julia, too,' she added as they went over to the dresser-bar. 'A brandy and soda, I should think, for both of us. Just a drop of brandy and plenty of soda.'

'I'll give Armitage another whisky.' Howell gave Daisy her drink, poured a small brandy and a hefty shot of whisky into tumblers, and carrying a soda syphon, took them over to the couple.

How long ago Daisy had discussed with him the principle of the syphon! How simple life had seemed then, just a matter of keeping Lucy from insulting their host.

She went to sit in an easy chair on the opposite side of the fireplace from Pritchard and Lady Beaufort. Both looked up to smile at her.

'Got everything you need?' Pritchard asked.

'Yes, thanks.'

They returned immediately to their earnest, low-voiced conversation. Howell came and dropped with a sigh into the chair next to Daisy's. He, too, had a drink, but it was as pale as Daisy's, more something to do with his hands than anything else.

'What a day!' he said. 'I'm afraid you haven't had the pleasant visit my uncle hoped for.'

'I'm just glad it wasn't Lucy and I who brought the scourge upon you. Rhino being the scourge,' she hastened to explain.

'Good lord, we don't hold the Beauforts to blame. My mother was to some degree responsible. Believe me, Uncle Brin is quite capable of having sent him off with a flea in his ear if he wasn't so soft-hearted as to give in to Mother's wish to entertain a real live lord.' He hesitated, and Daisy was desperately trying to think of something kind to say about Mrs. Howell when he continued in a lowered voice, 'You were present when my mother . . . at her outburst, weren't you.'

'Yes. I'm sorry. Having Rhino about the place must have been a great strain on her nerves.'

'She always did dislike the grotto. If you ask me, it was hearing of the use Lord Rydal and Lady Ottaline intended for it, even before the explosion, that sent her over the edge.'

'Some kind of nerve storm, I suppose.' Daisy wasn't very sure what a nerve storm was, but it seemed a tactful thing to say.

'She'll have to see a specialist,' Howell said sombrely. 'Don't you think a rest-cure would be the thing? By the time she gets back, I'll have set up a house for her in Swindon. She may complain at first, but in the end she'll be much happier there. She likes the idea of living in a mansion, but she really prefers town life.'

'I suppose it would be a bit difficult for her to stay on here after what she said about Mr. Pritchard. Will you go and live with her?'

'That would never do! As a matter of fact, I've been making plans to set up my own household for some time now, only I just didn't know how to break it to Mother that I'm going to get married.'

'Married?!' Daisy hoped she sounded more interested than astonished. After all, why shouldn't Owen Howell marry? He was well off, not bad looking, not too old; she had even seriously considered him as a husband for Julia.

'You may well be surprised. My fiancée is getting tired of keeping it secret from Mother.' He followed Daisy's glance at Pritchard. 'Uncle Brin knows. He's met Jeannie. He thinks I should have told Mother ages ago, but ... Oh well, this situation is dreadful but it does make things easier for me in that respect!'

'Your uncle will miss your company.'

'I daresay Jeannie and I will be in and out. They like each other. But in any case, I hope Uncle won't be living here alone for long.' Howell gave a significant look at Pritchard and Lady Beaufort, still in animated conversation.

Once again, Daisy was astonished. 'Good heavens, you think ... ?' Was that why Mrs. Howell had taken against both of them, afraid for her position in the household? 'Well! I did notice right away that they seemed to get on very well together, but – '

'Nothing is settled,' he said hurriedly. 'You won't mention it?'

'Of course not. It would be a very good thing, though, especially if Julia's going to be emigrating to Canada. As long,' she added with foreboding, 'as Boyle doesn't go and arrest both her and Charles.'

Alec found DI Boyle looking pleased with himself.

'I'd lay odds the Canadian did it,' he said, rubbing his hands together. 'I never heard a thinner story in my life, taking off tramping over the hills when there's rain on the way, just to see a bit of an old grass-grown bank. It's not even like this here Barbury Castle is a real castle, you know, with towers and battlements and such.' He started folding the ordnance survey map spread out on the desk.

'Armitage is a historian,' Alec reminded him.

'Armitage! Your good lady hasn't told you, then? His real name's Appsworth,' Boyle said triumphantly.

'Great Scott! Masquerading under an alias.'

'Well, not exactly. Pritchard knew all along, but no one else, not even Miss Beaufort. Or so they say. What I say is, it shows a talent for deception.'

'For what purpose?'

'So's not to cause a lot of rumours about a missing heir come to claim his inheritance. Or so he claims.' Boyle handed the half-folded map to DS Gaskell. 'Here, you deal with this damn thing.' He leant forwards over the desk and stabbed a finger at Alec. 'And when I ask the girl to show me on the map which way they went to get there, to confirm what Appsworth told me, she claims she can't read it.'

'Perhaps she can't. She has lived in France since the War, in rather restricted circumstances, I gather. Besides, some people just have difficulty relating a map to the actual landscape.' Alec's facility in that regard, together with his name, had led to his RFC nickname during the War: Arrow. In his single-seat spotter plane, a fabrication of canvas, balsa wood, and piano wire, he had almost always come back with information about exactly the target he had been sent to observe. But the very fact that his ability to home in on his target like an arrow had resulted in the nickname suggested that many pilots failed to do so.

'You don't believe she's protecting Appsworth?' Boyle snorted. 'Not that I'd blame her, mind, a young lady in love. But it's accessory after at least, if not before. I suppose you'll tell me next you don't believe he blew up Lord Rydal.'

'I have an open mind on the subject. I'm not half so convinced of his motive as you are. He seems to have come to an understanding with Miss Beaufort some time ago. Rydal was an irritant, not a threat. As an irritant, the man spread his net wide.'

'Yes, just about everyone here loathed his guts, servants and all – '

'Speaking of servants, I'd better pass on what one of the housemaids told my wife.'

'Your wife!' Boyle was outraged.

Alec decided to suppress the butler's role in sending Rita to Daisy. 'It happens,' he said apologetically. 'Witnesses see her as a more sympathetic listener than the police, yet they can be sure the information will reach me if necessary.'

'If Mrs. Fletcher considers it necessary,' the inspector growled.

'Yes. Unsatisfactory, I know, but I've learnt there's really nothing to be done about it, short of ignoring what she tells me. If she refuses to listen, the chances are they won't be coming to spill the beans to me themselves, or else they'll waste my time with completely irrelevant waffle.'

'All right, what did this maid have to say?'

Alec related Gregg's threat. The inspector came to the same conclusion as Daisy – though Alec didn't tell him so: The chauffeur might have stayed to see Rydal suffer, but was not likely to have set things in motion.

'He was hanging about the servants' quarters till after one o'clock,' he said. 'You haven't seen their evidence about times yet, have you. Here, see what you make of it all.' He passed Alec a handful of papers, but didn't give him a chance to study them. 'I don't think it was Gregg. You don't think it was Appsworth. Who does that leave us? Lady Ottaline and Mrs. Howell. Explosions – that's not a woman's crime, to my way of thinking. You mark my words, Appsworth is our man.'

'You've no proof, I take it.'

'Not a smidgen. Nor I don't see how I'm ever going to get any, not what you might call solid evidence.'

'What's your next move?'

'My next move? Not to say *move*, but you and me and Sergeant Gaskell here are going to make sure we've all of us got all the information, seeing we've been working separately. Then Sergeant Gaskell is going to drive me home, and on the way we're going to have a bit of a think and a bit of a chat. I hope you'll have a think, too. I daresay you'll have a chat with your missus. I'd rather you didn't, but I can't stop you. Tomorrow I'm going to let them all stew in their own juice for a few hours. First thing in the morning, I'm coming back with every man I can muster and search the hole and what's left of the grotto.'

'I hope it'll have stopped raining by then. It's going to be a hell of a job even if it's not pouring. You're looking for the gas taps, are you?'

'If we can find 'em all and see how many were turned on, it might – might, mind you – narrow down the time.'

'Did you test the ones we found for dabs?'

'Not yet. As a matter of fact,' Boyle said sheepishly, 'Thomkin seems to have gone off with it in his pocket. How he can have failed to notice it . . . !'

'I expect Lucy – Lady Gerald was rushing him.'

'Do you really think fingerprints would tell us anything? We know they were all in there at one time or another.'

'Except Mrs. Howell, I believe. Hers would be definitive. It seems to me unlikely that anyone other than Pritchard, Howell, or Appsworth would touch the taps in the ordinary way of things.'

'So Appsworth's wouldn't amount to proof.'

'If they were smudged?' Gaskell contributed his first mite. 'Meaning someone else touched them after he did.'

'Or he did it wearing gloves to mislead us,' the inspector pointed out. 'Let's wait and see what we've got before we start speculating. I hope Lady Gerald gets a move on bringing back my only concrete clue, my sergeant, her photographs, and that young man who did a bunk.'

'Yes,' said Alec thoughtfully, 'I'd like a word with Carlin. I can't help feeling we're missing something somewhere.'

CHAPTER 33

Considering all that had happened at Appsworth Hall on Saturday, Sunday breakfast was amazingly normal. Daisy was surprised, however, that both Mrs. Howell and Lady Ottaline, both of whom usually breakfasted in their rooms, came down to join the rest, as did Lady Beaufort.

Mrs. Howell was very subdued and avoided meeting anyone's eyes. She was all in black, not – it transpired – in mourning for her deceased noble guest, but for Chapel. Her son and Pritchard wore black suits for the same reason.

'I'll go with Winifred and Owen,' Pritchard said to Lady Beaufort. He didn't seem to hold any grudge against his sister-in-law. 'Madison will be waiting to drive you down to the village to Church when you're ready.'

'Thank you.' She beamed at him. 'Daisy, you'll come with us, won't you?'

'Er, I think not, Lady Beaufort. I have to make a fair copy of some notes I took yesterday. Besides, I'd better be here when Lucy gets back, in case . . . um . . . in case she needs my help explaining her photographs to the inspector.' Not for the world would Daisy miss Boyle's reaction to a certain one among the photos.

Lady Beaufort seemed a little puzzled, and Alec gave Daisy a suspicious look. Julia and Charles, knowing just what she was referring to, exchanged a glance. Daisy smiled at them all sunnily and spread marmalade on another piece of toast.

Outside the sun was peeping through the last ragged remnants of the storm. A beautiful day for a walk, and Daisy was keen to inspect the damage to the grotto – not the bit that had caved in on Rhino, but the entrance. She decided that would be pushing Inspector Boyle too far. He was searching it this morning, she vaguely remembered Alec telling her when at last he came to bed last night. She had been half asleep.

What on earth did he hope to find there?

Her thoughts returned to the present as Julia said, 'I'm glad you've recovered so quickly, Lady Ottaline. You've really been in the wars the last couple of days.'

'I'm not an old crock yet!' Lady Ottaline snapped. Then she pulled herself together and said with a strained smile, 'Sorry. I'm nervy and I ache all over but the doctor said there's nothing very wrong and if I stay in bed too long I'll stiffen up like a board.'

'Did he really?' said Daisy. 'I wouldn't have thought he was capable of stringing so many words together.'

'He succeeded in conveying his meaning in two or three brief phrases. I gather you and Miss Beaufort rescued me from my second mishap, Mrs. Fletcher.'

'Not really, did we, Julia? Charles carried you halfway. When he met us, he left you with us and went back to help Alec and Gerald. We were expecting servants to come along after us, you see. But you were getting awfully chilly, and we were just wondering whether we'd be able to carry you between us when Madison arrived. So he carried you till we met the gardeners, then he handed you over to one of the gardener's boys. Fred was his name, wasn't it, Julia?'

Julia laughed. 'No, that was what Madison called him, and the head gardener got shirty about the chauffeur giving his lads orders, remember? The one who actually carried you to the house, Lady Ottaline, was Billy.'

'I seem to have been passed round like a parcel. You'd better hand out a few hefty tips, Des.'

Sir Desmond grunted. He looked, if anything, less well than his wife, as if he had spent a sleepless night. It didn't seem to have affected his appetite, however, and what little he said was as suave as ever.

Neither he nor Lady Ottaline made any mention of church-going, but Charles said he would join the ladies. At once Gerald looked up from the heaped plateful he was methodically demolishing, and caught Alec's eye.

'I'll accompany you, if I may, Lady Beaufort,' Gerald said. 'It's been a while, I'm afraid. You won't mind guiding me through the Prayer Book. I bet I remember the hymns, though. Had them thoroughly drummed into us at school.'

Daisy guessed that Alec had asked him to keep an eye on any suspects who left Appsworth – which meant Charles was still on the list, alas. She wondered about the chapel-goers. She was pretty sure Pritchard and Howell were in the clear. Perhaps Alec had asked Pritchard to make sure Mrs. Howell didn't flit. He might not hold a grudge, but he had no cause to love his sister-in-law. In any case, her chances of getting far under her own steam appeared slight.

In fact, she was such a wishy-washy person, Daisy simply couldn't believe she had the gumption to blow up the blasphemous grotto, with or without the immoral Rhino and his mistress in it. Her outburst against Pritchard, if not a fit of madness, had been more spite than a deliberate attempt to implicate him.

People dispersed. Daisy felt she ought to have a go at the few notes she had made for Boyle, having given them as an excuse for skipping church. She had been too tired to tackle them last night. She took her notebook to the library, where she sat and stared at the hieroglyphics. Her mind was elsewhere. She had a familiar feeling she was missing something vital, some clue, some observed quirk of character or behaviour, that would change the picture entirely. The more she sought it, the more elusive it became.

Alec came in. 'I'm going over to the diggings, love, the place where the hillside collapsed, to see if Boyle's found anything. Want to come?'

'Seriously? Don't you think he'll throw a fit if I turn up?'

'He can't stop you going for a walk. He can keep you at a certain distance, and of course he doesn't have to tell you anything. Or if he makes you shake in your shoes, you could hide behind a tree – '

'Darling, honestly! I'm not *afraid* of the man. I just don't want to queer your pitch. But I'd like to come. I was thinking earlier that it's a beautiful day for a walk.'

'Let's go, then.'

They went out by the terrace. As they crossed the paving stones, Daisy's nagging sense that she was forgetting something returned.

'Your forehead's all wrinkled,' Alec said. 'Better hope the wind doesn't change. What is it?'

'That's the trouble, I don't know. I'm sure I do know something helpful, something important, but what it is . . .' She shrugged helplessly.

'You, too? It's far more likely to be valid in your case than mine, though. You've known these people longer than I have, and you were here yesterday morning.'

'Yes, but you know much more than I do about what they claim they were doing, and what they say about each other. I missed lots of it.'

'I told you pretty much everything last night.'

'I was half asleep, darling. Suppose you start again from the beginning now. Perhaps it will spark an idea in one or t'other of us.'

Alec sighed but obliged. In general, he was much more obliging in this investigation, which wasn't his own case, than when she 'meddled' in an affair for which he was responsible.

'That's the lot, I think,' he ended. 'Why don't you give me your views of all the people involved and their relationships with Rydal? Come to think of it, I missed a lot of it the first time round. When you were telling Boyle, I was trying to wash the chalk out of my hair.'

'Right-oh. As long as you're not going to make a fuss if I go round in circles a bit. Relationships simply can't be described in a straight line.'

'Make it as straight as you can, Daisy. We'll be there in five minutes.'

They had started on the path to the grotto but taken a branch to the right well before reaching the bridge. It climbed more steeply than the other, without any steps to aid the ascent. Now they came to a drystone wall with a stile made of flat stones sticking out. Alec gave Daisy a hand over, but she managed to catch one stocking all the same.

'I'm going to start wearing trousers for country walks,' she said, regarding the ladder with disgust. 'I don't care who thinks they're improper.'

On the far side of the stile, the path was no more than a sheep-track across the short, wiry grass of the slope. No sheep were in sight. Doubtless they had made themselves scarce because of the thumps and shouts coming from the excavations, ahead and uphill.

Daisy talked faster and faster and increasingly breath-lessly. They stopped for a couple of minutes before they reached the site so that she could finish the story of the night outing and mass ducking, which she hadn't got round to describing to Boyle.

Then they had to wait a couple more minutes for Alec to recover his gravitas.

'It's all very well laughing,' Daisy said severely, 'but I wouldn't be surprised if Lady Ottaline was pushed, by either Rhino or Sir Desmond. Lucy's inclined to think that Rhino might have been pushed, by either Sir Desmond or Julia. Of course, by the time he went in they knew it wasn't really dangerous,' she added. 'Charles – unless it was Carlin – called up that the water wasn't very deep, just enough to break the fall.'

'No water in the stream-bed now,' said Alec.

'No. But darling, that makes me think – '

'Tell me later. I want to know whether Boyle's chaps have found those gas taps.' He set off over the last rise.

Daisy followed. In her view, her sudden insight made it virtually impossible that Charles had caused the explosion. If only she could be sanguine that Alec and the inspector would be equally convinced.

She caught up as Alec called down into the dell, 'Any luck, Inspector?'

Boyle yelled back. 'All but one tap, and the chauffeur's bowler.' He climbed the steep, tumbled slope towards them, leaving eight or ten men behind him at the bottom.

The hole in the ground wasn't very large or very deep. About as deep as the hermit's room had been high, Daisy supposed. 'Not so deep as a well, nor so wide as a church-door' – a cathedral door, anyway – but it had served to kill Rhino.

'How could anyone have known the roof wasn't too thick to fail?'

'If the blast had been contained,' Alec said, 'it would have been much stronger. That alone could well have done for Rydal. As for who could have foreseen the actual effects of the explosion, as far as I can make out most of it seems to have been sheer guesswork.'

'That's what I . . .' But Alec had turned away to give Boyle a hand over the rim of the crater.

'Morning, Mrs. Fletcher. All but one,' the inspector repeated to Alec. He was lightly dusted with white, but didn't look as if he'd played an intimate part in the digging. 'Two large, the fireplace and the water-heater, presumably, and two small, two of the three lights. They're all turned on, so the third light probably was, too. We'll have to consult Pritchard and Howell, but we can assume that narrows the time period we have to consider.'

'Good work! The hat's not going to help us much, as we know Gregg was there.'

'No, only if it'd been in the back room, which it wasn't.' He gestured. 'Over there it was, which I reckon to be the middle part, where you found him. We're not likely to find anything more. A proper mess it is. We can't turn over every lump of chalk or limestone or whatever the muck is, hoping it's just a coating on something of interest. The rain last night washed a lot of it off the brass taps and copper tubing and they shone in the sun, is the only reason we found them. Did you talk to Gregg, sir?'

'Yes. Sullen, but of course he can't deny having been there. He swears he just wanted to embarrass Rydal by bursting in on him and his lady-friend. In any case, intending blackmail isn't a crime, and he didn't have a chance to commit it.'

'I can't see how anyone could have proposed to blackmail Rhino,' Daisy said, 'when what he was up to was known to everyone at Appsworth Hall and half the population of London.'

'That's a point, Mrs. Fletcher, though villains are often much stupider than you might expect.'

'It's hardly fair to call Gregg a villain,' Daisy protested. 'To all appearances he was a perfectly blameless manservant. I wouldn't blame him for talking about blowing off Rhino's eyebrows – '

'But the only way we'll prove he went further than talk is if his dabs are on the gas taps.' Boyle looked down at a figure who was toiling upwards, a canvas bag in one hand, and called, 'Got those safe, Gaskell?'

'Yes, sir,' the sergeant said hoarsely, and coughed to clear his throat. Clad in a bulky overall, he was caked with grey-white soil.

While they waited for him, Daisy made another attempt to share her revelation. 'Alec, you said no one could have been sure what would happen when Rhino walked into the hermitage with a lit cigarette. It was sheer guesswork.'

'Yes, but with all the taps turned on, it was liable to be pretty drastic. A fire if not an explosion.'

'But don't you see, it was just a guess that he would arrive before Lady Ottaline. Or rather, no one could know who would arrive first. She smoked quite a bit, too. It was odds on that she'd have a cigarette burning. That means – it *has* to mean – that the person responsible didn't care if *she* was blown up, instead, or as well.'

'That's what it was!' Alec exclaimed. 'I knew something was out of key.'

Boyle frowned. 'Unless she did it herself.'

'I wouldn't put it past her,' Daisy agreed, 'but don't you see, the important thing is that Charles Arm – Appsworth had absolutely no motive for doing away with her. If anything, he had cause for gratitude to her for taking Rhino away from Julia. It's inconceivable that he'd risk killing her by chance.'

'It does seem highly unlikely,' Alec agreed.

Boyle's frown deepened. 'What we don't know is whether they'd arranged it that way, that he'd arrive first to warm the place up, say. It wouldn't have been cosy. The servants were asked who knew about the meeting and when, not whether they knew or discussed the details of Rydal and Lady Ottaline's plans. Maybe Appsworth found out she was going to follow him later. Gaskell!' He turned to the sergeant as the latter reached the top, huffing and puffing.

'All safe and secure, sir,' he gasped, patting the canvas bag.

'Get everyone out of there and out of their overalls. There's no point going on mucking about here. We've got work to do back at the house.'

'You'd better hop it, Daisy,' said Alec, 'if you don't want to find yourself surrounded by large, dirty men undressing. You're right about Lady Ottaline. We should have thought of that. But Boyle is right, too. We've got some questions to ask.'

At least Alec hadn't already decided that Charles was guilty, Daisy thought mournfully as she made her way back down the hill, hitching up her skirt to scramble over the stile. Unfortunately, Boyle still seemed to be keen to arrest him. She hadn't much hope of being able to prove him innocent. If only he and Julia hadn't decided to go for a walk just then!

CHAPTER 34

Walking through the gardens, admiring the daffodils nodding in the sunshine, Daisy noticed that the grass round them had been recently mowed. Not today, Sunday, a day of rest; not yesterday afternoon, when it was raining and in any case all the gardeners were busy digging up Rhino; it must have been done yesterday morning.

Surely DI Boyle must have asked the gardeners whether they had seen anyone? Yet all Daisy had heard about was the information garnered in the servants' hall. She knew she had missed a fair bit of what was going on, partly just because she hadn't been present, partly because of the innate tendency of the police to keep things to themselves. But *had* Boyle questioned the gardeners?

He had arrived late on the scene and had been very busy all evening. With Alec involved informally, there was no clear line of command, no coordinating strategy (or did she mean tactics?). The more Daisy thought about it, the more likely it seemed that the gardeners had been overlooked.

After a glance at her shoes, she went into the house by the side door. When she reached the hall, Barker was coming out of the drawing room. He looked irritable, though his face smoothed into his customary blandness the instant he caught sight of Daisy.

'What's the trouble?' she asked.

'Trouble, madam?'

'Come on, tell me. You never know, perhaps I can help. The household must be all at sixes and sevens, and I'm afraid it's going to get worse. Inspector Boyle's got another round of questions for the servants.'

The butler went so far as to utter a groan – not a loud one, but definitely a groan. 'I beg your pardon, madam. I must confess, I am a trifle put out. It's not what one is accustomed to. My immediate difficulty is – er – one of Mr. Pritchard's guests. He desires a drink before luncheon, very much before luncheon, and, to tell the truth, more than one drink. Yet being a gentleman, he refuses to help himself to his host's spirits. This is the second time he has summoned me from duties which are pressing.'

'Sir Desmond's intent on getting blotto?'

'Such would not be an inaccurate way of putting it, madam.'

'Well, I'm sorry if I led you to expect my assistance, but I'm not prepared to help him on his way. Barker, do you happen to know whether the coppers had a go at the gardeners last night?'

'I cannot say for certain, madam, since in normal times they come to the house only to bring garden stuff to the kitchens. However, I doubt it. I believe the man Boyle arrived after Mr. Simmons's assistant and the two boys went home to the village. Mr. Simmons himself has a cottage over near the greenhouses. I cannot speak for him.'

'Of course not, but you can direct me to the cottage, if you'd be so kind.'

Barker obliged. 'Will that be all, madam?'

'Yes, thanks. Barker, I don't want to appear to try to teach you your job, but if I were you, I'd fail to hear the bell next time Sir Desmond rings. Either he'll pour for himself, or he won't, which would on the whole be a good thing, don't you think? Is Lady Ottaline with him?'

'No, madam. I believe her ladyship is writing letters in her room. Goodness knows,' he added gloomily, 'what she's saying about Appsworth Hall.'

'Goodness only knows!' Daisy agreed.

The butler hurried off. Daisy turned towards the door by which she had come in, then changed her mind and headed for the front door. If Alec had been about, she would naturally have pointed out the necessity for questioning the gardeners. But he was unavailable, no doubt tramping down from the hill with Boyle and his crew. If she went out the back way, she might meet them heading for the servants' entrance. Boyle would not be happy, she told herself, to have it pointed out to him in front of his men that he'd overlooked several possibly vital witnesses.

She was doing him a favour, avoiding him.

The gardener's cottage was easy to find but hard to see, being overgrown by a huge wisteria already in full bloom on the south-facing wall. Daisy ducked under the drooping purple clusters, still dripping with rain, and knocked on the door. It was opened by a thin, spry, elderly woman enveloped in an apron as thoroughly as the wisteria enveloped her house, and equally flowery.

'Mrs. Simmons? I'm Mrs. Fletcher, a guest of Mr. Pritchard. I'm hoping for a word with your husband.'

'Simmons is out the back, madam, staking some of his

blessed p'rennials, but I'll get him in in a trice. It's a labour of love with him, you see, all the same if he's working for the master or himself. Come in, do, madam, if you don't mind me getting on with the pudding for his dinner. It don't do to let it sit once you've beat in the eggs, that's what I say. Best to get it into a hot oven quick as – '

'I don't want to disturb you,' Daisy broke into the flow of words. 'Suppose I go round the side and find Mr. Simmons.'

'Well, you could,' Mrs. Simmons said doubtfully, 'but the path's overgrown something dreadful with them blessed flowers. Won't trim 'em till they finish blooming, he won't, and that won't be till – '

'That's all right. I'll manage. Thank you!'

No Sunday best for Simmons. He was wearing an ancient tweed jacket of indeterminate hue, with sagging pockets, and moleskin trousers tied at the knees with the same twine he was using to stake his plants. He looked round as Daisy pushed open a creaky gate.

His garden was crammed with colour. Spring bulbs – daffodils, narcissus, iris, hyacinths pink, white, blue, and yellow – vied with polyanthus and nodding columbines, violets and pot marigolds. Even the surrounding fences were starred with clematis. To an artistic eye, Daisy thought, it probably was a horrendous hodge-podge, but she didn't claim to have an artistic eye so she was allowed to enjoy it.

She introduced herself. 'I expect you know my husband is helping Detective Inspector Boyle with the investigation. I have a question for you.' The truth and nothing but the truth, if not exactly the whole truth. She took out her notebook to make herself look more official. 'Were you or any of your staff working in the gardens behind the house yesterday morning?'

'Yes, madam.'

'Who? All of you?'

'No, madam. Just young Billy, the lad you took to carry that ladyship to the house.' He sounded as if he still resented her endorsement of the chauffeur's illegitimate order to the gardener's boy.

'He mowed the grass round the daffodils?'

'Yes, madam. He's good with a scythe, and I told him I'd use it on his ears if any of the daffs got cut down.'

'Did he mention seeing anyone while he was working?'

'Not to me. He'd no business looking about him, nor doing aught else but concentrate on his work.'

'Mr. Boyle's going to want to talk to him. Where is he to be found today?'

'I can't speak for what he may be up to on his day off, but he lives with his parents in the village.'

Daisy wrote down the address, thanked Simmons, and headed back to the house. Three factors made her decide against going in search of Billy. First and least important was Boyle's ire. He would already be annoyed with her, and a little extra annoyance wouldn't hurt either him or her. Second was that she didn't know how long a walk it was to the village. It hadn't seemed far when she and Lucy drove through it on the way to the Hall, but Lucy's speed made apparent distances deceptive.

The third difficulty was decisive. She remembered being unable to understand more than one word in three of Billy's Wiltshire dialect. A fat lot of use it would be to question him if his answers were incomprehensible to her. One of the local police would manage better.

By the time Daisy had finished with the police, receiving a little grudging gratitude along with the expected telling off, the Church-goers had returned. She joined them in the drawing room. Lady Beaufort was talking to Sir Desmond, who looked as if he wasn't hearing a word. Daisy wondered whether he had started helping himself from the bar when Barker quit answering the bell.

Gerald left Julia and Charles and came over as Daisy entered. 'Lucy sent a wire,' he told her. 'She's expecting to get here shortly after two. She says, "watchdog collared bureaucrat." Telegraphese! What's she talking about?'

'The inspector sent a sergeant with her, didn't you know? He's the watchdog. His original purpose was to stop her flitting to the Continent, but when Boyle heard about Carlin, he told whatsisname – DS Thomkin – to get hold of him and bring him back.'

'Carlin? That's Wandersley's secretary?'

'Yes. He left from Swindon to go and play in a golf tournament. As he must have heard what happened here before he caught the train, Boyle is understandably unhappy.'

Carlin. Daisy didn't imagine for a moment that he had blown up Rhino, but he had some connection with whatever it was she was trying to recall. Something he'd said? Something he had done?

'I hope Lucy's photos cheer him up,' Gerald interrupted her thoughts.

'I shouldn't think so. I don't see how they can help him

much. One of them, if she really intends to show it to him, if it doesn't make him laugh – well, there'll be another explosion. I wonder if it worked. I can't wait to see.'

'Daisy, what are you talking about? It's not something he could arrest her for?'

'Blue? No, not at all. How could you think such a thing! Feelthy pictures are not at all Lucy's style.'

Gerald laughed. 'Oh, you know Lucy. Always experimenting. I live in dread.'

The arrival of the Chapel party put an end to the topic. Pritchard and Howell started to dispense drinks. Sir Desmond perked up.

Barker came in. In his discreet butlerian undertone, he said something to Mrs. Howell that sent her scurrying out of the room, her lips pursed. A night's sedated sleep seemed to have calmed her *crise de nerfs*. At least she wasn't foaming at the mouth.

Barker next spoke to Pritchard, and then came over to Daisy. 'Mr. Fletcher desired me to inform you, madam, that he will be lunching with Boyle. I understand they have much to discuss.'

'Thank you, Barker. Bother!' she said to Julia as the butler bowed and turned away. 'I wonder what . . . ? I suppose I'd better not go and try to find out now.'

'I wouldn't. But I'm a suspect, not an amateur detective.'

'Darling, I'm just trying to work out what really happened. I know you and Charles weren't involved, so the sooner we nail whoever did it, the better.'

Pritchard came over to see if they wanted their drinks topped up. 'Barker let you know your husband won't be eating with us?' he asked Daisy. 'I told him to give them the same as we're having, but he said they requested sandwiches.'

'Easier to eat at the desk,' Daisy explained.

Lady Ottaline came down last, alarmingly bright-eyed and bursting with energy.

'I hope I'm half as merry and gay when I'm as old as she is,' Julia whispered to Daisy. 'How does she do it, after what she's been through?'

'Some kind of pills, I expect, or cocaine.'

'No, surely . . . !'

'It wouldn't surprise me. Don't tell anyone I said so, even Charles.'

Mrs. Howell rushed back into the room, her face now a mask of tragedy. 'The police are pestering the servants again! Brin, how can you allow it? Right before lunchtime! I dread to think what the meal will be like.'

'Perhaps Alec's the lucky one,' said Daisy.

The soup was too salty. The beef was like boot-soles, the roast potatoes limp, the gravy lumpy, the carrots bullet-hard, the brussels sprouts grey mush. The Yorkshire pudding had gone flat and was burnt round the edges. Remembering Mrs. Simmons, Daisy was prepared to bet her pudding had turned out beautifully and wished she'd invited herself to the Simmonses' midday dinner. Mrs. Howell wrung her hands while everyone else tried to pretend the food was edible, though Lady Ottaline didn't eat a single morsel.

They were sitting pushing soggy jam roll round their plates when Lucy sauntered in.

'Hello, all,' she drawled. 'Do you mind if I abstract Daisy, Mrs. Howell? I need her support to face the massed constabulary.'

'Lady Gerald! Have you eaten? I'll have something – '

'We stopped for a bite on the way, thanks.'

'You're early, Lucy,' said Gerald.

She smiled. 'Darling, the time I told you was based on the fact that Sergeant Thomkin refused to let me drive back.'

Gerald was aghast. 'You let him drive my car?'

'No, I thought you'd prefer Carlin at the wheel. He treated your car with tender care, but poor Thomkin! He must have assumed a civil servant would drive sedately. Carlin's time wasn't much slower than mine.'

'Young Carlin?' Sir Desmond frowned. 'What the deuce is he doing back here? You brought him, Lady Gerald?'

'Depending on how you look at it, I brought him, he brought me, or the police brought both of us. He's talking to Alec and the Boyle man now.'

Sir Desmond looked confused, as well he might. Lucy's oracular explanation on top of his libations – he had done well by the wine with lunch – was enough to confuse anyone. 'Boyle – the inspector? I haven't spoken to him. Fletcher asked me a few questions.'

'Much more fun, darling,' said Lady Ottaline with a coy, girlish giggle.

'If you ask me,' Daisy whispered fiercely as Lucy tugged her from the room, 'it's a pity she didn't go up with Rhino.'

'Don't take any notice of the poor old thing, darling.'

'If she goes round saying that sort of thing, it could ruin Alec's career.'

'Bosh, no one pays her any attention.'

'Lucy, does she take drugs?'

'I should think so. Lots of people do. How else could she

keep up such a killing pace? Come on, Boyle is panting for my pictures.'

'Did your experiment work?'

'*À merveille*. Wait till you see it. They're all pretty good. There are three I'd like to use for the book, if they go forward with it, and three or four that should do for your article.'

They reached the door of Pritchard's den. Daisy put her finger to her lips, Lucy nodded, and quietly they went in.

CHAPTER 35

To Daisy's disappointment, as she and Lucy entered the den, Boyle was saying, 'Thank you for your help, Mr. Carlin. Not that it helps much, but that's not your fault, I suppose.'

'I can't see why you had to drag me all the way back, make me miss the tournament, for that! My partner's furious.'

Daisy had missed hearing his evidence, but the sound of his voice brought back to her the last time she had heard it, at breakfast the day before. Surely he couldn't have told everything, or Boyle wouldn't have been so disappointed. Unless he had already heard from someone else? But in that case he should be glad of confirmation.

Daisy decided she'd better wait until Carlin left the room before she cast doubt on the completeness of his answers to Boyle's questions.

'I suppose I can leave now, after this totally unnecessary journey,' Carlin said sulkily.

'I'd prefer that you not leave Appsworth, sir,' the inspector said. 'And I'd be obliged if you'd stay just now and give us a hand. Good timing, ladies. Let's have a look at these photographs.'

DS Thomkin went to Pritchard's blueprint drawers and took out a large sheet printed with what turned out to be a ground-plan of the grotto's three caves. Boyle picked up a large manila envelope and opened it as the sergeant spread the plan on the desk.

'Here, let me,' said Lucy, reaching for the envelope. She took out a sheaf of photos. 'You said you wanted to see all of them, didn't you?'

'I did.'

Alec pulled his chair closer.

'These first few are of the front of the house.' Lucy spread them before Boyle, who pushed them aside with a grunt of irritation. 'All right, here's the stream.'

'Now dried up,' said Daisy.

The inspector contradicted her. 'Not any more it's not. There's a fair trickle in it. All that rain last night, it broke through again. The stream, that's another thing I want to talk to you about, Lady Gerald, but let's see the rest of the pictures first.'

Lucy laid out several shots of the grotto entrance from outside. Boyle glanced at them, but it was the interior he was interested in. He had Lucy, Daisy, and Carlin try to place the location of each photo, one by one, on the plan. They had a few disagreements.

'We'd better get Pritchard or Howell for this,' Alec suggested, 'or even Appsworth – '

'Appsworth?' said Lucy and Carlin together.

'Armitage,' Daisy enlightened them. 'It turns out he's really Charles Appsworth.'

'Really!' Lucy was sceptical. 'The long lost heir, I suppose.'

'No, he's – '

'Please, ladies! Mrs. Fletcher, you can explain later. Lady Gerald, you haven't got people in these photos, except the ones of the entrance, where he's too small to identify.'

'Oh, that's Armit – Appsworth. For that sort of shot one wants a figure to show the scale. The others, well, I wasn't taking holiday snaps, you know.'

'So I – Strewth!' The inspector had reached the last of the grotto pictures.

Lucy's ghost had come out beautifully. The white statue of St. Vincent Ferrer, cowled, marble flame in hand, was distinct against a dim background. At his shoulder stood a doppelganger, a murky, blurred figure, but definitely another monk.

'Very nice, Lucy,' said Alec dryly.

'Do you think I can sell it to the Society for Psychical Research?'

'Probably. Who is it?'

'Appsworth again. Wouldn't you expect him to haunt his ancestral home?'

'Very good at play-acting, that young man,' Boyle growled.

'Not really, inspector.' Daisy was well aware of the natural distrust of the police for acting ability. 'Lucy told him exactly what to do, and with that robe and hood to hide inside, anyone could have done it. You'll have noticed that the statue is of a Catholic monk. He's the patron saint of plumbers. That's what got Mrs. Howell carrying on about Papism.'

'And the others are heathen idolatry.' He shuffled through the images of gods, goddesses, and half-clad nymphs. 'Thank you, Lady Gerald. Now, while I have the three of you here, what's this Mr. Fletcher tells me about people being pushed into the stream?'

'Pushed!' Carlin exclaimed, startled. 'Lady Ottaline fell in. She was wearing high-heeled shoes, completely inappropriate for the path. Mrs. Fletcher turned her ankle earlier in spite of wearing walking shoes.'

'Mr. Carlin was the first to jump in to rescue her,' Lucy said. 'Quite the hero.'

Carlin flushed at her mocking tone. 'Nothing heroic about it. The water was only four foot deep or so.'

'But you didn't know that,' said Daisy, 'and it was dark.'

'And you might have landed on top of her, for all you could see,' Lucy pointed out.

'I was careful to jump in upstream of where she fell,' he said indignantly.

'Charles – Mr. Appsworth – was ahead of us,' Daisy went on, 'already past the corner. He heard Lady Ottaline scream and ran back, and he was the second to jump.'

'A positive multitude of heroes. There stood Rhino on the brink, pretending to take off his coat, with Julia on one side of him and Wandersley on the other. Nothing will persuade me that *he* wasn't pushed.'

'Would you agree, Mrs. Fletcher?' Boyle asked.

'I'd agree that he wasn't at all keen to go in. He was so slow that Julia made some remark about his being too elderly for such exploits. He did take his coat off then, and next moment down he flew. He could have decided he'd better show willing after such a comment from the woman he loved.'

'Much more likely Sir Desmond pushed him,' Lucy insisted.

'You believe Lady Ottaline was also pushed?'

'For heaven's sake, Inspector, I don't know! Perhaps it was

her shoes. But considering she was with her cuckolded husband and the lover who wanted to ditch her – well, perhaps one of them succeeded.'

'Succeeded?'

'Ditched her.' Lucy was so pleased with her pun that she actually asked Boyle's permission to go to the grotto. 'I brought some more plates and I'd like to get a couple of shots of it the way it is now. Not for any particular purpose, more for my records. For the history books.'

Boyle glanced at Alec, who shrugged.

'I suppose . . .' The inspector paused. 'Yes, why not? Don't go up there alone, though, please. Take someone with you in case of accidents.'

'Daisy?'

'Of course, darling, but not right now.'

'I'll go with you, Lady Gerald,' Carlin offered, nobly in view of her sarcastic comments on his heroism.

'Right-oh. I expect Gerald will, too. We'll wait for you, Daisy, if you're not too long.'

'Just a couple of minutes. Get my coat for me, will you?'

Lucy and Carlin departed.

'What now, Daisy?' Alec asked.

'You have information for us, Mrs. Fletcher? About Carlin?'

'Yes. He may have told you already . . .'

'Never mind. At worst you can confirm his statement.'

Her pointing out of the overlooked gardeners seemed to have raised her in Boyle's estimation. 'Well, first, it's something he said at breakfast. Howell was complaining because Sir Desmond hadn't come down yet, thus delaying their business in Swindon. Carlin said something – I can't remember his exact words, I'm afraid – about it being no use trying to hurry him, because he always went for a stroll after breakfast for the sake of his digestion. If he missed it he got dyspepsia and became thoroughly disagreeable.'

Boyle perked up. 'Sir Desmond always took a walk after breakfast?' He exchanged a look with Alec.

'So Carlin claimed. Howell could confirm that he said so, I'm sure, because it annoyed him. Julia and Charles were there, too, I'm pretty sure, though whether they were listening is another matter.'

'Do you know whether Wandersley actually did go out for a walk?' Alec asked.

''Fraid not. Shortly after he came down at last, Lucy and I left. That was just after the second thing I thought I ought to make sure you know. Carlin was the butt of one of Rhino's sneering insults and departed in a huff.'

'Well, now, he didn't happen to mention that, either, Mrs. Fletcher.'

'In exchange, I hope you're going to tell me whether Billy saw anyone in the gardens.'

Alec smiled. 'He saw Julia and Appsworth making off over the hills, in the direction of the area of the later explosion. They didn't go anywhere near the grotto's entrance.'

'Thank heaven! Anyone else?'

Boyle regarded her for a moment, his face expressionless. Then he said, 'Billy saw someone going towards the grotto. He only caught a brief glimpse, between bushes or hedges or whatever, because he'd come to a tricky bit of mowing and had to watch his scythe. He didn't recognise the person.'

'Man or woman?'

'I've told you all I'm going to, Mrs. Fletcher, and probably more than I ought. You've been very helpful. Have you got any more questions, Mr. Fletcher?'

'Just one. Let me make sure I've got it straight who was in the breakfast room when you and Lucy left. Howell, Rydal, Wandersley – anyone else? Pritchard?'

'No, he went off earlier. Carlin left just ahead of us, and Howell was close behind him, I think. Julia and Charles were still there, if I remember correctly. Yes, they must have been, because Julia told Rhino he was appallingly vulgar. Can you believe it, he said she must be thinking of someone else and he started blethering about his quarterings!' Seeing Boyle looking blank, she explained, 'The bits of an escutcheon – a family's coat of arms – that show which noble families they've married into. He said with pride that the Earls of Rydal hadn't married a commoner in centuries, which, come to think of it, was a sort of backhanded insult to Julia.'

'He insulted everybody,' said Boyle, 'but insults just rolled off his back.'

'Exactly. Small wonder he got blown up! I wonder if anyone will truly mourn him. What has he got in the way of family? Perhaps he's another person at home, kind to dogs, children, and his aged mother.'

This flight of fancy alarmed the inspector. 'He has an aged mother? We haven't done anything about informing next of kin. It's impossible to get hold of lawyers on a Sunday, even if we knew who his lawyer was.'

'I haven't the foggiest about his mother. I can't imagine him having anything so normal as parents or brothers and sisters, which may sound unkind but you didn't know him until he was dead. Mr. Pritchard probably doesn't run to a

Peerage. Mrs. Howell might possibly pore over one in the solitude of her room. Lucy probably knows, though she'll never be as omniscient as her Great-aunt Eva.'

'I'll ask Lady Gerald later,' said Boyle impatiently. 'If you've no further revelations for us . . .'

'None that come immediately to mind. May I tell Miss Beaufort and Mr. Appsworth that Billy's saved their skins?'

The inspector shrugged. 'If you want. Don't tell anyone else, though, and tell them to keep quiet about it.'

'Right-oh.' Daisy blew a kiss at Alec and whisked out of the room.

In the drawing room, she found Lucy, Carlin, and Gerald only waiting for her arrival to go out. So were Julia and Charles, who had decided to join them for a breath of air. Lady Ottaline wanted to go, too.

'I'd have thought you'd had enough of that place,' Sir Desmond said, sounding bored. 'Not to mention that you ought to take it easy till you're fully recovered.'

'Do stop fussing, Des, I'm perfectly all right. I might get an inhibition about grottoes if I don't go. I can tell you, though, I shan't smoke in there.' Waving her cigarette holder, she said to the hovering butler, 'Barker, have my maid bring down my coat.'

'I suppose I'd better come with you,' her husband said, 'as your usual escort is – unavailable.'

Carlin, standing near Daisy, whispered to her, 'D'you think I ought to offer to take his place?'

'Absolutely not. You steer clear of that imbroglio.'

Looking relieved, he nodded. 'Besides, you'll need me as Mr. Fletcher isn't going with us. He's splendid, isn't he? Not at all like that inspector chappie. You know, I rather wish

I'd gone into the police instead of the civil service, only the parents wouldn't have heard of it.'

Which would have sounded like an insult in the mouth of Rhino, Daisy thought, but from the baby bureaucrat was merely a wistful musing.

Pritchard now made up his mind that he must brace himself to see his ruined grotto for the first time. 'Better get it over with in company, don't you think, Owen?'

'I want to see it in ruins,' said Mrs. Howell malevolently. 'Owen, wait while I change my shoes.'

Lucy had waited for Daisy, but she wasn't about to wait for anyone else. She gathered her chosen companions together and shepherded them out through the French doors. Behind her, Daisy heard Lady Beaufort say placidly, 'No, I think not, my dear. I'll come and see it again when you have restored it – and installed a few seats along the path.'

CHAPTER 36

'I hope Mrs. Fletcher isn't going to come up with any more inspirations.' Boyle was thoroughly disgruntled. 'We're getting nowhere fast.'

'We're getting along nicely,' said Alec. 'We've eliminated Julia and Appsworth – '

'That may look like progress to you, sir, but to me it looks like we just lost our most likely suspects.'

'We have plenty left to work with, more than we had a few minutes ago. Look, man, if you think the Yard expects to clear up a murder case in twenty-four hours, I can assure you you're mistaken. You're getting along nicely. We have Wandersley and Carlin to replace the two that Billy cleared, and Mrs. Howell and Lady Ottaline are still in the picture. More's the pity. I'd rather have got rid of them.'

'Billy did think the person he saw was a big man, but he's on the scrawny side so anyone might look big to him. Anyway it could have been Rydal off to make preparations for his love-nest. Or if it was Sir Desmond, likely he was just going for his stroll, like he said. I just can't see a Principal Secretary going round bumping people off. And a "Sir," too.'

'Principal *Deputy* Secretary. Somewhat less exalted. Not that I think civil service rank has any correlation with murderous tendencies, or the reverse. He's spent his life repressing his feelings, in his marriage as well as his profession, apparently – '

'Oh, that psycho-stuff. I don't cotton to all that rubbish.'

'It has its points. As for his having been knighted, neither knighthood nor nobility ever was or ever will be a guarantee of virtue. The Wandersleys both have strong motives.'

'Carlin hasn't got much.' The inspector was determined to look on the gloomy side.

'Not for long premeditation. Unless there's something in their past dealings to be dug out.'

'Which we're not likely ever to dig out.'

'It shouldn't be very difficult. But let's cross that bridge if we come to it. Let's suppose a flare of temper when Rydal insulted Carlin. He leaves in a huff, as Daisy said, then he remembers Rydal's rendezvous and the talk of explosions in the grotto. He himself has already announced his intention to go up to town from Swindon without returning to Appsworth . . . It might look like the ideal way to get his own back without risk of consequences. Probably without any idea beyond singeing Rydal's eyebrows.'

'Like the chauffeur,' DS Thomkin put in.

'I can see he might think it up,' said Boyle, 'but I'd expect him to cool off on the way to the grotto. Still, we'd better have another go at him after what Mrs. Fletcher told us.'

'Perhaps we ought to confirm Daisy's story first,' Alec said diplomatically. 'She said Appsworth and Julia were still at breakfast with Wandersley and Rydal when she and Lucy left.'

'Right, sir. Thomkin, go and get those two.'

Alec and Boyle barely had time to start discussing

whether any of their suspects could have foreseen the dire consquences of turning on the gas, when Thomkin returned.

'They've gone to the grotto, sir,' he reported. 'They've *all* gone to the grotto, with Lady Gerald, like you said she could. All 'cepting Lady Beaufort.'

'Bloody hell!' swore Boyle. 'What the devil are they playing at?'

'I don't know,' Alec said grimly, 'but if Daisy's gone to the grotto with a bunch of dodgy characters against one of whom she's liable to have to give evidence, I'm going after her.'

Daisy stopped on the platform at the foot of the steps, facing the much diminished waterfall. Lucy went ahead up to the grotto, followed by Carlin bearing her impedimenta. She'd been muttering all the way about swarms of people getting in the way of her photography.

'You can't really tell what it was like,' Daisy said to Gerald. 'The waterfall was very pretty, and marvellous at night, lit from behind. And that statue up there in the middle had a head. I wonder if it fell in the pool.'

She went to the edge and, hanging on to Gerald's arm, peered over. The once-charming pool was an expanse of mud with a trickle winding across it. Tethys's spattered face stared blindly up at her.

'Nasty business,' said Gerald.

'The explosion, or the collapse, must have shaken the whole hill. I hope Mr. Pritchard is able to restore the grotto. For the second time, poor man! But look, Gerald, I do believe the flow is increasing.'

'Possibly,' Gerald said cautiously.

'The stream must be gradually washing away the debris blocking it.' Hearing voices, Daisy looked back as Julia and Charles came round the bend.

'Of course you don't have to,' Julia was saying passionately. 'Who cares what anyone says. Let alone what they think.'

'You don't understand. It's not that, it's what I –. Oh! Hello, you two.'

'What's wrong?' Having averted an arrest, Daisy wasn't going to put up with misunderstandings where she had been counting on a wedding.

'Nothing,' said Charles.

'Yes there is.' Julia was too upset to pretend.

'Julia, don't!'

'Charles was buried alive in a collapsing trench during the War.'

'I know,' Gerald mumbled uncomfortably.

Julia turned to Daisy. 'When the grotto blew up, it reminded him, and now he thinks everyone will say he's a coward if he doesn't go back in.'

'Of course he's not,' Daisy said firmly.

'That's what I keep telling him.'

Gerald shook his head. 'It's not you he has to convince, Miss Beaufort. Not us. It's himself. If what it takes is going into the grotto, don't make it more difficult for him.'

Without another word, Charles started up the steps, his face set. Julia went after him.

'I suppose we might as well go, too,' said Daisy.

'Don't crowd him.'

'Oh. Right-oh.' She turned back to the waterfall, just in time to see it suddenly double in size with a whoosh. 'Look! The water *is* breaking through.'

The trickle in the mud became a rivulet. Daisy watched fascinated as new geographic features were carved in miniature before her eyes. Then she heard voices again.

'Here come the others. Let's get out of their way.'

Glancing up at the grotto she saw no sign of Charles lingering near the mouth. Lucy had probably roped him in to help. Being obliged to do something – anything – was usually the best antidote to an excess of emotion of any kind, in Daisy's experience.

She started up the steps, but Gerald stayed below, doubtless to avoid embarrassing Charles after Julia's outburst (to be blamed on the French influence, perhaps?) about his weakness. Daisy thought Gerald had handled the situation with unexpected delicacy. He was usually such a taciturn chap that when he did open his mouth and reveal glimpse of his character, it quite often surprised her.

Halfway up she looked down. Gerald was pointing out the fallen head of the river goddess to Pritchard and Howell. Mrs. Howell stood with her back to the cliff, staring up at the headless torso with an expression of grim approval. She didn't appear to have any desire to inspect the destruction of the idols from a closer vantage point. Daisy wondered if it was wise of Pritchard to stand on the edge with his back to his sister-in-law. Then Lady Ottaline and her husband came round the corner, crossed between Mrs. Howell and the men, and approached the steps.

With the sound of the waterfall so much diminished, Daisy heard Lady Ottaline say sharply, 'Come along, Des.

I'm the one who was battered. Twice. If I can manage the climb, so can you.'

Why she was so insistent on returning to the scene, Daisy couldn't imagine. Having no desire to speak to Lady Ottaline, Daisy hurried up the rest of the way and stepped into the grotto. She couldn't see much for a minute as her eyes adjusted to the dimness. Julia came to meet her. Further back, Charles and Carlin were apparently clearing a space for Lucy to set up her tripod.

'Daisy, I'm so sorry,' Julia said in a low voice. 'I shouldn't have blurted out . . . what I did. Charles had just told me and I was so upset I wasn't thinking straight.'

'I know. You needn't be afraid I'll tell anyone else. Even Alec.'

'I gather Alec already knows, as Lord Gerald does. My poor Charles had to explain why he couldn't help them in here right after the explosion. I feel such a fool for embarrassing him and you –. Oh, blast, here come the Wandersleys.' Julia took Daisy's arm and stepped backwards into the shadow of the headless Tethys.

Following, Daisy looked back. Lady Ottaline came into the grotto. As Sir Desmond reached the top step, she moved further in, out of his way and turned towards him. The moment he was clear of the railing, she gave him a vigorous shove.

For a moment he tottered on the edge. Then, with a shout of terror, he toppled over.

Julia screamed.

How deep was the mud? The question hammered in Daisy's mind. How deep? The depth might be the difference between life and death.

'Daisy, get away from the edge!' Charles yelled.

She hadn't realised she was approaching the edge, hadn't consciously wanted to see what had happened to Sir Desmond. Julia grabbed her and pulled her back as Charles and Carlin pounded past Lady Ottaline and down the steps.

Lady Ottaline was laughing, high-pitched, hysterical. Grabbing the end of the stair-rail, she hung on and leant forwards to look down.

'She pushed him!' Daisy cried.

'No, darling.' Lucy seemed to think Daisy was also hysterical. 'That was the other evening, and I said he pushed her into the stream, but I wasn't serious.'

Instantly Lady Ottaline stopped laughing. 'Not serious?' she hissed. 'He *did* push me. I felt his hand on my back, and then I was flying through the air.'

'It could have been Rhino who pushed you,' Lucy pointed out.

'He wouldn't! He loved me. That's why Des blew him up, the bastard. Not jealousy. Oh no, he didn't care about me. His reputation was all he cared about.' Lady Ottaline stared from one to another of the three facing her, and alarm flickered in her eyes. 'But you're wrong, I didn't push him over. How could I? A big, heavy man like Des! I'm not strong enough.'

'I saw it, too,' said Julia. 'You caught him off balance. If he's dead, you – ' She broke off as a peculiar roaring noise came from behind them.

Daisy swung round just in time to see a surge of water burst through the rear wall. The gaping sea-serpent, already missing several teeth, cracked and crumbled. The renascent stream swooshed along its bed, flinging spray over the low wall, rushing towards the drop into the mud puddle, soon to be a pool once more.

A pool with people in it. Even as the realisation dawned, Daisy dropped to her knees and stretched out full length with her head and shoulders over the edge.

'Water coming!' she shouted, waving her arms. 'River's rising! Flood! Ring the alarum-bell! Blow, wind! Murder and treason!'

Somehow Charles and Carlin had already got down to the fallen man. Knee-deep in mud, they seemed to be trying to sit him up. Alive, then, Daisy thought thankfully. At her shout, they looked up, then redoubled their efforts. Gerald, lying flat on the platform – perhaps he'd lowered the other two? – called to them and they changed their tactics. They grabbed Sir Desmond under the armpits and started to drag him towards the side of the pool.

The waterfall arrived. As it hit, mud fountained upwards.

'She's getting away!' Lucy cried, releasing Daisy's ankle. Until she let go, Daisy hadn't noticed that Lucy and Julia were both hanging on to her. Julia let go, too, and they stood up.

Daisy rolled over and sat up. 'Who? Oh, Lady Ottaline!'

The lady in question was stepping carefully but swiftly over Gerald's outstretched legs. Pritchard and Howell, kneeling on either side of Gerald, didn't notice her sneaking by behind them. Mrs. Howell stared at her but made no attempt to stop her. Why should she? She couldn't have seen what had happened up above.

Round the corner came Detective Inspector Boyle, followed by Alec and two hefty detective sergeants.

'Thank heaven,' said Daisy with a sigh, relaxing. 'They'll take care of everything.'

Julia gripped the railing, as Lady Ottaline had, and leant over for a better view of what was going on directly below. 'They've got Sir Desmond over to the rushes. It's shallower there, but the water's rising. I'm going down.'

'Phew, what's that foul smell?' Lucy demanded.

Daisy sniffed, and wished she hadn't. 'They must have stirred up the bottom mud.'

'It's disgusting. I hope Gerald stays out of it. I'm going to get on with the photos before I'm asphyxiated.' With the arrival of the police to take charge, the single-minded Lucy had lost interest in mere mayhem. 'Come and hold the flash for me, darling.'

Daisy hadn't lost interest, but she was in no hurry to report what she'd seen and heard to Inspector Boyle. Besides, a certain amount of mud was bound to be splashed about in the course of the rescue of the men in the pool, and though less fastidious than Lucy, Daisy had no desire to be on the receiving end.

'Right-oh, darling,' she said.

CHAPTER 37

'It's a damned awkward situation,' Alec said irritably, wrestling with his collar stud. He hated wearing his dinner jacket, and stiff shirts were anathema.

Mrs. Howell, having lost three of her more distinguished guests to death and the police, had chosen to show the flag with a decree that the rest were to dress for dinner. She would not reign at Appsworth Hall much longer, but for the moment Pritchard was still prepared to indulge her.

'Let me get those studs for you, darling,' Daisy offered.

He held his arms out to allow her access. 'I don't know why I let Boyle inveigle me into being his unofficial assistant.' At least for once he wasn't blaming Daisy for his entanglement. 'I must have been mad.'

'If Superintendent Crane gets to hear of it, you can always plead temporary insanity. Is that what Lady Ottaline's going to do, do you think?'

'Who knows? With your and Julia's evidence, she can't avoid a charge of assault and battery, but there was no grievous bodily harm, just an unbelievable amount of mud.'

'I'm glad you didn't have to go in to help. Charles and Carlin both still have a faint miasma floating round them.' She fastened the last stud and his arms closed round her.

'Mind my frock!' she yelped. 'And your shirt.' After a careful but thorough kiss, she resumed: 'Mmm, very glad you didn't land in the pool, darling. You're quite sure it was Sir Desmond who killed Rhino, I suppose? All you said at tea was that he'd been arrested.'

'Not everyone wants a review of the evidence with their scones and Welsh-cakes.'

'Freshly baked scones! I do think Barker is a marvel to keep the household running so smoothly with all the upsets the servants have been having.'

'No, we are not getting a butler.'

'I wouldn't dream of suggesting it, even if we could lure Barker away, which I doubt. I don't think he'd approve of us, what with your irregular hours and the twins. Besides, Mrs. Dobson would be terribly hurt. Sir Desmond . . . ?'

'For a start, your friend Billy – '

'My friend!'

'That's how Boyle refers to him: "Mrs. Fletcher's friend Billy." He saw a big man hurrying down through the gardens from the direction of the grotto. He had no notion of the time – he works till he's finished the job or the head gardener calls him for his dinner. Of course, Rydal himself could have gone up there for some reason. Billy wouldn't necessarily have observed anyone else going or coming later.'

'But Sir Desmond and Rhino were the only two notice-ably large men. Until Gerald arrived.'

'Yes. Still, it's not proof. Wandersley could have been taking his daily stroll, as advertised. Howell confirms that Carlin told him about Wandersley's digestive difficulties. Julia and Appsworth agree that when they left the breakfast room, shortly after you and Lucy, only Wandersley and Rydal remained.'

'A combustible – not to say explosive – combination, especially as Rhino had just made that remark to Carlin about bone-lazy bureaucrats. I wonder if that's when the idea of actually blowing him up occurred to Sir Desmond.'

'It hardly matters, from a legal point of view. He can't very well claim there was no premeditation. Still, it's always awkward arresting a bigwig. I must say, Boyle handled it with suitable dignity and solemnity.'

'Good for Boyle. But you have no real proof, just circumstantial evidence.'

'Circumstantial evidence is perfectly valid in a court of law, though juries tend to prefer eyewitnesses, however unreliable, and fingerprints, however smudged.'

'He might get off. I have to admit to a certain sympathy.'

'For a murderer? And you the wife of a copper?'

'You didn't meet Rhino.'

'True. He seems to have made a present of motives to practically everyone. The manservant is clear on technical grounds, but unfortunately, we haven't been able to completely rule out the other two remaining suspects.'

'Lady Ottaline and Mrs. Howell. No dabs on the gas taps, I take it.'

'Nothing useful. He was probably wearing gloves, or else he gripped them by the edges. What we do have is a confession – '

'Well, what more can you want?'

' – Of sorts. Not to a sworn officer, unfortunately. Wandersley told Appsworth and Carlin, when they were extracting him from the mud, that he wished he'd bagged

Lady Ottaline in the explosion, but he had failed to take into account her persistent unpunctuality.'

Daisy couldn't help laughing. 'She is practically always late.'

'But now he's shut up and won't say another word without his lawyer's advice,' Alec said gloomily.

'I suppose you couldn't find the torch.'

'Torch? What torch?'

'Darling, he must have had an electric torch. It was pitch-black in the back room, no natural light, and he could hardly use an open flame to find the taps when he was about to turn them on, could he?'

'Great Scott, Daisy! I must phone Boyle at once – no, he won't have reached Swindon yet. Why didn't you say something sooner?'

'Actually, it's only just dawned on me.'

'It should have dawned on me or Boyle. One gets so used to clicking a switch.'

'I was remembering getting Lady Ottaline back to the house after her ducking, because even soaked and freezing, she managed to delay us. Julia had a torch she'd taken from Charles's pocket. Barker put it on a shelf by the side door – back door, whatever you want to call it. The one in the passage next to the drawing room. I suppose it's kept there with the lamplighter's pole, for whoever goes out at night to light the lamps in the grotto – '

'I'll check there first.'

'And for daytime, an electric lantern behind a nymph at the back of the first cave. Rhino probably knew about that and counted on it, but I don't see how Sir Desmond could know about it. The only time he went was at night.'

'Oh hell!' Shrugging into his dinner jacket, tie untied, Alec dashed off.

Running down the stairs, he wondered what Boyle would say if Daisy's belated stroke of genius meant bringing all his men back to search the grotto, the area of the explosion, and the gardens for an electric torch. He would have to do it, on the slim chance of finding incontrovertible evidence – not only the torch but Wandersley's fingerprints on it.

Unless . . .

The dining room door stood ajar, and Alec heard a sound of movement within. He looked in to find, as expected, the butler straightening a fork here, giving a glass an extra polish there, making sure his domain was in perfect order for dinner.

'Barker, I need your help.'

'Sir? Your tie, sir. Allow me – '

'Devil take my tie. You keep a torch near a side door to the terrace, Mrs. Fletcher tells me?'

'Yes, sir. If you take the passage on your left as – '

'Show me. I may need a witness.'

'Certainly, sir. This way if you please.'

The passage was too narrow to be called a hall, too wide for a mere corridor, just wide enough not to be obstructed by one of those curious pieces of furniture, that combine a pair of umbrella stands, hat and coat pegs, a looking-glass, a small cupboard, and a shelf. One umbrella stand contained three umbrellas, the other a lamplighter's pole, but Alec had eyes only for the chromed-steel torch on the shelf.

'Here it is, sir.' Barker reached for it.

Alec gripped his wrist. 'Don't touch it!'

'Very good, sir.'

'May I?' He whipped from the butler's shoulder the snowy napkin with which the man had been buffing up silver and glasses. With the cloth enveloping his hand, Alec picked up the torch by the lens end and held it up to the none-too-bright electric light, turning it this way and that. 'Fingerprints!'

'Indeed, sir!' The butler looked quite put out. 'The third housemaid is required to polish it daily.'

'Thank heaven she didn't. I'd like a word with her.'

'So,' muttered Barker grimly, 'would I. In the circumstances, sir, perhaps you had better come to my pantry.'

Alec had dealt with enough butlers to appreciate the honour of this invitation. 'Thank you, that will do very well.'

Bearing the torch, he followed Barker through the green baize door.

The third housemaid was the child who had reported Gregg's threat against Rydal's eyebrows. Rita came in eyes wide with apprehension, summonses to the butler's sanctum being associated with reprimands too severe for the housekeeper to handle. Her eyes flew to the torch, displayed on the napkin on the table where Barker was wont to do his serious silver-polishing.

Alec got his question in before the butler's rebuke could frighten her out of her wits. 'Rita, when did you last polish this torch? It's the one from the hall stand by back door.'

She addressed her reply to the butler anyway. 'Oh, Mr. Barker, I tried and tried but I just cou'n't get ever'thing done what wi' the p'lice an' all, the way they kep' coming back.'

After a pregnant pause, Barker said judicially, 'It has been a trying time for all of us. Be a good girl and answer Mr. Fletcher's question.'

'Oh, sir, I reckon it must 'a' bin yes'dy morning, like every day 'cepting today.'

'What time, do you know?'

Barker answered. 'The ground floor rooms are supposed to be finished before the master finishes his breakfast.'

Long before Wandersley finished his, Alec thought. There was something to be said for an old-fashioned household. It was still possible that Sir Desmond had used some other torch and thrown it into the bushes on his way back to the house, but who else had had need of a torch since early yesterday morning?

'And what I need now is a telephone,' said Alec.

Twenty minutes later he dashed back upstairs to find Daisy waiting for him. While she tied his tie and made sure he was in all respects respectable, he told her about finding the torch.

'Boyle's sending a sergeant to fetch it and to get statements from Barker and me. He's as convinced as I am that the fingerprints on it must be Wandersley's.'

'I hope that means we can go home tomorrow,' said Daisy as the dinner-gong rang through the house. 'Come on, we're going to be late. I'm dying to see the babies. I feel as if I've been away for weeks.'

Hurrying down the stairs, Alec said, 'Yes, everyone's free to go. You'll undoubtedly be called at Lady Ottaline's trial, but Boyle's promised to do his best to do without my appearing in person as a witness. He's not a bad chap, but I must say I'll be glad to shake the dust of this place off my feet.'

'And out of your hair.'

Alec grinned. 'And out of my hair.'

'I don't expect Mr. Pritchard will manage to have the grotto rebuilt before we come back.'

'Come back? I've no intention of ever returning to Appsworth Hall!'

'Darling, you can't possibly miss the triple wedding.'

'Great Scott, Daisy, what – ?'

'I had a feeling you weren't really listening at tea-time. Julia and Charles, and Lady Beaufort and Pritchard – '

'What? So that was her secret!'

'Yes. She wouldn't tell Julia she'd given up on Rhino because then it would have looked very odd if she hadn't decided to return to town at once. I'd guess she needed time to make sure she and Pritchard were really thinking along the same lines.'

Alec grinned. 'To bring him up to scratch.'

Daisy gave him an old-fashioned look. 'To continue: and Howell and his ladylove. They're all going to tie the knots en masse, before Julia and Charles leave for Canada, and we've already been invited.'

'Great Scott!' Alec repeated. 'Church or Chapel?'

'I don't think that's been decided yet,' said Daisy, opening the drawing-room door as the last reverberations of the gong died away.

Pritchard stood up with a smile. 'We were just wondering – '

His sister-in-law interrupted him. 'Since Lady Ottaline isn't here to come down late for dinner,' Mrs. Howell said acidly, 'I suppose I should have expected that someone else would follow her example. I'm sure I don't know what the aristocracy are coming to!'